ALWAYS SCOUT BEFORE INVADING

✛ ✛ ✛ ✛

A man wearing ornate armor, waving a discharged pistol, stumbled out a doorway. Peirol knew him not, guessed he was from one of the other warships. The man's face was bleeding, and blood spouted from his left forearm, where his hand had been. The man was babbling in terror and pain. He managed, "Inside! They were waiting, and—"

A dark rope whipped out of the doorway, wrapped twice around him, yanked him out of sight. It wasn't a rope, Peirol realized, but a tentacle, like that of the tiny cuttlefish he so dearly loved sliced in rings and fried in garlic and oil, but a tentacle five times or more the height of a man . . .

✛ ✛ ✛ ✛

ALSO BY CHRIS BUNCH

The Demon King
The Seer King
The Warrior King

THE EMPIRE STONE

CHRIS BUNCH

ASPECT®

WARNER BOOKS

A Time Warner Company

WARNER BOOKS EDITION

Cover design by Don Puckey
Cover illustration by Steve Youll
Cover hand lettering by Ron Zinn
Book design by H. Roberts Design
Interior map by Neil Hyslop from a sketch by Karen Eisenberg

Warner Books, Inc.
1271 Avenue of the Americas
New York, NY 10020

Visit our Web site at
www.twbookmark.com

. A Time Warner Company

Printed in the United States of America

First Paperback Printing: June 2000

10 9 8 7 6 5 4 3 2 1

For
Margaret Macrae
and
Cunégonde and Doctor Pangloss

Thanks to Jerry Keenan, Mr. Diamond, Astoria, OR,
and Tim and Jim Gannaway,
Gannaway Brothers Jeweler, Warrenton, OR.

And thanks to Lloyd Eshbach
for the spark.

NAMELESS LANDS

N

THE SEA OF COTEHL

PARASSO
■ Beshkirs

RESTORMEL

Sugat River

■ Restormel

Arzamas
■ Tybee

Manoleon Peninsula

🏰 Lord Aulard's
Castle

■ Isfahan

Diamond Fields of Spada

Map not to scale

"*They called it the Empire Stone. Big it was ... is, if it still exists, wherever it's been stolen to. Double the size of both m' fists,*" the boy's father said. "*M' grandsire's grandsire's grandsire saw it oncet, when he was in Thyone, and th' king passed through, all so'jers an' tootlin' bands an' gold.*"

The man laughed harshly, drank from the battered pewter jack no one else in the family was allowed to use. A chill wind whistled through the cracks in the rickety moor-house, and the boy smelled snow on the way. His brother and sisters were curled asleep around their mother like so many kits. His father was not drunk. Not sober, but not seething with that unknown rage that'd smash out at anyone.

"Long time ago, that," he went on. "When there

was a king in our land, an' Thyone was a city, not a shamble a' stones."

"How did the king carry the Stone?" the boy who'd later name himself Peirol asked, waiting to duck away from a blow. "In his crown?"

"Haw. Bust his fool neck if he tried. Carried it 'top a two-handed scepter."

"What did your granda say it looked like?"

"Some say it's a clear stone that catches and reflects colors, many colors, not just the six we know, but colors that aren't like any others on this earth," he said. "It's luminous, they say, like foxfire.

"It's round, cut perfect. They say it's got a thousand facets, but that's hoobly-shit, for if a diamond's cut with more than the perfect fifty-eight, it throws light away, doesn't reflect it back."

The man wasn't speaking in his usual tinman's crude rumble, and the boy wanted him to keep talking like this forever.

"Who cut the Stone? Does anyone know?"

"Gods . . . or maybe demons," his father went on, then laughed dryly. "More likely, a real nervous man, some lord behind him with a bare sword, waiting for him to make one mistake."

"Where'd it come from?"

"Nobody knows."

"When the sea-rovers sacked Thyone, they stole it?"

"Aye. And with the Empire Stone gone with the men of the black ships, those who tried to rebuild Thyone were doomed to be defeated by every barbarian looking for a little loot, a few slaves."

"Did the Empire Stone have powers?"

"Course it did," the man said, returning to his usual accent. "Any rock like that's got to have powers, or legends don't get made. Th' Empire Stone brings riches, brings power—power for evil, for what man without the law would do good if he doesn't have to?"

"Is it gone forever?" the boy asked.

"Who knows. There's tales of brave heroes who journey out in search of th' Stone, but they never return.

"Which is a damned fine lesson for anybody with sense t' work his set till it's naught but waste."

The man drained the jack, shook the small wooden barrel beside it, listening to emptiness.

"Shit," he said once more. "We'll sleep now."

He blew out both guttering candles, and sprawled down by the boy's mother.

The boy sat, listening to the wind.

"Brave heroes, who journey out . . ."

O N E

*

Of Dead Gods
and Serpents

Twelve wolves sat in the center of a great courtyard, shattered columns on either side reaching toward the winter moon's wane.

Peirol of the Moorlands huddled behind one toppled column and sourly considered how few blessings the Year of the Mouse had given him.

First he'd fallen in with Koosh Begee and his gang of tricksters, merely because the thief-lord's wife, Lorn, had once—only once!—invited him upstairs when Begee was out of the city of Sennen on some nefarious errand. The night had been exhausting, ecstatic, and lasted for a thousand years, he admitted grudgingly. But Peirol should never have hung on, waiting for a second chance at Lorn's delights, pretending to be interested in gaming. Pretense grew into fascination. The yellow felt circle became a snare worse than any woman, and he'd spent hours, days, in its spell, losing, always losing.

Quite suddenly he realized the whole thing, from Lorn's conveniently offered charms to Begee's pretended friendship, had been a trap. First he'd lost his tiny shop, then a chance to travel east with some traders to the legendary diamond mines of Osh. A trap—and this was the night it'd been sprung, with the help of Peirol's own so-clever tongue, sending him into these supposedly monster-haunted ruins of Thyone after a god's sapphire.

A wolf yipped sharply, and its fellows trotted to him, backs to Peirol. The slight breeze, smelling of some unknown, overly sweet flower, was blowing toward him, so the beasts shouldn't scent him. Peirol slipped through the shadows toward his goal.

The moon casts strange and lying images, but Peirol's shadow was true. Above the waist young Peirol of the Moorlands was nearly perfect—long, carefully tended blond hair, with the noble forehead and clear gaze of a young statesman, gleaming teeth revealed by his frequent smile through sensual lips, a dimpled chin.

His chest was a warrior's, heavy, sharply defined muscles tapering to a slender waist.

Then the gods' jest began. His legs were short, misshapen, bowed, although very strong. He stood almost a handspan below five feet, and the moon's shadow mocked his hitching, rolling gait.

A wolf turned its head, and Peirol ducked behind rubble and became one with the dead stones. The wolves, if they were sensible, normal creatures, should have abandoned this absurd vigil and gone about their hunting. But they still hung about this ruined temple. Peirol refused to admit they could be waiting for . . . for anything.

He thought of calling them—years ago he'd learned, from a witch of the moors who might or might not have been his blood kin, how to mimic the yaps and even baying of the wolves of the moor, enough to call or even, once or twice, frighten them away from a scent. But that was a long time, nearly fifteen years ago, and the penalty for inept mimicry would be awful. He settled back to wait . . . and remember.

Koosh Begee had cast his net with skill, asking Peirol if he feared demons, after a long, wine-filled dinner companied with half a dozen of Begee's henchmen, their doxies, and Begee's entrancing wife.

"I've never seen one," he'd answered honestly, "and it's stupid to worry about the unknown. Mostly it's nothing but the imaginings of fools and beldames."

"And the gods," Begee pressed. "You fear them, of course."

Peirol had smiled, twistedly. "After what they did to me at birth, of course I fear them. Fear and hate them. They're malignant thugs, I believe, and so should be treated with contempt, as any back-stabbing worm must."

The table hushed, and one of Begee's men glanced upward, as if expecting a thunderbolt through the tavern's roof. Even Begee licked his lips a bit nervously.

"There is a tale," Begee said, clearly changing the subject, "of a great gem, a huge blue star sapphire, somewhere in the ruins of Thyone, a sapphire—"

"I've heard the story," Peirol interrupted, the wine speaking for him. "Supposedly, when the black ships came and destroyed the city, the priests of whatever god the sapphire belonged to cried for salvation. The god took mercy, and the earth opened, and the temple sank below ground. The god then sent demons to hide the temple, and in an hour, perhaps two, a single slab of stone roofed the pit where the building was.

"The invaders never found the hidden entrance to the buried temple or the sapphire, but slew all the priests, as they slew throughout the city, taking any loot that presented itself."

Like the Empire Stone, his mind whispered suddenly, resurrecting that tale of his father's, years gone by. Peirol shrugged the memory away.

"The jewel was left in darkness, the temple guarded by whatever devils the tale-tellers had enough brandy to people it with."

"My sister told me the story," Lorn said. "The god was named Slask, and he was—is—the Lord of the Underworlds.

"And there were guardians set. Big old serpents, as long as this building, double-fanged with a poison that killed if it ever touched your skin, or the snakes could just crush you in their coils. Be careful, Peirol," she warned. "Slandering our creators is foolish."

Peirol ran a hand through his long-brushed, soft blond hair and turned slightly, so Lorn could admire and hopefully once more want the pressure of his oiled and scented chest muscles.

"Then I'm a fool indeed," he said. "For I don't think the gods, if they even exist, listen, not to our prayers, not to our laments. And by the way, every gem I've ever heard of bigger than my thumbnail always has some sort of evil tale attached.

"I've bought them, I've sold them, and look at me? Do I look cursed? Doomed? Demon-haunted?"

There was laughter.

"There needs only be one such for you to meet a horrible doom," Lorn said stubbornly.

"So where is this one stone?" Peirol said. "Somewhere beneath Thyone? And why have you told me about it, Koosh? Do you think I'm a miner, like my father? Would you have me drilling around the ruins like a star-mole?"

"You owe me," Begee growled.

"I owe you greatly," Peirol admitted.

Begee picked up a parchment scroll from his seat, and Peirol felt his stomach knot. Too easy, too quick, too handy, his mind whispered.

"Someone *else* in my debt paid it with this map," he said, handing the scroll to Peirol.

"Tsk," Peirol said, untying its ribbon. "Any good treasure map's supposed to be ancient, tattered, and hopefully stained with many men's blood. You're not holding true to fable, Koosh."

Koosh Begee's smile, always as temporary as his good humor, vanished. "It was drawn less than a year ago," he said. "First there was a dream that my 'friend' had, then, after he had the courage to visit Thyone by day half a dozen times, he hired a sorcerer to draw this plan.

"It shows clearly the route to be taken through the ruins to the entrance to that underground temple, down to the great room where Slask's image waits, the sapphire in his extended hands."

Peirol examined the parchment. "The route seems clear," he said. "Obviously you wish me to go into Thyone and acquire this stone for you."

"I do," Begee said. "That will discharge the great debt you owe me, plus a bag of gold the size of my head as well."

"If there's no sapphire?" Peirol said. "I'll have chanced my life for naught."

"That is another gamble," Begee said, smiling again, but not in amusement.

Peirol tossed the parchment back to Begee. "No bargain," he said. "I'm not a fool."

"Then I must call in your debt," Begee said. "To be paid within a week, or else I'll visit the elders and have you seized and declared my slave, to serve until the debt is paid in full, which will be long years indeed."

Peirol's face remained calm. "I thought you were intelligent, Koosh. Obviously I overrated you. What service could I do as your slave? Make pretty baubles for your wife's ankles and wrists? Hardly a harsh duty, but I don't think you'd have the best bargain."

Lorn's eyes flickered.

"That'd not be what I'd order you to do," the thief-lord said. "I'd just send you back to Thyone—

and this time you'd have no profit when you brought the gem back."

"Do you really believe I'd do that," Peirol said, "and not keep right on going?"

"There'd be hunters after you if you did. I can command a thousand."

"By the time they chanced Thyone, I'd be far, far gone," Peirol said. "Now, let me make another offer. I'll go to Thyone, in search of this gem. I'll go tonight, in fact," he said, emboldened by the wine. "But here is our bargain. I'm to be free, whether or not I find the gem."

"Up a demon's arse! I'd be a fool to accept that," Begee sneered. "If you did find it, you could hide it, claim you found nothing, then return for it later."

"And how would we know," a thief said, smirking, "you'd even go all the way to this courtyard? A task like that'd take real courage. Maybe you'd just wait for a bit inside Thyone's walls, then come out and say you found nothing."

"Are you saying I lack courage, Reim?" Peirol said, right hand touching the grip of the sword sheathed down his back.

Reim shook his head hastily. He, like the others, had seen Peirol in anger, and knew the dwarf had not only the slender blade and the ornately jeweled dagger at his waist but other lethal surprises about his person.

"I meant nothing but a jest," he mumbled.

"Your purse-slitter has a point," Peirol said. "So to make sure there's proper trust among 'friends,' we'll go to Thyone with half a dozen men—I hope you'd include my brave friend Reim here—and they can wait for me. I'll descend into the temple, assuming the tunnel or whatever it is exists, and see what is to be seen. I'll return either with the stone, or with some dust gathered below-ground.

"I wager the sorcerer who drew this parchment could test the dust and determine that I actually went where I vowed."

"That sorcerer's dead," Begee said. "Something he cast disagreed with him. But there's no reason other mages couldn't do what you suggest. Perhaps Old Abbas, who's the best man I know in that wavering profession?"

Peirol kept a smile hidden. He'd once made a charm bracelet for Old Abbas's granddaughter, and the wizard had sworn to one day do him a service in repayment. "Excellent choice," he agreed. "Abbas is an honest man."

"Very well," Begee said. "We'll take ten men. You'll be one, Reim."

The thief whined, and there was more laughter.

"And I'll be one of the party as well," Begee said. "We leave within the hour."

Without a signal, the wolves rose and trotted across the great courtyard down a rubble-strewn street.

Peirol went fast, in his bobbling gait, down the courtyard to where the parchment had said the temple's entrance lay.

He noted the smoothness of the stones he crossed, remembered what Lorn had said about the temple being hidden "under a single slab of stone," decided there were excellent masons in the old days, and concentrated on the pile of stones ahead. It had been an altar, raised after Thyone was sacked, the scroll said, but storms roaring up the cliffs from the sea below had smashed it over the centuries. Peirol crouched in its shelter, considered the scroll's instructions. Look for a six-sided stone. Under that would be the way down, a narrow staircase.

Boulders, pebbles, rock-chunks, he thought. Some carved, some rough, some polished as if they were ocean-turned. Nothing, of course, and another legend dies—and then he saw the large stone, or rather pair of stones, that'd split apart. Put together as one, they were definitely six-sided, each side showing chisel-marks. Certainly though, he thought as he crept to it, there'd be nothing under or near. . . .

There was a crevice behind the broken stone, no more than a forearm's length wide. Peirol peered down, saw no stairway. He drew his sword, reached far into the crack, felt nothing. He took off his small pack, took out flint, steel, tinder, pulled off a bit of tinder, and struck fire. He dropped the flaming tinder into the crack. The small flame fell and fell, then bounced and was extinguished.

Peirol uncoiled a rope ensorcelled to have greater strength than it looked that was knotted at intervals of an arm span. He tied it off around the broken boulder, tugged. The stone didn't move. Peirol tied his sword sheath and belt to the rope's bitter end and let it slither down into blackness. He heard a distant thud.

Wiping suddenly moist palms on his tunic, Peirol lowered himself into the crevice. He slid down until his ribs were level with the courtyard stone, then stuck. He fought back panic, thinking what might happen if he couldn't free himself before the wolves returned, then pushed hard and slipped entirely into the crevice, into absolute blackness. His legs flailed and found nothing; then one arm caught the rope and he had it firm and went quickly down, hand over hand. A foot touched down; he reached with his other foot, felt nothing, almost slipped, then had a precarious stand on . . .

On what, he didn't know. He swung his free leg about, felt something solid, and cautiously let his weight down. He knelt, very carefully slid out of his pack straps, opened it, and took out a short wand of petrified wood. There was a dimple in one end that had been rubbed with oil and touched with steel and stone.

Koosh Begee said the spell would work every time, for anyone. Which means, Peirol thought, every time except this one, for everyone except me. He began muttering:

> *"Remember, wood*
> *Once you lived*
> *Grew strong*
> *Grew old*
> *Died*
> *And still are dying.*
> *Remember life/not life*
> *Sparks*
> *Strike fire*
> *Sparks*
> *Strike fire*
> *Burn now*

Burn always
Remember fire, wood."

Nothing. He started to growl, calmed, repeated the incantation again and a third time, then thought of just how he'd go back up that rope and push through the narrow crack to report failure.

Peirol blinked. His eyes were tricking him. But there was a glow from the end of the tiny wand, a glow and then a strong, flickering light, as if he held a tarred torch, and the wand writhed and grew in his grasp.

He looked about, gasped, and almost fell. He stood on a ledge not a foot wide, jutting from a wall carved with figures, inscriptions. On the three other sides was nothing but night. He pried at a bit of stone, dropped it, listened, counting. Peirol reached thirty before he heard the tick of it landing, far, far below.

Peirol wished he'd just looped his rope around that stone above, so he could pull it down to him and use it to descend farther. Then his mind mocked him—that would make getting back out interesting, wouldn't it? Do you really enjoy making your life more difficult?

He put his belt back on, slung his sword and pack across one shoulder. Peirol picked a direction, and moved carefully along the ledge, holding the torch high with one hand, clinging to the stone carvings with the other. He went ten feet, and the ledge ended. Peirol cursed, went back, and this time the ledge went on, step by step, downward, ever downward.

He chanced leaning back, holding the torch far away from the wall. He saw that the ledge went up to where a rockfall had smashed narrow steps. He was also able to make out some of the carvings, and shuddered. Either the priests of this forgotten god—Slask, that was it—had vivid imaginations, or else the god didn't care who worshiped him, in fact seeming to prefer the most fabulous monsters to mankind. Mankind *was* represented—either being punished by the nonhuman acolytes of this god, or else engaging in lascivious acts not even a tumbler could manage.

Peirol went on, then there were no more steps to reach for. He was on firm, level ground—a stone floor, he corrected himself. His torchlight reflected from the stones, and he knelt. Polished quartz, tourmaline, jadeite—each cobble was a polished semiprecious stone.

Peirol stroked his chin. If these priests could've afforded to pave their temple with rocks like this . . . No, he thought. Tales like this are never true. So let's make a quick tour and get out. You've more than repaid Begee's debt, just having courage to come this far.

He held the torch high. The room he was in—room, cavern, whatever—was huge. Something loomed ahead, and he started toward it. After a few paces, he thoughtfully unsheathed his sword. The object was almost twenty feet high. It was the statue of a shudderous god, crouched on four clawed legs, with a spiked tail curling high, a scaled body, and a face tusked like a wild boar, but with strange features, perhaps a man's, but stretched to fit a dog's skull. It also had two taloned arms that sprang from its shoulders, held palm up in front of its eyes. Slask's expression was somewhere between sneering arrogance and drooling lust, reminding Peirol a bit of Koosh Begee.

Reflected light glimmered from between the idol's forelegs. Peirol scooped up a handful of gems. All were uncut, unpolished. Black-green emeralds, dark rubies, citrine topaz. He tossed them in his hand and estimated that the biggest, cut and finished, might be just a bit over five *varjas*. Evidently the god of the underworld had welcomed offerings of jewels.

Pfah! A great idol, far underground, a monstrous deity in a haunted temple. Now all we need to make this situation utterly absurd, he thought, is for that godsdamned sapphire to be nested in Slask's hands. But if it is . . .

Peirol clambered up Slask's legs, sheathed his sword, and swung up to crouch on the idol's forearm.

Slask's palms were empty. Peirol laughed angrily. The sound echoed and reechoed, and his skin crawled.

What now? he mused. I suppose gather a bagful of stones, go back and tell Koosh Begee the truth, and then wake up Old Abbas to test me and remove Begee's suspicions. Perhaps Begee'd let me polish the stones and trade them, and perhaps that'd be enough to free me from debt, assuming he'd be patient for two, perhaps three Times, rather than wanting an instant slavey. Possibly. Now, if I took but *half* of those stones, left the rest, and came back in daylight—

Peirol heard a loud hiss in his ear, and became ice. He slowly turned his head, and the snake hissed again, louder, more threateningly. Its head was green and mottled black, about the size of his chest, and its body, thick as a ship's mast, ran down into darkness.

No, Lorn, his mind went wildly. I can't tell if it's double-fanged. . . . The ones it's showing are deadly enough, even if they're not dripping venom, nor can I tell if it's fifteen or fifty feet long.

The snake's mouth gaped further, and Peirol thrust his torch into its jaws, back-rolled off the idol's hands, and dropped to the temple floor, pulling his sword. The torch dropped beside him and rolled, sending light across the great chamber in dizzying spirals.

The snake struck, and he lunged, blade flickering in and out of the horror's neck. It seethed rage, slashed as if its teeth were sabers. He ducked, struck again, then the snake's body looped out of darkness around him, sending his sword flying, pinning one of his arms.

The coil lifted him into the air. He kicked helplessly, saw the jaws nearing, smelt the sourness of the monster's skin and the decay of its breath.

Peirol's free hand went to his waist, behind his elaborately worked belt buckle, and found a small dart, all metal, not much longer than a finger's length. *Do not miss,* he thought; *it is but a tavern game, a game of skill, a game of concentration.* Almost delicately, he tossed the poisoned dart into the snake's eye.

The serpent convulsed, throwing him high into the air, spinning, falling, and he bounced off the snake's body, hard, but better than rock, rolled off and away as the beast thrashed, shrilling in agony, like, he thought, an aelopile with a leak.

Somehow he found his sword and came back for an attack, but the snake was writhing, rolling, and he was unable to get close, and then it was whipping, thrashing, into the darkness that had birthed it.

He picked up the torch, listened to the snake's hopefully dying agonies. A smile began, and then he heard sounds, soft whispers, from another direction, sounds another snake, bigger than the one he'd half-blinded, might make as it approached.

He started to run, caught himself—*Not with nothing, I won't*—pulled a soft chamois bag from his pack, and hastily scooped it full of gems from beneath Slask's feet. He ran for the steps to the ledge, went up as fast as he dared as the whispers grew closer. Something smashed into the rock wall not half a yard distant, and he threw the torch at it. It bounced against the wall, fell clattering down the steps, then to the floor, and whatever it was, out there just beyond seeing, struck at it. He had the rope clutched in his hand, going up it hand over hand, as quickly as he'd climbed anything, even the crags of his native moors long ago, and something struck at him, hit the rope, and he spun back and forth like a pendulum. He felt rock above him, a narrow crack, and he held himself with one hand, shrugged off the pack and sword belt, forced himself into the crevice, never feeling its rough edges tear at him. He popped out of the fissure into the welcome haunted moonlight of Thyone's ruins.

Eventually his breathing approached normal.

All I have to worry about now is wolves, he thought. Two- and four-legged.

Peirol was just beyond the shatter of Thyone's onyx gates when the darkness beside the weed-choked road became ten separate shadows.

"The temple exists," Koosh Begee announced. "You were gone far too long for it to be otherwise."

"It does," Peirol said. "As does the idol. Lorn will be delighted to know her snake-friends do, as well."

"The sapphire?" Begee hissed, sounding related to the serpents below.

"That, my dear Koosh, either was never there, or was stolen by the priests if they were sensible, or else someone as brave as I came before."

"Search him!" Begee commanded, and two thieves had Peirol by the shoulders and a third patted him down.

"Here," he announced, finding the pouch and handing it to his lord.

Begee opened it, poured gems into his palm, eyed them in the moonlight.

"You did find it."

"I found *those* baubles," Peirol corrected. "But old Slask seems to have financed a drunk with the big one."

"You're lying!"

"Now why would I do that?" Peirol complained. "Don't be foolish. If I went down into that hell, which those beads suggest, and if the sapphire were there, wouldn't I have brought it back, all skipping and singing?"

"You hid it somewhere."

"Where? Inside Thyone? And then I came back to confound you? You're even stupider than you appear," Peirol said in a half-snarl. His only excuse was, it was very late, and Peirol became nervous around snakes.

Begee backhanded him across the face, one of his

rings drawing blood. Peirol licked it away from his lips.

"Do not ever do that again," he said calmly.

Begee hit him twice more.

"Now drag him off the track," he started. "We'll build up a little fire, hold this lying bastard's feet in it to make him—"

Peirol lifted his legs off the ground, the thieves holding him up too surprised to let go, and kicked Begee in the chest. The thief-lord went spinning.

Peirol's feet came back on the ground, and he drove a fist back into one thief's groin. The thief howled, clutched himself, stumbled away. Peirol back-butted with his head, smashing the second thief's nose, then he was free and his blade whispered out as Begee clawed for the heavy sword he fancied. It never came out of its sheath as Peirol's sword flicked into Begee's throat. Again Peirol lunged as Begee, confusion, anger, pain, and surprise racing across his dying face, went down.

Peirol spun, dagger coming into his hand, blade blocking the third thief's slash, the dagger going into the man's guts. Peirol pivoted away from a lunge, recognized Reim, spitted him, and ran. He saw a spark as someone uncovered a slow match and put it to his musket's pan. A flash and a bang followed, and a ball spanged off a rock.

"Get the little bastard! He won't get far! Come on—Koosh's dead—come on, you jackheads!" But Peirol wasn't listening as his head went back and he wailed loud, the prey-cry of a moor wolf.

He ducked around rubble, went between two narrow rocks, and was at a dead end, trapped. His lips pulled back in a snarl, he waited, sword ready, for the first man to chance the narrow way. Again he bayed into the night skies, hoping, having forgotten how to pray.

"He's in there—go on, in after him—hells with you—awright then, I'll go, spit the cocksniffer like he's—"

The wolves heard his cry, came as he'd called them years ago across barren, rain-drenched moors. A thief heard their howls and shouted in panic. Another musket banged, and dark gray shadows bounded out of the dark, snarling, tearing at Begee's marauders.

Finally the last man's death gurgle died away. Twice wolves sniffed at the passage, and he growled deep, telling them this was a den not to be entered without a fight. There was silence then, but Peirol waited for a time before creeping out.

Bodies were scattered in the moon's dying light, and he went from one to the next, taking gold and silver, rings and jewels, until he came to Koosh Begee's corpse.

Peirol scooped up the scattered gems, put them back in his pouch, and tucked it away. He looked down at Koosh Begee's face, dead eyes glaring back.

"You see," Peirol said quietly, "I do pay my debts. One way or another."

His smile died. "Now all I have to worry about is a thousand—rather, nine hundred and ninety—bravos who'll try to kill me as a boon to their lord's widow."

TWO

*

Of Green Emeralds
and a Vale

It was dawn when Peirol of the Moorlands went up the winding path to the sorcerer Abbas's tower, on the heights above Sennen. The gates stood open, for who would have the courage—or stupidity—to rob a wizard? There were a pretty pair of one-pound robinets on wheeled carriages with polished stone cannonballs beside the varicolored wooden door, but they were more for show than actual use.

Peirol considered his words, how he would make his plea, lifted the knocker, and the door opened.

A very beautiful girl stood there. She was perhaps sixteen, and her black hair fell in waves on either side of her doll-like face. Her porcelain complexion set off slightly rouged lips and green, inviting eyes. She wore a morning robe of silk and lace, and a smile. She had a thin scarf of emerald green silk tied around her neck. Peirol noted with a bit of a stirring, in spite of his fatigue, the gentle curve of small breasts.

"Welcome, Peirol," she said. "My grandfather is expecting you."

Peirol jolted away from a wisp of lustful thought. If no one robbed a sorcerer, certainly no one at all should consider . . .

"You're . . ." He let his voice trail off, not remembering the girl's name.

"Kima," she said. "You made this bracelet for me, three years ago." She held up her wrist, and Peirol, in spite of his better judgment, took her hand and pretended to examine the jewelry.

"If I'd known you were going to become this beautiful," he said, "I would never have put a price on it, but made it a present."

Kima giggled. "You said when you made it that one day you'd flirt with me. I see you do have the Gift."

"Not I," Peirol said. "Merely common sense." He brought himself back. "Abbas awaits? How could he know—" He broke off. "Stupid me. Wizards and that."

"Yes," Kima said. "Now, go into that first room on the right and wash. You look like you've been dancing with wolves all night."

"Would you believe that I have?"

"No. Grandfather warned me about you."

"Hmph." But Peirol obeyed, and came out a few minutes later feeling considerably better.

Kima led him up three curving flights of stairs, past paintings of times and cities he'd never dreamed of, onto a balcony that opened over Sennen and the river curling past the ruins of Thyone into the Ismai'n Sea. There was a beautifully worked table set for three. On the balcony beyond, the magician Abbas waited.

Peirol had never known why Abbas was called "Old," for he appeared in his mid-fifties, exactly as he'd looked when Peirol had met him, five years earlier when he arrived in Sennen. Abbas was big, six and a half feet tall, thick-armed and with muscled legs. His precisely curled and oiled beard and hair were the deepest black, falling over a wine barrel of a chest and proudly nourished stomach.

He was the most powerful and feared wizard in Sennen. Three times barbarians had threatened Sennen and he'd used his magic to confuse and divert them, which earned the people's gratitude. However, no one sought his company lightly. There had been times when lightning boiled around his tower and thunder clashed from a clear night sky. Some said they'd heard the scream of demons on moonless nights, and it was noted Abbas's enemies came to rather abrupt and unhappy fates.

Peirol preferred to have as little truck with sorcerers as possible. He feared them for their powers yet secretly held them in a bit of contempt, having consulted three over the years, paid their fees, and been told that the gods had doomed him to be a dwarf and they could cast no spells to change matters. Peirol always wondered what the reply would have been had he been richer. Sometimes he wished he had the Gift, but not often, having heard too many tales of magicians devoured by the demons they called up. And so, like most, he hired their services when he could afford them, from the cheapest of village witches to deadly thaumaturges like Abbas.

"After your adventures," Abbas rumbled, "I thought you might be hungry."

Peirol began to say he didn't have the time, then caught himself. He waited until Kima had taken a chair, then sat. There were three varieties of eggs nested in multicolored onyx cups, steam rising invitingly; a dozen kinds of bread, heated and cold; a platter of smoked meats and fish; a covered dish that held poached fish; a half ham; spiced kidneys; jams, marmalades, and comfits. Peirol stopped listing delights and ate.

"My attention was drawn toward Thyone last night. Koosh Begee will no longer bedevil the city streets. A pity, that," Abbas said sarcastically.

Peirol glanced at Kima.

"Don't worry about turning her stomach," Abbas said. "She knows men's hands are seldom blood-free."

"Koosh Begee being dead—Grandfather said you killed him—made me feel good," the girl said. "I once paid to ransom a girlfriend's ring from his gang. The man he sent had the audacity to think I was attracted to him, and made a rather crude suggestion."

"It was a pity," Abbas said, "the ransomer happened to trip and break his neck after the ring was returned. A great pity."

Peirol's eyes had been turning toward that cleft in Kima's robe but now returned to watching his fingers spread red jam on a piece of bread. Suddenly the jam looked exactly like the blood that'd bubbled from

Koosh Begee's throat. His appetite vanished, and his stomach curdled.

Abbas noted his expression. "Drink some of that herbed wine from that narrow-necked pitcher," he ordered. "It will settle your stomach."

Peirol obeyed.

"So Koosh Begee is dead, you are the cause, there was nothing but small gems in Slask's temple, Begee's toughs—or rather the woman who is Begee's widow, who now hopes to rule the gang—will be wanting your blood, and you have no idea what to do or where to flee. Or if you should flee at all."

"That is exactly the case," Peirol managed. "You seem to know everything."

"A sorcerer who doesn't generally finds his existence altered, and not for the better," Abbas said grimly. "Now, do you think the slight debt you incurred with me is enough to make me deal with those thieves?"

Peirol shook his head rapidly. "No, sir. I'm not a dunce. I just thought, you being wiser and knowing more of the world, maybe you could suggest what I should do."

Abbas picked up a bit of buttered toast, put a slice of smoked fish on it, chewed meditatively.

"Under normal circumstances," he said, "you could simply go live in the hills for a few weeks, until these jackals find a new master. Felons prate of revenge, but seldom follow through, unless it's in blood-heat or if there's possible gain. But there is"—the magician delicately cleared his throat—"the matter of his wife, who is ambitious and, for reasons we need not dwell on, most vengeful."

Kima giggled again. "He's blushing."

Peirol looked at the floor, drank more wine.

"I fear this widow will make certain you're not forgotten," Abbas went on. "And since she's from a thieving family, her words will be listened to.

"So, young Peirol, you must leave Sennen. The question is, in which direction? You could, if you hurried, catch up to that caravan to Osh that you stupidly didn't join. Assuming you're able to elude the bandits along the way. And assuming that you can somehow acquire greater gold than those jewels you found beneath Thyone will bring.

"I could provide that, if I wished. But I am not a philanthropic man. Especially when something more interesting offers itself.

"Let me ask something. Have you ever heard of a gem called the Empire Stone?"

Peirol jolted. This was the second time within hours the memory of his father's tale, years ago in that wind-ripped hut far to the south, had been forced on him.

"Yes," he said.

"Most have," Abbas agreed. "Gives the power of kingdoms, can doom or save its owner, and so on and so forth. I also assume you've heard there have been many who set out to look for it, none of whom have ever returned?"

Peirol nodded.

"So. I have, through my divinations, some inkling

as to where it might be sought. Does that interest you?"

Brave heroes, who journey out . . .

"It might," Peirol said cautiously, feeling the blood-thrill he'd had as a boy surge within him.

"Then let us discuss the actual mechanics of the deal before I become more specific. I would propose to advance you a certain amount of gold for your expenses, and perhaps a couple of charms or philtres, and you would take sail on a ship east, across the Isma'in Sea, the day after tomorrow.

"I will warn you, the journey will take you far to the east, into countries no man or woman from Sennen has ever dreamed of, let alone visited."

Peirol smiled wryly. "I'm almost twenty-five, sir, and I've wandered little beyond the three countries bordering the one of my birth. That isn't what I dreamed of when I was a boy."

"Good. So of course I needn't mention that a wizard should never be double-dealt with, for his vengeance is invisible, travels faster than the swiftest horse or ship, and can seldom be avoided."

Peirol's lips thinned. "And I," he said carefully, looking directly into Abbas's eyes, "have yet to break my word, when I give it in sincerity."

"Good!" Kima said, clapping her hands. "He doesn't draw back, Gran."

"No, he doesn't," Abbas agreed. "So if you secure the Empire Stone and return with it here, I shall make you richer than you can possibly imagine."

"I've got a *very* good imagination," Peirol said.

"No matter," Abbas said. "With the Empire Stone,

all—and I mean everything—shall lie within my grasp."

His eyes glittered strangely. He went to a sideboard and brought an oilskin pouch back to the table.

"All I have to do," Peirol said sarcastically, "is somehow . . . acquire this stone from its present owner. Since I assume he's attached to it, that means steal it."

"Just so. I wish I knew who holds it," Abbas said.

Peirol made a face. "That does complicate things somewhat."

"A bit. I know the Empire Stone is in a city called Restormel, about which no one knows anything. I assume there are powerful sorcerers there, for my attempts to investigate magically have all been blocked, as if I were trying to peer through a storm."

"The legend says anyone who holds the Stone can make himself a king," Peirol said. "Wouldn't you be better advised to send a magical army, or a real one, instead of a dwarf?"

"One man may succeed where an army fails." Abbas smiled. "Besides, to regain a stone whose value is beyond that of a nation, it amuses me to dispatch a single man."

"I hope," Peirol said, "I share your amusement when you tell me more."

Peirol finished the last page of notes and replaced the sheaf of paper in the oilcloth pouch. Abbas sat next to him, arms folded, waiting patiently. Kima curled on the floor, watching them.

"A far journey," Peirol said.

"As I warned you," Abbas said.

"The countries beyond Sennen to the east—at least the ones I've heard of—are all at each other's throats, from what traders have said."

"It will take a clever man to make his way," Abbas agreed.

"A clever—or rich—man. But I don't believe one man could carry enough gold to bribe and buy safe passage for that great a distance."

Abbas made no comment.

Peirol smiled wryly. "But as a trader, an artist, a man traveling in gems, the journey might be possible."

"Your very profession," Kima said.

"I would need the tools of my trade—balance, glass, cutter's, material for my special glues, some potions, polishing compounds, inks, cleaving knives, and such. All of which are in my rooms, which I dare not go to, for Begee's thugs are waiting. If I accept your task, I'll have to chance finding their replacements along my route."

"Not necessarily. Wait." Abbas left the room.

Peirol yawned, the night's struggles and the excellent meal catching up with him. He went to the balcony, looked out.

"It's a beautiful day," he said.

Kima came up beside him. "It is," she agreed.

"If things were not as they are," Peirol said, carefully not looking at her, "it would be a day for three horses, one for you, one for me, and one for our picnic. We could ride out into the hills, where I know a vale with a bubbling creek running through it, a vale with a pool in its center where otters sport and fish jump."

"How many others have you taken there?"

"No one, oddly enough. It was a place I discovered by myself, a place out of time, where I used to go to think . . . and dream. I never had the desire to take anyone else there. Not until now."

Kima turned away as Abbas came back.

"Your rooms have not yet been ransacked," he said. "But there are four men waiting at the stairs, another four inside. Two more hide at the back."

"As I feared," Peirol said.

"No fear is necessary. I've already dispatched my . . . agents to retrieve your tools, and clothing suitable for travel. There will be no problems."

Peirol blinked.

"I imagine, since I've been around jewelers enough, my representatives will know precisely what to take," Abbas continued. "I just hope my taste in your clothing will be acceptable."

"You're assuming I accept your offer?"

Abbas smiled broadly. "Do you see other options?"

"This entire day has shaken my belief in free will," Peirol grumbled.

"You mean you *still* believe in that?"

Peirol's smile echoed Abbas's, became laughter.

Kima showed Peirol to a bedroom and told him he could sleep as long as he wished. Their household, befitting a wizard, generally was active at night. Abbas was down for a nap, and she would follow.

"Dinner will be at full dark," she said. "But perhaps you might choose to wake a bit early and keep me company while Gran is in his study."

Peirol put on a very innocent face. Kima giggled and kicked him in the ankle.

"I'll bet I know what you're thinking, and you ought to be ashamed of yourself, and we barely know each other!"

"I was thinking of nothing," Peirol said, "except how nice that bed you just showed me looks."

"*Just* the bed for sleeping, sirrah?"

"Have a nice nap, Kima."

The setting sun was shining into the chamber when Peirol woke. But that was not what had brought him out of his sleep and troubled dreams.

He could faintly hear, from above, the grumblings of a great voice, far deeper and stronger than Abbas's. He listened but couldn't distinguish any words. Then he heard Abbas answering, and he shivered.

But the day was still warm, and the grumblings stopped. Peirol got out of bed, stretched, then saw his tools and clothes lying on a table. He prided himself on sleeping lightly, especially in a strange place, but whatever minion of Abbas's had brought them hadn't disturbed him.

He went into the next room, found a bath not only filled, but with water steaming, and again his neck hairs prickled at the knowledge of magic.

Peirol bathed, used the straight razor and soap he found, brushed his hair half a hundred times, dressed, and went upstairs, back into the dining area.

There was no one about, and now the household was completely silent.

Peirol thought of taking down one of the *grimoires* or scrolls on shelves but decided he'd best not, for fear of Abbas's displeasure or, worse, bringing up some horrid monster from the depths by inadvertently reading an incantation aloud. Peirol knew little of how magic worked, and wished to know less.

Instead he got the bag with the gems looted from Slask's temple and examined them. Some were cut, some rough. He considered which he wanted to work into a design, which might be easily sold when he reached the ship's promised first port of Arzamas.

He jerked back from his thought when a soft voice from behind said, "Isn't it lovely, how they catch the last of the sun and hold it?"

Kima now wore a black dress of the softest, finest wool that fitted close to her neck, followed her body's lines to her knees, then pooled at her ankles. It was a garment more suited for an older woman, but Kima evidently was the woman of the household.

"Good afternoon," Peirol said. "I hope you slept well."

"Until Gran started talking to his demons or spirits or whoever was making that horrid sound."

"It woke me as well." Peirol wanted to change the subject. He rolled the gems around the table. "Actually they catch and hold more than half of the light, not like glass or crystal," Peirol said. "Or so I was taught."

"Taught?"

"You don't think I just happened to be born knowing things about gems, do you? Dwarves," and here

Peirol put on a monstrous leer, "learn straaaange things when they're growing—or, in my case, not growing. But that's not one of them.

"I was apprenticed from the age of twelve for five years under the greatest jeweler in the world, a man named Rozan in Ferfer, to the south. Then for another two I was his journeyman. Some say I was destined by the gods to be what I am." Peirol made a face. "People that said that were the sorts who think the gods never take with one hand without giving with the other. I think I just worked harder than anybody else.

"Anyway, I took examinations before the Jewelers' Guild in Ferfer, was deemed qualified as a jeweler, and began traveling: sometimes selling, sometimes buying, sometimes crafting jewels.

"Three years ago, I came to Sennen, and met you not long afterward, when you were a mere slip of a thing.

"And now," Peirol made his voice ancient, quakey, "I'm gray and frail, and you're blossoming into womanhood."

"Who taught you to talk like that?" Kima said. "You sound like a romance."

"And what's the matter with that?"

"Romances are written by old poops to be read by fat, middle-aged women who never get . . . who don't know any men."

"Which is why you've never read even one."

Kima laughed again.

"So now you know all that's interesting about me," Peirol said. "How did you come to Sennen? Are your parents not among us?"

"Oh, they're still alive," she said. "My father—Gran's only son—turned out not to have any sign of the Gift. He loved cattle, though, and Gran bought him a great ranch in the Uplands and a title when somebody happened to die without any children.

"I could be up there with him, and with my stepmother if I wanted to."

"But you don't want to?" Peirol said. "Why not?"

"Cows? Bulls? Barns? The only excitement when somebody tries to steal some of the cattle, and the men ride them down and hang them along the road? Or getting to go to town—a little bitty town—three or four times a year?" Kima extended her tongue, crossed her eyes. "I died every day from boredom."

"Odd. You look quite alive to me."

"That's because Gran came to visit, and I guess he sensed the dull was going to kill me for real. And Da and Ma thought I was too wild for the ranch, and maybe a wizard could keep me in hand." Kima looked out over the balcony, smiled a secret smile. "He thinks he still can, too." She turned back to Peirol before he could respond. "You're a person of gems. They say that jewels have a secret meaning. Do they?"

"It wouldn't be a secret if I told you."

"Peirol! What does it mean when, say, you give me this stone?"

She picked up a cut blue gem.

"That's a sapphire," he said. "It means true friendship."

"Oh." Kima set it down, picked up another.

"What about this pretty black one?"

"That's an opal. It doesn't have any meaning, at

least not in the way you're interested in. Black opals are supposed to be unlucky."

Kima dropped that hastily. "This one? It's an emerald, right?"

"Right. That's given for faithfulness, for virtue."

"And these two red ones?"

"They're not the same. One's a ruby, the other's a fire opal. See, in the center of the opal, what looks like a flame? Hold it up to the sun."

"Oooh. And they mean?"

"Well, uh, passion," Peirol said.

"You'd give it to someone you wanted to make love to?"

"Or are making love to," Peirol said, "and you want to continue the affair."

Kima rolled the fire opal in her fingers.

"That's nice," she said. "I like that."

She set it aside reluctantly, picked up another.

"I know this one is a diamond. But why isn't it clear like the ones I've got?"

"It's what's called a fancy stone," Peirol explained. "The clear ones are generally the most prized, but there are ones even more rare. That yellow one you've got isn't all that valuable. The exotics are blue, the deeper blue the more valuable. There are red diamonds, too. I've only seen one in my whole life, and that was in my master's private collection.

"The rarest of all are the green ones. Some say they exist in nature, some say a diamond can be changed by magic. I don't know."

"And diamonds mean?"

Peirol found himself a bit nervous.

"They're supposed to ward off evil. They keep you from worrying. And they cure insanity too."

Kima lifted her head from the stone, gazed deep into Peirol's eyes.

"I like diamonds the best," she said, voice low, throaty, sounding quite older than her years.

The next day Peirol went over his notes, examined Abbas's maps, and considered what problems he might encounter. But mainly he rested. He realized the past few Times, deep in the heart of Begee's underworld, had been like winding a clockwork toy tighter and tighter.

The catch had broken with Begee's death, and he felt tension wash away and excitement build for his quest.

In early afternoon he found himself atop Abbas's tower. By night it would be threatening, with the great wizard chanting spells, and stars and comets answering him while demons swirled about.

But this day the sun shone down, and the winds from the sea were blocked by the parapet. He sprawled comfortably on a low, wide couch, a glass with ice, lime, and a touch of sugar at hand, wearing only shorts.

On another couch was Kima, seemingly asleep. A band of felt shaded her eyes.

Peirol had been considering her; he realized his body was displaying his thoughts, and rolled over on his stomach.

Kima raised her head. "Talk to me, Peirol. Abbas

thinks I'm a child, and won't talk about interesting things with me."

"What's interesting?"

"Tell me a story about . . . about a king's daughter, and about jewels."

Peirol thought, then began the story of a king's daughter, beautiful, of course, who lived in a great, lonely palace set in a huge, secret garden. All the servants were invisible—

"—Like ours."

Peirol thought, I hope not, fearing what demons served wizards, went on. The king was afraid his daughter would marry someone beneath her, which he considered everyone, and so the poor princess was most lonely.

Then one day, on her walk in the garden, she found a diamond. But she could see no one around. The next day, there was another diamond, and on the third day, another.

This went on for half a Time, and the poor princess, in addition to having a growing collection of jewels, was almost beside herself.

But every day she went to that particular garden and always found a beautiful jewel beside a tiny pool.

Then, one day, there was a rather large frog sitting beside the diamond.

She picked up the stone, and wistfully told the frog that she wished he could speak, and tell her about her unknown admirer.

" 'But I can,' the frog said, and the girl jumped in surprise. 'I am a noble prince, cursed to become a frog by an evil demon,' " Peirol went on. " 'It was only by the luck of the gods that I hopped into your garden, and was able to see your loveliness.

" 'Frogs have powers,' the creature went on, 'or at least I do, and one of them is to conjure up gems. I have no use for such, but thought your beauty deserves presents such as I've been giving you.'

" 'You are a lovely frog,' the princess said, 'and I wish I could reward you.'

" 'Actually,' the frog said, 'there is a way. For the curse can be lifted by the kiss of a beautiful virgin.'

"The princess snuffled a little at this, for she was indeed a virgin, having little chance to be otherwise and not liking her fate greatly.

" 'If I kiss you, frog, you'll become a great prince again? I assume you were young and handsome when the demon cursed you.'

" 'Of course,' the frog said.

"So the princess picked up the frog, and considered him, and he was a very ugly frog, even for a frog. But handsome princes didn't come calling every day, or any day for that matter.

"She puckered up her lips and gave the frog the most passionate kiss of her life."

Peirol picked up his glass and drank deeply.

"What happened then?"

"She developed a terrible wart on her lower lip," Peirol said. "Which proves you should never trust a talking frog."

Kima sat up abruptly, nearly losing her eyeband.

"That's really stupid!"

"You said you didn't like romances."

Kima stared at him, then started laughing. She broke off, stared at him for a long while.

"My grandfather is even wiser than he knows," she said. "You are dangerous. You can make a woman laugh."

Peirol shouldered a heavy pack. It held three sets of durable clothing, dress garments, boots, the oilskin pouch with Abbas's notes, Peirol's tools, the gems from Thyone, and a heavy bag of Abbas's gold. Abbas hadn't offered any explanation of how Peirol's belongings had been secured, nor did the dwarf get any chance to thank Abbas's unseen servants. He was somewhat grateful for not having to make their acquaintance.

Abbas had offered Peirol a matched set of pistols, powder, and balls, but he declined—they were too heavy, too unreliable, and would make him look very rich and hence a target the moment he produced them.

He did accept one thing, though. Abbas cast a spell, using herbs muddled in a mortar, then a bit of stone from the far north, mutterings, and rubbing the stone on Peirol's tongue.

"This'll give you a gift with words," Abbas explained. "You'll understand, and be able to speak, any language—or rather, any language the person you're talking to speaks and understands. This means you'll be able to talk in his dialect, his accent, even.

"You should attempt," the wizard added dryly, "not to talk to someone who's tongue-tied or has a cleft palate, at least one with a short temper, since you'll speak their language exactly as they do, and they might think you're mocking them. I could cast a more involved incantation that would let you know all of man's languages and perhaps that of a demon or two, but that takes two days and is a bit painful, since it requires making a dozen or so slits in your tongue." Peirol hastily said he was most content with the spell already cast.

Peirol looked down the road toward Sennen, then turned back to Kima.

"Well," he said.

Kima untied the green scarf around her neck, and handed it to him. "Here. A boon . . . a token."

Peirol took it, looked into her emerald green eyes, as green as her gift, then touched the scarf to his lips. "Thank you," he said. "When I return, you'll wear it again."

"Maybe," she said, "when we have our picnic."

She suddenly leaned over, kissed him on the lips, then pulled away and went inside and closed the door.

Peirol stood a moment, feeling the morning breeze ruffle his hair, and was ready for a crusade, any crusade, but felt the Empire Stone somewhere out there, somewhere beyond, waiting for him to seize it.

If I were anything but an imbecile, he thought, I'd take the mage's gold and flee hard to the east. Only a fool takes a wizard's errand, Peirol.

"You're right," he said aloud. "A fool indeed."

Whistling merrily in the winter sunlight, he started down the road toward Sennen's harbor, where the promised merchantman would sail west within the day.

THREE

*

Of Storms
and Intrigues

For the first two days, the wind bore fair, carrying them quickly across the Ismai'n Sea to the east.

One seaman growled that dwarves were bad luck, and two others looked worried. One said something about mayhap it'd be best to tip him overboard.

Peirol had quickly spiked that tale by saying *he'd* always heard men of small stature were quite good luck, and the mate, a darkly handsome rogue named Edirne, agreed, showing only Peirol his raised eyebrow and a grin, saying their quick passage proved the dwarf right.

That ended that, but Peirol still kept a dagger close by.

The merchantman, the *Petrel*, was a well-built three-masted caravel, with a lateen sail on each mast.

In addition to its cargo, the *Petrel* had fairly luxurious cabins for six passengers, of which two were occupied.

Its master and only other officer was a very experienced elderly woman named Todolia. The crew was a dozen men, the cargo assorted luxury goods for the great city of Arzamas, which, according to Abbas's maps—which grew vaguer and vaguer the farther from Sennen they got—was about a quarter of the way to Restormel, where the Empire Stone supposedly was.

Pride of place aboard the *Petrel* went to Zaimis Nagyagite, just eighteen, wildly beautiful, the intended bride of Baron Aulard, a very rich man who lived somewhere south of Arzamas. She was fairly small, slender but with full breasts, no more than a head and a half over Peirol, blond, green-eyed, with a perfect complexion.

Zaimis had almost everything else besides the great dowry carried in two of the other cabins—charm, poise, a purring voice, and the ability to give total attention to any man who spoke to her. Peirol thought her somewhat lacking in intellect, but most rich men didn't seem so much interested in a woman as companion rather than accoutrement.

Zaimis was of course a virgin, he was told, and Peirol nodded solemn agreement—the wealthy never married otherwise unless the bride-to-be was richer or higher-placed than the man. To keep it that way, Zaimis was guarded by a large, scowling eunuch named Libat.

Zaimis admired Peirol's strength one afternoon on

deck when he was exercising, and after that he never missed daily training, no matter what the weather, just outside the great cabin. He was acting a bit of the fool, he knew, but almost all the men did the same, going out of their way to pass by her quarters and be growled at by the eunuch, who hovered around his charge and slept across her doorway at night. Only Edirne seemed oblivious.

They reached the far shore of the Ismai'n Sea, threaded their way through the maze of islands.

Three times small boats put out from shabby villages, shouting dimly heard threats, but the *Petrel,* with a favoring wind, easily outsailed them. Peirol made sure when these would-be pirates appeared that he was on deck, armed, ready to defend himself and Zaimis, and hoped she noticed his prospective bravery.

He also took a private precaution, finding a small leather bag with double ties. He put the best of his gems in it and tied it behind his left knee, where no searcher would likely chance upon it.

No one slept much when they were among the islands, and when they cleared them, entering the Sea of Cotehl, they celebrated with a small feast.

Edirne sang two songs of his homeland, mournful melodies accompanied by tapping feet and crewmen echoing and holding the last word of each line; Peirol told three stories, two funny and one romantically tragic that pleased Zaimis, for she patted his hand when he finished, and left her hand on his. Emboldened, he slid a little closer to her along the bench, saw Libat frown and touch the handle of his sword. Peirol moved back to his former place.

They turned south to follow the chain for a week or so, then make an open-water crossing at the Straits of Susa, not daring the Sea of Wrath further south, to reach the Manoleon Peninsula, then north again, around the curve of a great bay to Arzamas.

One afternoon, Zaimis fell into conversation with Peirol, admitting that she knew nothing about dwarves and had only seen them in exhibitions.

"Some of my less fortunate brothers and sisters end there," Peirol said, angry at the implication he was some sort of freak or monstrosity.

Zaimis seemed oblivious. She looked up and down the deck, saw no one close enough to be listening.

"I've heard great lords—such as my intended, Lord Aulard—sometimes keep dwarves in their bed-chambers, and fondle them before going in to their ladies. I have heard it increases desire."

"Not dwarves, my lady," Peirol said, his anger broken by amusement. "Hunchbacks is what you're thinking of. And it does increase desire—for the hunchback."

She giggled. "You're clever. What is it you do?"

"I'm a man who travels in gems."

"A jeweler?"

"Sometimes a lapidarist, sometimes a trader."

"You know gems really, really well?"

"I like to think I have a certain familiarity."

"Come with me." Peirol, interested, obeyed, and the eunuch silently trailed behind. They went below into the great cabin, then into Zaimis's cabin, a flounce of pinned-up silks and cashmere. Zaimis bade the eunuch open a triple-locked case with keys from a chain around her neck. Peirol chanced peering, saw a promising-looking bosom. Zaimis saw him, giggled, made no move to discourage him.

She opened a soft cloth envelope, took out a necklace, and held it out to Peirol.

He gasped at the dazzle that caught the light from the two portholes, sent it flashing around the room.

"Blue diamonds," he murmured. "I've but seen those two or three times, and never more than singly, generally mounted as the centerpiece of a tiara or in a ring."

"Aren't they gorgeous? It's an engagement present from my husband-to-be, and he said it's but a small part of the jewels that'll bedeck me after we're married." She handed the necklace to Peirol. "Perhaps you'd be good enough to tell me what it might be worth—though I have no concern about that, but mere curiosity."

Her eyes gleamed with a most uncasual interest.

"Blue," Peirol muttered to himself, his suspicions automatically prickling. "Gold chain, of course, nicely turned, each link hand-forged, pure gold here, very soft. Thirty-two stones, from, oh, eight *varjas* down to one near the clasp—mine-cut, a bit old-fashioned, but still lovely—blue, oh so blue, aren't they." He lit a candle, pulled a curtain. "Still very blue."

"Is there something wrong with that?"

"Not at all," Peirol said. "Increases the value, and for me, the beauty. Just a minute. Let me fetch some of my devices, so I may give you a proper valuation."

He returned with his roll, opened it, took out a glass, examined each of the gems.

"Each stone is quite flawless—your lord must love you very much."

Zaimis simpered. Peirol scratched his chin, took another glass from his roll. This one was old, tarnished silver, a bit battered, with obscure letters around it. It'd cost Peirol half a dozen emeralds and a week's work setting them for the trader who brought him the glass and taught him the spell that went with it.

He screwed it into his eye and whispered its spell under his breath as he touched the glass to the smallest diamond.

> "See clear
> See fair
> Honest light
> Honest work."

The stone instantly lost its incandescence, was no more than a well-polished piece of, probably, quartz.

"Well, well, well," Peirol said, taking away the jewel, which instantly took on its former radiance.

"What do you think?"

"I think," Peirol said, picking his words carefully, "I think you have a totally unique work here, whose price is beyond value, and your lord-to-be should be taken as a man of most unusual qualities."

Zaimis beamed more brightly than her false gems.

The day afterward the skies were dark and threatening and a wind built, keening through the rigging.

Peirol sought the captain.

"Not good," Todolia muttered. "I'd suggest you lash down your gear, young man. There'll be a blow, coming down from the Sea of Wrath, and all we'll be able to do is reef sail, set a sea anchor, run before the tempest, and hope not to be driven too far north.

"Get yourself to the galley and eat hearty, for there'll be no warm food when the storm strikes."

Peirol obeyed, eating the thick pea soup the cook served until he could hold no more, then made sure his pack was filled and sword belt ready, in case they had to take to the cork rafts on either side of the poop deck.

He helped Libat the eunuch and Zaimis secure their possessions, wanting to stay and reassure her everything would be fine but knowing better than to think he could convince the eunuch to leave them alone, and went on deck and began helping the crew.

The sailor who'd wanted to pitch him overboard found himself heaving on a line with the dwarf. He grudgingly admitted he'd seldom seen anyone as strong as Peirol and guessed he'd been wrong, "Though we'll see what this tempest brings."

The winds grew, and Todolia, Edirne, the bosun, and the doubled steersmen fought the rudder, turning the ship north, back the way it'd come, and east.

"Better the open sea," Edirne shouted, "than being blown on a headland."

They streamed a long length of rope, tied in a bight, from the stern as a sea anchor, reefed all sail except for a hank on the foremast to hold the bow with the wind, and then waited.

The storm smashed down, and there was nothing

to do but go below and hang on. Peirol was pitched out of his bunk twice, snarled at the gods, pulled his bedding down onto the floor, borrowed some rope, tied himself into a corner, and tried to sleep.

He couldn't—the caravel was pitching, yawing, its wooden sides shrieking protest, trying to tear itself apart. He went into the passageway, stumbling, bounced from bulkhead to bulkhead, found seamen being sick in buckets and on themselves, almost threw up himself.

He pushed the hatch open, looked at the deck buried in green water, saw a greater wave coming aboard, hastily slammed the hatch, and went back to his cabin.

Eventually he slept, woke, went out, found some dry ship's biscuit to gnaw on, knocked on Zaimis's door to see if he could do anything, and was told to go away, with a groan added. He put on his heavy coat and went on deck, up the companionway to the poop deck. It'd been sea-swept, and the railings were gone, as were the rafts. Edirne stood at the binnacle, two seamen behind him at the rudder. They were soaked, eyes red from salt spray and lack of sleep.

Peirol asked if he could help and wondered why he was such an idiot.

Edirne leaned close and shouted over the wind's howl: "Good! Spell one man on the rudder. The other one'll keep the course. That'll give the other two of us a chance to go below for a breather."

Peirol obeyed, and the universe shrank to his watchmate, whose name he never learned; the leather-wrapped boom that was the tiller; smashing seas and winds howling about fear and drowning; fighting, pulling for an hour, a week; and then somebody was pulling him away, saying it was her watch.

He stumbled below, ate something, pulled off his sodden boots, slept, woke, stupidly put his boots back on, and went back on deck to that damnable rudder.

He didn't know if it was day or night. The crashing waves were phosphorescent, the skies always dark. Twice he heard a faint scream, once saw a man lifted high by a wave, dashed into blackness. The world was sleeping, eating, and nearly drowning, day after day after day.

Peirol didn't know if he was getting used to the tearing muscles, the crashing waves, or if the storm was lightening. Then Edirne told the other man on the tiller to go below, Peirol could handle it.

He felt a flash of real pride, grinned at Edirne, saw an answering smile. The mate clapped him on the back, went to the binnacle, peered at the swinging compass rose.

Peirol looked off to port at the choppy waves, tops still torn away by the wind, the water a frothing white. Then there was something else, something dark, and Peirol started to scream there were rocks, they were about to be wrecked, and that something dark lifted its head, and two huge eyes two feet or more in diameter—wise, knowing, below a curling red feathered crest like a monstrous rooster—looked at him. They saw the depths of his soul, then the monster was gone.

Edirne was beside him, shaking him, shouting, "What's the matter, man?"

Peirol was about to explain, shook his head.

"Keep the damned course," the mate snarled, and Peirol nodded.

Then one day he awoke and the wind was gone, and the seas were calming. He made his way on deck and saw that the *Petrel*, under light sail, was closing on land.

"Where are we, captain?" he called to Todolia.

"I don't know," she said. "We'll anchor inshore, and I'll see if it's on any of my charts while we make and mend from the storm."

They did, in a cove that encircled them like a protective hand. The sun came out and they made repairs, cooked, ate, slept again, and held death ceremonies for the two drowned sailors.

Todolia said she thought the *Petrel* had been carried far north, far off their course, she thought to the great island of Parasso, and they'd have to sail south. She looked worried, and Peirol asked why. She shook her head, refused to answer. He sourly wondered how far off his journey the storm had taken him, how much time would be lost before he could continue his quest.

Unable to sleep, Peirol stayed on deck for a time, listening to the three sailors on watch quietly talk between themselves. He heard one say something about "black ships," the other something about "sea dogs of Beshkirs," the third "better them than those murderous godsdamned Sarissans from the north," but then they noticed him and said no more.

He went below and was about to go to his cabin and try sleep when he noticed two interesting things. The first was, there was a light on in Zaimis's cabin; the second, that he saw no signs of the eunuch.

Peirol realized he must've recovered from the storm when he felt his body stir. He was about to tap on the door when wisdom took him. He combed the ship, looking for the eunuch. He couldn't find him, grinned tightly, went back to the great cabin.

He opened the hatch quietly just in time to see Edirne slip into Zaimis's cabin, the door closing behind him. Peirol waited for roars of rage from the eunuch but heard nothing for a while—quite a long while.

Peirol went into his own cabin, undressed, and crawled into bed. He managed to fall asleep just before dawn, but the two in the other cabin were very awake and noisy.

He woke a couple of hours later, put his breeches on, and went on deck to wash. Zaimis's cabin door was closed.

Edirne was on deck, naked, looking wrung out. He dragged a bucket up from the sea, dumped water over his head, and began scrubbing his body with a bar of soap.

Peirol stripped, took the line, and brought up his own bucketful. Edirne tossed him the soap.

"So now we sail north to Arzamas, to dispose of our cargo," Peirol said. "After a storm such as we went through, I wouldn't guess any of its owners would worry if there's a bit of . . . damage."

Edirne roared laughter.

"My friend, some of the cargo will arrive in exactly the shape it left in."

"Oh."

"That no-longer-a-man who was supposed to be

guarding certain cargo has vanished, by-the-bye. We're missing a small cask of wine, some dry rations. I guess he swam ashore during the night and fled."

"So my caution wasn't necessary," Peirol said.

"It slowed you badly," Edirne agreed. "Speaking of which, the lady Zaimis told me you appraised one of her presents, and told me exactly how you put your words. You *are* a careful man."

"It seems to pay."

"Sometimes yea, sometimes nay," Edirne said. "Perhaps nay with eunuchs, perhaps yea with barons with short tempers and swordsmen by the company on retainer.

"I find the situation amusing. Lord Aulard is known for his love of women and gems. I've heard he came by some of his gems in . . . interesting ways. Be that as it may, when he takes one of his wives into Arzamas, he drapes her with glitter, the tale goes. But if there's a theft, or a loss, he never seems to mind. That suggests something."

Peirol remained silent.

"What a good jest. False gems for false virtue." Again, Edirne laughed. "I would imagine someone aboard this ship might have learned to moan like a virgin and make a small cut for some blood at the proper time, wouldn't you?"

Peirol didn't answer, both because he considered himself a gentlemen and because something Edirne said had just struck him. "You said *one* of Lord Aulard's wives?"

"I did, did I not? I think there's a certain young

woman who may be in for some surprises about certain Manoleon customs, don't you?"

Peirol saw movement and hurriedly pulled his breeches back on as Zaimis, looking as pure as any temple virgin, came on deck. Edirne, laughing harder than ever, dressed quite leisurely, and Zaimis watched him as coolly as if she was considering a well-made statue.

Two turnings of the glass later, the *Petrel* sailed south. Half a day later, the black ships attacked.

FOUR

*

Of Piracy
and Rape

There were four sleek black galleys, each nearly two hundred feet long. They came from behind a headland, oars dipping in unison, skittering toward the *Petrel*.

Todolia looked up at the caravel's sails, slatting in the light wind, muttered a prayer, and shouted for the men to arm themselves and prepare for boarding.

Peirol obeyed, hurrying to his cabin. Outside came shouts and the thunder of feet.

"What's going on?" a wide-eyed Zaimis asked.

"Pirates, my lady," the dwarf said. "You'd best stay below, and not let them see your beauty and become more determined."

Even now, Zaimis managed a white-faced coquette before she went back into her cabin and closed the door.

Peirol went back on deck. The crewmen now wore motley leather armor and were armed with cutlasses and knives. One or two had javelins, another pair sporting bows.

Someone said in a low voice, "Best just surrender. There's no more'n a handful of us, against how many soldiers?"

"I count thirty, mebbe more," another said. "And a few hunnerd oar-slaves on each boat. And cannon. But we'll never raise a white flag. If th' skipper's right, and we're off Parasso, likely th' ships hail from Beshkirs.

"Th' mate spent half a dozen years on their damned galleys, and I've never known anyone who pulled an oar for them who didn't swear he'd rather die'n go back."

"Edirne must've assed somebody fair," a second sailor put in. "None of us'd end up a galley slave, as long as we can shinny up a mast and box a compass. Beshkir's hurting for sailors, always has been, always will be. As for bein' a slave, who hasn't gone overside in a fair port to get out from under an asshole skipper? Chains won't hold me for long, nor any of you, I'd bet."

"There you have it," a third said. "I'd *allus* rather take a chance on life over death."

There were mutters of agreement, but the sailors, at Edirne's command, drew heavy, wide-meshed rope nets from below and draped them loosely from the yardarms to the railings, so boarders would ensnare themselves.

Peirol stared, fascinated, at the oncoming galleys.

They were very narrow-beamed, and bulwarks were built overhanging the hull, rowing benches on them. He counted five slaves on each oar. Gleaming bronze cannon lay in a low carriage in the bows, with two smaller swivel pieces on either side. Men with whips trotted back and forth on catwalks, lashing the oarsmen while thudding drums gave the rhythm. The galleys were twin-masted, with huge, single yardarms on each mast hanging at an angle, sails furled, great banners on one end of each. On the stern of the galleys was a canopy, sheltering the ship's officers and rudder, and above it a huge ornate lantern.

Peirol admired their strange grace—but then the wind brought the stink of the ships, the unwashed, closely packed men, their shit and blood. His stomach roiled.

A sailor was praying loudly for wind, for a sea monster to rise up and save them, but the gods didn't appear to be listening.

Peirol went up to the poop deck, sword in hand. He hoped he didn't look as scared as the man at the rudder.

He saw a man in the bows of the second galley wearing robes, moving his hands back and forth. A feeling of weakness, of panic, swept across him, and Peirol realized there was magic being set against them as well.

A man in the stern of the leading galley shouted through a speaking trumpet. Peirol understood what he was saying and realized that Abbas's spell was at work, for the words changed as he heard them, and became familiar.

"What's he saying?" Todolia asked. "I don't speak whatever heathen language he's blathering."

"He wants us to surrender," Peirol answered, before Edirne could interpret.

The mate gave him a suspicious look but didn't have time for anything else, as the lead galley's cannon boomed, white smoke plumed, and a ball bounced across the water, just in front of their bows.

Edirne picked up a great double-curving bow, nocked an arrow, and sent the shaft arcing toward the first galley. It splashed just short of the ship.

"That's reply enough," he said, and two other cannon boomed from other ships. One missed, but the second smashed through the *Petrel*'s rigging, and lines snapped, falls clattering down to the deck.

"Bad," Todolia said. "Hear that whirring? They're using chain shot, shooting at the rigging. They're trying to dismast us, so they can take the ship intact for the cargo."

"And us for slaves," Edirne said.

"Damme, but I wish the futtering owners would've bought one piece, one frigging falconet, a crappy little moyen even," Todolia growled. "Damn them for the budget-minded butchers they are."

"One popgun wouldn't do much good against those culverin," Edirne said.

"No, but I'd feel like I was doing *something*."

Todolia shouted an obscenity at the galley, waved her fist. Peirol saw a small puff of smoke, heard the captain snort, like an angered bull. She turned, and Peirol gasped. The woman had no face, but a ruin of blood from the musket ball. She put her hand up, then it fell limply, and she sagged as if all the bones in her body had vanished.

"You men," Edirne bellowed at the sailors. "Shoot back at 'em! They've killed our captain!"

But he needed make no warning. Two sailors below were down in blood, writhing. A sailor hurled his javelin out through the netting. It splashed far short of the galley he was aiming at, and the two bowmen loosed shafts.

The galley cannons all fired, a ragged volley, and the *Petrel*'s mainmast snapped, sagged in its stays, and slowly dropped overside. The caravel listed.

"Cut away the rigging and the mast," Edirne ordered. "Get axes! We'll sail around 'em!"

He dropped his bow, went to a gear locker, took out a heavy ax. A javelin arched through the air and took him just below the ribs, the bloody spearhead jutting out through his back. Edirne screamed shrilly, clawed at the shaft of the spear, stumbled, and fell.

"Get the godsdamned white flag up," the sailor who'd speared him shouted. "Before they kill us all!"

Peirol went to Edirne, saw a spark of life flicker, vanish from his eyes as blood poured from his mouth.

"Are you another fool for fightin'?" a voice demanded, and Peirol saw a sailor with cutlass ready. Not trusting what he might say, feeling anger pound at his temples, Peirol dropped his sword, got up, and backed away.

"There's things worse'n bein' an oarsman," the sailor said. "Not that you'll ever pull one, havin' real talents with jewels. Somebody'll snap you out of the slave market on first showin'."

Two galleys were alongside, and grappling hooks dug into the *Petrel*'s bulkheads. Men in armor swarmed up the sides and cut through the netting. They herded the sailors and Peirol to one side, and broke into the great cabin. Peirol heard wood smash, and a scream.

A grinning man stuck his head out. "C'mon, boys, there's meat to share! Get your asses in line!"

There were shouts of glee, and two men dragged a struggling Zaimis out. Another rolled out the small cask of wine that stood in the cabin, smashed in its head with a dagger butt, and dipped himself a palmful. He wore, tied around his neck, the green silk scarf Kima had given Peirol.

A man took hold of Zaimis's dress at the bodice and ripped it away while the woman shrieked. The men watching roared amusement.

Then a pistol thudded, and the first would-be rapist contorted as blood gouted from below his armored waistcoat. He convulsed like a landed fish and lay still.

The others were very still as a large young man with cold eyes and blond hair and beard paced forward. He wore finely worked armor and an ostrich-plumed hat. He had a pistol in each hand, one smoking, two others in his waistband. He stuck the fired piece in his belt, drew, cocked another, blew its slow fuse to life.

"I believe my orders were to take the woman alive and unharmed, were they not? No man disobeys me, and remains healthy. I could've sworn you wretches had learned that lesson well by now."

The blond man nodded to two men, also finely dressed, beside him, obviously officers. "Help the baggage up, and assist her in getting dressed. I'll decide whether we transfer her to my ship or if she would be more comfortable where she is."

He turned his attention to Zaimis. "Don't be frightened, girl. I sought you for your ransom, not for your body. You'll not be harmed—at least not if your master is quick to reward me for saving your life."

Zaimis's eunuch Libat capered forward, beaming as if he'd had his manhood restored. The man leered at Zaimis, who turned away, sobbing bitterly. The man laughed, saw Peirol, and came toward him, as if expecting applause.

Peirol's mind said he was stupid, this would undoubtedly be his death, but his fingers were too quick, sliding behind his buckle, and tossing, underhand, a twin to that dart that had half-blinded the serpent. It flashed into the side of the eunuch's throat. Libat screamed rage, plucked it out, and lifted his sword. Then he looked very surprised as the poison worked quickly. He touched his throat, gaped three or four times, and went down.

There were half a dozen swords at Peirol's guts, and the blond man had a pistol aimed, very steadily, between his eyes. "That was a nasty surprise," he said, after seeing Peirol remained still. "Have you any more of those devices about you?"

"No," Peirol said. He hadn't time to hide another dart.

The man kicked the eunuch's body. "We *do* despise a traitor, don't we?" He didn't seem to require an answer. "Dwarf, listen well. I'm going to allow what you did, for I had no wish to reward this one who told us of his mistress and her value. A faithless servant deserves nothing but death.

"But do you have any ideas of continuing your no doubt quite noble pastime of revenge? If so, your value to me is slight, even though the not-man told us you had certain marketable skills, so I'll toss you overside now."

"No," Peirol said, tiredly. "I'm through with blood."

The blond man lost interest in Peirol, snapped orders to his men.

And so Peirol of the Moorlands became a slave.

FIVE

*

Of Markets
and Madmen

By the time Peirol reached the slave market at Beshkirs, he knew quite a bit more than he had, more than he wanted. He was now the property—and his mind roiled at the word—of Kanen of the Sporades, one of the Beshkirian warlords. He was precisely named.

Beshkirs, a pariah nation of slavers, thieves, fences, and pirates, had existed for half a millennium as a city-state without a real government. Instead, all its services, from garbage collection to war, were put out to the lowest bidder, and the winner's performance was reviewed annually by the city's property-holders. If unsatisfactory, the contract was rebid, and the former contractee subject to trial by ordeal if his performance had been overly incompetent or corrupt.

Beshkirs had half a dozen naval lords. Kanen was

regarded as one of the boldest—as witnessed by his having taken a few of his galleys out before the campaign season, while storms still raged—and luckiest, considering how Zaimis's eunuch had found his ships beached for the night and led them to the *Petrel*.

"Campaigning season?" Peirol asked.

"When we earn our keep," a captor said. "Taking merchantmen, mostly, from the Manoleon Peninsula."

"But this year, we'll likely earn it and more," another added. "We'll likely sail against the Sarissans, since they've been cuttin' into our gelt and the richies can't abide that for long."

The other men looked frightened. Peirol asked what were the "Sarissans," and was told to be silent; mere mention of them might bring them from nowhere.

Peirol asked if the black ships of Beshkirs were the ones that had sacked Thyone centuries ago. One seaman guessed that Beshkirs had stolen that tale to further frighten its prey, and the real black ships, the ones of legend, were either long gone or else from far to the west.

Peirol learned all this and more, for he was the only one on the *Petrel* besides the six-man prize crew. Kanen had decided that Zaimis would be best kept close, and the sailors from the *Petrel* weren't to be trusted, even chained up, so they were transferred to one of the galleys. But a mere dwarf was nothing to worry about. The bodies were dumped overside, the broken mast cut away, and the *Petrel* taken under tow by three galleys, with only a headsail on its foremast to reduce yawing.

Peirol still had the small bag of diamonds behind his left knee, but he knew better than to try to bribe one of the prize crew. It was known that he was a jeweler, and his bag of gold and lesser gems had been discovered. If he came up with another jewel, he'd likely be stripped, searched, and given a "Beshkirs smile," throat slit from ear to ear.

At least he'd recovered his roll of tools, cast aside as worthless when the raiders looted his cabin. So if all went well, and he found the master everyone said he would, Peirol would be able to work his craft, impress his master no end, and hopefully be manumitted.

Eventually the pirates reached Beshkirs and sailed into its harbor. It was at the end of a peninsula, a rocky hand curving around a deep water mooring. Low, thick-walled stone forts were built at either side of the harbor mouth, and the city climbed across the knolls behind them. To one side of the roughly rectangular harbor, more than fifty galleys were drawn up, sterns to a seawall. Behind the seawall loomed a great stone barracks.

"That's where the galley slaves are quartered when they're not afloat," a sailor said. "Free ships are over there." He gestured to the other side of the harbor, where merchant ships were anchored, or tied to wharves. "This bucket and its cargo'll be auctioned for Lord Kanen's and our shares. You and your friends'll be for the auction block."

Peirol had never considered slavery more than a natural part of the world like sunrise and wine, since he of course would never become one. He felt sorry for the slave with a harsh master, and for the poor traveler or soldier who got caught in a slaver's snares. Suddenly he realized being another's property, having to do his bidding forever, would be his doom. For an instant he thought of hurling himself overside, but his good sense caught him. There was always a way out, always something a clever man could do to improve or change his lot. And certainly Peirol of the Moorlands was a clever man. . . .

The slave market was a natural amphitheater in the center of Beshkirs. Stone slave pens that could hold one or a hundred bodies were behind the block, which was large enough to stage a masque. Milling around the front of the block were the traders and hangers-on, exchanging raucous jeering, insults, and lewdness. Behind them, row on row, rose seats where other, slightly more dignified spectators watched and bought.

The pens were crowded with men and women of a dozen shades and, it seemed, a hundred races. There were few children, and only two or three older men or women. Peirol assumed the old ones had some highly marketable skill, fairly sure what had happened to the middle-aged and ugly.

He asked one of the guards about Zaimis, but no one knew her either by name or description. Peirol assumed either Kanen had kept the woman or, since his reputed love was more for gold than sex, had successfully ransomed her to Aulard, her intended husband. He wished her well and hoped her marriage would be happier than he feared, given what Edirne had said.

The auctioneer, Jirl, was a fat, jovial man who carried a heavy staff and kept matters moving quickly.

Someone would be pushed up the stairs by the two guards, who wore studded, weighted gloves and had clubs and daggers at their belt, and blink bewilderedly or try to fix a smile while Jirl rattled off details of the person and announced a floor bid.

Young men, young women, pulled in the highest prices. Sometimes Jirl would allow a dealer or two onto the block, let him—and the dealers were always men—prod and pry the offering. Peirol noted when the man or woman was particularly attractive, however, none of these pit traders were allowed that indignity, no doubt to avoid soiling the merchandise.

He saw one trader of average build, quite normal looking, who bid just on children. Peirol, wondering what they'd be used for, saw the man's expression after his successful bid for a rather handsome boy about eight, shuddered, and looked away.

"TWO GIRLS," Jirl bellowed, and two young women—light-skinned, white-blond, in their early teens—were brought up. "Cirmantian, asserted to be virgins."

There was a howl of disbelief from the pit.

"Also purported to be of noble birth. Brought in by Lord Whaal, one of our most honorable dealers, who advises they have just been brought from their homelands, and neither has ever been a slave. A condition of offer is they are to be sold together. These are prime, my friends, and so I'll start at 500 gold coins. Each."

More lustful shouts, two men shouted offers, and the price rose and rose. A man, richly dressed, waved a fan.

"This is good, this is exciting, my friends," Jirl called. "Baron Clarmen is pleased to offer 2,000 as a preemptive bid . . . wait, I see an offer from Lord Nonac for three, three-five, four, four-five, eight, eight is the bid, eight, eight," and Jirl thudded the staff on the block, "and Baron Clarmen has two of the most beautiful, uh, house servants I've seen for many a day."

And so it went. Only one man struggled, and he was quickly bashed down and dragged back to his pen.

The sailors from the *Petrel* were brought out in a block, and bidding from the upper tiers was brisk. They were sold to a man Jirl called Captain T'thang, and vanished from Peirol's life.

Then it was his turn on the block.

"An interesting specimen, here," Jirl called. "Like the last lot, brought to us by Lord Kanen. This man is reportedly a skilled jeweler, and would certainly make his owner wealthy. Handsome, healthy, young—I'm afraid I'll have to start with an opening bid of . . . 600 gold coins."

"Dwarves ain't good luck," someone called.

"I don't believe that," Jirl said. "Bid on this man, and prove the tattle-talk wrong."

"If he's a jeweler, has he been checked by the guild?" a well-dressed man said. "Has Niazbeck approved his sale? I'd hate to try to market this man's work without approval from the Jewelers' Guild."

Jirl looked worried. "Magnate Niazbeck was supposed to be here, but his appearance seems delayed."

"He's off makin' noises with his toys," someone called.

"On condition Magnate Niazbeck approves, do I have 500 gold pieces?"

"He the man who killed somebody when he was took, after th' ship ran down its colors?"

"I'm, uh, not aware of any such report," Jirl said, stammering a bit.

There was silence.

"Four hundred. Do I have four hundred? Three hundred. Two . . . come now, someone, anyone, make an offer for this valuable artisan."

But no one spoke. Jirl smashed the staff down. "Remove him—next offering."

Peirol of the Moorlands was given back to Lord Kanen, and became a galley slave.

He was taken to the white stone barracks, given a numbered disk and a chain to hang it around his neck, told this was his mustering number and that he would be whipped if he was ever found without it. A barred door was opened, and he was led into a long, open-barred cage that was a sally port into the three-storied barracks with a huge central area and open cells at each level. The room was full of men, bearded, hair untrimmed, wearing everything from rags to soiled finery. A few—and Peirol noticed these were smaller, thinner than the others—were naked.

He sighed, knowing after what a couple of Koosh Begee's thieves had told him about prisons what was likely to come next. The inner door was unlocked; Peirol walked into the main room, and the door clanged shut. There were shouts, catcalls about dwarves, nothing Peirol hadn't heard from street urchins for years and years. He kept his back close to the cage, waited.

One of the better-dressed bullies swaggered up, flanked by three others. "Pay or strip!"

"Pardon?" Peirol asked politely.

"The way things are," a satellite thug explained in a not-uneducated voice. "If you have copper, or a bit of silver, Guran and we'll make sure you're taken care of, not hurt, get food when they serve it. If you're skint, your clothes'll serve for payment. I fancy that tunic—the embroiderin'll look good on me."

"So give," Guran demanded.

"And," another of his men said, "we'll have a look at that wee roll you're luggin'."

Peirol began to slip out of his jacket. Guran beamed, and Peirol spat in his face. Guran recoiled, and Peirol raked the side of his foot down the man's shinbone. He screamed, bent, and Peirol head-butted him in the face. Guran stumbled, fell on his back. His assistants were frozen. Hating what he had to do, but doing it, Peirol jumped forward and stamped hard on Guran's throat with the side of his foot. He felt cartilage, bone crunch, and the man flopped, was dead.

A sound came, somewhere between a hunting beast's roar over his kill and astonishment.

"You killed him," Guran's former toady whispered.

"Did, didn't I," Peirol agreed, forcing toughness when he wanted to vomit. Keeping his eye on the other three, but not very worried that they'd jump him, he knelt, swiftly felt through the corpse's pockets, found a scattering of copper, one gold and four silver coins, as well as a rather handy little knife that he pocketed.

"Lord Kanen'll have you skinned," a watcher said.

"No, he won't," Peirol said. "Guran slipped on the steps, fell. A true pity. I could tell he had signs of real leadership. Now listen well," he said, raising his voice. "Somebody talks to the guards, I'll have time to get you before they take me away. But nobody talks. Who needed Guran, anyway? These assholes who sucked around him? Nobody else. New rule. Everybody leaves everybody else alone. Or else I'll sic my new jackals here on you.

"Now you—"

"Habr," Guran's former aide said.

"Habr. Show me to Guran's cell. That'll do for me."

As Peirol had expected, none of the guards were very interested in the circumstances of the late Guran's passing. He kept the plug-uglies around, to alert him when the guards checked the upper tier and to get food and drink. He warned that any bullying he saw would be dealt with in the same manner as he'd handled Guran. Peirol wasn't naive enough to think the prison had become a delight of civilization, but life appeared quieter.

After a day's thought, peering deeply into the heart of the best diamond he had, which he'd heard gave strength, Peirol had an idea. He set out his tools, wishing he had either a pedal- or sorcery-powered lathe. He also lacked a crucible to melt and cast, so he gave one of his goons a silver coin and an iron spoon and set him to tapping the edge of the coin, turning it regularly hour after hour. Slowly the edge metal flattened, and the coin became a ring two finger-widths wide, needing only its center drilled out.

Peirol mixed glue from his roll, fastened a diamond to a stick, improvised a tiny vise, then began spinning that diamond against another, more perfect greenish-yellow gem, slowly cutting the stone round: what was known as girdling, or, in the case of this already worked gem, perfecting the "bearded," poorly rounded girdle it'd already had.

That finished, he used ink to mark where he'd make cuts, then glued the stone into a little cup. His "working" stone was used to cut a groove into the first diamond along the ink cuts. With his specially made cleaving knife, he made ready to cut the diamond.

Knife ready, about to strike the knife with an iron rod that'd been a cell bar, he whispered a prayer, aimed at whatever god or gods reigned in this land that he didn't much believe in. He was sweating slightly, just as he did whenever he made the first cut on a stone.

Peirol was very glad that he had never had to cut a great diamond, remembering the legend about the master cutter given a great stone who studied it, its lines, its grain, for a year, readied himself for the first cut, made it perfectly, and fell dead from the strain. Peirol didn't believe the story and had a perfectly strong heart; but still, he was glad he hadn't yet had to test it.

He struck, and the diamond split as he wanted.

Again he made a cut, and another cut, checking each facet. Then all that remained was to polish the stone with diamond dust and olive oil, detail the silver and cut its center out, and set the stone, and it would be ready as bait.

But the next dawn there was a tumult, and the slaves were turned out. Lord Kanen was ready to put to sea, on another preseason raid, and Peirol's education began.

A wing—ten galleys—pulled away from the wharf, Peirol's galley, the *Ocean Spell*, flanking Lord Kanen's *Slayer*. There was chanting from magicians afloat and ashore, and bands blared, and smoke of many colors plumed up from the harbor forts, gathered together, twisted and showed a magical sign of great good luck.

Peirol was told he was lucky not being assigned to Lord Kanen's galley, since the lord loved battle even more than gold and insisted his ship always be in the forefront. He was not *that* lucky, because he was taken by Callafo, Kanen's wizard, who was almost as battle-thirsty as his master, but who loudly said that dwarves were lucky.

Peirol was wondering where the hells these tales about dwarves came from. He'd heard none on the moors of Cenwalk nor in Sennen, and he thought wryly that anyone who considered his current state certainly should doubt the validity of the claim.

He learned other names to dread: the oarmaster, Barnack; the captain of the guard, Runo; and the ship captain, Penrith. The latter, he was told, seldom deigned to worry about galley slaves, "but ye're doomed if he does." But Callafo and Barnack were the most dreaded, Barnack because he was their immediate master and punisher; Callafo because he loved to see the lash come down, and would delight in having an oarsman whipped for any reason, or for no reason whatsoever. Callafo considered it a special delight if the slave died under the lash, and had been heard to say it would help his magic.

There were five slaves to a bench, the bench extending somewhat over the sleek side of the galley on the wooden superstructure. Along the outboard side of this decking was a huge thole pin beside each bench. The oars were in three pieces, the blade being separate, the shaft being in two parts, lashed around the thole pin, then the inner third, which would be lighter than the other pieces, with iron cleats for the oarsmen to pull on. An argument could always be made as to what kind of wood was best for the oars, but the longest-serving slaves held for beech, for its strength and flexibility. That mattered, because a lesser wood might be snapped by a storm wave and the jagged end flail the benches like a huge, murderous club.

Each slave was manacled at the ankle, a chain leading to a staple firmly mounted in the bench. Rowers stood, or in the case of the outer oarsmen, half-bent, pulling until they came back against the bench, leaned far back, then pushing down and coming back to their feet, bringing the oar forward for the next stroke. Slaves argued endlessly, in whispers, one eye cocked for the oarmaster and his whip, as to which was the worst rowing position.

Farthest outboard was generally agreed to be the worst, being the wettest and hardest on the back, since anyone of a proper size was forced to row half-bent. Closest inboard was the second worst, since that was nearest to the oarmaster's whip. In between was the most crowded.

"Crowded" was distinctly relative—the whole galley was crowded, 300 or more slaves at the oars, with another 200 soldiers, sailors, officers, and guards, all squirming for position like drowsy snakes when night fell afloat. That was one reason the galleys tried to beach themselves at night, although their fragility was even a greater one. A galley, Peirol heard, would be considered a credit to its builder if it lasted six seasons.

He asked what happened in the seventh. Another slave gave him a scornful look. "You drown when the ship breaks up, stupid. Or if you're unlucky you end up floating on the end of your bench, feeling the sharks nibble. Or if you're even less lucky, they pull you out alive, or your tub's scrapped, and you're pulling from a new bench. Best of all is if you're killed in your first campaign." The slave had been on the galleys, Peirol found, for thirty-seven years.

The jest was that no slave had to worry about trimming his beard—the oar was the best razor, never letting facial foliage grow beyond mid-chest.

Peirol was further unlucky, he learned, because he was set to the third oar, starboard side, of the twenty-five on each side. In a sea, this close to the bow would be very wet, and in battle one of the most likely to be smashed by a ramming enemy. "Or, since you're next to the great gun, to get your guts scattered if the gods-damned gunner makes a mistake and uses too much powder and blows himself up, or the swivel gunner beside him gets excited and puts your sorry ass between the muzzle and his target," he was informed.

Being short, Peirol was given the outboard station, able to begin his stroke standing. He thought he preferred to be half-drowned rather than lashed. He wasn't foolish enough to say he wouldn't stand for the whip, but he remembered his father's beatings.

Peirol's world was now nothing but the oar, to be pulled until he died and went overboard without ceremony or until the gods smiled. "And guess, little man," a guard said, grinning, "which is most likely to happen first?"

Peirol watched his fellows; learned that when the first drumbeat thumped, the oar came down into the water and was pulled through; then, at the second beat, was lifted, feathered, and pushed forward for the next stroke. At first it wasn't bad, then his muscles began to strain, then screamed. Peirol was, in spite of his strength, beginning to hurt, and worried about the oarmaster's lash.

But then drums thundered twice. The oars were lifted and brought inboard, and sailors lashed them down. Peirol heard a great slatting, and the huge squaresails were unfurled and took the wind.

Then there was nothing to do but talk, which the wizard Callafo didn't mind. Peirol's oarmates were—from inboard to his station—Baltit, a rangy ex-sailor, condemned to the oars for killing a man in a waterfront brawl. ("He had a knife, I had a bar stool, wouldn't have come to aught but he was a no-bleman's favorite and I wasn't"); Cornovil, a soldier with no discernible talents, captured on one of Beshkirs' interminable wars; Ostyaks, who no one knew much about, since he seldom spoke; and Qui-pus, who was noble and, Peirol quickly realized, quite mad, in a civil sort of way.

Quipus turned to Peirol after they were told to rest, introduced himself, asked Peirol's name, then said calmly, "When 'twere done, it was done well, if not a-purpose, for surely I hold no greater fealty than to Lord Poolvash, a man of great talents, certainly in recognizing me, and granting me station above all oth-ers, and surely you, being a dwarf of discernment, would hardly believe me guilty of what I'm accused of."

"Which is?" Peirol asked cautiously.

"No, no," Quipus said, "you're right, there's not a chance of it being anything other than a poor cast-ing, or perhaps that damnable gunner double-charged, or, oh yes, I have it, it must have been a miscast ball, damme for using one of the new-cast ones, instead of the reliable stone sort I've grown ac-customed to, perhaps the greater weight of the cast ball stressed the bronze, or no, no, it must've been a bad casting, casting, I vow the artisan, and I hate to gift the damnable fool with that, the man at the foundry must've had his eyes on a whore's skirts, or perhaps, greatest shame of all, was away from his station, futtering his heart away, leaving me with the shame, shame of it all, being thought a murderer, a plotter, the shame, the shame."

Peirol blinked, but Quipus had disappeared into a world of his own, muttering "shame, shame, shame," paying no further heed to his oarmate.

Two things broke Peirol's curiosity—the *Ocean Spell* rolled, dipped, and a wave drenched him; and the burly man on the catwalk shouted, "You! Dwarf! Your master wants you!"

Peirol gaped; the man growled, lifted his whip.

"He's new," Quipus said, suddenly reasonable. "Still learning. Have mercy, Barnack."

Barnack growled again, jumped down behind Peirol, went to his chain, lifted it, and whispered a spell. Suddenly the staple sprang open, and Peirol had an instant to vow he'd learn that spell somehow, someday, and then Barnack had the chain in one hand and was half-dragging Peirol to the catwalk. There were two guards there, with ready javelins. They prodded Peirol to the ship's stern.

Waiting was a thick-bodied man in elaborately worked armor, who he learned was Captain Penrith. With him stood a man not ten years Peirol's senior, who also wore armor, but this even more decorative, worked with stars and the signs of the zodiac. This was Callafo the wizard.

"Kneel," Barnack ordered, and Peirol obeyed.

"Stand, dwarf," the magician said. "Who are you?"

"Peirol of the Moorlands," the dwarf said.

"You claim to be a jeweler?"

"Yes, sir."

"Are you any good?"

"Very, sir. I apprenticed under the master Rozan,

whom I am sure you've heard of, then I worked in the great city of Sennen, my shop was favored by nobility, and even sorcerers like—"

"Enough," Callafo said. "All slaves have brags."

"But mine are true."

Barnack lifted his whip.

"No," Callafo said. "I'm amused, seeing someone of his size, having courage."

Peirol thought of saying that was all that seemed left to him, but realized he had spoken as boldly as anyone would allow and just nodded.

"I sought you for my galley because I believe small people have inordinate luck," Callafo said. "Also, I wonder if, in time, your talents might not be profitable to me. I might consider allowing you to open a shop on the waterfront, as other artisans are allowed, assuming you show no signs of rebellion, such as that eunuch you slew when you were taken."

Peirol saw a bit of future hope. "No, sir. I'm a peaceful man."

"We shall see." Callafo took something from a clip on his armor, touched a stud, and it grew into a wand almost two feet long, black onyx, with lights occasionally flickering its length. "But there is a more important reason I wished discourse with you. When I was casting our sailing spell, I smelled—detected, if you will—signs of other magic about. I traced those signs to you. Do you have the Gift, dwarf?"

"I do not," Peirol said, giving Callafo his most honest look, knowing little of Callafo's concern except he could guess there'd be but one wizard aboard this ship.

"Perhaps you have an idea why I smelled sorcery about you?"

Peirol, seeing that the land was a mere haze against the horizon, thought the truth, or at least a version of it, might be best.

"That is because"—he lowered his voice—"I'm on an errand for a magician. A great, great magician. You might, indeed, wish to engage me in the same quest, rather than for me to waste potential riches for all as a slave."

"Seeking what?"

"Have you heard," and now Peirol's voice was a mere whisper, "of the Empire Stone?"

Whatever reaction he'd expected, Callafo's was a disappointment. The man roared laughter, loud enough to, Peirol thought, billow the ship's sails.

"Great gods," he said. "You ask me to believe that mages in your part of the world still believe in that foolishness?"

"We . . . they do, sir," Peirol said, a little angrily.

"Your great, great magician is seeking a chimera, something that could never have existed. Consider this, little man," Callafo said; "why would the gods allow such a stone to exist, if ever it did, capable of upsetting the order they have given, making a man almost one of them?"

Peirol could have said he wondered if there were any gods, could have said if there were, why couldn't they play with men the way cruel boys play with broken-winged sparrows? But again, he held silence.

Callafo stared, and Peirol, surprised at himself, was able to return that stare.

"I think," Callafo said, "you are telling what you believe to be the truth. And no, dwarf, I'll not unchain you and let you wander away on your fool's errand. I'll keep you as an oarsman, perhaps one day a jeweler.

"Or perhaps one day, one of my greater spells might require a . . . participant." Callafo laughed again. "Barnack, return him to his station."

That evening, after they were fed stew and bread, Peirol, after noting that Quipus slept, chanced asking, "What in hells did he do?"

He'd expected Baltit, who seemed to know a great deal, to answer, but surprisingly, it was Ostyaks, the man who never spoke: "Lord Quipus fancied artillery. Had himself a company of cannoneers. He was showing off his brass and smoke to the lord who'd hired him, one of the greats of Beshkirs, named Poolvash, with his ladies and retainers, and something went wrong. The gun exploded, killed the lord, two or three of his wives, twenty retainers, and Quipus now pulls an oar. Lucky they didn't have him drawn and quartered."

Ostyaks lapsed into silence, not speaking again for a day.

The wing crossed the open water between Parasso and the Manoleon Peninsula, then sailed south along it, looking for prey. Four times they sighted sails, and the slaves were put to it, pulling until their hearts thudded in their mouths and the lash gave a harder rhythm than the drums.

Once Peirol almost fainted, and Barnack's whip shocked him alive.

Once they closed on a great galleass, and the guards and oarmasters brought vinegar-soaked sponges for them to taste, and drove them harder, and this time Peirol knew he would die, but the galleass outsailed them and was gone. The guards and oarmasters, bitterly disappointed, prowled the catwalks, whips ready, and no oarsman dared speak or even look at anyone unchained.

They sailed on, but the seas remained empty, no rich merchantman to seize. Once they raided a village, but their sails must've been seen as they approached, for the village was empty but for half a dozen snarling dogs by the time the soldiers splashed ashore. The soldiers killed the dogs, stove in the beached fishing boats, and tried to burn the huts, but mud burns badly, and the only things that caught fire were the easily replaced thatched roofs.

"One thing we know," Baltit said one evening, "is a muscle you don't use, don't work."

Cornovil and Ostyaks said nothing; Quipus nodded wisely and said, "With a light old-fashioned gun, such as a ribaudequin, always make sure the foundry provides two chambers, or refuse to make more than half payment."

"That makes sense," Peirol said. "What *you* said, Baltit, I meant."

"And the brain isn't any different. So we talk, and then we ask questions, like we were in school. Sooner or later, we might get a chance to . . . to go on about our own business," he said, glancing about. "Best we be learning, be stretching our head-muscles."

"Yes, yes," Quipus said, excitedly. "And there's someone new, someone intelligent, someone to *teach*."

And so it was that Peirol learned about cannoneering, as Quipus gouted knowledge. If the others had already heard about artillery, they said nothing. Quipus quizzed the dwarf after every monologue, seeming to think he was a soldier under his command.

"Gunner," Quipus would bark. "Load me this mortar."

Obediently, Peirol would reply, often not sure what the terms he was using meant, "First I elevate the muzzle to what degree I would have to perfectly assail the target, swab the barrel with water, dry it, then, once the piece is made clean, I put the powder in the chamber, and upon the powder I ram down a wad of rope yarn, hay, or whatever, then a turf of earth, cut on purpose, wider than the bore of the piece, just moistened to avoid premature discharge or explosion, and then the granado. Once ready to fire, I set fire to the fuse of the granado, see it burn well, then touch fire to the touchhole . . ."

Or:

"Gunner! With a great gun, commanded to deliver overhead fire, what is your best positioning?"

"Uh . . . first, try to set up on high ground, firing over the foot soldiers' heads, which is safest, giving you protection from a cavalry charge by the enemy, or in front of the infantry if so ordered, or if that is your only chance to strike your target true, or between their brigades."

Or:

"Gunner! Name me the types of guns and the weights of their shot."

"A syren, sixty-pound shot; basilisk, forty-eight pounds; a carthoun, also forty-eight pounds, bastard cannon, thirty-six pounds; half carthoun, twenty-four pounds; whole culverin, eighteen pounds; demi culverin, nine pounds; saker . . . uh . . . four pounds?"

"You were guessing! A saker fires an eight- or six-pound shot, depending on whether it is large or small. Begin again!"

Peirol sometimes found himself dreaming of cannon, of gunpowder, of being able to blow into smithereens various of his enemies, and that was a very satisfying dream for a slave.

The ten galleys were lying to, off a point, hoping to surprise some shipping when the sun came up. The seas were calm, the moon three-quarters. Quipus was the only one on the bench who appeared asleep.

"So where're you from?" Baltit asked Peirol.

"Cenwalk," Peirol said. "A long ways south. South and west. Beyond, even, the kingdom of Rokelle and its capital of Sennen."

"What sorta land is it?" Cornovil wondered.

"Bleak," Peirol said. "Dreary."

And so it was, long leagues of endless, rolling wasteland, dotted here and there with tiny villages, rocky outcropping or estates. Rain swept the land in sheets, and it seemed there was always a wind. The fortune of the lords who ruled Cenwalk was in sheep, black-faced, canny escape artists who roamed the marshlands and were rounded up twice a year for shearing by the shepherds following them as they wandered.

"Which your family was?"

"No. We were tin miners."

"Down the hole, and like that?" Cornovil asked. "Slavin' for the nobles?"

"No," Peirol said. "We were free men."

"Free?" Ostyaks snorted in disbelief.

"Didn't think anybody but sailors was free, and we're foolin' ourselves mostly," Baltit said.

A tinner could go and come as he wished, dig where and how he liked, according to an ancient charter with the far-distant ruler of Cenwalk. He'd find a promising piece of land, hire one of the roving magicians to cast a divination, and begin digging. Other miners might join him on shares. The landowner would get a share but could not interfere with the mining.

When a vein was worked out, the tinner and his family would move on. They had their own charter and courts, and the only tax they paid was on the metal.

Sometimes they would live in a village, more frequently next to the diggings, piling river stones for a rude hut or roofing a ruin with turf, laying heather down for bedding at night, the women and children cutting, drying peat while the men were underground. The tin would be taken to a nearby smelter, and then to a coinage town.

"Not a bad life," Baltit allowed.

Not a bad life? Peirol remembered his father, a drunken bruiser, his eight brothers and sisters, all with normal bodies, his mother, who seemed perpetually hunched against a blow. Tin men were known for violence and anger, and frequently crossed the line to become highwaymen, robbing and killing a traveler and tipping his corpse into an abandoned, water-filled quarry. Wary, brave men were the only travelers on the moors, moving in groups.

"How'd your family handle you bein' what you are?" Ostyaks asked.

To Peirol's older brothers and sisters, he was a bit of a pet, an oddity, especially since he was quicker in his mind than they were. But he found, as he grew, he'd as soon be by himself as not, wandering the mist-hung hills, feeling the wind's sadness against his soul. In the purling creeks, he found pretty pebbles, gifts that pleased his mother and sisters. Later he kept some of the prettiest for himself, discovered he could rough-polish them to a luster with certain kinds of sand, then hang them in rapids and let the water finish the task. Sometimes he pretended he was seeking the Empire Stone.

His father would growl that Peirol wasn't from his loins, but a changeling or fathered by an underworld spirit, a knacker. These were evil spirits, about three feet high, with squinting eyes and ear-to-ear mouths, who went about in groups, changing shape, vanishing or changing into black, scampering goats when a tinner came near.

His mother would protest the canard, and be struck.

His father seemed to hate Peirol, but for some reason talked to him more than to the other children, telling him tales of mining, underground sprites, the legends of the land, like the Empire Stone and the greatness of Thyone, before the black ships.

His mother favored him as the youngest and, she said, the prettiest, making sure he learned to read and write.

As Peirol got older, he began to fear his weird, going underground like his father, candle fixed to the brim of his hat, feeling the rock close about him, his mind being ground away by the drudgery with his pick, until he was no more than the others, a grunting, jostling animal.

Relief from the barren land and life were the assemblages in the coinage towns, four times a year, when the king's officers would buy tin, mark it with the royal symbol, and take it away to be rolled and stamped into coins. The biggest of these was the Midsummer Festival, a time of frolic and drunkenness, hurling, cockfighting, wrestling. Merchants would peddle wares, necessities and luxuries.

Peirol remembered the festival when he was just twelve, having disconsolately realized he probably would grow no taller, when he met one of the master jeweler Rozan's journeymen. The man—slender, young, a bit foppish—had rented a small shop for the festival and had a display of rings, necklaces, torques of gold, silver and precious and semiprecious stones for the staggering tinners to placate their wives and daughters into another dismal season in emptiness.

Peirol wanted to buy something for his mother but had of course only a few coppers, certainly no silver. He saw a discreet sign—I BUY GEMS—next to a necklace he knew his mother would love, a small diamond glittering at its center, set with other, red stones around it. He thought of his collection of beautiful rocks, knew none were really valuable, but ran back to his family's tent, pitched just beyond the town walls, and came back with his treasures.

The youth, whose name was Ty Lanherne, sorted through them with quick fingers, pushing most away, keeping a few. "This green one, now, is a garnet. Not really that valuable, it's quite soft, but it's big, which helps, and it can be fashioned into a bauble for a trader's daughter, far prettier, once it's been cut and polished, than its price would reflect. . . . Ah, now this one's worth a bit of silver, a cat's-eye. Nice, reddish, which isn't that common, the eye shows well . . . looks like you did a careful job of polishing . . . you can see how clear it is when you hold it up to the light. . . . It'll make a nice gem for a man's ring, or perhaps a pommel for a dress dagger."

"I thought I saw something in there, in the heart of the stone, when I found it," Peirol said proudly. "And I worked as carefully as I could, getting that color-slit, what you just said was a cat's-eye, to show."

"You have a bit of talent," Lanherne murmured, continuing to finger the bits of rock. "These three are zoite, notice how blue they are, almost like a sapphire . . . this pink one's beryl. . . . Hmm. I'll give you five pieces of silver for the lot."

It of course wasn't enough to buy the necklace, but it was more money than Peirol had ever seen, as much as his father sometimes made at a coinage sale with his tin. He picked out a lesser necklace, gave back the coins.

He didn't want to go back out into the drizzle and bluster, back to that crowded tent to wait for his drunken father to stumble in, so he lingered in the shop. Lanherne didn't seem to mind, answered Peirol's questions about the various gems.

"What about those," Peirol finally asked, pointing to two small diamonds. "Where are those found?"

"Not around here," Lanherne said. "But many places. Sometimes deep underground, in veins, they say, called pipes, which I've never seen. Some of the biggest pipes are in Osh, and some say to the east. Sometimes diamonds are found in creeks, in streambeds. But you'll not see them like this, for it takes great skill and art to turn diamonds in their raw form into gems like these."

Peirol suddenly blurted, "I could spend my life doing what you're doing, traveling, handling jewels."

"I studied for five years as an apprentice before my master, Rozan, let me accompany him on a selling expedition like this," Lanherne said. "And it was three more before he trusted me to go on my own. In two, perhaps three more years, I'll go before my guild, be tested, and maybe then be allowed to call myself a lapidarist."

"How did you get into your master's service?"

Lanherne grinned like a boy.

"I bothered a journeyman who was selling stones like I am now when he came to my village until he lost his temper, told me to go away. I followed him, when he left, until he reached Ferfer, which is Rozan's home. Then I sat on the master's doorstep for three days, getting kicked when he went in and out. Finally he took me in as an apprentice, sleeping on straw, eating but twice a day, having only ten feast days a year."

Peirol thought it sounded far better than the life he had.

"Let me ask you this, boy. Who's *your* master?"

"I have none," Peirol said.

"What of your parents?"

"They care little what I do," he said, a guilty thought of his mother coming, being pushed away.

"And your age?"

"Fifteen," Peirol said.

Lanherne looked skeptical, then made a face. "As if I'm an expert at judging the age of the little people." He thought a moment. "It's hard work, requiring a careful eye and a love for detail, and you've got to develop a way with people, with the rich, being able to listen to their chatter and snootiness and not arguing back."

Peirol said nothing.

"Take your purchase, my friend," Lanherne said in a friendly manner. "And the best of luck be with you."

Two days later the Midsummer Festival ended, and Peirol's family went south, back to the moors and their mine. In his mother's bedroll, unknown to her, was a silver necklace, with a worked gem in its center. Peirol hoped she mourned his running away, but not for long.

Ty Lanherne, pack on his back, silver in his pouch and a sword loose in its sheath, traveled north toward Ferfer. He glanced back, saw the small figure of a dwarf trudging about a quarter league behind, grinned, and broke into song.

Peirol was still there, half-starved, boot soles worn through, stumbling, when Lanherne reached Ferfer.

Peirol came back to the present, to the galleys, when Ostyaks muttered, "Like Baltit said. Not a bad life."

Quipus said suddenly, "Because you were free."

No one spoke again for the rest of the night, and eventually Peirol slept.

The next morning, Lord Kanen's galley came alongside, and a long boarding gangplank was dropped between the two ships. Kanen came across the narrow plank, surefooted. He was grim, lips pursed.

Callafo met him, trying to keep a worried expression from his face, and the two went into Callafo's cabin in the poop. Slaves close to the stern said they heard Kanen's voice, harsh in anger.

A turning of the glass later, and Kanen came out and returned to his ship. A young girl, very young, was led out of his cabin by two guards. She wore slippers and a heavy robe, and looked frightened. One guard slung her over his shoulder, trotted across the gangplank to the *Ocean Spell*, led her to the foredeck, and waited beside the gleaming brass cannon.

Callafo came out of his cabin, wearing traditional sorcerer's robes, carrying a leather case and his wand. He ordered the foredeck cleared, and a small tent, blazoned with strange symbols, was pitched by the guards. He pushed the terrified girl inside, pulled the tent flap to after him. A few minutes later, he started chanting. Incense of different colors and scents drifted from the vent in the top of the tent. The chanting grew, and it was as if a chorus was inside the tent, for Peirol heard many voices, almost in a plainsong.

He looked at the others on the bench, saw the fear. The direction of the chanting changed, and it seemed to come from all around the galleys, from the sea itself.

Then the girl screamed, high, piercing, in utter agony, and the scream cut off at its peak.

There was silence for a while, except for the plash of the waves against the galleys hulls.

Callafo came out, and all men, sailors, slaves, soldiers, ship's officers, looked away. Peirol thought he saw stains on the wizard's robes.

Callafo shouted for Lord Kanen. The corsair came to the bow of his *Slayer*.

"South, four points off the Warrior's farthest star," Callafo said, without preamble. "Two ships, heavily laden. We'll sight them just at dawn."

Sail was made, and the rowers told to sleep, for they'd be required during the night. Peirol didn't think he could, but when he opened his eyes it was dark, and a bell marked the third glass of the second watch. He moved Quipus's foot from his leg and tried to find a more comfortable way to lie.

He saw motion, where the tent still stood on the foredeck. He heard men mutter, saw guards' armor. The tent came down and was hurriedly rolled. The two men picked up something limp, carried it to the side, and tossed it overboard. It struck with a splash, and the clouds fell away from the moon.

Peirol looked into the water, saw a white face bob up for an instant, a blood-streaked face torn by slashes, then the body was pulled under the keel, vanished.

There *were* two ships, as Callafo's spell had foretold, fat three-mastered flutes, slow and heavily-laden, following the coast's curve. Their captains saw the ten black ships closing, far faster than the flutes could travel, raised all sail, prepared for battle, and no doubt prayed hard.

The gods weren't listening, any more than they'd heard prayers from the *Petrel*.

Kanen's signal flags went up, and the slaves manned their oars. Another set of flags, and the wing swept wide, pulling ahead of the flutes, then turned like wolves, driving the ships toward the shore. The flutes tried to run toward land, but the wind was in their throats.

Peirol heard a growling sound from the soldiers waiting to storm, the sailors, and even some of the slaves.

A cannon boomed, and the ball arced through the air, no pretense at a challenging shot, and smashed into the rearmost flute.

"Hit her, gunner, strike her hard, for she'll be ours before noontide," Quipus shouted gleefully, and then screamed as Barnack's whip cracked across his shoulders.

"Serves y' fiddlin' right," Cornovil managed, and then the drum cadence came faster, and they were rowing too hard to talk, to think, nothing but the feel of the iron cleat in their hands, tearing away calluses, making blisters and breaking them, the wetness of blood, the tear of muscles. Guards cascaded buckets of salt water over them, and it was welcome. Their own cannon fired, and again Quipus rejoiced, and then a shadow fell, and they were alongside the flute, another galley nosing to the stern. Soldiers, shouting, scrambled over the *Ocean Spell*'s bows and up the flute's sides. Peirol heard screams, shouts of men fighting, dying, and a spear thudded down into the deck beside him, but none of the slaves paid mind to the battle, slumped over their oars, gasping for air.

Cries came for quarter, for surrender, and it was all over.

The other merchantman was hove to not far distant, three galleys alongside it, one the *Slayer*. That ship's cargo was different from the bales and boxes of the craft the *Spell* had seized.

There were passengers aboard. Merchants, nobles, who knew? Peirol was never told. But he saw the cold-blooded sorting that Kanen made. Young men and young women were put to one side for the slave market, and those richly dressed who might be ransomable to another. There were a few boys aboard, evidently not suited for the block, for Peirol heard them scream as swords spitted them, and the bodies were thrown overboard.

He saw four women standing alone, close enough for him to see they were in their middle years, and saw Kanen point to them. The soldiers aboard that ship howled, broke ranks, and tore at the captives. Peirol looked away, tried to block his ears against the screams.

Two of the women, he was told, lived long enough to be cast down into the *Slayer*, reward for the oarsmen, and Peirol heard mutterings of envy from the rowers.

The wing, carrying its prizes, made its way back to Beshkirs, and again Lord Kanen of the Sporades was hailed for his luck and skill.

Peirol remembered only the screams and the face of the nameless girl Callafo had sacrificed for that "luck."

Two days after the galley returned to Beshkirs, Peirol finished his bait. He held the ring out to the barracks guard he'd taken aside, turned it carefully, so the silver caught the reflections from the sun shining through the barracks skylights, shot them into the heart of the diamond, which reflected them out in shatters of red, orange, yellow, green, blue, and violet.

"Where'd y' get that?" the guard wanted to know.

"I made it."

"From what?"

"From the sun, from the moon, from the metals of the earth," Peirol said. "We dwarves have many powers."

"'Ats what I heard. Whacha want me for? You gimme that for a present?"

"No. But I'll reward you well."

The guard's eyes gleamed.

"I've heard of a man named Niazbeck," Peirol said.

"No shit. Magnate Niazbeck. Jewels is his main interest, but he's got others."

"I want you to take this to him, to his shop, offer it for sale. Tell him or his representative a man of the galleys made it, could make many more, far more beautiful, if his circumstances were different."

"What's cir-cum-stances?"

"Job. Life."

"You mean, you want me to tell him you want to be his slave?"

"Yes."

"I get caught doin' that, sayin' that, liable Lord Kanen or Callafo'll have my skin for a shield-cover."

"You can keep half of whatever the ring brings."

The guard made a sound deep in his throat.

"Don't cheat me," Peirol warned. "As I said, we dwarves have powers. Strange powers. Some night, your sword might come alive, dance in your hands, leap for your throat. Or your dagger, when you're sharpening it, suddenly turn, and dive into your guts. Or your spear—"

"Shut yer yap! Sounds like you're layin' a curse! Gimme that ring."

He held it for a time, turning it back and forth. He clearly wanted it but kept glancing, worriedly, at Peirol, fearing his curse.

"I'll do it," he said finally. "First time I get a free shift."

Peirol hid his grin. If his plan worked, he could be one small step closer to continuing his quest for the Empire Stone. At any rate, he'd be better off than he was now.

But Peirol heard nothing, didn't see the guard before the slaves were told off to be ready to sail.

This time it was to war with the Sarissans.

SIX

✳

Of Sarissans
and Black Cities

Peirol had never dreamed of so many ships. All the galleys and other warships of Beshkirs were ready for the summer's campaigning, plus auxiliaries, which meant any merchantman a couple of tiny robinets or even moyen could be mounted on, as well as ships manned by Beshkirs's allies of the moment, some of the tiny sea-kingdoms dotted like cancers up and down the Manoleon Peninsula, after prestige or loot.

The galleys sailed first, to give flank security for the fleet assembly, which had to be done at sea, for Beshkirs's harbor couldn't hold a quarter of the fleet. Ships arrived singly and by squadrons. Someone said there were five hundred, another said a thousand.

Peirol overheard one of the ship's officers say

they'd be better off with half the ships and a tenth the warlords, but had no idea what the man meant.

Everyone was awed by the splendor, and even Barnack lashed a gaping slave more lightly than he might've otherwise.

Baltit said, wryly, "Don't it say something about man that his greatest show is when he's about to start killing his brothers?"

"If," Quipus said, sounding very sane, "the Sarissans are men, after all."

He was quickly hushed.

By now, Peirol had pieced together mutters and whispers about the strange ones from the north. They were tall, majestic in appearance, a head taller than a man. They were covered with long, silky hair of a yellow-auburn color. They looked a bit like the lions of the far northern deserts, if lions stood on two legs and had arms and hands, with glaring slits of eyes, like great snakes. Their sex was either hidden in their bodies or by their hair, for no one knew which were male, which female, or if there were more or less than two sexes.

They were fierce warriors, and seemed to love battle even more than man. They neither gave nor sought quarter in battle. Sometimes they raided, sometimes they conquered land, with no seeming logic to their plans. No one knew what happened to the people of the lands they held, but the lands they raided were left black and barren.

The Sarissans had been unknown until a bit more than a generation ago, when they'd appeared from the jungles of the Unknown Lands to the north. No one seemed to know where their name had come from, or what it meant, since no one had ever learned their language. They'd conquered the Unknown Lands and erected huge cities along the coastline seemingly overnight, which proved they were not human.

Emboldened, they built strange ships and sailed out as raiders against any human ship or village they came upon. At first they had no cannon, depending on the old tactics of ramming and boarding, but they learned quickly, and now had guns at least as powerful as any in Beshkirs.

"Yes, yes," Quipus had added dreamily, "great, great guns, with cast shot, and none know the secret of their powder, if it be natural or sorcerous. 'Tis said they mix it with seawater, but that cannot be, cannot be, for wet powder will not burn, nor explode. Perhaps they use a secret wood for the charcoal, or have the purest of nitre, or unknown spells, but none knows, none knows."

There had been attempts made to talk peace, but diplomats never returned from their parleys. There was great fear the Sarissans had the temerity to want to own the world, when all knew it was man's. Since the island of Parasso and the city of Beshkirs lay close to the Unknown Lands, the Beshkirians—in spite of not yet finding profit from fighting the strangers—were loudest in demanding their destruction. With the Sarissans destroyed or driven back, Beshkirs could return to its normal position as king of the freebooters.

"Poor Lord Kanen," Cornovil said. "Havin' to be content with glory, 'stead of gold. That was the way I thought, once." He clinked his chains to make the point.

The battle fleet was to sail east around the tip of Parasso, then northeast, across open water, until it closed on the Unknown Lands. Then it was to bear along the coast until they found ships to attack, or, better for the possibility of loot, one of the Sarissans' stone cities, which were said to be huge, monolithic.

The weather was clear, the sun warm, the sea dappled, and the wind behind them, so the oars weren't manned except at dusk and dawn, when the galleys beached and the other ships anchored offshore from them.

Ostyaks broke silence to say, "I feel luck all about me, luck and gold." Peirol snorted, having come to the conclusion there was no such thing as luck in his world save bad.

This was also true for Quipus. When the fleet reached Parasso's end, ready to make the jump across the open ocean, the *Ocean Spell* was sailing just behind Kanen's *Slayer*.

Callafo, in his impressive robes, held a ceremony on the ship's forepeak, to implore guidance and help from Parasso's gods as men crossed to the Unknown Lands. There was the usual smoke of various colors, incense of various odors, chanting, flashes from the water like strange lightning, and in the middle of the ceremony, Quipus started laughing.

Callafo broke off his chant, looked at the slave in disbelief. "Silence down there!" he roared. Quipus broke off, owl-eyed the wizard, shook his head, laughed on.

"Quiet him!" and Barnack and two soldiers leaped down from the catwalk, hammered the madman.

Callafo finished the ceremony, stalked back, looked down at Quipus. "Two, no, three dozen lashes," he snarled. "A lesson for insolence."

"But he's mad, sir," Baltit said stupidly.

"And a dozen for this man as well. Impudence is evidently contagious. Barnack, I want to hear those strokes in the stern, so lay on well!"

Callafo glared at the others on the bench, who were looking properly humble.

A few minutes later, two gratings were lashed to the mast, and the whip-crashes began. Baltit held silence, as befitted a sailor, but very strangely, when the first stroke landed on Quipus, he began laughing once more, and his laughter didn't stop until the sentence was complete and he was cut down.

Peirol watched not the victims but the sorcerer, noting his enthralled smile, and a flashing, absurd, impossible promise streamed through his mind, was gone.

The two were dragged to their bench and remanacled. A bucket of salt water was cascaded on them, less further punishment than a balm, and the voyage continued.

Now, on open water, Peirol realized the galleys' lack of seaworthiness, as the *Ocean Spell* wallowed and took green water on as long rollers came aboard. Ostyaks was seasick, throwing up on the bench, and other slaves did the same. Peirol tried to ignore the smell, concentrating on the blue sky above and the green seas. He was grateful for the waves, for they washed the slaves clean. But cursing sailors on the pumps behind the mainmast felt otherwise.

There was no sign of land, no place to beach the galleys, and so they slept head-to-toe as the sails above cracked in the strong winds.

Four days later, the lookout in the mainmast's crosstrees shouted "Land!" and Peirol saw the Unknown Lands. They weren't that dramatic: low, rolling dunes, with green splashes here and there. The land was not quite a desert, but appeared infertile.

The fleet turned east, staying well offshore, for fear of running aground on uncharted bars, and Captain Penrith put two experienced seamen in the chains to watch for the changing color of rapidly shoaling water. The *Slayer* passed close by, and Peirol saw Lord Kanen in the bows, wearing armor, eager for battle.

Even though they were close to land, none of the galleys beached that night, nor anchored, but drifted, sails lowered, and half of the crew remained on watch. But nothing happened, and at dawn they raised sail and went on, the fleet streaming behind them in motley formation.

It was almost midday, and Peirol was feeling an appetite for the stew he could smell heating when a lookout cried, "Sail on the sta'board quarter, two enemy ships, more," and they'd found the Sarissans. Peirol wondered how the lookout could tell they were enemy, but the drums sounded and the whips cracked, and again the oars bit into the water, sent the galleys skimming.

Peirol chanced losing the stroke, saw why the lookout had been so certain. The four ships fleeing ahead of the Beshkirians were of no human design. Their mainmast rose from the forepeak back at an angle, with a single lateen sail. There was a second mast coming up from midships, pointed forward, with four triangular sails on either side, sheets running to booms extending from the bow and stern. A fifth sail, also triangular, was set from the tip of the main mast to another boom on the stern, extending straight aft.

Baltit, face wizened from the pain of his wounds torn by the rowing, said, "They're using magic to move, or else I don't know aught about sails. Damned things should be stealin' each other's wind." The whip cracked close beside him, and he cramped his mouth shut, pulled harder.

Slowly the galleys closed on the four ships, and Peirol could see yellow-brown dots on the decks.

"Gunners to your stations," Captain Penrith shouted, and the cannoneers scurried. "Load your weapons."

Quipus started laughing again. "Now, now we'll see it, we'll see the dragon," and Peirol, wondering what the hells he was talking about, elbowed him to shut him up.

Quipus laughed on, but quietly, under his breath.

"Do you have a range, gunner?" Penrith shouted.

"Not yet, sir."

"When you do, take good aim for their rigging, to bring down their masts. I'll give you the order to fire."

Then the four enemy ships, as precisely as if in a regatta, bore to port, toward shore. The land had changed without Peirol being aware. Now there were headlands in sight. Here and there, close in the shallows, Peirol saw what looked like buoys.

The Sarissans drove hard for land—to beach themselves and flee, Peirol thought. Then he saw them zigging through those buoys, in a dredged channel, toward the wide mouth of a bay. There were shouts from the poop deck, and the sails clattered down. Other commands were shouted to the port and starboard oarmasters.

"If we miss the channel and strike at this speed," Baltit muttered, "it'll rip our keel off, and we'd best hope it'll be shallow enough for wading."

But the *Slayer*'s master and Penrith made no mistakes, the other galleys falling in line behind, and they were through the channel, land on either side, and the bay opened. It was huge, leagues across, big enough to anchor their fleet and many others beside. Then Peirol caught his breath.

At the far side of the bay rose a great stone city, black and looming, and it was for this the enemy ships were scudding.

The oarmasters shouted for more speed, whips thudding on flesh, and the slaves rowed as they never had, but the Sarissans' ships pulled steadily away. There were docks ahead, but the ships didn't turn for them, beaching themselves at full sail on the black sand, one ship's mast cracking, going down with the impact. The sailors jumped overboard, waded ashore, turned back to shout what must be curses.

"Fire!" Penrith shouted. The main gun boomed, and the ball lofted high, smashed into a stone building on the waterfront without appearing to do any damage.

The Sarissans chittered, strange language that would've sounded better coming from an eagle, and Abbas's language spell gave no translation. One Sarissan cast a spear that landed many lengths short of the *Slayer*. Then they ran up city streets and disappeared.

"Back oars," Penrith shouted, as the gunners reloaded, and the two leading galleys slowed, then backwatered a dozen yards, sat rolling in the small surf.

"Here we are, in a fine, fine trap," Quipus crooned, "for none of the bravos thought the enemy has guns, oh, but they will, they do, great guns, far bigger than any rowboat like us, like us, could carry, and now they'll rend us like we were toys on a pond."

But nothing happened, no cannon were rolled out from hidden arsenals to shatter the galleys. Peirol, looking back at the headlands, saw no sign of forts guarding the gateway to this huge city. The larger ships in the fleet were carefully entering the harbor, spreading out, ready for battle. But none was brought.

For a very long time, nothing happened. The slaves sat, oars out, waiting. The soldiers stood, weapons ready, waiting. The sailors stood at their posts, waiting. The cannoneers stood, fuses in hand, waiting.

"Stick about, with yer thumbs up your ass, walking on your elbows, when the enemy's close about, and men'll start dying," Cornovil muttered. "That's the way I got captured, bein' on the losin' end with a lord who wouldn't shit if his breeches were full."

At last, small boats started rowing back and forth between flagships. Lord Kanen came back from a conference aboard one, had his boat brought close aboard the *Ocean Spell*, shouted, "Volunteers, men! We've been picked to scout the city."

"Picked," Baltit said, "or that bastard drew the short twig."

"No, no," Quipus said merrily. "He did really, really volunteer. Men like that do things like that."

"Mmmh," Baltit said. "You're likely right."

"Of course I'm right, right, right, when it comes to important matters like dying. You'll see, you'll see, you'll be with me at the last."

Evidently the sailors and soldiers made the same analysis, for there was a distinct shortage of volunteers, except for officers. Aboard the *Ocean Spell*, Callafo shouted vainly, was forced to detail twenty men, including ten musketeers, from the soldiery. Gangplanks were dropped into the shallows, and men clattered down them, splashed ashore. Callafo paused, saw Peirol.

"You, dwarf! We're after the Sarissans' treasure. You're to come with us. If you know your gems, your metals, you'll be rewarded. If not . . ." He didn't finish, but followed his men.

Barnack hurried up, knelt, whispered the unlocking spell. Peirol was bending close, and caught three of the four words—"*Toas cugs namde . . .*"—but he missed the final word. He couldn't guess at it, since the phrase was in no language he'd heard, and Abbas's language spell gave no assistance. The manacles fell away, and Peirol straightened.

"Come on, dwarf," Captain Runo of the guard shouted. Peirol staggered down the gangplank, almost falling, but then he was on land, dry land, wearing no godsdamned chains. He saw some of the ships in the fleet lowering boats filled with armed men.

"Follow the wizard," Runo ordered.

"Could I have some sort of weapon?"

Runo laughed harshly. "Slaves don't get weapons, so you'd best stick close to the wizard and hope he'll defend you if our furry friends start trouble."

Peirol grimaced, trotted after Callafo. Other galleys were beaching themselves, more troops landing. Other, bigger ships sailed close inshore, turning so their cannon could broadside the city.

This is a great city, Peirol thought. Perhaps as big as Sennen. Certainly the buildings I see are as great as anything on Sennen's wharves, and far taller. But where are the people—the Sarissans? They should be fleeing, and we should be hearing screams, and their soldiers should be trying to drive us off. But there is nothing.

He shivered.

The buildings around him appeared of solid stone. He remembered the legends about builders of myth, who would quarry and shape huge stones with magic, use other spells that laid them in place atop one another, so no mortar was needed and a fingernail wouldn't fit between the stones. He went to one building, saw, with an odd thankfulness, where mortar had oozed and dried, leaving a good small-finger's-width between the blocks. The paving stones he walked on were strange, completely smooth. He knelt and touched them, and they were polished, slightly greasy, resilient. He thought, oddly, of bits of meat in aspic.

"Dwarf!" Callafo shouted. "To me!"

Peirol scurried, and the columns moved deeper into the city. The streets were wide at first, then narrowed, turning, twisting. The soldiers kept close watch for ambushers. But there was nothing.

The shops Peirol looked into, if shops they were, had neatly stacked items like none he'd ever seen. Triangular bottles, strangely colored cloth in rounds, not bolts, utensils and tools he couldn't see the purpose of.

As the streets curved back and forth, leading deeper into the city, he was reminded of traps the shepherds on his moorlands set when it was time to shear their wily flocks: wide V-shaped lines of piled heather with rocks behind them, so the sheep would amble, unthinkingly along, slightly chivvied and worried about the shouting men and dogs behind, and then realize, too late, they were in the shearing pen.

Or, he thought, on the killing floor, as the street opened into a huge square, as big as some towns he'd been in. In its center was an enormous squat building, with strange, yawning portals. They weren't shaped for men, nor for the Sarissans to enter easily, but were low, slotlike. A strange light gleamed from within.

The raiders debouched into this square from several avenues and stood looking about, wondering what should next be done.

Peirol noted round posts, no taller than he was, set in the flat stone of the square at irregular intervals, like posts to hitch horses, oxen, or zebras to.

He saw the glitter from them, about the time someone shouted. Callafo was one of the first to stride forward, examine them.

"Dwarf! What of these?"

Peirol goggled as he came nearer. The posts were made of some crystal, cut and worked like gemstones. But Peirol couldn't imagine why anyone would use jewels as hitching posts. He tried to figure how many *varjas* each jewel would be but failed. He knelt, looked deep into the crystal, tried to think of a conventional stone it reminded him of, could not.

"What would be the value of these?" Callafo demanded.

"Reshaped into normal configurations . . . if the stones find worth in the eyes of those who value gems, they are of incalculable value. Or, if they fail to find favor, who knows?"

Callafo licked his lips greedily.

"If these monsters put jewels of this value outside, what must be in that building?"

Peirol gave him a slave's blank look of stupidity, calculated to enrage an owner without going far enough to merit a beating, and had the pleasure of having Callafo snarl. He stamped toward the nearest entrance as Lord Kanen, at the head of a hundred or so troops, trotted into the square. "There, men," Kanen called. "There's their palace, and we'll all be rich within the hour. After me!"

He ran forward, ducked through the entrance, his men after him. Peirol noted Callafo hesitating at the entrance. Captain Runo stuck his head out of the building.

"Sir! M'lord commands you to join him."

Callafo looked about, perhaps seeking Peirol, who ducked behind a scatter of soldiers. Callafo hissed annoyance, went inside.

Peirol suddenly realized there were no more than half a dozen soldiers in the square—the rest had heard Kanen's call to gold and obeyed, hundreds of them. Peirol had a chance to run. But where? Deeper into the Sarissans' city, hoping to throw himself on their mercy? Into the desert beyond, and hope for the succor of sand-demons?

The air seemed suddenly thick, thick and beginning to blur, as if an invisible pot was starting to fill the square with steam. Then came a scream, high, drawn out, as if a woman had made it, but Peirol knew it to come from a dying man's throat. Another scream echoed from the huge building, then the clash of steel against steel, the thud of gunshots and shouts. The square, except for the handful of soldiers, was still empty, and the sound of distant battle rang clear, echoing off the great stones.

A man wearing ornate armor, waving a discharged pistol, stumbled out a doorway. Peirol knew him not, guessed he was from one of the other galleys or perhaps one of the warships. The man's face was bleeding, and blood spouted from his left forearm, where his hand had been. The man was babbling in terror and pain. He managed, "Inside! They were waiting, and—"

A dark rope whipped out of the doorway, wrapped twice around him, yanked him out of sight. It wasn't a rope, Peirol realized, but a tentacle, like that of the tiny cuttlefish he so dearly loved sliced in rings and fried in garlic and oil—but a tentacle five times or more the height of a man.

More screams came, and more soldiers poured

like ants out of their drowning hill, out of the doors of the building, a building Peirol thought of, for some unknown reason, as a temple. Some ran, afraid to look back, others backed out, weapons ready. Tentacles came out of the building, took them, pulled them back. Musketeers shot at the tentacles, which seemed impervious to harm.

Lord Kanen stumbled out of a doorway, a sword in one hand, a pistol in the other. A tentacle looped after him, he shot at it, and it jerked back. Another tentacle came out, lifted, curled, like a snake about to strike. Kanen's eyes were on it, sword raised, and a second tentacle took him around the waist.

Kanen slashed, but the arm seemed to feel no pain, and then the upper appendage came down, whipped twice around his helm, and pulled Kanen's head off. Blood fountained high, and the body was tossed away.

Peirol saw a sword lying on the cobbles, a loaded pistol nearby, seized them. He was starting to run when Callafo pelted past him.

"Gods, gods," he sobbed, dignity and magic gone. "The Sarissans aren't the rulers, no, others, beyond them, greater ones, we must away . . . pray, pray to gods I never knew, never dreamed, power, they have all the power, my spells gave nothing, no warning, no clue, empty, empty . . ."

Not having the slightest idea what Callafo was babbling about, but not caring, fear keening, Peirol followed, running as hard as he could and cursing, not for the first, not for the hundredth time, his stubby legs. There were other soldiers running with them, and tentacles came out of the shops, out of the windows above, harvesting men as they ran. Peirol ducked under one tentacle, slashed at another, saw the harbor three, no, four blocks away, and there were no more than a handful of men still alive and fleeing.

A wall opened where there'd been no portal, and Sarissans attacked them. They brandished strange swords whose points curled, one in each hand. One ran at Peirol, and he shot him, flattened as a sword whipped overhead. Peirol rolled to his feet, lunged with the clumsy blade he'd picked up. The sword cut deeply into the tawny one's chest, and those slit eyes blazed fury, then blanked, and the creature fell, pulling Peirol's sword away.

Peirol spun, running as hard as he could for the beach, running past men wounded, men winded. Somehow he passed Callafo, and there were no more than a handful of men left in the street. Peirol heard an agonized screech. He turned, and saw impossibility. The street was becoming liquid, just as aspic will melt in the sun, and Callafo was sinking into the stone, up to his waist.

"Help me, dwarf! Help me, for the love of the gods!"

His hand was outstretched, and Peirol could just reach it, and he was stretching for it . . .

. . . *the dead face of that nameless girl, slashed to ribbons, floating away, under the galley's keel . . . Quipus's beribboned black, blood runneling down . . .*

Peirol's hand jerked back, as if he'd touched fire, and Callafo screamed again, this time as much in rage as panic, and something came up like a great fish through the stone and pulled Callafo down, and there was red spreading across the liquid stone, like blood on water after a shark's strike.

Peirol ran on, feeling the stones pull him down, wading, and then he was on solid sand, galleys in front of him and ships lifting their anchors, trying to flee the nightmare.

Barnack was at the end of the gangway, paying no attention to Peirol, eyes wide in horror at something behind the dwarf. Peirol was past him, up the catwalk and into his station, jumping down onto the bench, pulling with the others as the *Ocean Spell*'s keel grated off the sand and the ship was afloat.

Other galleys came free of the land, turned, oars flailing like the legs of frightened waterbugs to get away. Galleys crashed together, careened, spilling slaves, soldiers, sailors, into the bay, and fanged creatures came into the shallows and took them.

There was open water in front of the *Ocean Spell*, and far away, leagues away, the bay's mouth. The other, greater ships in the fleet were putting on full sail, canvas flapping, unfurling, reaching for the gentle wind.

Peirol looked back, almost screamed at what he saw. The city had become something like a dark sea anemone, tendrils waving, beckoning—but it wasn't, was still dark stone. But each window, it seemed, had a reaching tentacle, and the stones he thought for an instant were moving, coming toward the water, the city itself in motion. But everything shimmered; the delusion, if that's what it was, vanished, and the buildings were still once more, except for those groping, reaching arms.

The drums were thundering, oarmasters shouting, and Captain Penrith and his mates bellowing, when the Sarissan fleet appeared from nowhere. Not from nowhere, Peirol realized, but from caverns in the low hills, sea caves with entrances cleverly hidden by sand-colored nets with green brush painted on them. The ships were the same strange style as the four they'd chased into this trap, but far larger, as large as the biggest human galleass, with cannon lining their sides. They were on both sides of the human fleet, closing like pinchers, the mouth of the bay unreachable leagues distant. As had the four ships—bait, Peirol now realized—they moved precisely, as if on tracks like mine cars, or moved by some invisible puppeteer.

Guns boomed, and smoke boiled from the bows of the Sarissan ships. Ranging shots and cannonballs arced through the air, smashed into ships. Men fired back, and here and there an enemy ship was struck and smashed like a toy of light-wood.

Now Peirol understood that officer's complaint about too many admirals as squadrons broke away from the fleet, crowding on full sail, trying to reach, like trapped flies, for the mouth of the bottle, not realizing their only hope was unity, fear breaking, tearing them.

He was pulling at the oar, shouting, and the others on the bench were pulling as well, no need for the whip or even the drum. If they were trapped here, they'd die horribly like the sailors in the city, or maybe worse.

The great gun just in front of him slammed, and Quipus whooped in pleasure. The gunners reloaded as the two swivel guns cracked. Peirol realized something must be closing on them, but couldn't, wouldn't look up, nothing but the iron cleat in his hands, beechwood scraping his knuckles, breath sobbing in, out, with the oar's sweep. Then he heard a scream, and that forced him to lift his head. The galleys had sped through half of the shambles that'd been a fleet, and the bay's mouth was in front of them.

With something blocking it. Something rose from the water, and Peirol thought, for one insane instant, of a monster, a dark sea monster, an ally or the god of the Sarissans. But then he saw it wasn't flesh but dark wood and metal, a huge ship, a two, no, three-tiered galley, somehow capable of traveling underwater—or maybe it'd been masked by a spell of the Sarissans.

He thought it capsized, then realized the galley was roofed, armored with curving timbers up its sides, looking like a turtle, stub masts above the armored bulkheads with huge cannon mouths menacing them. Smoke from the guns boiled across the waters.

Peirol saw, veering toward them, one of their own galleys, masts drunkenly overside, one sail still holding the wind, its oars shattered, weaving like a crippled bug. Then it was on them, ram sweeping down the starboard oar bank, wood splitting, smashing, oars sailing through the air like snapped toothpicks and men screaming. Something caught him, sent him flying, and still unchained, he rolled, landed hard on his side on the *Ocean Spell*'s catwalk as the other galley raked down the ship's side.

Peirol saw his bench, his world, his only friends, ripped into the boiling water, spinning in the galley's wake for an instant, heavy wood and chains dragging the bench down.

The last he saw was Quipus, arm waving, and he swore he heard the madman's laughter; then he was gone and water was gushing into the *Ocean Spell*.

The galley had been ripped in a full circle, still had way on. Barnack was in the bows next to the gun, and ahead loomed that monstrous enemy ship, guns bellowing at them—at *him*, each trying to kill Peirol. Grapeshot swept the bows of the *Ocean Spell*, and Barnack was shredded, body knocked overside with the dead gunners.

Ahead was death, death in white smoke and black, round metal.

Peirol was staggering with the *Ocean Spell*'s crazy rolling, stumbling toward the bow, toward that great gun. It was as if Quipus were beside him, lecturing calmly, as he had so many hours, days, while they sat behind the killing oar.

—If the gun be in battery—

"It is!" Peirol shouted.

—make sure it is swabbed out, then load with your powder—

Peirol's hands were fumbling with powder bags, tearing them open, pouring them into the open mouth of the gun, finding the ram, half-smashed, praying it'd not break in half on him, pushing the powder down the gun's muzzle, then finding the cotton pad . . .

—Wadding, 'tis called—

Wadding, then lifting a ball, heavy stone, shoving it down the muzzle, then pushing, pushing with the ramrod until it could be pushed no more.

—with utmost care, sprinkle a bit of powder in the touchhole, covering it with your thumbstock so there'll be no backblast—

"Too wet," Peirol cried, "and there's no time to look for that damned thumbstock."

—the gun is then brought into firing readiness—

And how could he work the pulleys to haul the gun forward into position?—impossible, except the galley rolled, cannon muzzle almost going into the water, and the gun carriage rolled forward as if of its own will to the ends of the breeching rope, ready to fire. The *Ocean Spell* rolled back, and there was nothing but darkness and gunfire above him, prow almost touching the hull of the Sarissans' great galley.

—taking care and caution with your fusee, at the proper command of "fire," bring the fusee to the touchhole—

Scrabbling, finding the bucket with the smoldering fusees, and ramming one against the cannon's breech.

The gun bellowed, bucked back, and the ball smashed into, through, the enemy ship's armor, deep into its heart, and the *Ocean Spell* turned, spinning down the other ship's rows of oars. Then it was free but foundering, small waves slopping over the gunwales.

Peirol paid no mind, still following that ghost-voice, telling him to sponge out, reload, be careful, have the enemy in your sights and FIRE, and again the gun went off, and then a third time. The world, the universe, time, exploded and he could hear nothing, and was knocked away, blood in his mouth. He forced himself to his feet, clutching the railing of the ruined *Ocean Spell*, feeling it sinking under him, as white flames, impossibly hot, boiled from the galley of the Sarissans as the ship writhed, racked by blast after blast.

There were soldiers, sailors beside him, and he faintly heard them shouting, pointing at the other ensorcelled ships of the Sarissans as they went out of control, twisting, ramming human ships, each other, wrecking themselves, the puppeteer's strings torn away, and someone, Captain Penrith, was cheering, cheering him. It made no sense at all. Peirol of the Moorlands decided his war was over; he cared not who'd won, letting himself collapse, embracing darkness.

SEVEN

Of Magnates' Hobbies and Family

The fleet shattered like exploding crystal, captains shouting for full sail, galleys with their oarsmen whipped into a heart-bursting pace, each ship for itself, out of the trap, each man afraid to look back, afraid the Sarissans and their dark masters or gods were pursuing. But there was no pursuit.

Peirol came to aboard one of the cannon-equipped merchantmen and was permitted the freedom of the ship until home port was reached. He wondered how great his reward would be, dreaming of gold, possible titles, an escort to accompany him on his quest for the Empire Stone. But there was none, not even manumission.

The Sarissans had roundly defeated Beshkirs and their allies. Whether another, stronger expedition might be mounted in a month or a year, or great magic brought against them, no one said. But very suddenly any mention of the leonine raiders vanished from all conversations.

Peirol was escorted back to the white barracks and told he was of course still a slave, and would be auctioned off shortly with the rest of Lord Kanen's possessions by his only survivor, a pinch-faced niece who was a Guardian Virgin in the temple of Aballava, Goddess of Mercy and the Downtrodden. Peirol considered the irony, quickly realized there would be none apparent to the people of Beshkirs, and slumped into a black depression.

He was brought out of glumness by a dream, if dream it was. He saw nothing except swirling clouds and gentle colors, and felt contentment, happiness. A soft voice came: "Peirol, you must hold fast. Nothing can last forever. You will be free soon, free to continue, free to find the gem you search, free to find riches and then return."

He woke, smiling, smelling jasmine and roses, remembering the voice of Kima. He wondered if it was a dream, or a spell sent by Abbas to bolster him.

Peirol gathered his strength and his wits and considered what to do next. He still had the tiny bag of gems tied behind his knee, but his jeweler's roll had been lost when the *Ocean Spell* went down. No matter. Tools can be bought or fabricated, spells can be recast.

Two days later, he and the others who'd belonged to Kanen were taken back to Jirl's slave market.

Peirol was kept aside from the others as Jirl chanted their virtues and the required opening bid.

"A dwarf," Jirl intoned at last. "A good man at the oars, but more important, a hero of the engagement that cost his master his life—gentlemen, this man has the courage of a lion and the tenacity of an eagle, handsome, healthy, in the prime, I must insist on a floor bid of 1,000 gold coins for a man of his experience and ability."

Peirol felt his stomach come up.

"One thousand, for a man any seaman among you would be proud to have as oarmaster on his galley. . . . I see one thousand, twelve hundred, fifteen hundred, two thousand, even, two thousand once, two thousand twice . . . and another bid of twenty-five hundred from Lord Whaal, are there any other bids . . ."

Peirol remembered Lord Whaal as the slave raider, and he cursed the dream that'd given him a moment of hope. To be an oarmaster, the man with the whip? Never. Peirol vowed he'd throw himself overboard, take his chances with the musketeers and the sharks, first.

"Two thousand five hundred one time, two times, and—"

Jirl broke off as a small, officious man in green robes bustled up.

"One moment, gentle ones."

Jirl came down from the block to whisper with the small man, and there was interested speculation from the crowd. Jirl nodded, and the little man in green scurried to an enormously fat man escorted by four grim swordsmen. They conferred, and the large one lifted a hand.

"The dwarf is hereby withdrawn from this market," Jirl said. "Another arrangement has been made."

"By who?" somebody shouted, and another voice called, "And for how much?"

Jirl ignored them, jerked his head at the guards, and Peirol was led back down the steps, where the man in green waited.

"Do I need to have you chained?" the man asked.

"No," Peirol said, wondering what doom had come.

"Good, good. I am Guallauc."

"And I'm—"

"I know who you are," Guallauc said. "Peirol of the Moorlands, sometime jeweler. Follow me to meet your new master."

"Who is?"

"Magnate Niazbeck, the one you sent that bit of silver to, of course. I am his chief factotum."

Peirol felt the world change around him.

Magnate Niazbeck was the fattest man Peirol had ever seen. His head with its jolly wrinkles was the roast suckling pig at a holiday, his body the barrel of wine that was rolled out, his legs drumsticks from a fabulous bird, his thighs rolled roasts, his fingers cream-filled macaroons.

His smile beamed across the carriage at Peirol, and all appeared jollity. "I'm sorry, boy," Niazbeck said, in an incongruously squeaky voice, which made Peirol wonder, considering the man's bulk, if he was a capon. "I wasn't able to rescue you before you went off to war, but then, if I hadn't, your great secret would never have been revealed, now would it?"

"My secret, sir?"

Niazbeck chortled. "There's no need to dissemble. I've had a full report of your ability at the great gun. Why didn't you tell the late Lord Kanen about your talents? He surely would have found a place for you as a gunner, instead of at the oars."

"I didn't think anyone would believe me, sir," he said. "Besides, the god of artillery isn't the god I prefer to serve."

Niazbeck's smile turned chilly. "And what is the matter with an honorable service such as that? Keep in mind, boy, that is the greatest reason I'm paying an outrageous sum both to Lord Whaal to withdraw from bidding and to Jirl for special consideration."

"I don't consider myself more than a journeyman," Peirol lied. "In my land, sir, the gunners are so skilled, so talented, I thought yours would be at least as talented, since you're a greater kingdom, and I didn't want to look like a fool or a braggart."

Niazbeck eyed him carefully. "That is interesting, indeed. Your homeland?"

"Once Cenwalk, but I learned what little I know of the Great Art in Sennen."

"I have never heard Sennen noted for its cannoneers," Niazbeck said. "Have you, Guallauc?"

The little man jerked his head back and forth.

"I thought it was a land of magicians, cutpurses, and other rakehells," Niazbeck said.

"And jewelers, sir," Peirol added. "That was the calling I preferred."

"One which you'll have full opportunity to indulge," Niazbeck said. "That was where I made my reputation, and my first millions. But that opportunity will be interrupted before fall," he said. "And you'll be serving in your previous trade, for war threatens."

"War? With the Sarissans again?"

"No," Niazbeck said. "We'll not war with them until someone devises a better strategy than Lord Kanen had. Our destiny lies south, across the straits, on the Manoleon Peninsula, against the shameless people of Arzamas."

"Shameless," Guallauc snickered, "and, fortunately, wallowing in gold."

Niazbeck gave him a look, and the factotum shrank back. "I, for one, need no further riches," Niazbeck announced. "I have raised a company of artillery because I am a true son of Beshkirs, even if adopted, and wish to see us expand, grow, move into the land of our rightful destiny, and bring the gift of freedom and peace to those poor wights south of us, end the rapacious warrings of their bandit kingdoms." He looked closely at Peirol. "I assume you have heard tales of the evils of Arzamas?"

"I have, sir," Peirol said quickly. "I was much afraid when I heard those stories on the ship from Sennen, because Arzamas was my destination before I was seized by your pi— by Lord Kanen's warships."

"What was your business there?"

"I had begun a search for a great stone, sir, somewhere far to the east, in a city named Restormel, of which we in Sennen knew nothing but the name."

"A single gem?"

"Called the Empire Stone," Peirol said.

"I know it not," Niazbeck said. "Forget about it. Serve me well, and I'll give you the chance to design and work with greater gems than any you could have dreamed of.

"Serve me badly, and . . ." Niazbeck shrugged, said no more.

Peirol decided, in spite of Niazbeck's jolly manners, he liked him not at all.

Niazbeck's estate, one of many, was built around a naturally defensible rocky cove. Thirty-foot stone walls, wide enough for guards to walk on them, closed off the land. To sea, the cove was guarded from raids by pirates or competitors by sea chains hung between three lighthouselike towers. The water was warm, clear, and green, and the sands of the beach impossibly white. Within the walls were lavish gardens and pools around the sprawling great house, two stories of gray stone and many rooms. The estate was lit and the buildings heated by what some called sorcery, others clever mechanics. Coal was brought from the interior, turned into a gas by Niazbeck's wizard, a quiet man named Tejend, sent through copper pipes, and ignited. On one side of the main house were greenhouses filled with exotic flowers. On the other were the work rooms and slave quarters. A showroom sat close to the outer wall, and a winding tunnel-like passage reached from an outside entrance to it.

Niazbeck's gems were so valued he was able to make the elite of Beshkirs come to him, rather than opening a plebeian store within the city. Unfortunately

this made it impossible for Peirol to plan an escape—
not that he had the slightest idea of how he would be
able to get off the island onto the Manoleon Peninsula,
especially after he learned the Parassan peasants were
well rewarded for the return of any escaped slave,
with no interest being taken in whether the escapee
was alive or dead.

Peirol was taken to his quarters, a cubicle about
ten feet on a side, one of thirty such, opening on a
common room. It was furnished with bed, table, and
chair, and there were pegs to hang clothes on. Ablu-
tions would be done in a stone room off the common
room, and meals would come from Niazbeck's own
kitchen, Guallauc explained. He had an hour before
the meal, and should take himself to the seamstresses
to have new clothing made.

The seamstresses had a giggling great time fitting
him for the blue clothes that slaves wore, to be ready
on the morrow, and managed to find a tunic big
enough and cut down a pair of trousers as a temporary
measure for him. Peirol asked to have his shipboard
clothes burned, and took himself to the washroom.

There were three different kinds of scented soaps,
rinses for hair, and perfumes, so he guessed everything
would be coeducational. Peirol stripped, found a tub of
heated water, washed from a bucket twice, rinsed his
hair three times, and found a forgotten partially
toothed comb to rake out the worst of the tangles before soaking for a few minutes. He found himself
yawning, forced himself out, and toweled dry. The
washroom's back door revealed a lawn, green as any
emerald. He remembered emerald eyes, the smell of

jasmine and roses, and walked out, stretching, feeling the late spring sun warm on his bones.

Peirol felt himself being watched and realized he was foolish, going out naked when he knew nothing of Niazbeck's customs. He ducked back inside and found his breeches. On the second floor of the main house, he saw movement, sunlight reflecting something, a flash of red hair. Faintly came the clack of metal, then a door opened, closed. He wondered who'd been spying on him, hoped he hadn't offended, worried a bit that he might have pleased.

No one in the jewel works quite knew what to make of Peirol, since he'd been the personal acquisition of the magnate. But he'd worked in enough places to know how to behave. For the first two weeks he kept his mouth shut, hurried to do anything anyone suggested, and was careful to take on the most menial jobs. Slowly the slaves began warming to him, accepting him as one of their own.

The shop overseer was a small, shrewd old man named Klek, who'd been Niazbeck's slave for twenty years, and Peirol quite liked him. He asked, as casually as he could, what Niazbeck's policy was on manumission.

Klek snorted. "If he, or his father before him, ever freed anyone, it's beyond my knowledge." He leaned close, lowered his voice. "In fact, the magnate's known for being quick to send someone back to the market if they displease him."

"What are ways to avoid his displeasure?"

Klek smiled twistedly. "The only one who seems to know the rules is Magnate Niazbeck."

The magnate spent no more than a day or two per week in the shop, passing most of his time at his country manor farther up-island, where he had his artillery company quartered. But when he did appear, Peirol noted, he paid close attention to both the shop and his accounts.

He learned Niazbeck was most dyspeptic, unable to do more than taste his vast collection of wines and digest the simplest foods, although his family and guests were encouraged to dine in the most lavish manner.

There were only two in his family: his daughter, Reni, who was about seventeen—she of the red hair—and Niazbeck's third wife, Ellena. Ellena was about Peirol's age, and Peirol lifted an eyebrow.

Klek explained, "The first one, I understand not bad-looking, worked herself into the grave helping him build his business; the second could have given a serpent the horrors, but gave him the riches to become a magnate with interests in many areas and then was set aside; and now this one. They've been married just at two years."

"Without children?" Peirol said.

"Without children," Klek nodded. "Although they try hard enough. The carpenters not infrequently have to repair their bed. And I have a suggestion for you about both wife and daughter: don't go into rooms with them where there are corners."

"What's that mean?"

Klek grinned, refused to elaborate.

Peirol considered his options. He didn't think escape from the estate would be that good an idea, quite likely impossible. He hoped Niazbeck had been wrong, and there would be no war and hence no call for him to perform again as a cannoneer.

But the year was dragging on, and the Empire Stone felt farther away than ever.

The best thing to do was to change his circumstances. Peirol got permission from Klek to hunt about for a project of his own.

"Although," Klek said, "I must warn you not to be *too* artistic. The magnate has been known to feel irked when, shall we say, a smaller light threatens to eclipse his own."

"And what happens then?"

"You've gone before Jirl twice," Klek said. "I assume you'd find a third visit tiresome."

In a storeroom where Niazbeck kept his breakages and faults, Peirol found something interesting: a large chunk of purple amethyst, a big man's handspan in size. It had been partially cut, and one facet had a great crack down one side. He took it to Klek. The man winced.

"I remember that well. Niazbeck once purchased a man who claimed to be a journeyman jeweler. I don't even remember his name now. Anyway, he convinced the magnate of his talents and was purchased. Magnate Niazbeck had recently acquired that gem, and thought to have a goblet made, since he'd been told amethyst will drive off poison."

"So I've heard," Peirol nodded. "Without a spell attached, that doesn't sound likely to me."

"Nor me, but I was certainly not about to argue with the magnate. So with flash and fuffle, the journeyman began to cut the gem. You see what happened. Too great an angle, too much force, and the stone's ruined."

"What happened to its cutter?"

"He was gone within the hour," Klek said. "I asked Guallauc what happened, if he'd been taken back to the slave market, and he just looked at me, eyes wide, as if I'd made him remember something monstrous. He begged me not to ask, not to mention the matter again."

"How very nice," Peirol said. "Of course, no one else would try to salvage the disaster."

"Of course not," Klek hissed. "Gems collect luck, some good, some bad. That one's already brought one man's doom, why should it collect another's?"

"I disbelieve that," Peirol said. "Would there be any objection if I used it for something?"

"Not at all. And if you ruin it, there'll be no need for Magnate Niazbeck to know, though if he did know, I doubt if he would care."

"I have an open field," Peirol said gaily, "and nothing but good fortune can attend."

"If you say so," Klek said dubiously, and gave him his own bench and tools.

Peirol clamped the flawed gem in his vise and sat staring at it for a day and half a night, making sketches, throwing them away, drawing others. No one came near him, which was perfectly acceptable to the dwarf when he was planning. At last he went to Klek and asked if Niazbeck had access to a wizard. "Not one of the first rank, even," he said. "But I think I need some magic." Thus he learned about Tejend, the quiet magician, and went to his lair, at the far end of the garden.

The magician considered Peirol carefully. "Magnate Niazbeck told me he'd bought a dwarf, one with great talents, almost magical. What do you require of my magic, young man? I must warn you, I'm under oath to report anyone who visits me. Even for a simple love philtre," he said. "The magnate is a most careful man."

"It's not love nor villainy I'm interested in," Peirol said, and explained what he wanted.

Tejend nodded. "That's quite an easy matter, and I know an easier casting than the way you have suggested. But your gem must first be faceted, almost ready to be set, as I think you craftsman put it. Return with it then."

Peirol went to work. Klek winced when he realized the savagery Peirol was about to commit. He used a chisel to cut the stone in two along the crack. Then he cut the stone again parallel with the first cut, so he had a jagged slab a child's palm wide, and almost a finger-width thick. Again and again he cut the stone, then cemented it in his lathe and turned it until he had girdled it into a disc. He measured, marked, and cut facets into the side of the disc. By now the stone was as big around as a man's thumb and forefinger put together, about fifty *varjas*.

"Why inward facets?" Klek asked. "That'll just swallow the light."

"Maybe not," Peirol said, working his neck back and forth to ease a cramp. "Maybe it'll cast light out."

"What light?" Klek said. "No stone does more than absorb and reflect what's around it."

"Not in Sennen," Peirol said smugly.

Finally the facets were finished and polished. Peirol cast a wrist torque from gold and spent three days cutting an intricate abstract pattern into the metal. He convinced Klek to give him twenty tiny diamonds, again from the waste bins. They'd been cut in an old-fashioned seventeen-facet cut, which allowed light from the top to escape through the sides instead of concentrating it, making them "sleepy" stones. Since they were too small to recut, they were almost value-less to a jeweler like Niazbeck, who offered only the most expensive baubles. Then he went to see the magician again.

The estate path curved through flowers, and the world was bright with early summer, sunlight dappling the wavelets in the cove. Peirol took a moment to wish this place was his, without slaves, and with only, well, perhaps Kima to company him.

"And while I'm at it," he muttered, "why not the proper legs the gods should've given me as well?"

He saw a flicker of red, rounded a curve, and there was Reni in front of him, carrying a basket of flowers. Not sure of the protocol a slave should show his master's children, he jumped off the stones and ducked his head as he assumed a proper underling should.

Reni laughed, a rather pleasant sound in this quiet

place, and Peirol thought it might be all right to look up. She was not much taller than he was, quite perfectly proportioned for her size, and her hair was caught in a gold tie, then fell halfway down her back. She wore a linen gown with flowers embroidered on it, and sandals with straps that reached up her ankles.

"You needn't be so formal, dwarf."

"I'm still learning my place, mistress."

"I have a name, you know."

"Again, something I didn't know if I was allowed to use, Reni."

"And you are?"

"Peirol of the Moorlands," he said, as formally as if they were equals.

"My father's told me of you, and I've been meaning to visit the shops, to see what you look like." She giggled. "Although I have a fairly good idea of that already."

Peirol pretended innocence, guessing that the clash of metal he'd heard when she realized he'd seen her was a seaman's spyglass being closed.

"You don't look like the warrior my father says you are."

"I'm not," Peirol said. "What I did was only to keep me alive. My first love is jewels."

"And your second?" Reni looked slyly at him.

Alarm bells clanged in Peirol's mind.

"That is a good question, mistress," Peirol said. "And I admire your cleverness, for no one before's ever asked me that, and so I have no ready answer."

"Think on it," she said. "For I've heard . . . interesting things of dwarves."

Hoping he'd misunderstood, Peirol ducked his head. "If you'll pardon me, now."

"*Interesting* things," Reni said again, and licked her lips.

Peirol wished he could have found a better description of the way he left rather than "scuttling."

"You've been gone over a Time," the wizard Tejend said. "I thought you'd failed, or lost interest." He examined the disc. "Now I see what you're attempting. Very interesting indeed. So let us make preparation."

He drew a series of circles on the floor of his workroom and inscribed a different symbol in each. He put three small braziers equidistant from each other, then a fourth in the center.

"We'll burn young oak, for when it's wet it can be easily shaped, as we want to shape your gem. Cypress for its powers, some pine knots since they burn brightly, and we'll dust the fires with, oh, skullcap and vervain for movement, rosemary, wintergreen, and yellow dock.

"Now, for an incantation. Umm. Ah, I have it. Now put your stone in the center of that great brazier. Don't worry, it won't be harmed by the flames."

Tejend gestured, and the four braziers flamed to life. Smoke curled, wound around the room. He chanted:

> *"Fire burn*
> *Fire bring a gift*
> *A gift of memory*
> *Warmth to the heart of this stone*
> *Alarat, Mentmana, Carral."*

He repeated the names, if names they were, three times, then chanted for another minute in a language Peirol's spell didn't translate. He waved his hands, and the fires flickered three times in unison, went out.

"Pluck the gem from the brazier. It won't be hot." Peirol obeyed. "Now, look into it. Is that the effect you wished?"

"It's wonderful, sir," Peirol breathed. "Fine, very, very fine, better, much better than I thought it'd be."

"So you're satisfied."

"I am and more," Peirol said. "But . . . how do I pay you, or rather, since it's intended for sale, how should you be recompensed?"

Tejend smiled, a little sadly. "Forget about it. It let me exercise my mind. As I said before, I spend too much of my time doing nothing but love philtres."

Peirol didn't think it would be seemly to ask for whom, thanked the wizard again, and left. Helpful and friendly though Tejend was, Peirol remained nervous in the presence of magicians.

The disc was set in the torque, with the diamonds around it at equal intervals.

"Here," Peirol said, handing the bracelet to Klek next to a window. He stared into it, as hypnotized as Peirol had been. In the heart of the disc a purple fire seethed and curled. The diamonds caught the sunlight, concentrated it, and shot it into the disc, and the fires burned higher.

"I've never seen anything like it, Peirol. You were far more than a journeyman where you came from."

Peirol nodded.

"Never anything like it," Klek whispered, turning the torque back and forth. "Incredible. Just incredible. Magnate Niazbeck will be stunned."

Peirol heard nothing for three days, then Klek told everyone in the shop they were to be honored by a visit from Magnate Niazbeck and a client. The client was named Vel, younger than Reni, lovely in a calculating sort of way, with her husband-to-be, a trading magnate perhaps four times the woman's age.

She'd insisted on meeting the man who made the bracelet that won her heart and made her more than willing to become the trader's second wife. Klek presented Peirol, who bowed very deeply.

"You have much talent beyond your size," Vel said. "I've never seen such beauty in a piece of jewelry. You are an artist."

"I thank you," Peirol said, bowing once again. "But the true artist is my master. I'm but an artisan, who carries out his designs."

Niazbeck was startled, hid it well. Klek had to turn away, to hide a bit of coughing.

"Perhaps, one day," Vel said, "you, or rather Magnate Niazbeck, will devise something equally striking, and my dear husband might choose it for me."

The trader looked a little worried. Vel seemingly didn't notice and passed down the benches, cooing at other slaves' handiwork. The trader leaned close to Peirol.

"My Vel mentioned you possibly making something striking someday? Well, such a piece would find favor with me, quite immediately. But not for her: for my first wife, who I'm afraid is behaving in an unreasonably jealous manner about our wedding plans."

"Something my overseer, Klek, told me about one of Magnate Niazbeck's earlier works, something he himself might have forgotten, has sparked an idea," Peirol lied. "Perhaps, in a week, perhaps two, I might have something not totally unworthy of your attention."

The trader beamed, hurried after his wife.

Magnate Niazbeck eyed Peirol. "You are very clever, my lad."

"Nossir," Peirol said. "I meant what I said. You've given me a space for my horizons to widen, to grow, and I'll be cursed if I don't express my gratitude."

"I see," Niazbeck said. "Don't worry. If you can drag another commission out of Tightfist, well, you'll be properly rewarded. I promise you."

Peirol bowed, rose as Niazbeck waddled away, noted Klek still standing there. "Clever, clever," the older man said, "I just hope not *too* clever."

"I shall try to avoid that."

Klek nodded. "What do you need for your next masterpiece? Assuming, that is, you truly have an idea."

"I do," Peirol said. "First, I'll need a colorless diamond, decent sized, perhaps three *varjas*. And, I think, a dozen moonstones. Big ones. This time, I'm going to make a necklace."

Peirol really hadn't much liked what he'd done with the amethyst. It was clever, but far too garish for his own tastes. But he'd learned long ago, shortly after he'd been accepted as an apprentice by Rozan, that wealth in no way suggested good taste. In fact, the master jeweler had said, the fresher the gold the bigger the bauble should be, "for most men who've just made themselves rich want to trumpet it to the world, if not the tax collector."

Peirol thought about what the trader's first wife might appreciate, and set to work. He chose the clearest and second largest of Niazbeck's diamonds, which had already been cut pear-shaped, and took it to Tejend for a dose of sorcery. The spell was simple, but the effect was exactly as Peirol had wanted.

Since the wizard still wouldn't accept any sort of payment, Peirol, hewing to his own ethics, made him a small wand out of a length of bicolored tourmaline that had been simply faceted and polished. He told the magician there wasn't any magic in it, but he imagined Tejend could provide that.

He then carefully, remembering their delicacy, worked the moonstones into simple ovals and set them in silver around the diamond. "No gold," he told Klek, "even if the client's six kinds of a vulgar bitch. I have a few standards."

Klek, when the necklace was finished, showed it to Niazbeck, who chortled gleefully and summoned the trader and his first wife. Peirol was amused to note that the woman, thirty years ago, would have looked a twin sister to Vel. The woman gasped three times, then took the necklace with trembling fingers. The trader clasped it around her neck, held out a mirror.

"Oh merciful goddess," the woman whispered.

It *was* fairly special. The diamond had been ensorcelled while Peirol moved a succession of multi-colored candle flames close to the stone, then away into darkness, waiting a moment before holding up another candle. Forever after, it would echo those reflections to anyone who peered into its depths.

The moonstones were magicked to simply reflect bits of the candle glow, no more.

The trader was as impressed as his wife. "Magnate," he said, "you were always a genius, it appears."

Niazbeck looked humble.

"Now, magnate, you might now do me a great favor," the trader said. "Don't come up with any more brilliances, at least not until I make a dozen or so successful ventures so I can pay for your baubles."

Everyone laughed, but Peirol wondered how much gold Niazbeck had charged for the jewels.

"You're to be rewarded," Klek said the next morning. Behind him was Guallauc.

"Thank you, sir."

"Follow me," the factor said, and strode out. Peirol obeyed, and saw, sitting in front of the great house on the drive, a carriage.

Just a look at the world beyond these walls is reward enough, he thought. Maybe enough to bring me the beginnings of a plan to get away.

Quite a hobby, Peirol thought.

"I knew the proper reward for you wouldn't be gold or anything else, but the chance to watch my cannoneers' evolutions," Niazbeck said.

"You understand me well," Peirol said, trying to

keep from shivering in the chill wind from the ocean. There were sixty men on the grassy slopes above the water, drawn up behind the four objects of Niazbeck's adoration: ribbed tubes eleven feet long, each weighing more than all their eight main attendants.

Niazbeck had insisted Peirol be given the "honor" of inspecting the artillery group—a battery, he called it—he'd personally raised, outfitted, and paid. "Some think it's but my silly hobby, but soon enough they'll realize I can scent the wind well, and have the best interests of my adopted kingdom at heart."

The cannoneers held a dizzying array of trades, from gunners to matrosses and their assistants, blacksmiths, harness makers, carpenters, pioneers, guards, cooks, sutlers, and trumpeters, all wearing the Niazbeck-designed uniforms of purple and white, with high green boots. Peirol thought, if he had to choose a trade among them, he would've been one of the kettledrummers, who had their own cart to hold the great drums, with the trumpeters leading the horses.

The men glowered uniformly at Peirol, correctly thinking that if it weren't for this damned dwarf, they could be in a nice warm taphouse with some mulled wine, trying to cozen a wench for their knee. The horses, twice as many as the men, were far friendlier.

"Your opinion, Peirol?" Niazbeck asked.

"An astonishing turnout," Peirol said honestly.

"But you, a man far more experienced at practical gunnery than any of us, must have observed *something* not quite right," Niazbeck pressed.

Peirol wanted to groan, was about to beg off again, when he noticed the hard, examining look in

Niazbeck's eye. He hastily scanned the assembled troop and their guns, casting back in his mind for more of Quipus's mad wisdom. The guns looked like small culverins—demi-culverins, he thought they were exactly named. The bore was about the size of his fist, which meant they would probably fire a stone shot of about nine pounds. Ah.

"You chose to buy wrought iron, instead of bronze guns?"

Niazbeck made a face. "The best foundry I located who would cast my culverins in bronze was on the Manoleon Peninsula, which I disliked, plus it required full payment in front, and a two-year wait."

Peirol echoed his grimace, turned his attention again to the guns. Something else came.

"Ah, but I see your wisdom," he said, "in that even though you couldn't get the best metal, you did have your reinforces made stronger than is the general custom."

"You noticed that," Niazbeck said proudly. "Yes, the master founder suggested that, and for a few more silver coins, I could have better safety. You are a true cannoneer, Peirol, with an eye for the piece. Would you care to call the firing order?"

Peirol's mind scrabbled back—remembered the drills aboard the galley.

"Gunners, take your stations," he shouted, and the six men per gun scrambled forward.

"Load your guns and report!"

"We use the order to load your guns and stand back," Niazbeck said. "But continue."

"I said, report!"

Four men shouted the guns were loaded.

"Target—" and Peirol turned, looked out to sea. "That floating log, one hundred yards distant! Gunners, take aim, and report!"

Metal bars were used to move the guns from side to side, then to elevate them, one man peering along the cannon barrel.

"Do you have your targets?" Shouts. "Stand away from the guns . . . gunner, you may fire when ready!"

Each gunner picked up a length of smoking fuse from a bucket, touched it to the hole. The cannon crashed and rolled back on their single trails, and the air smashed at Peirol's eardrums. Four splashes rose, neatly bracketing the log.

"Good, very good shooting indeed," Niazbeck said. "I assume Guallauc told you that you're also to be a guest at the family table for dinner?"

Peirol brightened. Now *that* might actually mean something, instead of this freezing and dancing around chunks of metal.

Peirol was very curious as to how a magnate dined. He hoped the stories were right and Niazbeck didn't make guests share in his dyspepsia, serving naught but soft-boiled eggs, buttered toast, and milk. After all this time as a slave, if he had to eat another bowl of gruel, this time at a rich man's table, he was sure he'd burst into tears.

Niazbeck wasn't that sort. While he, indeed, had bread soaked in milk and a barely boiled, buttered egg, the dinner consisted of a spiced vegetable soup, baked fish with nut stuffing, asparagus with vinegar and oil dressing, cherry tomatoes in cream, and a spring berry tart. Niazbeck selected and poured a different wine with each course, seeming to take as much enjoyment in other people's pleasure as if he were able to drink himself. Peirol cautiously sipped the wine, not because he didn't want to swill like a hog, but because he'd been sober so long, he feared its consequences.

At the table were a dozen household members, of which Peirol knew Guallauc, Tejend the sorcerer, Niazbeck, his wife Ellena, and Reni. Peirol had instinctively moved to sit with the servants, but Niazbeck told him no, he was being honored this night and should sit above the salt with Tejend and the family.

Niazbeck's wife was tall, stately, a trifle imperious, and it was clear she came from a noble line. She was quite curious about Peirol's history. The dwarf couldn't figure if it was because she'd never been around someone like him, or if everyone at the table had heard everyone else's stories time and again and desperately wanted something new. Maybe the vaunted country estate could be a trap, seeing the same faces, hearing the same voices, day after day. Perhaps he was right in hewing to the city. When he'd made his millions, maybe Peirol wouldn't want something like this. Or perhaps he would.

Niazbeck started a story from his early years, when he'd been unfortunate enough to take in, as collateral, a notorious gem which half a dozen men had died for. Peirol, interested, asked for the full story and, when that one came to a rather dull climax, for other tales. The magnate told them eagerly, and Peirol looked about, gauging the reaction, trying to find a key to his situation. Reni acted as if she hadn't heard some of them, Ellena as if she had heard them all twice, was being incredibly polite in listening yet again, and wanted everyone to know it. Tejend, who'd been polite if little more through the meal, excused himself as quickly as possible. The servants listened raptly, as if nothing so clever and exciting had ever been told.

Niazbeck looked at the decanter with the dessert wine as if it held his soul, and his pink, catlike tongue licked his lips every time he poured another glass.

Reni kept Peirol's glass full, and insisted he drink with her, in spite of his protests. She poured another, and Peirol knew it must be his last, for there was a slight bitterness to it, and when drink changed its taste, it was time to end the evening.

Niazbeck was in the middle of what was actually quite an interesting story, about the bandits to be found on the trading routes on the upper reaches of the Manoleon Peninsula, when the room around Peirol gently lifted and moved back and forth in a rather stately rhythm. Peirol blinked, squinched an eye until the room stabilized, managed to make it until the end of Niazbeck's story.

He stood, keeping one hand firmly on the table. "Magnate, I'm desperately sorry, but the conshtraints of the day sheem . . . seem . . . ." The room spun once, in an unexpected direction, and dumped Peirol backward. He missed his chair and sat down firmly on the carpet.

Ah gods, now I've done it, he thought, and it's all

that bitch Reni's fault, I should've said I drink not at all . . .

If his legs and eyes weren't in full order, at least his ears were:

"Taken drunk." That was Guallauc's voice. Sneering a bit.

A giggle. Reni? Ellena?

"That's all right," Niazbeck's voice came heartily. "He's made us near a million with just those two pieces of jewelry, so he can drink half my cellar, throw up on the table, and earn no shame, as far as I'm concerned."

"I'll call servants take him back to his quarters." Guallauc.

"No need," and that was Reni. "Here, summon servants and have him taken to one of the spare guestrooms. Let him have a final bit of honor before he goes back to the slave quarters with a thick head."

"Why not?" That was Ellena. "Especially since you think so highly of him, my lord."

"Why not, indeed?" Niazbeck laughed again, and Peirol's ears decided it was all right to go to sleep like the rest of him had.

Peirol woke slowly, in a great, soft bed with silken sheets. He expected to be sick and was pleased to note his stomach was still in place, even if the world was a bit swimmy. He was also in a state of great arousal, he noted.

Lips swept across his stomach, and he realized this wasn't the first time he'd been kissed. His eyes snapped open. He was in a richly furnished room. He was naked, and there was a single candle burning. There was red hair piled on his chest, and the lips continued moving downward. He snorted in surprise, and the head lifted.

"I thought that would wake you," Reni purred.

"We can't be doing this," Peirol whispered hoarsely.

"Why not?"

"Because . . . because your father'll turn me into a eunuch if he finds us!"

"So I shouldn't scream, and say I was merely checking on you, to make sure you weren't sick, and you leaped upon me?"

"Uh . . . no. No, I wouldn't like that at all."

"Do you like this?" Reni kissed him again, lingeringly, well below where he'd discovered her.

"I . . . of course I do. But—"

"Hush, then. Save your energies, for you'll need them in a bit."

Just before Reni's body swallowed him, he remembered Tejend complaining about love philtres, and the bitterness of that final glass of wine.

Someone was pulling at Peirol's ankle. "You're insatiable," he murmured.

"What's that?" The voice was grating, if female. Peirol's eyes slid open. It was daylight, and the woman pulling at his leg was middle-aged, fat, and had a mustache that would've made a soldier proud. "Get your unspeakable ass out of this bed," the maid said, sounding as if she were gargling broken glass. "And get back to your quarters. Damned work slaves get one night of privilege, dining with the master, and there's no damned telling what liberties they'll want next!"

Peirol hoped the night with Reni was no more than an impulse but was proven very wrong the next day, when she came through the shop and passed him a note, to meet her after evening meal in one of the greenhouses. He obeyed, seeing no other option.

She was naked, lying on a bed of flower petals, quite lovely in the light from the setting sun. "Come here," she whispered. "Prove to me it wasn't the philtre."

And so their affair began. Reni was not only fairly insatiable, but wanted to make love in hazardous situations. Twice she ordered Peirol to evade the night guards and climb up to her bedroom; three times in the cove just out of the guards' earshot; once standing up in the great house's main hallway, minutes before her father returned home. Peirol assumed all the slaves and servants knew what was going on, knew they wouldn't tell unless there would be some great advantage to them, little caring, as most slaves did, what their masters did, considering it all bad and evil.

It appeared no overseers knew, especially not Guallauc. Peirol worried less about discovery than what had happened to his predecessors. He wasn't Reni's first, nor, he guessed, twentieth lover. When she became bored, what would happen then? He spent hours remembering bawdy tales, scatological engravings, trying to constantly surprise Reni with a new position, a further bit of exotica. His real work, his jewelmaking, was suffering, but no one else seemed to notice.

Peirol knew this situation could not continue forever. He was quite right.

At first, he thought the drumming was his impassioned blood as he moved in Reni's body. Then he realized the thunder came from outside. They broke apart, hastily dressed, and left the gardens by different paths.

The drummers were from the artillery battery, and Magnate Niazbeck stood in front of them, waiting for everyone on the estate to assemble before squeaking out the news in a triumphant voice.

War had been declared on Arzamas an hour ago.

EIGHT

✳

Of War and
Other Complications

ord came that an expeditionary force was being mounted; would Magnate Niazbeck consider allowing his artillery battery to be part of this first incursion across the straits? Niazbeck was ecstatic.

Klek heard of the magnate's joy, made a face. "I was in a war once," he said. "And I was lucky enough not just to be on the winning side, but to get into it very late in the proceedings. All those eager young fools who rushed off when the trumpets first started singing had gotten themselves dead or maimed by then." He spat into the small crucible hissing beside him, and lowered the bucket of gold scraps into it.

Peirol thought it was all very well for Niazbeck to rush toward the sound of the guns—but did he have to take other people with him? Particularly other people he thought were master gunners. But Niazbeck didn't summon Peirol, and the dwarf was quite ignored in the flurry of preparation.

Three days later, Magnate Niazbeck was hoisted into his carriage, already heavy-laden with viands for his delicate constitution, with promises more would be sent on every boat that went from Beshkirs to supply the army. Everyone, slave, free, family, went to the port to see him off, and the men and women from Niazbeck's other estates joined them. Peirol looked for a chance to break away, but the guards were most alert.

Niazbeck went up the gangplank of the ship he and his cannoneers had been assigned to, and the transport was hauled away from the jetty by a galley.

Guns boomed, kites flew, women wept, and children old enough to understand sobbed with their mothers or if younger played happily, wondering what the excitement was about. Ellena and Reni cried more loudly than most, and waved frantically.

Guallauc had been told to stay behind and help Ellena with the household, and so he took charge as Niazbeck's ship sailed out of the harbor, marching the slaves and servants back to the estate.

Peirol was completely lost. If Niazbeck had bought him for his supposed ability as a gunner, why wasn't he aboard that ship? Had he done something to anger the magnate? Or, he thought hopefully, had he so proven his ability as a moneymaker that Niazbeck had no choice but to keep him at home to defray the costs of the battery?

He decided the morrow might provide answers. At least, he thought wearily, massaging his feet after the long walk in what were little better than house slippers, Reni hadn't summoned him when they got back to the estate. But the next morning, as he was going from first-meal to the workshops, she was waiting along a path.

"With father gone," she whispered, "we'll be able to have more time together." Peirol pretended eagerness. "Tomorrow night then? In the orchid house?" She especially liked to make love there, liked the humidity and heat, the way sweat oiled their bodies as they moved together.

"But of course," Peirol said heartily, and blew her a kiss, grateful for another evening to rebuild his strength and devise new gymnastics.

Just before second-meal, Guallauc came to him. "My mistress, the Lady Ellena, would like your opinion on whether we should take advantage of this crisis and stockpile our precious metals. After dinner, in her chambers." Peirol blinked, nodded.

"I know nothing of the current market," Peirol complained to Klek after Guallauc left. "Why would she want to consult me? I'd guess, wars being what they are, it'd be a good idea to stockpile almost anything. But anybody could've told her that."

"Perhaps Magnate Niazbeck told her to consult a well-traveled man such as yourself," Klek said, grinning.

"Why the humor?" Peirol asked suspiciously.

"Just remember what I told you about corners."

Peirol quizzed other workers about what they knew about precious metal prices, left his bench early, ate a hasty meal of bread and cheese, then bathed, sweetened his breath, and put on clean tunic and breeches. A servant took him upstairs to Ellena's apartments.

Niazbeck's wife met him at the door, told the servant there'd be no further need of her services and ushered him inside. He heard the lock click behind him. Ellena's apartment contained four rooms: the sitting room he was in, a lavish bedroom, an equally large dressing room, and, connecting the bedroom and dressing room, a bathroom. There was a table in the sitting room, but none of the paperwork and account books Peirol had expected.

Just as he realized how awfully naive he was, just what Klek had meant by corners, he also noticed Ellena's garb: a silver mesh dress extending only to mid-thigh. The meshes were very widely spread as well. It appeared there was nothing under it. She was barefoot, and her blond hair came down in carefully brushed waves. She smelt of woodland flowers and musk and was very beautiful. Perhaps Peirol's appreciation showed, for Ellena laughed, a low, sultry chuckle.

"Sit down, Peirol of the Moorlands."

He obeyed, at the only chair at the table.

"Would you care for a glass of wine?" He nodded dumbly. She poured wine from a chilled bucket into two glasses, gave one to Peirol. "Do you like being served by the lady of the house?"

"I just wonder," Peirol managed, "what I've done to deserve such an honor."

Ellena curled on a lounge, tucked her feet under.

"Try your wine," she said. It was not a suggestion. Peirol sipped it, licked his lips. It was a little bitter for his tastes, and he suddenly remembered another such glass, a dessert wine.

"The honor?" Ellena mused. "Perhaps because you've been able to satisfy my unbelievably randy step-daughter for over a Time. That is why I asked my darling Niazbeck to let you remain behind with Klek for a while, to make sure the business was well supplied, since you knew about wars and scarcities. I didn't mention what scarcity is uppermost in my mind."

Peirol choked a little. Ellena laughed again. "Reni is very poor at hiding things, especially when she has a secret longing, I think, to be caught in an embarrassing situation by her father. When I discovered she was lifting her skirts for you on an almost nightly basis, I was intrigued. Not that I wasn't . . . interested in you when you first appeared here. I've always been drawn to the unusual.

"Generally Reni's infatuations last a week, maybe a bit longer before the poor man—or woman—is so exhausted he cares little what happens, or else my stepdaughter's learned his repertoire. Once there are no surprises, she has no use for him, so he finds himself sent to one of the outer estates, or sold. There are a few exceptions who've managed to remain here, and are brought back to perform on sentimental occasions, but not many.

"Tell me, Peirol, what is your secret? Are you equipped like a stallion, perhaps?"

"I . . . I don't think so," he said, blushing furiously and feeling even more like a fool.

"Hmm," Ellena said. She went to him, gently pulled him to his feet. "You have," she said amusedly, "an expression very much like a yearling deer I once saw, trapped in nets."

Peirol found anger and his voice. "Wouldn't you, my lady, if you were decoyed into a situation like this, fed what I suspect is one of Wizard Tejend's love potions, and had wit enough to look into the future and see the best that can happen is being returned to Jirl's slave pens?"

Ellena, instead of becoming angry, laughed quite long. "Oh, my poor, dear dwarfling. First, don't you think that I have a bit more cunning than that child? When I decide I want to cuckold my husband, as I do from time to time when someone interesting visits our country prison and circumstances permit, I'm extraordinarily careful. I may not have as much to lose as you, but if I'm discovered, don't you think Niazbeck would set me aside as quickly as he did his last wife?

"I have no desire to return to that brothel I was clever enough to escape from in the first place."

Perhaps the potion was working, for Peirol found his mind veering.

"Niazbeck met you there?"

"Of course not," she said. "The poor dear would faint if he thought any other man has been with me. No, I heard he was searching for a tutor for his Reni and applied for the position, pretending to be an innocent freshly arrived from a country temple. I quickly ensured I found another position, though." Ellena poured him another glass. "I'm glad you're not looking like you're about to face execution any more. That young buck that I mentioned? I cut him free of his nets, and he ran off. I sometimes thought I saw him again, when I would rent a horse and ride out into the country. You see, Peirol? I'm a romantic."

Peirol, in spite of the lust beginning to surge through him, doubted if he'd ever met anyone as unromantic, but decided that wouldn't be the brightest thing to say.

"One question," she said. "If you fathered a child, would he or she be a dwarf, too?"

"No," Peirol said. "Or, not necessarily. I've heard of people like myself who had similar children, but not often. I was the only one in my family, as far back as anyone could recall. Perhaps that was why my father thought I'd been sired by a changeling," he said bitterly.

Ellena made a harsh sound. "We're more alike than we knew," she said. "My father—after he'd had his will with me for three years—was the one who sold me into the skin trade. Why are parents such assholes?"

Peirol shook his head, having no answer.

"And haven't we managed to break the mood," she said. "I guess it's my fault. Would you like a kiss, dwarf?" Peirol would, and took one. Ellena lifted her head away.

"I begin to see some of your talents. You kiss exceedingly well. Come over here." She led him to the couch.

Very late in the night Ellena whispered, "You think I'm perfectly heartless, I suppose. But I'm doing more, I hope, than just satisfying base lusts, although that's certainly part of things. I want a child, and I think Niazbeck's seed cannot sprout. We've tried often enough, including with magical help. That was why I asked about whether dwarves breed true. If you'd said they did, I would have taken precautions. But since that's not the case . . . I would not object to having a son with your features, your hair, your strength."

"And what would you tell your husband if you became suddenly pregnant?"

"As for the timing," Ellena said, "it's still very close to his departure, and I made sure he pleasured me several times before leaving. I've also told him my family is known for giving birth prematurely. I wanted to prepare myself in the event I wished to have an adventure or two."

"You think of everything," Peirol said, not meaning it as a compliment.

"I try. Now hand me that pillow. There's something I thought of that needs attention."

As the night ebbed, Ellena prodded Peirol, who'd just dozed off. "Now, my stallion, get out of here. There'll be no one in the halls to threaten you, and should you meet anyone, do not greet them or speak. I find you more than satisfactory, and think as long as these foolish men insist on going to war, we should have a world of love. Return the night after next, and I shall show you some other things you might not be aware of."

Peirol dressed. As he reached the door, she said: "One other thing, my love. Feel free to continue your liaison with Reni. It amuses me to think of you showing her things I might have taught."

* * *

So it went for a Time and a half, as summer dragged toward fall. Peirol was very proud he was able to continue both affairs and perform after a fashion at the work bench.

He'd thought war would mean Beshkirians would be less inclined to fripperies, but he was completely wrong. There was always someone in the shop eagerly dropping his profits from selling war goods to buy gems, the more gaudy and expensive the better. Peirol's designs were the most sought after of all. The dwarf also found time to cut and polish more than half of the stones in his bag, the gems he'd found in the underground temple of Thyone.

He wondered what would happen next, saw nothing but disaster and doom. He desperately wanted to find a way to escape, to get to the mainland, past the damned armies and on toward Restormel.

But he saw no way out that wouldn't bring that disaster down even more quickly.

Word came from the Manoleon Peninsula: the armies had landed, been hit hard, both with conventional soldiery and magic, and been driven back, north of the landing grounds. They'd rallied, took back their old positions, and were now moving south, closing on Arzamas.

And then word came: Peirol of the Moorlands, sometime artillerist, was needed by his master, Niazbeck.

The war had stretched out its bony hand, and dragged him in, and Peirol was very grateful.

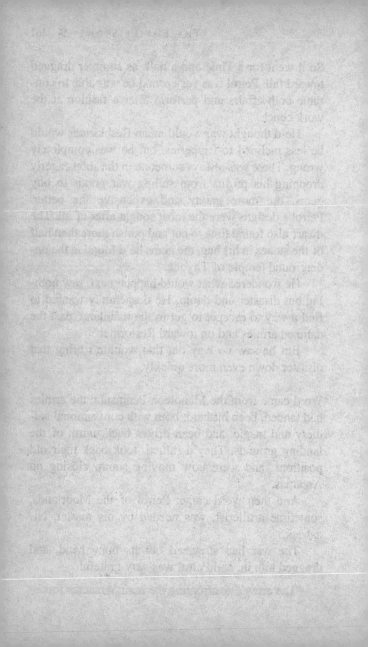

✳

NINE

Of Cannon
and Battles

The landing port was aswarm with ships unloading lines of victuals and replacements, who formed up to bellowed orders and plodded off, heavy-laden, through the fishing village now crowded with whores, blackguards, and opportunists, the flotsam behind the fighting lines of any army, toward the interior and the sound of guns.

Peirol, for a change, was not one of the burdened herd but was met by Guallauc with a pair of horses.

"Magnate Niazbeck needs you desperately. He's most unhappy he listened to the Lady Ellena. Beshkirs needs you far more than a simple jeweler could. Now is no time to think of yourself, but of your homeland."

Peirol thought it was nice someone wanted him for something other than his animal talent.

"The army's confronting the main Arzamas force,

just four leagues north of their city," Guallauc explained. "And the lords told Magnate Niazbeck if we hit them hard, their lines will shatter, and we can take their city. That is where you will fall, for we need someone clever and experienced, who can move from gun to gun and bring fire where it is most needed. Magnate Niazbeck, in view of his, well, physical circumstances, is obviously not capable of such athleticism."

They rode south, with the soldiers, through the shatter of war. The villages they passed through were stripped of anything valuable, edible or combustible, then burned. They saw few civilians, and those few were old, begging, with nothing to steal and nothing to fear. Fall was closing, and rain drifted across the land. Peirol was grateful he'd been able to equip himself before leaving Beshkirs, and huddled in the warmth of a blanket-lined oilskin, trying not to meet the eyes, see the plea, of the ruined ones they saw beside the road.

But there were things that burned into his mind: A line of pushing, half-drunk men outside a hut. Peirol saw the reason—a tatterdemalion whore, no more than fifteen, with dead eyes, someone's daughter who hadn't run fast or far enough.

A mewling kitten who approached their fire one night. Peirol held out a bit of meat, and the kitten snatched and inhaled it, came back for another. Peirol fed it two more pieces, then the kitten came back a fourth time, bit him hard, then shot away.

A crater with half a cannon barrel near it, broken wagon wheels and bits of wood from a caisson around, rotting horse carcasses that had been rough-butchered for stew meat, and high in a bare-limbed tree something strange, which Peirol realized with a gulp was the decaying naked lower torso and legs of a man.

Once they saw a ragged band of bandits or partisans being chased by Beshkirian cavalry, another time a squad of musketeers leading two bound men toward a convenient wall that was already blood-spattered, a harsh-faced priest behind them, offering no last prayers.

Five days after Peirol landed on the Manoleon Peninsula, they reached the army.

Arzamas held the heights, a C-shaped range of low hills curving around the city. From the hills, the land sloped down to a valley. Across that valley were the Beshkirian lines, Niazbeck explained. Not only did the enemy hold the high ground, but they had well-mounted cannon, huge syrens and basilisks, far larger and longer-ranged than anything the Beshkirians had in their arsenal. The army needed to smash the enemy lines and keep the offensive going to stop the Arzamanians from retreating into their walled city.

"For then we'll have a siege," Niazbeck said, "and the attacker is always at a disadvantage, or so the treatises I've read and the grand lords with our army tell me. Such a nightmare could last for years, decades, and would be as likely as not to fail, especially if Arzamas gains new allies, who could surround and wipe us out."

The problem was not only attacking uphill into cannon, but the magicians of Arzamas, who cast their spells from just beyond range of the Beshkirian artillery. Their sorcery was also stronger than Beshkirian magic, and counterspells had not been effective. These three, in deadly combination, had broken four attacks. Bodies of men and horses were scattered up the hills, but no Beshkirian had gotten closer than a sixth of a league.

"We are stalemated," Niazbeck said. "And winter is coming fast—I told them over and over we should have begun the war in spring, instead of mounting that preposterous expedition against the Sarissans. The odds are increasingly favoring those bastards from Arzamas.

"We must do something, and since I believe in my heart of hearts cannon is the key to all victories, I knew it was time to summon you and depend on your experience."

"Mmmmh," Peirol said, trying to sound wise. "First I must spend some time with the battery, and then acquaint myself with the battleground."

"You have four days," Niazbeck said. "No more, for the wizards are predicting serious weather."

Four days, Peirol mused. But if he had an idea that would end the war, Arzamas would surrender, and possibly the Beshkirian gratitude would be great enough so they would call for Peirol to be freed. Niazbeck couldn't resist something like that. Or, in the victory celebration, he might be able to slip away.

Since Arzamas wasn't counterattacking, the battery wasn't on the front lines, but in a hollow a sixth of a league behind them. Peirol thought they were living as roughly as any tin man on the Moorlands. The campaign's toils had been hard. Of the sixty men, only forty still served. Three had been killed by the enemy, eight wounded badly enough to be sent home, and the others had died of various plagues and fluxes. There were replacements on the way, the battery's second-in-command—a young lord named Poolvash—told him. Perhaps they were marching up even now with the replacements Peirol had passed. Poolvash . . . Peirol's mind chewed at the name, wondering where he'd heard it before, remembered suddenly that was the nobleman the mad Quipus had blown apart, thus getting himself sentenced to the oar. This Poolvash must be his son. Peirol decided not to bring up the past.

The cannoneers' scarlet, green, and white uniforms hadn't lasted past the first encounter with ribaudequin, small multiple-barreled cannon firing grapeshot, and the now-wiser artillerymen had dyed their finery the color of the dirt around them. The guns appeared in perfect shape, the horses almost as good, and the wagons and leatherwork were in good repair.

On the next day Peirol went forward to the front lines, into the infantry pits, crude holes roofed with saplings and whatever cloth or canvas could be found, and studied the enemy positions. He wasn't sure what that gave him, never having seen such before. The lines curled around the hills, and the earth was bare, chewed up. The infantry around Peirol were as ground-up as the land: hard staring eyes, quick movements, and little speech. All appeared half-starved, but Peirol saw uneaten food around them.

Peirol watched until a storm broke and sheeting rain blocked his view, then went back to the battery.

Where before he'd felt sorry for them, living under canvas with nothing but campfires for warmth and cooking, now he realized there were always greater depths of misery, such as he'd seen the sullen infantry wallowing in.

The problem was simple. They had to kill the enemy to win the war, which they could only do if they got within range of him and used cannon, got closer and used muskets and bows, still closer and used spears, then they would be on him with their swords, pistols, and daggers. But they could not get within range without taking the most severe casualties. A stalemate, of sorts.

The best solution would be to have bigger, longer-range guns brought up, but they were back in Beshkirs. Peirol thought of using more powder in the battery's guns, remembered Quipus telling him what happened with overcharged guns. He had no desire to echo Lord Poolvash's fate, and imagined neither did the man's son. He remembered one of Quipus's babbles, about the guns of the Sarissans and their power, and how some said they mixed gunpowder with salt water, which was impossible. Even Peirol knew wet powder didn't burn, let alone explode.

He wondered why he gave a damn about either side. The Beshkirians were proven scum, and he didn't know anyone in Arzamas from a rock. But as soon as the war was over—or better, as soon as he could create enough madness to escape from it—he could return to his pursuit of the Empire Stone.

Peirol had another idea. He ran it through from several angles, and decided that it just might work.

The only problem was, it also could get Peirol handily killed; he was pretty sure Niazbeck wouldn't let him delegate the mission to a cannoneer of "lesser ability." But he came up with nothing better, and went to Niazbeck.

The magnate was impressed, especially by Peirol's courage. As the dwarf had thought, Niazbeck assumed Peirol would lead from the front. He went to the heads of the army with the idea, which of course would be presented as his own. Peirol had asked for some time to prepare for the mission. He and Poolvash the Junior, as Peirol kept thinking of him, chose the two sturdiest cannon, the best horses, the quickest crews, then moved these "volunteers" back behind the lines so they couldn't be seen and rehearsed them over and over. Even though powder was scarce, they were permitted to actually fire their guns at targets the size and range of the ones they'd face.

Poolvash finally told Peirol they were as good as they could get; any further drilling would simply exhaust the men and, more importantly, the horses. Peirol bowed to the other's hopefully superior knowledge. There was nothing to do but return to their tents and wait for the army lords.

Two days later, the decision came. A grand attack was ordered in three days, and Magnate Niazbeck's cannoneers were given the honor of beginning the battle.

Dawn came slowly, with drizzles. Peirol hadn't slept, didn't think many in his tent had. He'd laid down fully dressed, as had the others, and had no toilet to make but splashing some muddy water on his face, rubbing a soapy finger across his gums. Magnate Niazbeck sat outside his carriage, fully dressed. He nodded a greeting. No one felt like talking. Everything was gray: the world, the muck, the army and its banners. Peirol even thought death was gray.

There was a heavy meal prepared by the battery's cooks, and Peirol found himself, surprisingly, very hungry. He was starting to load his tin plate when an old matross stopped him. "Eat light, sir," he said. "If you're belly-cut, it makes healing easier, and death not quite so likely, or anyways, not nearly so messy." Peirol gave his plate to a recruit, had only bread dipped in sour wine.

Drums rolled, echoed, and the armies went into their attack lines. Peirol thought he saw them sway forward, back, as if eager yet reluctant for the other's embrace. Cannon thundered from the Arzamanian lines, and one lucky hit sent mud and a scatter of scouts tumbling.

Peirol scorned a man's cupped hands for a step, pulling himself into his saddle with his arms. He carried only a dagger and a pistol. If heavier weapons would be needed, the battle was almost certainly lost, and there'd be more than enough dead around for him to rearm.

"Now, m'lord?" Poolvash asked.

"Go," Niazbeck said. "And win this battle and this war for Beshkirs."

Poolvash touched his knuckles to his forehead, Peirol remembered to bow to his master, and they rode to where the two cannon waited. Their single trails, heavy, elaborately enameled balks of lumber curving down and back from the guns, were already hitched to the two-wheeled tumbrels to keep them clear of the ground while moving. Sixteen horses, twice the usual number, were hitched to the tumbrels. Behind the guns were two wagons of powder and shot, also double-teamed. The cannoneers would run beside the guns when they went forward.

The rain grew harder, and Peirol didn't know if that was enemy magic or just chance. He missed the command, but heard and saw the lash of the whips, and the battery went forward, slithering through the puddles, bouncing in the ruts, down the trail toward the front lines. A wave of fear swept over him as he saw a cannoneer stop, ready to flee, heard a warrant shout, "It's naught but their damned magic, boy! Keep moving." The artilleryman recovered, went on, but hanging back, white-faced.

Peirol craned through the mist, across the valley toward the enemy, and saw a knot of men around banners, men in robes, chanting—magicians. They were where he'd been told they'd been in the last attack, almost in the enemy's most forward lines. Jouncing on his horse, he lifted a twig that he'd notched twice, peered again across the valley. When a certain tree over there reached from one notch to the other, they'd be within firing range. This was something Peirol'd learned on his travels, but from whom, he couldn't remember.

They reached the Beshkirian lines. The infantry-men looked shocked as the cannon went past them, past the scouts, until the two guns were closer to the enemy than any Beshkirian. There was a great whir, and a cannonball bounced toward them. Peirol thought it looked like a harmlessly bouncing ball someone might stop as a memento; then he saw it smash a man into bloody jam, and fragments behead his partner as neatly as a farmer kills a fowl.

The tree was the proper size in his twig measurer, but Poolvash shouted the halt before Peirol could give an order. Instantly the horses were brought around by their teamsters, the ropes holding the trails to the tumbrels unlashed, and the guns, already loaded, were muscled into firing position. The ammunition wagons were drawn up, behind them, at a safe distance.

"Gunners, take stations!" Poolvash bawled. "Target . . . Group of men, on t'other hillside." This was the way of the army, point out the obvious, even though every man on the guns knew what his target would be. The two lead gunners crouched, sighting along their guns' barrels, waved one way, another, up, down. Handspikes moved the guns precisely, until both were aimed at the Arzamanian magicians on the farthest hill.

Peirol felt nausea, wondered why he was here when Poolvash was quite capable of ordering the men and getting killed if something went wrong, wanted to boot his horse back toward safety. His stomach roiled once more and he knew another enemy spell was on its way.

Arzamanian cavalry trotted out on the flank, coming steadily through the mire, ordered to wipe out these insolent cannoneers before they could do any damage.

Trumpets blared from behind, and the Beshkirian army marched forward, into the attack. The two gunners, paying no mind, intent on their duty, shouted readiness.

"Stand back from your guns. . . . Fire!" Peirol shouted.

The guns bellowed, and white smoke gouted from their barrels. Peirol rode forward a little into clear air, saw men down to the side of the magicians.

"Right a trifle," he shouted, wondering if that was any sort of military order. Men were swabbing out the guns, pouring powder down the muzzle, putting the wad down, and ramming the ball home.

"Aim right," a gunner shouted.

"Ready! . . . Ready!"

"Stand back from your guns. . . . Fire!"

This time the guns struck home. The sorcerers' tiny canvas enclaves were slashed to bits, and the stone balls hit boulders, spraying fragments. Wizards in mid-spell, their acolytes, and their attendants, were broken, torn apart.

Something moved in the corner of Peirol's vision, and he turned, caught only a flash of something awful, something red. Men cried as they, too, saw the demons. Then the demons were gone as if they'd never been. The cannon crashed, again on target, and more men died, and the magic Peirol felt swirling about him vanished.

"Gunners . . . new target . . . attacking horsemen to our right . . . load grapeshot . . ."

"Ready . . . ready . . ."

"FIRE!"

The stone balls, more than three dozen to a cannon, scythed through the cavalry, not fifty yards distant. Horses reared, screaming like women, multicolored guts coiling across the muck, men falling, dying, screaming louder than their mounts. Then the infantry was past the guns, attacking into the smashing fire of the Arzamanian heavy guns, but Peirol and the battery were safe. Creaking toward them was Niazbeck's carriage, the battery's other two guns behind them. Niazbeck leaned out, shrilly shouting patriotic nonsense.

The army hit the enemy lines at a walk, and the Arzamanians fell back a little and regrouped just as the Beshkirians shouted for the charge. The walk became a trot became an unstoppable run, and the Arzamas lines broke, curling back. Again the battery took up firing positions, blasting any enemy formation they saw.

Peirol found himself shouting victory, that the war was over, as the Beshkirian juggernaut went up that hill. He rode past dead men in starry robes and their assistants. Braziers, cases of gear, were being smashed open and ruined by vengeful infantrymen, the air thick with perfumed powders. Arzamas's magic had been broken, and now the Arzamanians must be finally defeated. But the Arzamanian officers regained control, and their army retreated slowly, stubbornly, in spite of suicidal attacks by the Beshkirian cavalry. The gates of their city swallowed them, leaving only a rear guard to bravely die where they stood. The Arzamanian army was safe.

In spite of Peirol's plan, Beshkirs had failed. The great city of Arzamas, well supplied, well guarded, almost impregnable, was now under siege, and soldiers wondered how many would die under its walls.

TEN

✳

Of Sieges
and Betrayal

By midwinter, Peirol was an experienced soldier—not in killing, but in surviving a mad world where everyone seemed intent on killing him.

The soldiers dug elaborate earthworks surrounding Arzamas, sealing it from relief. But the walls of the city overhung the besiegers, and any soldier who dared step above ground would be obliterated by the huge murtherers on the battlements, guns with a bore bigger than a man's head, hurling stone balls weighing more than a hundred pounds.

Magic also stalked the soldiers. An innocent root in a trench wall might reach out and strangle a passerby. Weird creatures stalked the night, creatures found in no bestiary but in a wizard's fever dreams. Sometimes they were innocent nightmares; other times, when a more potent spell eluded the counter-sorcery of Beshkirian wizards, they killed with their fangs and talons.

Even the lords of Beshkirs wanted to kill Peirol. Half a dozen times futile attacks had been mounted, suicidal frontal attacks shattered even before scaling ladders could be emplaced. Mines had been dug, and countermined, so the sappers far underground were buried alive. Peirol shuddered at that death, although he'd seen none that were exactly appetizing.

Disease raked the men. More than fifteen of the battery, including young Poolvash, died thrashing in delirium. Others' minds broke, and those men were taken away, babbling or silent in a lost world of their own. A sign of the times was that the casualties were replaced not by free men, who'd originally formed the battery, but by slaves freshly bought by Magnate Niazbeck or taken from his estates, who of course made indifferent warriors.

Everyone seemed content to allow the slave and dwarf Peirol to actually command the unit. No noble officer was interested in coming this far forward and chancing death, even though, as always, the cannoneers were far safer than the infantry in the very front lines. The battery was positioned on the southern side of Arzamas, far distant from the supply lines to the landing port and home. There were Arzamanian units outside the city to their south, but they'd done nothing more than mount occasional ambushes and keep the Beshkirians from marching farther south. Niazbeck had commandeered a small hut, refitted it into luxury, and lolled far behind the battery's position with a staff of servants. Peirol didn't grudge him that—the winter had brought gout to cripple the magnate, although Peirol wondered if he'd be healthier if he lost some weight. But delicacies continued to arrive for him by the cartload from Beshkirs. At least, unlike some of the other lords, Niazbeck sent some of this bounty to his men.

But that didn't improve matters much. The siege dragged on as storms raged. The countryside, once green and fair, was nothing but mud and misery. Men would die, sometimes be buried, and a barrage would, as likely as not, raise them from their shallow graves into the company of their former fellows. Men could complain, but the horses could only endure, eyes and coats dull, perhaps wondering what they'd done to deserve this mire, instead of green paddocks and sunshine.

Peirol no longer shuddered at bodies, pieces of bodies, nor the rats that dined on them. Now he truly wondered why some men prized this horror so greatly, told tales and sung epics about this catastrophe called war.

He vaguely remembered another life, a life of women's voices, clean clothes, glistening jewels. Once in a while he took out the gems he still carried, rolled them about, tried to find comfort. But they were glistening rocks, no more, without value in this land of death. He remembered Abbas the wizard and Kima, doubted if he'd ever see them again, let alone continue his quest for the Empire Stone, a gem he now thought mythical. He thought of Ellena, of Reni, and was further discouraged to feel no particular lust. Of course, if someone had offered him a chance to go back to the estate, even with its perils, even continuing as a slave, he would have leapt eagerly. But he thought of those days but seldom, and they felt years, not Times, distant.

All that kept him together was the battery. Niazbeck might send foodstuffs, but no one cared how or whether the drummers, gunners, matrosses, carpenters, and the rest lived. Peirol spent his waking hours and deep into the night chivvying them, not letting them give up, making them hate him if that was what it took, checking their feet for sores, their fingers for frostbite when it snowed, not letting the cooks get lazy and dollop out swill, although the rations of unleavened bread, soup from dried meats and vegetables, leavened occasionally with half-cured bacon or beef about to go bad, were terrible material for the most talented chef.

He wondered why he did all this. The gods knew he was no soldier, no warrior, no leader, and his men were brutal thugs, little better than state-sanctioned murderers and bandits. Wondering, he continued leading them, day by day. It would have been better if they had tasks beyond digging trenches, improving their positions. But the guns were too light to punch through the stone walls of Arzamas, and so they remained hidden, waiting for a task to be assigned. But none came. Rumor had it that huge siege cannon were being built, would arrive any day. But the guns never appeared.

The only brightness Peirol could offer his men—

and, perhaps, himself—was the slow, dragging approach of spring. Other than that, there was nothing.

A sense of disgust came after Peirol found himself learnedly discoursing with Gulmit, his senior gunner, about the various types of lice infesting them, the long gray louse with a spot on his back, the black fat one that squirmed in slimy knots, the more common head louse; and whether it might be possible to convince them to war on each other.

He had to do something to keep his mind alive, even if his body was likely to be destroyed in the next bombardment. He thought about making jewelry, but who would send him tools? Then he remembered the notes, now lost, he'd taken from Abbas on what he could expect in his travels.

That gave him something. He found parchment, ink and pen, and dredged his memory for Abbas's words. At first nothing came, then a flash, a phrase, here and there. He forced his mind into its corners, remembered more and more, sometimes starting awake with another instruction from the magician. He kept the parchment rolled, close at hand, ready for any opportunity. But that wasn't enough.

Another idea came, the one he'd already toyed with: Quipus saying the Sarissans' gunpowder was supposedly steeped in seawater to gain potency. Of course the power of their cannon he'd witnessed came from magic, not salt water, which had been more of the madman's driveling. Nevertheless, he acquired a small powder cask and began experimenting. Nothing happened except fizzles and saltpeter smells for a week. An empty cylinder, a finger in diameter, that once held spices was his testing machine, a cork his means of measuring the potency of powder. A tiny measure of normal, dry powder, compressed and lit, had power enough to blow the cork out of the cylinder and about an arm's-length into the air. The salt-water powder almost never budged the cork at all.

Then, one night, he'd drenched powder with salt water, the salt carefully added to boiled water until it tasted like the ocean he remembered. But he'd been called for. There were problems with a quartermaster who'd found brandy and, instead of doling it out, had split it with his three best friends. Roaring drunk, he now wanted to unmask the cannon and duel with the great guns of Arzamas. By the time he and his drunken compatriots had been quelled and chained to wagon wheels to make them aware they'd committed some breach when they woke, Peirol was too tired to continue his experiment.

He awoke, remembered his experiment-in-the-making, examined the powder. It had dried into a cake, sitting not far from the lamp he'd left burning in his dugout. He thought about discarding it but decided to try it, rolling the cake back and forth until it broke into miniscule clumps about the size of peppercorns so the powder would fit into the cylinder. Expecting nothing but failure, he packed his cylinder, put in a wad, rammed it home, and stuck the cork in place. He lit a twig, held it to the touchhole he'd bored in the cylinder. There was an audible crack, and the cork exploded across the dugout and buried itself in the dirt wall. Peirol gaped, repeated the experiment. Again and again it worked. Quipus may have been mad, but he wasn't crazy. This powder, probably because of the manner it was corned together in the drying and rolling rather than the presence of salt water, was markedly more powerful than before.

The question was, What to do with this discovery? He knew better than to use this water-powder in a one-to-one ratio to normal gunpowder. It'd likely explode his cannon, or at least sear out the touchhole. However, since they were always low on gunpowder, he'd be wise to make some up, so when supplies ran low, they could use less powder than normal and have a reserve to fall back on.

He decided to say nothing of his accidental discovery to anyone, not even Magnate Niazbeck, but set his men to mixing. Of course, they thought him deranged. But Peirol the dwarf was considered lucky—the battery hadn't suffered nearly as many casualties as other units. So they obeyed, Peirol watching closely, and put the dry, kerneled powder into casks marked with black crosses.

Peirol stared, hypnotized, at a small yellow bird, singing on the log roof of his dugout. There might be a chance there would be a spring, and he might live to see it. Then Guallauc rode up through the ravine that kept the battery's approaches from being seen and shelled.

"Magnate Niazbeck wishes you immediately!"

Peirol's back prickled. He'd tried to warm up the officious little man, thought he was succeeding, but Guallauc's voice was as imperious as it'd ever been.

"What seems to be the problem?"

"You delaying, when your master wishes your presence!"

"Do you remember this man?" Magnate Niazbeck said, almost crooning in his high voice.

Peirol looked at the man behind Niazbeck, thought him vaguely familiar, no more.

"This is Narack, formerly one of my house slaves, who arrived with the latest draft. He worked in the kitchens over the past two years, and has told me there were irregularities after I departed. Are you aware of any such?"

"Of what nature, sir?"

"I asked a question," Niazbeck said. "I did not expect it to be met with another question."

"I'm sorry, sir. No, I know of none. As far as my own small responsibility, concerning the purchase of—"

"There are irregularities beyond the financial," Niazbeck interrupted. "Some might find a more serious label for them, such as low treason."

"I beg pardon, sir?"

"You heard me."

Peirol pretended thought. "No, sir. I'm certainly not aware of any problems, least of all something serious enough to be called treason."

"I thought *you* wouldn't. You may go."

Peirol bowed low, left hastily. He knew what treason was, knew it was generally applied to an act of disloyalty to a high lord or king. Low treason, he supposed, would be deeds committed against any lord, perhaps any householder. Among those deeds might be adultery. Peirol knew he was doomed.

The manner of his fate was announced a day later, in front of the assembled battery, by Magnate Niazbeck. It appeared an honor. Again, the magnate's battery had been chosen for a heroic action, a way of breaking the stalemate. Not coincidentally, Niazbeck said, voice gloating, the hero of the first action, the slave Peirol, had been chosen to command this daring undertaking.

Peirol was ordered to take a single gun far forward, into positions he would prepare himself, and attack the walls of Arzamas. A ripple ran through the ranks, and silence was shouted for by Peirol and the warrants. Niazbeck caught one word from the rumble.

"Foolishness, you said? Not at all. This is the great subtlety of my plan, which the lords have approved. We've all seen woodpeckers tacking at a tree, and laughed. But peck by peck, a hole is made, enlarged. Since my battery is known for the precision of its shooting, there'll be one gun, well hidden, firing at exactly the same point, time after time.

"Now you see it, don't you? One gun, too small for the huge cannon on the parapets to seek out, can peck by peck, ball by ball, batter its way through any wall. When the wall is breached, my friends, my servants, my companions, then the war will be ended, and Arzamas will be ours within a day. Is that not a great plan?"

Some men, the newer soldiers, cheered, but their cheers broke off when they saw the still faces of the veterans.

"I knew you'd understand," Niazbeck said, turning a truly malevolent smile on Peirol. "This venture shall ensure that you all will be rewarded as you deserve."

The battery's worst troublemakers and malcontents were detailed off with Peirol for the great honor. At least his best, most senior gunner, Gulmit, insisted on sharing Peirol's fate.

A week later, Peirol was ready. He'd gotten permission to prepare the site where and as he wished, and further, to command the firing when and how he felt it to be most opportune. Niazbeck assented, almost giggling in glee. It tickled him well for his slave to squirm on the hook, knowing there was no way to escape.

But Peirol had decided there was no such thing as inevitability. In the long boredom of the siege, he'd watched musketeers as they crawled far forward, using every bit of cover to snipe, as they called it after the marsh birds that had to be carefully stalked. Once in position, the musketeers would lie patiently, weapon aimed, to make that single shot and kill their target on the battlements above. Generally they missed, but Peirol had noted successful shooters would make several kills in time, whereas the others made none. Some called it a hunter's instinct. He'd talked to the successful snipers, heard how they measured their powder precisely, weighed their lead balls so they were all the same, discarded any with visible flaws. Now Peirol thought of himself as one of those snipers with a hunter's instinct, but using an eleven-foot-long demi-culverin, a musket with a fist-sized bore, shooting at a target more than a bit larger than a man.

Peirol toured the entire perimeter with one of his pioneers, an experienced mason. Halfway around, the mason had pointed out a portion of the wall. "See how the rain's run down the wall, into crevices, and how the stone's discolored here and there? That's from the mortar being washed loose and out. Sloppy workmanship. Or else the fiddle was the builder's, mixing his mortar on the cheap, or using sandstone instead of granite." He grinned, rubbed thumb and forefinger together. "Nice to see the Arzamanians're no more honest than the rest of us."

Rather than take a position directly in front of the hopefully vulnerable section, Peirol went to one side. He guessed the impact would be lessened if the ball struck at an angle, but his position would be less obvious, less likely to be instantly destroyed by the murtherers. He found a watercourse, knee deep in mud, about fifty yards in front of the infantry lines and had pioneers drain it by digging a ditch to the side, working at night. The walls of the course, good clay, were patted hard, and bags of sand piled up in front and to either side. The course was floored with more sandbags, and boards laid on either side of the gun's position, these for the men to work from. Dry brush was positioned around the end of the course for camouflage. Gray stakes were pounded deep into the ground a yard on either side of the course's end, just in front of where the gun was to go.

His carpenters built a special cradle for one of the cannon, a cradle set within a trough. In one night it was positioned, staked, and bagged in place. Over the next two nights the gun, which weighed more than a ton, was moved forward through the lines, thirty sweating men trying not to curse above a whisper or make noise and bring down death from the wall only two hundred yards to their front. The gun was slid into its cradle and lashed securely by its trunnions. Sorcerers in the front lines droned a bad weather spell as they worked, and the rain crashed around them, drowning sound.

Then they were ready. A dozen archers from the infantry had been grudgingly detailed, to keep an Arzamanian patrol from slipping out the gates and slaughtering the artillerymen while they were intent on their gun.

The cannon was loaded with a precise amount of gunpowder, previously weighed and sewn into cloth bags, the wad forced down on top of the bag, and a ball, again chosen to be exactly the same dimensions and weight as its mates, rammed home. The cannon's cradle was slid forward to the end of the trough and aimed, in the dimness, at where the pioneer had noted the faults. The distance from the muzzle to the stakes on either side of the barrel and to the stake underneath it was recorded. A canvas tube was extended ten feet forward beyond the gun's muzzle, held up by withes.

A slow match sat in a covered barrel beside the cannon, and when Peirol whispered readiness, a man held his cloak in front of the gun, hiding the glow as Gulmit brought it to the touchhole. The cannon bucked, nearly deafening Peirol, the flash mostly hidden under the hood but still enough to night-blind him.

The cradle slammed to the rear of the trough against silencing pads of cloth, stopped by the ropes.

Everyone lay silent until the cloud of smoke blew away. Peirol waited on, until he was sure no one above had seen them. Two loaders went out then, swabbed the gun, reloaded it, and the cannon was pushed back into firing position. Once more the distance to the three stakes was measured and the gun barrel reaimed, the hood that had been blown away by the blast replaced. All this had taken a full turning of the glass.

Peirol fired once again. Again he waited, loaded, measured, fired. He shot five times that night at irregular intervals. Twice the Arzamanian cannon on the walls bellowed, firing blindly far overhead them, into the front lines. He would have shot more, but the canvas hood ripped. Gulmit wanted to keep shooting, but Peirol forbade it. They covered and camouflaged the gun, slid back to the main lines, and returned to their battery.

Food was waiting, as was a dozing Guallauc, who seemed surprised Peirol and the others still lived. He left without saying anything to give the bad news to Niazbeck.

When it grew lighter, Peirol went back to the lines with a glass and minutely examined the wall. The stone was broken, dented in a wide patch about the size of two men's bodies. Only one ball had gone wide and printed away from the target. Well content, he returned to the battery and slept well. He woke in the late afternoon, smiling, having dreamed of Kima.

That night, they went back with a spare hood and fired eight times. On the way, one of the loaders said,

"Hope when th' wall's down we'll be allowed our choice of wimmen, even if we don't get in with the first wave."

"What does that mean?" Peirol said.

"When we loot the city, sir," Gulmit said patiently.

"I thought," Peirol said hesitantly, "that if . . . when . . . we smash the wall, they'll surrender."

"Not likely. First we'll have to storm the city, for there's times I've been told the defenders still held firm and saved the day, even with their wall breached," Gulmit said.

"Storm the city, wait for the white flags," the loader nodded, "then it'll be ours to sack. Anyone, anything's ours."

Peirol was shocked.

"What's the matter, sir?" Gulmit wondered.

"I thought, once there was a surrender, they'd pay tribute and, I guess, swear fealty to Beshkirs."

"All of that, sir," Gulmit agreed. "But the army'll have the city for its own for a time. A day, a week—that depends on how angry the lords are about this damned siege that's gone forever. But looting's part of our bargain, our pay. You don't think any soldier'd live in this shit if there wasn't the promise of as much gold as he can steal, as many women as he can rape, now do you?" Gulmit and the loader laughed loudly at Peirol's innocence.

Eleven shots the next night . . . eight . . . four, when a patrol sought the gun, and they had to lie low . . . six . . . ten. Now the wall was chipped, the face breaking away, and a cleft clearly apparent. They had to shoot more carefully, for the infantrymen behind were only too aware of their progress and, in spite of their officers' commands, cheered the cannoneers when they shot.

Magnate Niazbeck summoned Peirol and listened to his progress, lips tightly pressed together. "You are lucky," was all he said.

"Thank you, sir," Peirol answered. "I hope so, sir."

"No man's luck lasts forever."

"No, sir."

Peirol left the man brooding, twisting the rings on his fat fingers.

Three nights later, as they fired their fourth shot, there came a great cracking, then a rumble, and something enormous smashed into the ground not far distant. They instantly covered the gun, slipped back to the lines, and waited for dawn. First light showed a long crack in the wall, from their target area up to the parapet, where a whole section of battlements had broken away and fallen, a part of the parapet and one of the huge murtherers crashing down. The parapets on either side of the breach were now strongly guarded, and Peirol saw men in elaborately worked armor—officers, lords—considering the damage. Periodically someone would see something below, and cannon fire and musketry would be brought on it.

Peirol gave orders for the gun to be withdrawn that night, went to Magnate Niazbeck. "Sir. We've completed the mission."

"*What?*"

"The wall's nearly broken down. Half a dozen

shots, maybe some more, and the whole section'll crumble."

Niazbeck was amazed. "You're sure?"

"Yes, sir. I didn't think we should finish the job, but wait until the army's ready to attack, so the Arzamanians won't have time to reinforce the wall or seal that section off."

Niazbeck stared for a long time, then that harsh smile came. "Good, Peirol. You do not know how well you did. Now you may go."

The smile remained as Peirol left, afraid, not knowing what would come next.

Over the next four days, the army of Beshkirs made ready for the grand assault. But Peirol witnessed none of it, for within an hour after reporting success, he was seized by royal dragoons, dragged off to the hastily constructed prison, and chained to a wall.

"It ain't much of a dungeon," the warder said. "But we don't need much of one, for there's but one penalty, and you'll be hanged within the day."

But Peirol wasn't hanged. Instead, he was watched closely by a succession of wary guards. The warder permitted men from his battery to bring him food and wine. They asked what he'd done wrong, how he'd offended Niazbeck, but Peirol gave no explanation. They said they'd help him escape, they weren't afraid of any godsdamned warders, but Peirol counted the number of guards, told his men no, there'd be but one death for him to worry about, and told them to leave him to his prayers. He didn't want them to see the tears in his eyes for these brave fools, ready to chance death themselves trying to free another idiot who didn't know how to stay out of corners.

Strangely, Peirol felt no fear, but a dawning hope. These bastards from Beshkirs had tried hard enough to kill him by now, in every way from piracy to rowing his heart out to this latest disaster. This would be the last time, and once more it would fail. Without any facts, any reality, he knew that. He didn't pray, didn't have any gods he believed in enough to pray to. Instead his mind churned like a mill wheel in a torrent. He saved the fat from the horse steak his men brought, hid it in his tunic pouch, remembering something a thief had told him about warders and their chains.

On the third day guns began bombarding Arzamas, and Peirol realized part of him wanted to be with them, hurling death at that other set of bastards he illogically felt were also responsible for his plight.

That night, men came. Peirol thought them Niazbeck's killers, readied himself to die fighting. But they unchained him from the wooden log wall, tossed him in the back of a wagon. His face was in the filth of the wagon floor, and he tasted dung, smelled half-dried blood. He paid no mind, busy stretching, twisting, taking the hidden fat out of his tunic and hiding it in his sleeve.

The wagon bounced over rough ground, eventually came to a halt, and he was dragged out. He saw gunfire flicker, realized he was in the front lines before Arzamas, watching the final bombardment before the wall came down, and madness and rapine took the city for their own.

There was another wagon, a two-wheeled tumbrel, sitting nearby, and the men chained Peirol to its back, left without saying anything. He waited for an hour, perhaps longer, saw the sky begin to change.

Peirol heard the creak of a carriage, craned his neck, and saw Magnate Niazbeck waddle toward him. "As I told you, Peirol, no man's luck lasts forever," he said.

"So it seems."

"Perhaps you'd like to know what comes next."

"I think I might prefer it be a surprise."

"The lords of Beshkirs have given me a great honor, finally confirming the many great things I've done for my adopted city. The honor of making the final breach in the walls of Arzamas has been given to me, and to my battery. I shall fire that cannon myself, when the lords of the army arrive and give the order."

"The *battery,* at least, deserves that honor," Peirol murmured.

Niazbeck paid no mind. "When it becomes lighter, you'll be able to see your former companions march past, not a dozen yards away. Your awful fate, though they'll never know your real crimes, will keep them disciplined.

"You, slave, for your crimes, which are unspeakable, are to die, since the imbeciles in Arzamas didn't manage to kill you as I'd planned. So it's left to me to give you the death you deserve. When the wall comes down—in one or two shots, as you said—the army will make its charge through the gap, and destroy the city.

"My battery will fire one more shot. After the lords have ridden forward into Arzamas to witness the triumph, I shall have you chained to the muzzle of one of my guns, and that gun will fire one more shot, in celebration of victory." Niazbeck smiled his awful smile. "Not even a trace of you will be left after that shot is fired, but a rather garish spatter of gore.

"Now I shall march my battery past in a few moments, so they can see your degradation. They'll move this cart forward with them, so you'll be close at hand for the final cannonade, witness my greatness, and realize you'll be nothing, not even remembered, in a Time. Are you satisfied with what you've brought about, Peirol of the Moorlands?"

Peirol thought about replying, decided not.

Niazbeck shifted from foot to foot, then stamped away. His dramatic departure was marred when he caught his foot and sprawled, staining his colorful silks. He stood with Guallauc's assistance and got in his carriage.

Peirol realized with wry amusement that he wasn't that angry with the magnate. He would die, and nothing would be done to Reni, to Ellena, although what had happened was as much their fault as his. Niazbeck would continue being cuckolded, his wife and daughter maintain their roundheeled ways, taking lovers for a minute, then casting them back to the slave market. But that was the way of things, and how could Peirol of the Moorlands be stupid enough to expect justice in this world?

It grew lighter, and Peirol heard horses, saw the battery. Niazbeck's carriage took position at the formation's head. The men, afoot, saw Peirol, and he heard shouts, questions. A squad of men ran toward him. Gulmit was at their head.

"We were told to secure this tumbrel, sir, and bring it with us. They also said you were to die."

"So it seems."

"What'll we do?"

"There's nothing you can do," Peirol said. "But I thank you for wanting to do—wait. I *can* think of something." He gave quick orders to Gulmit, who nodded understanding.

"Get as far away as you can when everything's set," Peirol said. "If it happens at all, don't worry about anybody asking questions."

"Nobody'll ask," the gunner said. "That sort of thing happens often enough. But what about you?"

"That'll give me my chance. Now, haul away, you men. I want to make sure I have a good view."

The tumbrel was man-hauled forward another quarter league, positioned to one side as the artillerymen set up their guns. Instead of the usual straight line, the cannon were set in a diamond configuration. Peirol guessed Niazbeck would fire the gun at the forward point, hoped Gulmit would be able to do as Peirol had asked.

The artillery barrage around the perimeter grew louder, and Peirol saw stirring in the lines as the troops readied themselves for another attack. Horsemen rode toward the battery, men in elaborate armor, horses richly caparisoned. The lords of the Beshkirian army, and their staff, had come to witness the firing. Some looked curiously at Peirol as they rode past, but no one queried. Peirol wondered why the damned Arzamanians didn't see the lords and send in a barrage, guessed wizards had cast a spell of confusion or overlaid an illusion.

The artillerymen were assembled in front of the lords, and Niazbeck gave a brief speech. Peirol was too far away to hear what he said. Powder kegs were rolled to the forward gun and opened with rubber mallets, and the gun was loaded. Peirol couldn't make out any details of the kegs. A gunner knelt and sighted along the barrel.

Magnate Niazbeck readied a slow match.

Peirol had the fat in his hand, rubbed his wrist in it. He pulled, making his hand small, as that thief had shown him, felt rough metal scrape, was stuck, pulled harder, not caring about tearing skin, had one arm free.

The familiar commands were shouted. Niazbeck touched the match to the hole, and the cannon boomed, bucked. The shot was not badly aimed, slamming into the wall about ten feet away from the crack. Stone tumbled, and Peirol imagined he could see the wall itself move.

Peirol had his other wrist greased, was pulling. This arm must have been slightly larger than the other, because he couldn't get it free.

Again the gun was loaded and aimed. Niazbeck reached with the match, held it to the touchhole.

Peirol was never sure how much of what happened he actually saw and how much his trained mind told him had happened in that instant.

Flame shot up from the touchhole, searing Niazbeck. Peirol thought he heard him scream, saw him stagger back as the gun barrel opened like an evil flower, muzzle spreading, red fire, black smoke building to a ball, as that special powder he'd concocted blew up, the powder he'd asked Gulmit to load the cannon with, the blast swallowing the magnate.

Peirol saw Gulmit and the other gunners running hard, diving into ditches, saw the flames reach the powder kegs behind the gun, saw them catch. His hand was finally free, and he flattened as the gunpowder blew up.

Lords of the army were tossed here, there, hurled spinning as a kitten tosses a bit of yarn, attendants falling as the hot wind killed them. A vast, twisting ball of red, black, and gray boiled over the battery, and the shock washed over Peirol, knocked the tumbrel aside.

He saw no more, for he was on his feet, running back, back through the lines, running hard, as the army of Beshkirs milled in confusion, terror, some fleeing, some attacking, most numbly waiting for the orders that would never come.

Peirol paid no mind to men in his path, cut around them, ignored the shouts of warrants, officers, paid no heed to the musket ball that buried itself in the mud in front of him, fleeing the army of Beshkirs away from Arzamas, into the unknown lands between the armies.

Peirol ran on, small legs churning the ground, feeling no fatigue, no fear, breathing the sweet air of freedom.

ELEVEN

✳

Of Desolation
and Ravens

Eventually fatigue came, fatigue and terror, for now Peirol found himself in a dangerous wasteland both armies had patrolled and raided through. He took stock, which only needed a minute. He had the brown-dyed uniform on his back, his boots, which were fortunately in good shape, and his hidden pack of jewels. Those were completely without value in this wilderness, for even if he found someone who wanted them, they'd simply put a sword at or through his throat.

His body reminded him of thirst, hunger. Peirol found a trickling stream, drank, kept thinking. His confidence was still strong. If all he had was his cunning, so be it. Food, warmth, weapons, all that could be acquired. He wished he'd grabbed a spear or sword from one of the corpses he'd passed in his mad flight, but he hadn't. He found a stout, nearly straight stick that'd do for a walking staff and weapon.

In the distance, he heard what he thought at first was the moan of the wind; then he realized it was the baying of a wolf. He could always try to call it and its pack and hope they'd attack his attacker—if they didn't devour him first. Wolves weren't particular in that regard.

The desolate road suddenly looked like a place wolves *and* bears would appreciate, bears also quite fond of small men with tangled golden hair and scruffy beards. Without further ado, Peirol began his march south at a rapid trot.

The land had been picked clean by the foragers from the Beshkirian army, so he found nothing worth stealing. But at least the land wasn't quite as ruined, with trees on either side beginning to bud. He had to hide once as a patrol of dragoons galloped up a side road. The dragoons, wearing a uniform that was neither Arzamanian nor Beshkirian, thundered past, intent on their own business. Peirol waited until they were gone, then went on.

After a while Peirol came to a crossroads, where there'd been six huts, now just burned shells. It was getting colder and darker, and he wanted a fire; he thought about taking shelter in those ruins. But he caught himself. Anyone else abroad in this desolation might think the same. When night came, he stopped by a brook, drank deeply, then found a hollow tree not occupied by anything slithery and settled in for the night. It was long and cold, and shivering woke him frequently. He paced back and forth, waving his arms vigorously until he convinced himself he was warm, went back, and dozed again. It was long after dawn when he awoke, frozen through, his legs aching from the unaccustomed running.

He listed all of the things he wanted, from his own castle with servants—not slaves, servants—and so on, down to a simple cup of hot water. No godlets materialized to offer him any of these, and so he set out once more.

It was a very lucky day. He'd gone no more than a league when he heard the creak of a cart. He found cover, and the vehicle, a shabby wreck high-piled with rags, rounded a bend. It carried one man, a bearded peasant looking perhaps ten years older than Peirol, although he could have been half that age in actuality, considering the way the world treated the poor. No one else appeared, nor did the man appear to have any weapons. As he closed, Peirol came out of the bushes.

"Sir," he began. "I pray you—"

The peasant screeched "YAAAAAAH," leapt from his seat, and pelted back the way he'd come. Peirol knew he'd been living hard, but he didn't think it showed *that* badly. Perhaps the peasant had a problem with dwarves. In any event, he jumped up into the cart and ransacked it. The rags might've been rags to him two years earlier, but now they were finery, especially since they didn't look anything like a uniform. He found child's breeches that looked as if they'd fit, a flannel shirt with only two rips, even a battered slouch hat. Better, there was a warm coat whose only sin was being baby-excrement yellow.

Peirol discovered the cart's seat lifted. Inside was

the peasant's meal of bread, cheese, and an earthen bottle of beer. Next to it was a shabby leather purse. He opened it, saw one silver coin and half a dozen coppers. He thought about taking them, having no money at all, but stopped.

He looked at the cart horse, an uncurried old gray, who was looking back at him. "All right," he muttered. "I know, I know." He started to put the purse back, then took out his pouch and put a small stone into the purse. "You!" he shouted. Nothing but a slight echo came back. "You are honored for helping the, uh, God of Wit and Handsomeness, Hamma Salbamus, and have been rewarded!"

No movement. The horse nickered. Peirol left the horse and cart, feeling faintly virtuous for not being *that* great a thief, and went on, seeing no signs of the peasant. He kept thinking about that huge packet of bread and cheese, letting his mind build it into a banquet until he could wait no more. Then he took to the bushes, telling himself he would only eat half of the bread and cheese and save the rest for dinner. He came back to himself as he was chasing crumbs around the package, a little tipsy on the strong home brew.

Two leagues later, he saw a sign, almost obscured by brush, its paint peeling. He peered at it, saw

then a third symbol he couldn't make out, very windy and weather-worn. "This way" and "water" were obvious. There might have been a path beside the sign—he scuffed dirt, saw cobbles, and followed them, pushing through brambles. A place to bathe and change, at the very least. It was more, much more: a long-abandoned hot springs, its wooden buildings sagging, smelling of rot. He disturbed various furry creatures, making sure there was nothing to loot, found a bathstone, took it to the hottest pool he could stomach, and began to soak.

He scrubbed, soaked, scrubbed and soaked, until he was pink and painful. Yawning, still full, he thought of a nap but forced himself to dress in his new finery and keep moving. Any day that began this well couldn't help but end that way. At midafternoon he found his first sign of real life—a village, walled with thornbushes. With thoughts of an inn, a real bed, hot food, he turned off the track. Peirol was a dozen yards from the village's gate—dead pricker-bushes tied to a wooden frame—when the voice came.

"Far enough."

He stopped. "Good morrow," he said cheerfully. "I'm Peirol of the Moorlands, seeking lodgings."

"Seek on, Peirol. There's nothing for you here."

"But I'm but one, and small at that. I can pay. How can I harm you?"

"Maybe you're magicked."

"I vow I'm not."

"We'll not take the chance. Move on."

"But—"

An arrow thunked down two feet from him.

"Ah," Peirol said. "And may the gods be as good to you as you were to me." Not waiting for a response, he went on, mood not that spoiled. The country was improving. At least they hadn't tried to hit him—he thought.

He passed three other villages that afternoon. One was walled with logs and made no response to his halloing; the other two were empty, abandoned and stripped bare.

In late afternoon he saw a man working in a field. He approached him cautiously, called. The man jerked in surprise.

"Sir," he quavered. "I mean no one any harm. I'm but a poor farmer, working my barren fields to feed my six, no, seven children, with never a mother to take care of them, nor any horse to plow, but my own muscles—"

"Stop," Peirol said. "I mean no harm either. I'm a starving traveler, heading south, and wish only food or even whatever you're growing. I'm willing to work."

The man came up from his supplicating crouch. "Just one?"

"Just me," Peirol said.

"You have no weapons?"

"You see me as I am, far worse than you are."

"No, no," the man muttered. "Not worse, never worse, for I've had everything taken, and have nothing."

"What about your seven children?"

"Oh. Oh, yes. Them. They're starving too." The man considered Peirol. "A traveler, willing to work. That's rare, in these times. Do you have a name?"

"Peirol."

"Peirol. That's a good name. They call me Wym."

"May I work with you for my meal?" Peirol was starting to think the man simple.

"Work, yes, you may work, help me, and I shall feed you, feed you with my children, I meant that not the way it sounded, but that we shall dine together, not that I am offering you a chance to dine on my own flesh and blood. I am seeking the potatoes in this field. You move just ahead of me and point to likely growths, they'll be half-buried, and then we can share, or at least I shall give you a portion after my five children and I, starving we are, take what we must have."

"Good," Peirol said. "For I'm sure four eyes are better than two." He wondered what a peasant with nothing was doing with a hoe, whether the field belonged to him or not, decided that wasn't worth worrying about, any more than how many children the man actually had, and bent to work. He moved up the row ahead of Wym, half-kneeling, staff in one hand, found three, then four potatoes, rather unappetizing and somewhat shriveled tubers, but better than nothing, dug them out, and tossed them to one side, moving to another promising location.

He saw a blur out of the corner of his eye, reflexively rolled to the side, and Wym's hoe buried itself in the dirt beside him. The man yanked it free, lifted it high in the air, its V-tip gleaming sharpness. Peirol rolled, spun the staff, and hit Wym hard on the knee. Wym howled, dropped the hoe, grabbed his knee, and fell. Peirol was up, staff end in both hands, struck down once, twice, and Wym was sprawled unconscious. He had to stop himself from striking until the man's skull split, remembered his children, thought what it must be like, one man with everything stripped from him.

But he still knelt and searched the man's pockets. He found flint, steel, a battered tin case with kindling inside, a comb, a folding knife, a dozen gold coins, one silver.

What was a man in a field by himself doing with gold? he wondered. If he had gold, why couldn't he feed his children? Were there any children? Was Wym some kind of snare for bandits or such?

Peirol looked around the edges of the field, saw no movement. He pocketed the gold coins, felt a fool for leaving the silver for the children who couldn't be real, grabbed Wym's bag of potatoes, and ran to the road.

That night he slept warm, a small fire beside him, his belly full of roasted potatoes. For a time.

He dreamed, but knew it wasn't a dream. He was in Abbas's study, and the sorcerer was glowering at him. Behind the wizard was a window, and a storm shot lightning across the sky. "You please me but little," Abbas rumbled.

"I'm sorry for that," Peirol said. "What wrong have I done?"

"I dispatched you after the Empire Stone over a year ago, and my avatars tell me you are still on the Manoleon Peninsula! A snail could have crawled from Sennen to where you are by now!"

A primary rule in dealing with wizards is to always be respectful, if you wish to have a continued and placid life. Nevertheless Peirol exploded in anger.

"You're talking like a godsdamned fool! Sir!"

Abbas's brows gathered, and the storm raged harder. "I shall not destroy you until you explain."

"A year? My year of slothful leisure as I lazed from palace to palace? I've been taken by pirates, enslaved on a galley, almost taken by demons, nearly drowned, enslaved once more as . . . as what it doesn't matter! Then I've fought a war, almost gotten myself executed, and now I'm in the middle of a godsdamned wilderness with nothing but rags, a couple of potatoes, and my cunning, and you chivvy me for being slow? You're lucky I'm still here, still alive! I thought that was why you sent me that dream of encouragement Times ago, so I wouldn't give up hope!"

"My granddaughter asked me to do that," Abbas grumbled. "I had no idea where you were at the time."

"This quest of yours is hardly going well," Peirol said. "Everything you gave me has been lost, I've almost died a dozen times, and . . . and . . . and now you accuse me of laziness!" He broke off, almost in tears.

Abbas grunted, then grunted again. "Kima has often chided me for moving before I know all the details," he said. "Although why I'm confessing that to you is beyond me. I do not apologize, do not ever go back on my words. But let us assume that I spoke not, that I inquired as to how I might help continue your quest. Assuming you haven't lost heart and have given up."

That thought *had* been in Peirol's mind, but he hadn't been able to come up with any other plan. He assumed wizards could take revenge over great distances.

"I haven't given up," Peirol said. "As to how you might help—I could use gold, a cavalry escort through these barbaric lands, an invisibility spell—almost anything."

"And I'm afraid I see no way of giving you anything," Abbas said. "I could strike you down, but help you—sorcery has its own limits."

"Then why did you trouble me with this vision?" Peirol almost shouted.

Abbas stared hard. Without answering, he vanished, and Peirol woke beside a dying campfire. Excellent, he told himself. Now you've angered your only . . . friend? No, Abbas is hardly your friend. Kima? He couldn't know, could only hope he still had *someone* wishing him luck.

For a moment he thought of that secret, hidden vale, with the bubbling creek and the pond where the otters sport, and again felt like crying.

Brave heroes, who journey out . . .

Oh, horseshit!

He was on the road early, in a sour mood. He'd only gone a short distance when he heard the calling of ravens and saw two, swooping overhead. They followed him, curveting through the trees, and Peirol admired their grace. He appreciated their company, thought they'd give warning if there was danger ahead. But as the day went on, and the ravens showed no sign of turning away, he began to worry, trying to remember if the birds were lucky or unlucky. Vaguely he remembered they were messengers, but for whom, he couldn't recollect. Giants? Wizards? Demons?

Probably not demons—the birds were too full of themselves for spirits to tolerate. He wondered if Abbas had sent them but remembered the wizard had little power in this land.

A road intersected the track, and the ravens swooped up it, back, then up it again. Perhaps he was being led into a trap. Perhaps not. Peirol went up the road. Less than a quarter of a league later, he came on a tiny village. The houses were perfectly kept, recently painted. The village square was as green as if it were summer instead of spring. But he saw no life, not man, not cattle, not even cackling chickens. Perhaps everyone was indoors.

Keeping his staff ready, he went on. He sniffed the air. Very strange. He smelt musk, jasmine, sandalwood, scents never found in the country, smells for incense and magic. The tiny hairs at the base of his spine prickled. The ravens called, dove close, then perched in a nearby tree, spectators for what would come next.

None of the houses on the square were businesses but one, and that had a discreet sign of a man being devoured by some sort of fabulous monster. Attractive draw, that, Peirol thought. I'll meet you at sundown for a glass of wine at the Dragon Fodder Inn.

"Good morrow," a woman said. It was easily the most lovely voice Peirol had ever heard, including Kima's. He jerked around. Standing outside one of the houses was a young woman. Her hair was dark blond, cascading down to her waist. Her face was heart-shaped, and her smile was knowing innocence. She wore a simple peasant woman's dress, except the dress was made of the finest, shimmering peach-colored silk that held close to her voluptuousness, matching her sandals.

"Welcome to my village," the woman said. "Welcome to Casaubon. I am Kilia."

"And I Peirol of the Moorlands." He bowed low, and one of the ravens squawked.

"I assume those are yours?"

"My friends," Kilia said. "My only friends."

Peirol looked around. "What of the others who live here?"

"There are no others."

"Then how does it stay so clean, so, well, perfect?"

"Because it wishes to," Kilia said. "I speak to the wood, to the nails, to the paint, and they listen."

"I, uh, see."

"You are alone in your travels. My friends told me that. Where are you going?"

"A far place called Restormel," Peirol said.

"I know it not. But that doesn't bother me, for I'm content here, within Casaubon."

"It's very lovely."

"Lovely now," Kilia said.

"Is that an inn where I might break my fast?"

"You could." She laughed. "There are fruit juices, barley soup, black bread, and cheeses I've . . . devised."

"That sounds wonderful," Peirol said.

"Then come with me."

The inn was small, as immaculate on the inside as out, the wood paneling gleaming, the brass lamps polished. Peirol sat at a table, and Kilia went into the back and came out in minutes with a tray, as if it had been waiting, which she put before him.

"Could I convince you to join me?"

"No," Kilia said. "I shall sit with you, but I eat privately."

Peirol began eating. It was one of the stranger meals he'd devoured. Kilia sat silently, watching closely as he chewed. The food was tasty, except once, when it was as if he was chewing on nothing but the blandest of farmer's cheese, no more. Then, as Kilia turned back to him, his mouth was filled with the taste of herbs.

"You serve no beer, no wine, in your inn?"

"No," Kilia said. "Nor meat, fish, fowl, or eggs. I take nothing from the earth that doesn't give it freely."

"Cheese given freely?" Peirol joked. "Once, when I was a boy, I helped the wife of a man whose land my father was mining make cheese from sheep milk, and it was one of the hardest jobs I've done. Ever since I've always respected those with the skill and patience for that job."

"I find it easy," Kilia said, indifferently. "Where do you hope to end your day's travels?"

Peirol shrugged. "Where the sun finds me when it sets, I suppose."

"There are empty houses here." She smiled.

Wondering why his skin crawled, he smiled as politely as he could. "I wish I could stay," he said. "But Restormel grows no closer when I just sit."

"I sensed that," she said. "You are one who prefers the real world."

"I beg pardon?"

"I do not," she said. "For it has handled me badly."

"I'm sorry to be thick-witted," Peirol said. "But I still don't understand."

"Do you wish to?" Her eyes were piercing.

Wanting to say no, Peirol said yes.

"You've finished your meal. Come outside, and I'll show you." Peirol followed her into the sunny square. "I ask again, do you wish to see what is real?"

"I think so."

"I ask you a third time, do you wish to see the world as it truly exists?"

Peirol nodded. Kilia pointed, moved her arm up, then in two semicircles. The neat row of houses across the square changed to blackened, rain-soaked rubble. There was grass growing through the cobbles, and in front of the largest house were scattered skeletons: half horses, the other human. Kilia moved her hand again, and the houses were bucolic perfection.

"As it was, as it is, as it shall be, as long as I live," she murmured.

"What happened? Are you a witch?"

"A witch? I do not know. There was one who called herself a witch, before the men came, but she couldn't stop them."

"The men?"

"Soldiers. They rode in and began killing, without words, without explanation. I saw my father die, heard my sisters scream, and I ran, ran into the fields. But half a dozen, perhaps more of them, ran after me. They found me, and they dragged me back, threw me on the ground while Casaubon burned around me. Then they hurt me, laughing, said even one as ugly as I was wouldn't be spared. I lay on the ground, bleeding, their seed inside me, my body torn, wanting to die, and then I knew I would not die, that I'd live, and felt the power come.

"Then *they* died, all of them, died screaming in agonies worse than any they'd brought to me or to my people, and I fed on their deaths, felt the power grow, and all changed, all went back to the way it was before. I healed my body, then decided I would change myself too, I would be as the prettiest ever was, even though she lay dead with a spear through her chest. Am I not beautiful?"

"You are," Peirol said, honestly, trying to keep his voice from shuddering.

"Is Casaubon not lovely?"

"It is."

"Why, Peirol of the Moorlands, why do you think, when I've offered others a chance to see things as they are not, a few even to join me here, in this paradise that shall last forever, or until I die, if I yet live, none have taken my offering?"

"I don't know," Peirol said. "Maybe we're fools."

"The road goes on for you now," Kilia said. "I am sorry you chose that, instead of me."

"Maybe," Peirol said, almost in a whisper, "maybe I am, too."

Kilia laughed gently, and a breeze came across Peirol's face. When it had passed, there was no one in front of him. The village remained, empty, perfect in its beauty. The only life was the two ravens in their tree.

Peirol realized his stomach was also empty, wondered what, if anything, he'd eaten. He picked up his staff, started back the way he'd come.

"Good-bye, Kilia. I'll dream of you."

His words echoed, and one of the ravens cawed, and Peirol felt the world's sadness in the sound.

Four days later Peirol reached a small city, whose gates, amazingly enough, weren't barred. Two guards laughingly challenged him, gravely decided he would be of no harm to the greatish city of Tybee, and allowed him entrance if he promised to wreak no havoc. Peirol, wishing that the myth that dwarves could work magic was true—if it were so, he'd cheerfully change certain sentries into goats—entered Tybee in a growly frame of mind.

He quickly cheered, feeling cobbles under his feet, smelling human ordure and garbage, listening to marketplace shrillings and tavern music. He'd always be a city lad, he decided, and determined to find a peaceful inn, have three or six glasses of good wine or perhaps even brandy, then seek lodging and a bath. He saw a sign for the Inn of the Bare Bodkin, went for it. Two men, rough, dirty, carrying both swords and daggers, half-drunk, blocked him.

"No beggar lads allowed in here."

"That's the long and short of it," the other said, and both bellowed what they thought was laughter.

Peirol looked at their sneering grins, thought of his innate peacefulness, considered what he'd been put through in the last year. One end of his staff caught the first thug on the ankle. He howled, grabbed it, leaped

to and fro. Peirol, not pausing, rammed the other end
of the staff into the second's stomach and rapped him
hard on the back of the head. That man fell on his face
in the muck and began snoring. The first tough saw his
mate down, reached for his dagger, and got the staff
between his eyes as if it were a lance. Cartilage
crunched, and he fell, clutching his face. Peirol let him
moan while he quickly searched his unconscious companion, then did the same to the first.

It said something about the district that passersby
noted what was going on but made no effort to inter-
vene on anyone's side.

Peirol ended with a rather nice haul of cutlery and
a quarter bag of copper and silver coins to add to his
loot from the potato field. He thought of stripping the
roughnecks naked but decided he didn't want to get
his hands dirty. Instead, he located an armorer's. A bit
later he came out with a nicely balanced shortsword
with a baldric he could use as a shoulder sling, a belt
for one of the desperado's daggers that he fancied for
its nicely carved onyx handle and balance, even a dart
similar to the one he'd used to kill Libat the eunuch.
He'd been offered a brace of pistols, but the price was
exorbitant. He was left with a few coins and directions
to a public bath and a tailor.

Some time later, clean-bodied and shaven, wearing a hastily cut-down pair of leather breeches and
linen shirt, he went back to the Bare Bodkin. Wym's
gold had made the tailor very civil, and two more sets
of clothes, plus a cloak guaranteed weatherproof by
the best spells, would be ready in a day or so.

The two lummoxes were gone from the doorway,

and he entered. The inside was smoky, smelling of lees, spilt wine, sizzling meat, and cheap perfume. Peirol dragged it deep into his lungs, feeling his mood soar. He found a table where he could put his back to the wall, put his new dagger in front of him, and ordered chilled red wine, a snifter of brandy, and two roasted capons. He smelled the brandy happily, sipped at the wine, and began pondering what would come next, after he slept in a real bed.

Again, no idea came but pursuing the Empire Stone, although Peirol thought he was at least obsessed, most likely cracked, given what the quest had brought. But this was adventuring, was it not? Peirol wondered if adventuring wasn't more comfortable being heard from a bard instead of actually taken part in; he drank more red wine. His fowl arrived, and he ate heartily until nothing but bare bones gleamed, then ordered fruit and ices to finish.

Perhaps the thugs outside were gone, but someone must have noted what happened to them, for he was left severely alone. A wench swayed up and inquired his pleasure.

Peirol thought about it; then, for some unknown reason, Kima's face intruded. "A bit later, perhaps," he said, and tossed her a coin. She smiled, showing very bad teeth, and went elsewhere, as did Peirol's flash of lust.

Stomach full, he allowed himself to drink the brandy, ordered one and only one more, having a very good idea what might happen to a Bare Bodkin patron who drank himself into a stupor.

A rather tattered wall map of the Manoleon Peninsula hung over a nearby table, and he examined it. He grimaced at how far he had to go before even reaching the mainland, let alone Restormel. Then a small name caught his eye. An idea—or more correctly a scheme—came, and he admired himself for its nefariousness as well as its arrogance.

He asked a barmaid about the name and got a shrug, but she directed him to a more traveled person, a man who guarded the merchant caravans up and down the peninsula. He bought the man a drink, and was given a warning to avoid that area as if it were demon-haunted. But his guess about the name on the map was confirmed.

Three days later, well rested, nursing a slight hangover, and wondering if he should feel guilty for having visited a rather plush brothel, Peirol left Tybee, pack full of clothes, cooking gear, and dried victuals.

Four days after that Peirol saw a castle looming menace from a nearby hillside. Just past its turnoff, a peasant was hammering away frantically, repairing a broken cart wheel, his small wagon levered up on a pile of logs.

"Help you, sir?"

The man stared suspiciously, then nodded. "I'll thank you, for I'm cursed, stranded by this den of devils."

Peirol set his pack down and went to work. He thought it was amusing that both he and the wagoneer made sure their backs weren't turned to the other.

The wheel repaired and remounted, the man

pulled away the lever, and the cart thumped down on its wheels.

"Now I'm far gone," he said. "Would you ride with me? My nag's not fast, but it's quicker than being afoot."

"Perhaps," Peirol said. He pointed at the castle. "What's that over there?"

"The lair of a murdering bastard," the carter said. "A man without pity or mercy, who holds this land under his thumb, taking what he wants when he wants it."

Peirol asked if the murderous bastard had a name, was told it, and held back a smile as the teamster raved on. "Yes, and may the demons hear me and seize him by his throat and balls and tear him apart! Stranger, don't chance his hospitality, for he knows no kindness and will likely kill you just because he's never murdered a dwarf, and will wonder if it's the same as slaughtering a full man."

"That sort," Peirol said, "is the very sort of man I seek," and he went up the road toward the castle while the carter gaped, then whipped his spavined horse away at full rattle.

✳

TWELVE

Of Old Friendships
and Bloody Gems

The castle wasn't that prepossessing. Its stone bulk sat atop a hill, surrounded by artfully tended grape vines. Instead of arrow slits, generous glassed windows studded the angular cone-topped turrets at each corner of the walls. The huge gates thudded open, and a dozen armored men galloped out, lances lowered. Peirol pulled up and waited.

The men smoothly surrounded him, and Peirol was at the center of a nest of lance points. Their evident leader, a bushy-bearded man with a scar down his face where his right eye and most of his nose should have been, bayed a laugh a wolf pack leader might have envied.

"It's nice when the prey comes to you, even if it's nothing but a bearded child."

" 'E's a dwarf, Honoro," another man said.

"Dwarf, changeling, what matters it? What tribute do you have for us, little one?" Honoro bellowed.

"Not a copper," Peirol said.

"Then your life is forfeit."

"Perhaps you'll let your lord, Aulard, the one I seek, decide that," Peirol said.

Honoro jerked in surprise. Instantly all the lances were lifted. "You have business with him?"

"I don't think it's any concern of yours," Peirol said haughtily. "Where I come from, lackeys listen and obey, no more."

Two or three of the riders laughed. Evidently Honoro was no better liked than most bandit leaders. Honoro started to scowl, met Peirol's steady gaze, dropped his head. "Sorry. Sir."

"Now you may escort me to him," Peirol said. "And I find you a good and proper guard."

Honoro, insulted then praised, didn't know what to do. Eventually he touched his free hand to his helmet in salute, and the dozen men, Peirol in their center, rode back up to the castle. Over the sallyport a motto was carved in the stone: HELD NOT BY THE MIGHT OF MY STONES, BUT BY MY LORD'S STEEL. Peirol glanced into the moat as his horse clopped over the stone bridge, then looked more closely. There was no water below, only green grass, but the moat was an even deadlier guardian than normal. There were at least half a dozen huge bears patrolling the strip of land. Two were worrying over bones, and there were other bones scattered around the sward.

"Lord Aulard, when it strikes his fancy, or when

the beasts hunger, tosses one of his prisoners over," Honoro said.

"Are there always prisoners?" Peirol asked.

"Generally," Honoro said. "But if there ain't, we grab a peasant. They do fine. And if we get lucky, and it's female, we get pleasure of our own before the bears."

Lord Aulard was a perfect example of the sort Peirol had always feared and, secretly and ashamedly, envied a bit. He would have been a huge baby, always growing faster and larger than his fellows. Boys and men like him had always found Peirol their natural prey, and it wasn't until the dwarf had learned the equalizing power of a stick, a rock, or later, a small knife, that he could come and go undisturbed. Now in his thirties, Aulard bulked over his retinue, and his long dark hair and beard made him even more menacing. He wore a dark red silk shirt, leather breeches, and an incongruously jesterlike baggy red cap. A sheathed sword stood beside his ornately carved chair.

His receiving room was hung with weaponry and trophies of the hunt, both four- and two-legged prey. Fires burned in great hearths on either side of the room.

A servant hurried up with a crystal decanter and four glasses, two filled with chilled water. Aulard poured brandy into the two glasses. He dipped a finger in each, flipped a drop over each shoulder. "Give a bit to the gods," he explained, "and they'll reward you tenfold."

"Of course," Peirol said. *Good*, he thought. *A superstitious man. That moves my goal a bit closer.*

Aulard pointedly sipped from each glass, proving neither was poisoned. "I honor you, Peirol of the Moorlands," he said. His voice was gruff, boisterous, in keeping with his size. "Even though you're not a minstrel, as I hoped when my men, er, escorted you here."

"I'm sorry to disappoint, lord," Peirol said.

"You do indeed," Aulard said. "We have no troubadours, nor sorcerers or even a witch for entertainments. You have no idea how bored my women become, without gossip to twitter about in these hinterlands, nor anything but the passing seasons to look forward to, and how miserable their boredom can make my existence."

Peirol didn't voice what he was thinking—men who prized women as decoration seldom thought they had to provide anything to ward off boredom.

"It's all this stupid war those damnable Beshkirians have mounted on Arzamas, which has unloosed every barbaric son of a bitch to loot and pillage to his heart's content. Normally the winter would find all of us, save the garrison of course, spending time in the capital and regaining perspective on what it is to be a man instead of a bumpkin. But travel in this time is absurdly dangerous, and I chance it not."

But you sit here like a hawk on its perch, swooping on every other poor fool that must go abroad, Pierol thought.

Aloud he said, "I understand the problem well,

lord, and agree with you. For I myself was a slave of those Beshkirians until I was able to make my escape."

Aulard grinned, drank brandy. "Which means you're a free man. Any slave who can outrun his captors should automatically consider himself free, in my eyes. Of course," and Aulard's eyes glittered, "should he then be misfortunate enough to be captured by other slavers, he might revert to his old status, and curse whatever made him continue his flight beyond the bare necessary."

Peirol stiffened at the implied threat, but his voice remained calm. "Even an escaped slave can have hidden fangs to make his new captor regret his actions."

Aulard grinned, settled back in his chair. "So what, sir, made you seek *me* out?"

"I, sir, am a man who travels in gems," Peirol said. "I first heard your name aboard ship, and was impressed by what I heard."

"So my—I won't be arrogant enough to say fame, but let us say reputation—has spread abroad?"

"In a sense," Peirol said. "The teller of the tales was a beautiful virgin named Lady Zaimis Nagyagite."

Aulard, surprised, sat up straight. "You were aboard the *Petrel* with her?"

"I was, sir, and both of us were captured by those Beshkirian pirates. I became a galley slave, and have no idea what happened to the noble lady, except I hope she survived her travails and is now safe in your household."

"She is," Aulard said. "I now recollect she said something about a dwarf jeweler of great charm and knowledge, but she was afraid he was killed. Obviously—"

"Obviously," Peirol agreed, drinking brandy.

"Let me ask you this, before we proceed to your business. What was your impression of milady? Speaking in utter confidence, man to man?"

Aulard was not a subtle person.

"I was quite impressed with your choice of brides," Peirol said. "I found her modest, yet outgoing and quite witty. She kept mostly to herself, and the only man she spoke of was you, her intended."

Aulard beamed.

"I'm glad the Lady Zaimis was ransomed," Peirol said. "Before the pirates took us, she told me she'd drown herself before letting anyone chance her virtue."

"I ransomed her," Aulard said. "And it was a good lot of gold, too. And now she is indeed part of my household. A very spirited part, too. Sometimes . . ." Aulard didn't finish his sentence, but drained his brandy. "I've thought again on what I said," the big man said. "Perhaps your business might be entertaining to my ladies, since they are always fascinated with baubles. As I'm sure you know, I have quite a collection, which I assume is what brought you to me."

"It is, my lord."

"I'll have a servant take you to your quarters. Dinner is a glass past sundown, and I'll send someone for you."

"An excellent idea, my lord," Peirol said. "I don't know if I can amuse your ladies, but certainly discussing diamonds and such, and their possible uses and gifts, generally interests anyone, especially if there's a good profit for them in the offing."

The trap was being laid.

Peirol went up steps, down corridors, following the servant with his saddlebags, who looked as much a bandit as valet. Suddenly a voice came from an alcove: "Peirol! It *is* you!"

Zaimis caught him around the shoulders, holding him close, saying his name over and over as if he were a lost lover instead of a momentary companion in misfortune. He'd just begun to consider how her breasts felt even better next to his cheek than he dreamed when she pulled away.

Zaimis was more beautiful than he remembered, her blond hair now cut short, her perfect face not needing makeup, but her lips lightly rouged. She wore a floor-length linen gown that buttoned chastely at her throat.

"You're safe! You're here! I thought you were dead."

"I was," Peirol said. "But the memory of your beauty brought me back to life."

She giggled, looked at the scowling servant. "You. I assume milord is putting him in the second tower?"

"Yes, milady."

"Good. Go, await us there, for I've some memories to share with Peirol, and you would be bored."

The man hesitated, then bowed and walked away.

"It would have been simpler to just dismiss him," Zaimis said. "But not with a bedchamber in the offing. My Lord Aulard trusts me no more than the rest of his wives, which is to say not at all," she said, a little bitterly.

Peirol remembered the dark mate Edirne, and a night full of moans. "That's too bad," he said piously. "For a man who doesn't trust a woman as clearly honorable as you is to be pitied."

Zaimis looked up and down the corridor, then tucked her hand under his arm. "I thought I saw you killed, after you gave that wretch Libat his due."

Peirol told her what had happened from the bloody decks of the *Petrel* on, omitting details he thought might be embarrassing, such as Niazbeck's wife and daughter.

"You have the luck of the gods."

"So I would hope," Peirol said truthfully. "But there were times I despaired of their existence."

"Don't ever do that! I myself have prayed and prayed, and now you've arrived and I know, somehow, you'll help me."

"I would be only too delighted," Peirol said, "if I knew what troubled you."

"It's Lord Aulard," she hissed, looking from side to side like a trapped wildcat. "He didn't tell me, or rather my father, the truth when he wooed me."

"How terrible," Peirol said neutrally. "In what way?"

"He never said that he has eleven other wives, to begin with," Zaimis said. "Nor did he say that he's not much better than that pirate who ransomed me. Worse, for Lord Kanen was certainly fairer to the eye than Aulard, and his home wasn't in the middle of a barren, like this horrible pile of stones. I should have . . . never mind."

Peirol wondered what she should have, and said banally, "Yes, well, sometimes things aren't quite the way we expect them. But at least Aulard gives you a safe home, which is a great deal these days."

"Piffle," Zaimis said. "I have enough faith in myself to know I could make my own way, if I had to. At least I'd have my freedom.

"If only—"

Zaimis broke off and said, calmly, "Aulard is quite more than I'd expected, dear Peirol. Not just in"—and she simpered disgustingly—"in the ways you men talk about all the time, but as a companion and protector as well."

Peirol, wondering if she was mad, felt pressure on his shoulder from her hand and saw her finger pointing to the side. He looked, saw nothing but a tapestry of a lion hunt. Then he noted the dead lion, and how the yellow thread appeared thinner than in other places. He saw movement behind the tapestry—an eye? part of a face?—then nothing. They moved on.

"You see?" Zaimis said fiercely. "The walls have ears and eyes, and anything that's said in range of them is reported to my sneak of a lord, and he then applies 'appropriate disciplines.' Sometimes with his bare hand, sometimes with a whip. I . . . I confess at first I thought it exciting, a different kind of loveplay. But then . . . there were, until two Times ago, thirteen of us. That one—we're forbidden to even think her name—was given to the bears." Zaimis shivered. "I'm so afraid, Peirol. *So* afraid, and I don't know what to do. But you'll devise a plan, won't you?"

"What sort of plan?" Peirol temporized.

"You'll think of something. There's your room, just ahead. I'll see you at dinner, and hope you'll be staying for a few days." She started away, then turned back. "Do you remember, back on the ship, the night before those pirates came?"

Peirol still cursed his caution.

"I've sometimes wondered foolishly, thinking you were dead, but now the idea comes fresh, what could have happened if—well, I thought when Edirne knocked that it was you, and opened the door gladly. Perhaps things would have been better if they were different." She smiled sultrily and was gone.

Peirol, appalled, stared after her. Better? Edirne had been game until the sun rose. What miracles did she think dwarves were capable of? Now he was wondering if he shouldn't have taken that carter's advice and kept on moving, instead of following his ever-so-crafty plan. Why couldn't Zaimis have been fat, pregnant, and happy?

"Now this particular ruby," Peirol told his rapt audience, "has a most evil tale behind it. Perhaps, Lord Aulard, I should not give details, for fear your wives will not sleep well this night."

"Go ahead," Aulard rumbled. "*I* determine how my wives sleep—if at all." He guffawed in an unseemly manner, and his swordsmen, now waiters, echoed the mirth.

Peirol noted that only about half of the twelve

women in the room seemed to find the remark funny. The dozen women ranged from Zaimis's twenty years to thirty for the oldest. All, in various shades and colors, would be reckoned great beauties.

The meal was straightforward, a warrior's feast of spiced beef, roasted fowl, and sweet potatoes. Aulard ate heartily, if somewhat mechanically, most of the women less so, as if the menu were the same night after night.

The wives clamored for tales of the outside world, of travel and glamour. Peirol obliged, lying when necessary. When the meal finished, he brought out a small bag and scattered a few stones on the tablecloth. He held up the ruby.

"Now, as I'm sure Lord Aulard knows, it's possible to change the color of a ruby by heating it. That deepens the red, makes it more alive," Peirol said.

"Risky business, that," Aulard said. "Too hot, and the stone shatters."

"True," Peirol agreed. "I think it's best to have a magician in attendance, and let him 'feel' the stone as it heats. However, the history of this stone is very different. Note how the red has somewhat of a dark, brooding note to it. That's because the jeweler who first cut it also practiced dark magic, and when the stone was finished, he used a young virgin's blood in the spell."

There were *oooh*s, and even a couple of the swordsmen shifted uneasily.

"That brought a dark curse," Peirol went on. "The murderous jeweler died when the jewel passed from his hands, and the tale is that anyone who owns the stone will die when he sells or gives it away—unless a woman who's close to him dies, no matter the cause, in which case he's safe."

Of course the ruby in question had no such tale connected with it. It was just one of the stones Peirol had stolen from the great snake who'd guarded Slask's underground temple in the ruins of Thyone.

"But what about you?" a woman asked. "Aren't you terrified that the curse may strike you?"

"Little people," Zaimis said, before Peirol could say anything, "have powers of their own, and I know Peirol to be very, very brave, able to stand against even magic."

Lord Aulard gave her a dark look. Peirol cut in before the situation could worsen. "I thank you, my lady. But technically I do not own this stone, but am acting as a middleman for its owner. He's very noble, but I cannot mention his name. I'm taking this stone east to a big city, where I'll sell it without mentioning its reputation."

"Won't that doom someone in the new owner's household?"

"I don't think so," Peirol said. "For I've noticed the power of gods and demons ebbs more, the farther from their realm you travel. Halfway across the world, will that curse still have effect? I don't think so, as I said. This is my specialty, taking jewels with dark reputations to places where their full value may be realized, without possibly false rumors lessening the stone's worth."

"Dark reputations?" Aulard said. "Could that also

include gems that have been, let us say, acquired in extralegal manners?"

"Possibly," Peirol said. "I judge my clients by what I think, not by what the world says."

Aulard stroked his beard.

Peirol told half a dozen other stories, each bloody, each total fiction, before Aulard yawned, stretched, and drained his wine. "Time for sleep," he announced, looked down the table. Some of the women smiled eagerly, others looked away. "You, Zaimis. I give you this night's honor."

Aulard stared at Peirol, as if expecting a challenge. "Good night, noble lord," Peirol said.

Aulard grunted, took Zaimis by the hand, and walked out, flanked by two guards. Peirol wondered why he felt shamed, as if Aulard had seized a woman companioning him. Completely absurd, and so he pushed the thought away. But it still came back, as he tossed in his own chamber.

The vault, Peirol admitted, looked prepossessing, with four huge brass locks. However, he remembered what he'd learned from thieves: that a lock's size means less to a skilled robber than its internal complexity. He was proven right when Lord Aulard took out four equally heavy, ornately cast keys that were simple skeletons in design.

"I have been considering your profession," Aulard said as he swung the iron door open with a clang. He set the large lamp he was carrying on the table in the room's center. Drawers lined the walls, and Aulard took out several. Peirol noticed all came from the left wall.

"Yes," Peirol said. "I was . . . impressed with the jewel you sent Zaimis to pledge your troth."

The pause was deliberate. Aulard looked at him carefully. "Impressed? In what manner?"

"In the manner of its careful construct."

"I find your choice of words interesting."

Peirol smiled.

"Let me ask in another manner," Aulard said. "If I'd brought you that jewel you told Zaimis was beyond value, if I quote you correctly, and also said that it had unusual qualities, just what would you allow me on it?"

"Oh, perhaps a dozen pieces of silver," Peirol said. "More if I knew of a collector of . . . curiosities who might be interested in such a finely wrought piece."

"Just a dozen pieces of silver?" Aulard pretended outrage. "For a blue diamond?"

"For a blue *stone,* to be precise."

"There are few men in the jewel trade who could have recognized that object as mere crystal."

"I thank you, lord."

"I'm especially impressed you didn't expose my small and meaningless romantic gesture to Zaimis. Men have died for less at my hand."

"So I understand."

"You're not only clever, but careful."

"Someone of my physique learns that early," Peirol said.

"Yes, I suppose you would, wouldn't you?"

Aulard said. "The jewels, or mock-jewels, such as Zaimis was given, are kept in cabinets on the right. I find it very soothing to know, when I go out or to the city and my women accompany me, that the gems they gleefully wear are such that if they're lost, stolen, or as has happened, kept by a woman who's decided to go her own way, I'll lose little sleep. Not that that has slowed my revenge, my pursuit of someone who's shamed me publicly, either male or female," Aulard said, a bit of a growl in his voice. "Enough playing. Your profession appeals, because there are certain gems I possess that I'll never be able to show, nor wear myself, nor allow any wife to display. Only a few have legends such as you told last night, but the reasons they must be kept in secret aren't your concern.

"My current situation is such that I desire greater gold, to take advantage of this war and purchase various properties around me whose owners—hardly friends—are in distressed circumstances. I would like to be able to convert these gems into cash, but I can hardly do something that crass myself, nor would I want my name associated with them."

"I see," Peirol said, holding back a grin. The bait was taken. "Let me ask some questions and make, perhaps, some qualifications. Of course I'd be interested. That is in fact why I came to your castle."

"I surmised that," Aulard said. "Therefore, neither of us should think the other a fool. What are your qualifications?"

"First, another question. Is the reputation of these gems you wish me to handle of recent acquisition?"

"None," Aulard said shortly, "have been . . . acquired . . . over the last year, except for two, and those were gained under circumstances no one will ever suspicion."

"Good," Peirol said. "A qualification is, no stone should have a dark reputation to the south or east, since that is the direction I travel. I hardly want to return them to, and I misuse the phrase, the scene of the crime."

"You could indeed have chosen better words," Aulard said. "But that limitation is not a factor, since I know well the history of these jewels, and hardly wish to blow your gaff."

Peirol noted the use of thieves' cant, hardly appropriate for noblemen.

"Now let me bring up two questions of my own. What will be your commission?"

"Thirty percent of the sales price," Peirol said. "Plus a suitable expense, which I guarantee will not exceed an additional ten percent."

"That's ridiculous! I'm willing to pay ten, perhaps fifteen percent, but no further."

"Then we should return to the receiving room, share a final brandy, and I shall be on my way, thinking well of how gracious a host you are."

"I could just throw you to the bears, take your jewels, and add them to my collection."

"You could," Peirol said, voice indifferent. "But do you really believe none of my gems are cursed? Do you really think I'm foolish enough to go into the den of a man who keeps bears for amusement without certain safeguards? Do you really think I'm such a fool as to travel these roads truly alone?" Peirol stared into Aulard's eyes until the nobleman pulled them away.

"No," Aulard grudged. "Of course not. Twenty percent."

"I'm known as a man who's bad at bargaining, so I set a price and stick to it. Thirty percent was what I said, and what I meant. However, considering your courtesy, and that I'm excited by the possibility of handling some of the jewels I see on that table, I'll lower my expenses to five percent of the final price."

Aulard growled wordlessly, nodded. He reached into a tray, raked jewels with his fingers. "That's one of my questions," he said. "There is another. As I said, neither of us are fools, so the question came: What is to keep you from simply going on, once you've sold my gems, and never returning with my share of the gold?"

"Why," Peirol said, "my innate honesty."

Both men smiled humorlessly.

"Exactly," Aulard said. "Then, deep in the night, a solution came. You appear to like my wife, Zaimis, and she has an attraction to you, I've discovered. I consider that somewhat perverse, but I've learned women are always receptacles of such wickedness. But that gave me my safeguard. First, I'll send a man with you: Honoro, who I trust absolutely, who owes me his life and has sworn blood loyalty. He can bring the gold back, if you don't desire to return on your tracks.

"Second, I'll have Zaimis as a hostage against any . . . difficulties. I promise, if you don't come back, or rather if my gold doesn't, she shall die an unimaginably slow death, until, at the last, she shall be screaming for my bears to deliver her from torment. I have certain definite ideas—dreams, rather—that I would dearly love to develop, and Zaimis, as young and perfect as she is, would be an ideal subject." Aulard's smile was inward, terrible.

"I don't think that you're like me in any way," he went on. "*I* could listen to such a threat with equanimity, since women have never been more than an amusement. But I don't think you're like that. I think, Peirol of the Moorlands, you're one of those people men like me were meant to have power over."

"You're a man of hasty judgments," Peirol said, holding back his temper.

"But I'm almost invariably right," Aulard retorted. "I can accept your conditions. Can you accept mine?"

After a moment, Peirol extended his right hand, and Aulard clasped it.

"Very good," Aulard said. "Partner."

Aulard muttered as he sorted through his gems. Peirol found the muttering instructive: "That bastard's son's still alive . . . too well known . . . the dwarf said nothing to the south . . ."

Aulard chose first smaller unset stones, which would be easy to move, then larger gems, which would be harder to sell but would produce greater profits. Peirol decided he'd wait on the bigger gems until he struck a city at least the size of Arzamas, where there'd be someone anonymously wealthy to afford those baubles.

Aulard set aside four particular gems: two diamonds, a fiery black opal, and a third, most unusual pin. All were very large, at least thirty *varjas* each, and very striking. The settings of three also held other, varied jewels.

"This first diamond," he said, "supposedly brings doom, a slow, coughing death, to its owner, although it's done no harm to me. This other one carries a curse of sterility. I'll admit I have no sons yet, so perhaps it's well I'm rid of it, although I have little interest in creating someone who'll grow to be a danger to me as I was to my father.

"This opal passed through a long line of bandit chieftains before I acquired it, none prospering once they'd killed to obtain it."

He picked up the pin, considered it. "This . . . no. This one stays, not just because it's the pride of my collection, in legend if not appearance. I'm hardly superstitious, but there's something . . . strange about it, although nothing's happened to me."

"May I examine it?" Peirol asked.

Aulard hesitated, passed it across. The stone was unlike any other Peirol had seen. It might have begun as a raw brown diamond of forty or more *varjas*. Rather than being conventionally cut, its facets had been made in the shape of a wolf's head, baying. The pin was mounted directly to the stone, with no silver or gold setting. Peirol glassed it against a light, thought it dull, reflecting little fire, then brief flashes came, went.

"There's been magic laid on this stone."

"Magic and more," Aulard said. "I don't know what sort of stone it is. It's not a diamond, but far softer. Also, you'll note the brown carries throughout, unlike most of the fancy browns I own, with no pale shades; and the brown coalesces to black where the wolf's eyes would be."

"Interesting," Peirol admitted. "Quite valuable to the right buyer—almost certainly a man. Why, other than because it's a remarkable work, don't you want to sell it?"

"As I said, I'm not superstitious," the superstitious Aulard said. "This stone purportedly gives the sorcerer who owns it, who knows the proper spells, the ability to call changelings to him, make them do his bidding without their savaging him. The man I . . . acquired the stone from wasn't magical, and knew none of those incantations, so I've been reluctant to wear it for long."

Peirol wondered what Aulard would do if he told him he'd been called a changeling himself as a child, and could sometimes call real wolves to him, as he had in the ruins of Thyone against Koosh Begee and his thugs.

"Again, this is cursed with bad luck, a truth, not a legend. Reason enough not to wear it, and keep it here in this vault with spells set around it. Here it can't wreak any harm. I keep it because . . . because of its very uniqueness.

"None of my wives like it, save Zaimis, and I think she said that just to be perverse."

"There is no problem," Peirol said, handing the pin back. "We have a sufficiency with what you've selected to make you far wealthier than you are now. Keep that in its vault until you find a rich magician."

Aulard smiled tightly. "All appears to be going very well. I'm pleased. Because of this, I'll add a bonus. If you do as you claim, I promise I'll give Zaimis one of my better stones—a real stone, not crystal. But I would suggest you not tell her that. Women confuse easily."

A day later, after a proper feast, where Aulard got very drunk and amorous, carrying off two of his wives at the end, Zaimis being one, Peirol and Honoro were ready. Aulard showed no damage from the night before, and was most jovial. His retainers were assembled, and Aulard stood on the courtyard steps. He bade Peirol good speed and trading, and a swift return, "for fear of misunderstandings."

He laughed hard, looking pointedly at Zaimis, who looked a little piqued. But she laughed heartily, and Peirol could not imagine she'd been told of her role as a hostage. He'd had no chance to speak to her alone, unable to find out what she'd wanted for a "plan."

Aulard took Honoro aside and whispered to him, looking frequently at Peirol. Then he said, loudly, "And you're the best I have," clapped him on the back, and the two mounted. Each had his horse, plus a packhorse with supplies.

Peirol had Aulard's jewels in a pack under his tunic. He'd found a mail shirt that fit him exactly, which Aulard gifted him with. His own gems were, as usual, in the pouch tied behind his knee. Peirol bowed to Aulard's wives, thought he saw Zaimis wink, then made obeisance to Aulard. He and Honoro stepped up into their saddles and rode down to the highway.

Peirol's plan had worked perfectly. His cant had made Aulard give him enough wealth to carry him to Restormel comfortably, trading here and there. He wasn't happy with the idea of Zaimis being a sort of hostage, but assumed, if he did as he'd told Aulard, made a sufficient profit and sent it back with Honoro, that she'd be in no danger and might just be treated a little more specially.

Peirol had consulted a map of Aulard's; he decided the first city he'd trade in was Isfahan, at least two weeks' ride south, almost at the head of the Manoleon Peninsula.

Two days beyond Aulard's castle, the countryside grew richer. Peasants in their fields no longer fled at the sight of armed horsemen, and they even passed unarmed riders. There were more villages, some with inns, although both Honoro and Peirol were very cautious before allowing themselves the luxury of a real bed out of the weather.

Five days from Aulard's castle, Honoro said something odd, in a very quiet voice, as much to himself as Peirol: "Vows are vows, and promises are promises, but good steel is the only thing worth trusting."

Peirol asked what he meant, but the scarred rogue just shook his head.

That night they camped not far off the road in a ramshackle, abandoned byre. Honoro's bow had brought down a large bird, and Peirol gutted it, stuffed it with rice, seasoned it with herbs plucked along the road, and spitted it for roasting over the low fire. Honoro took a flask of wine from his packhorse, filled leather jacks. They sat, stretching occasionally after the ride of the day, in fairly companionable silence.

Honoro said suddenly, "What're you going to do with your share of the gelt?"

"I beg your pardon?"

"Your half of what we get from selling that shithead's jewels," Honoro said carefully, as if talking to a slow-witted child.

Peirol's heart turned, and he looked to where his sword belt lay, across the fire, on his bedroll. *Too far, too far.*

"I still don't understand," Peirol said. "We ride back—or possibly you ride back alone—with sixty-five percent of whatever we manage to make."

Honoro gaped in disbelief, then started laughing. "Damned funny," he said. "Very damned funny. You're the wanderer, the misshapen one, the one no one in his right mind would believe for an instant, the one who, if he has any sense, would sell Aulard's gems and ride on, laughing at the fool he'd rooked. I'm the faithful retainer, the one who was saved from the gallows by Aulard, who swore a death-oath he'd serve honestly as long as he lived, a rogue, but one who never betrayed his bargain, waiting until he had the right chance. Opposites rule, don't they?"

"The reason I am going to behave as I am," Peirol said, "is, Lord Aulard told me Lady Zaimis would die a terrible death if I didn't come back."

"Is Zaimis your sister? Was she once your leman?"

"No to both," Peirol admitted.

"Then what of her? She's naught but a foolish slut who thought she was making a good marriage when her father betrothed her to Aulard. I know she feels promises were broken, but what of that? Since when does any man tell the truth to a woman when all he wants is what's between her legs? Why are you such a gentleman? Or fool?"

"I don't know," Peirol said. "Maybe I've seen enough bodies, and don't want to be responsible for any more."

"Then kill yourself right now," Honoro said. "For what is life but the strong taking from the weak? Man is kept alive by bestial acts, you know."

"No," Peirol said. "I don't know."

"Very well," Honoro sighed. "I guess there's no point in reasoning with you, since what I propose should be obvious. We'll continue on, and when our business is finished, we'll split the gold, and you may do what you will with your share. Remember, I would kill you here, except I'll need your knowledge to get a goodly price."

Honoro drained his jack. "No," he said. "I am thinking again. Assuming you're a man of your word, what I've said must now have made you my enemy. The reason I've lived as long as I have in hard conditions is I've either fled my enemies when they were too strong for me, or . . ."

A long dagger glittered in Honoro's grip. "I am sorry, dwarf," he said, getting up. Peirol was on his feet as well. "Don't try to fight," Honoro said. "That way, I can give you the easiest death, and you'll not suffer—"

Honoro stumbled, made a strange noise. His hand opened, and the dagger clattered down to the stones. He opened his mouth, and a trickle of blood ran out. Peirol saw the flash of metal in the center of Honoro's chest, then it was hidden by gore.

Peirol realized the flash was an arrowhead's point. Honoro made a bleating sound, spun half around, and crashed into the middle of the fire, very dead.

THIRTEEN

※

Of Revenge and Creatures of Smoke

Z aimis came out of the darkness, holding a small target bow in one hand. She wore breeches, riding boots, and a hooded jacket, all in brown leather.

"Did I . . . is he . . ."

"Dead, indeed, my lady," Peirol said as an unpleasant smell came. He realized the late Honoro had begun to roast. He dragged the body out of the fire, accidentally turned it over, and saw the charring face. Zaimis made a sound and was shudderingly sick.

Peirol dragged the body into the bushes, rescued the fowl, then went to the now-sobbing Zaimis, reached up, and put his arm around her. She put her head on his shoulder, cried harder.

"You saved my life," Peirol said soothingly. "Please don't cry anymore."

Slowly the sobs lessened, and she lifted her face. "I never killed anyone before . . . even if that bastard was willing to let me be tortured to death."

"Killing people's not a good habit to form," Peirol agreed. "Here. Let me get a cloth and some water and wash your face. Have some wine. Sit down, and tell me how you escaped."

Zaimis snuffled, nodded obediently. Even with her face scrubbed bare and red eyes, Peirol still thought her one of the most beautiful women he'd ever seen. She drank about half of the jack of wine, and Peirol upended the flask into her cup, got another from Honoro's bags.

"Now I understand what kind of plan you wanted from me," he said. "I'm sorry I wasn't able to find one."

Zaimis shook her head. "That's of no matter. My father always told me a good plan is something that you come up with on the instant, and that's what *I* made." Peirol couldn't begrudge her the slight emphasis on *I*. "Aulard was very boisterous after you two left, talking about the lands he'd buy, the neighbors he'd drive into destitution. He ordered a special meal." Zaimis shuddered. "I may never be able to look beef in the eye again. I swear that's all the man eats. At any rate, we dined. I had my idea then, and put a small powder into his brandy."

"What sort of powder?"

"My nurse was a bit of a witch," Zaimis said. "She collected herbs—some for good, some for evil—and taught me how to recognize, dry, and use them. The one I gave Aulard was meant to loosen his bowels. I think I gave him too much, because I was wakened by moans and groans coming down the hall from his bedroom. With the others, I ran to see what I could do, and he was sitting on a chamberpot, saying his guts were falling out his bum, and what did he do to deserve such a sickness, he would never eat that much again, and then more groans. I swear, if men ever suffered the way women do, every month . . .

"Anyway, no one paid me any mind, so I took his key chain from where it hung. Then I dressed in my riding outfit and went below stairs. The household was up and in alarms, sure their lord was dying, and the cooks were making various concoctions to cure him. I could have told them the herb would run its course in a day, and he'd be fine, only a bit weak. But I said nothing, went to his vault, and took what I needed.

"I relocked the vault and dropped the keys on the floor so he'd think he'd but misplaced them and not check his vault for a time. Then I took a pack from the armory room, stuffed it with provisions from the larder, went to the stables, and saddled my horse.

"The gods were with me, for the gates were open, and some of the guards had gone to the closest village to bring back their witch. I rode hard and didn't pause all that night, or the next day except to water and rest my horse and buy grain where I could. I asked travelers, village guards, if they'd seen a small man with a single guard, and some of them had noticed your passage.

"Today I found I was very close, since I was going as fast as I could without foundering my horse. I saw you just at dusk on the road ahead, held back until I saw you make camp, then crept close with this little bow. When I was a maiden, I used to shoot at wooden birds with my sisters, and was very good.

"I thought maybe I could disarm Honoro, or possibly creep in after he slept, waken you, and we could flee together. Instead—"

She started leaking tears again, and once more Peirol comforted her, telling her over and over she'd done no wrong and he was proud of her.

Zaimis drank more wine, hiccuped. "You're right, Peirol. Now we must flee together."

Peirol remembered Aulard's words about pursuing anyone who shamed him. He brought Zaimis's horse into the cowshed and unsaddled, fed, and watered the animal. As he did, a shuddersome thought came.

"Uh, Zaimis? You said something about taking what you needed? What was that, precisely?"

"Something to ensure I wouldn't be a beggar or whore," Zaimis said. "Something for myself—and for you, I hope." She took a small pack from her saddle, opened it, and a double handful of gems threw firelight at Peirol.

"I was on to the bastard's tricks," she said, "and knew all those drawers on the right held glass beads, and the real gems were on the left. I'd also asked him to show me his most precious, and noted their location. I took a double handful for you," she said. "And also this."

She turned over the lapel of her jacket, and Peirol saw again the wolf's-head gem. "This was always my favorite, and Aulard owed me at least this for taking the best two years of my life, giving me nothing in return."

"You realize he'll come after us."

"Of course," Zaimis said. "But I'm with you now, and I know anyone as clever as you are will keep me safe."

Peirol tried to keep from moaning.

He woke Zaimis before dawn. They'd been curled together, in his blanket roll. Zaimis had a bit too much wine, then, to Peirol's surprise, announced hunger. He'd managed to gnaw a leg of the fowl and the woman had gone through the rest of the bird as if she hadn't eaten for a week. They'd gone to bed, fully clothed, in the event they had to wake and travel fast. She'd giggled, said something about love, then gone instantly to sleep. Peirol had worried about Aulard's pursuit, then realized it was inevitable. Finally he slept as well.

They washed, ate bread Peirol had bought before in a village, and rode off with a change of mount apiece. Honoro's horse had been skittish, so they turned it loose in a field. As for his body, they had neither time nor inclination for burial ceremonies.

"Where are we going?" Zaimis asked.

"We're going to Isfahan, which is a big city about five days away, I'd guess, if we push hard," Peirol told her. "We'll be able to sell the gems, decide what to do next."

"Is it big enough for us to hide from Aulard?"

"I don't know," Peirol said. "But with what

you"—he almost said *stole*—"took from Aulard, I'd be more inclined to lean on richness than anonymity."

"I knew I was right, putting my life in your hands," she said.

Peirol, about to say something gracious, looked back across the long valley they'd crossed. Far distant, near their camp of the night before, he saw dust. Riders, coming fast. Zaimis paled.

"Maybe it's just some merchants hurrying to market," Peirol said. "But let's move on." He thought of disguises, of stopping in a village to buy new garb. But that would ensure remembrance, and besides, there was nothing he could do about his appearance. If he'd been a midget, he could disguise himself as a boy, the male traveler's son. But not as he was.

"What are we going to do?" Zaimis said. "Are there public guards in this land? An army?"

"I don't know." He didn't say that either watch-keepers or soldiers would likely bring them a quicker doom. He didn't know what rights women had in this land, but doubted if one was husband-looting. With Honoro dead, Aulard would claim both were thieves. The best to be hoped for was an end as two dangling corpses from trees beside the road. The worst . . . Peirol remembered the bears, and Aulard's threat that Zaimis would welcome death at their hands. Before that happened—before that, he had a dagger and, hopefully, the strength to use it on them both.

They were riding into hills, and it was hot, dusty. He thought he saw a building topping a distant hill, and hoped it might be a castle where they could find or bribe shelter. An hour's further travel, and he could see it was indeed a castle.

They rounded a bend and saw what looked like a festival. In open fields, some strange plant twined up around thin rope. Men and women were walking among the plants on stilts. They wore brightly colored clothes, and children ran amid them with baskets.

Puzzled, Peirol pulled into a field, and a jovial woman stalked over. "Good morrow, friends," she said. "It's good luck for travelers to join us, and we have more than enough bread, cheese, beer."

"Thanks," Zaimis and Peirol chimed, then Zaimis added, "But we're traveling hard, and must put miles on."

"That's a pity, for the harvest goes well."

"What are you harvesting?" Peirol asked.

"Hops, to season the finest beers, which our district produces," the woman replied.

"Thank you for educating me," Peirol said. "One further thing. That castle over there? Could you tell me anything of its lord?"

"He was an evil man," the woman said emphatically. "From an evil breed. And the gods, or perhaps his demons, struck at him and destroyed his castle on a night of no storms and a clear sky."

"Do you know if there's enough in the way of ruins for us to shelter in?"

"You're welcome to stay with us," the woman said.

"No, we cannot," Peirol said. "Uh . . ."

"We have a vow," Zaimis said smoothly, "to travel

a certain number of leagues a day, and I'm afraid even that castle might be too close."

"You wouldn't want to tarry there in any case," the woman said. "For the curse of the lord lingers on, and strange creatures—changelings—haunt the ruins, dooming anyone who dares enter the walls. I've not seen them, but my cousin's grandfather's sister did. No, travelers, monstrous things happen inside those walls."

"I thank you, lady," Peirol said, and bowed in the saddle. "We'll certainly heed your advice, stay far distant from that castle, and continue to a village beyond it, where we may find lodgings."

He dug a coin from his purse, tossed it to her. She caught it, one-handed, without swaying a bit. "I thank you, but I did nothing to deserve a reward."

"Use the money," Zaimis said, "to drink a beer in remembrance of thirsty wanderers, who cannot pause."

"Oh. Now I understand. You're cursed yourselves! No, no. Coins from such as you might bring wickedness." She spun the money back to Peirol. "Now be on your way," she said, suddenly unfriendly. "For my people have enough troubles to contend with."

An hour later the castle loomed over them, battlements jagged daggers against the afternoon skies.

"Up here," Peirol said, pointing to where a lane might have been, winding upward between rows of tall trees.

"Toward the castle?"

"Exactly."

"But what about the curse?"

"I don't believe in changelings," Peirol said. "But I do believe in Aulard."

"Then why'd you tell the woman . . . oh. Aulard will ask and be misdirected," Zaimis said. "Clever dwarf."

"I hope so."

Whoever or whatever had ruined the castle had done a fairly thorough job. Only some of the ringwall was still standing, as were two round towers set into it. All else, including the center keep, was little more than heaped stones. Peirol and Zaimis guided their horses across the granite outcropping the castle had been built on to the far wall and tied them, still saddled, in a nook.

"And now?" Zaimis asked.

"Now," Peirol answered, "we find a peephole, and determine just how clever this dwarf is."

It was twilight when they saw, far below, a cluster of riders. Moving at a trot, they rode past the turnoff to the castle.

"Clever indeed," Zaimis said. "After they pass, what will we do?"

"I'm not sure," Peirol said. "I'm not much concerned about this ruin being haunted. There isn't a pile of rock anywhere in the world that doesn't have ghastlies hanging about it, which were last seen by somebody's grandmother's cousin's grandfather's aunt's uncle. Perhaps we'll stay here the night, then look for an east–west road, and then another track going south. Or perhaps we could be very cunning, like a fox I saw once, and follow the good Aulard from behind. He'd never think of backtracking, and his band of thugs would scare off any banditry that might be lurking ahead of us."

"Clever, clever, clever. Perhaps we should begin thinking about a suitable reward for a clever dwarf." Zaimis leaned over, ran a tongue in and out of his ear. "Perhaps we *should* spend the night here."

Peirol was about to turn and kiss her when he saw the riders turn back.

"Gods*damn* it!" Peirol swore. "And we covered our trail so well!"

"Maybe he's just being careful and checking the side roads," Zaimis said hopefully.

"No," Peirol said. "See how he's got outriders in front? If I crane hard, I can see they've got bows ready. He knows he's onto something." He looked again. "There's a woman with them. Would he have brought one of his wives? And why?"

"I can't think of who . . . wait a moment. Aulard sent for a witch when he was sick."

"And she's sniffed us here," Peirol said.

"Do we have another plan?"

Peirol shook his head. "Nothing."

"Let's run."

"No," Peirol said. "They'd just ride us down. And I don't know where we can run to." He rubbed his chin. "About the best I can think of is we wait until the middle of the night, then slip out afoot and make our way cross-country, hoping they aren't master trackers."

"Aulard is a great huntsman," Zaimis said

gloomily. "Perhaps if we remain still he'll think we're not here. Or if there is a curse on these ruins, maybe it'll confuse the witch's scenting powers."

"Maybe," Peirol said, looking out again. The riders—there were eleven of them, plus the witch and Aulard—stopped short of the castle, dismounted, and began making camp.

Aulard strode to where the castle gates had once been and stood, hands on hips. "Cower in your nests," he shouted. "I know you're in there. But it's getting dark, and I'll not chance one of my men tripping over a stone or giving you the chance to backstab him. I'll give you the night to think of the ways you'll suffer, as I have been planning them. After dawn, I'll come for you. Pleasant dreams." He roared laughter and went back to where a campfire was smoldering into life.

"I'll not wait to be killed," Zaimis said.

"Nor I," Peirol agreed. "We'll try to slip out in the wee hours."

But that never happened.

They waited in a stone cubicle Peirol thought might've been for a prized horse, since it was larger than a normal stall. Or, his mind thought, since the castle's builder had supposedly been in the thrall of demons, it might have been some fabulous monster chained within. He decided not to dwell on that subject. At least the stall was next to the ringwall, and there was a chest-sized hole they could squeeze through and flee down the back slope.

Neither slept, and they kept their weapons at hand. It was clear, with a three-quarter moon, when Peirol wanted rain and thunder. But again, the gods paid no attention to a dwarf's prayers.

The night dragged, lasting for years. Peirol crept out from time to time, peered out at Aulard's fire. It guttered down, and he began to hope, then someone threw dry wood on it. It flared up, and he saw two alert men walking back and forth on guard.

It was just around midnight, Peirol guessed, when he heard the first baying. Zaimis's eyes went wide in the moonlight. Peirol smiled reassuringly. If there were wolves in the hills, that was the least of their worries. He wondered if he should chance calling to them, if they'd come and possibly attack Aulard. That had worked once, but only by pure luck, and he was afraid to try again. It would be far more likely the beasts would steer well clear of armed men with fire and go after two running, harmless ones, he thought, remembering how wolves dearly loved mice as appetizers to their main feast. He tried to guess which direction the pack was, but was puzzled. The baying was very faint, but seemed to come from all around them.

There weren't that many wolves in the world, he knew. It must have been a trick of the stones around him, miscasting the sounds. The baying came again, still louder.

"Are they coming here?"

"I don't know."

Peirol slid his sword out of his sheath, looked into the keep. It was very light, just as, he thought, it'd been light in the ruins of Thyone, showing those wolves clearly. Peirol shuddered reflexively, and Zaimis saw the movement, whimpered.

Out there, in the moonlight, something was moving. It shimmered, like heat waves over a furnace, and then came to life. Peirol couldn't make out what it was, exactly. Its form kept shifting. He thought it to be a man, then some sort of beast.

"Look," Zaimis whispered, and another being appeared beside the first, then there were half a dozen, more. Peirol heard low muttering, a sound more like apes would make than wolves. Then a bit of cloud came across the moon, and the creatures moved toward the stone cubicle.

Very suddenly, Peirol believed in changelings.

The creatures drifted toward them as if being blown by a gentle wind, and then one lifted its face— snout?—to the sky and bayed loud, and the others echoed him. Zaimis screamed then, and the creatures came closer.

Peirol wondered if his steel would cut them, or if he needed some magical weapon, which he was a bit short of at the moment.

One of their horses, tied across the way, echoed Zaimis's scream as it, too, saw the unnatural monsters. Again the pack bayed, this time in unison, and Peirol thought of calling back, hopefully confusing them. Then he remembered the pin Zaimis wore, the wolf's-head pin Aulard had told him was meant to call changelings. Perhaps that had summoned them. Or perhaps they just . . . came when they sensed prey. But he had no spell, knew nothing of magic.

"The pin," he managed. "Give me that wolf-pin!"

Zaimis stared, then understood and fumbled the pin off her jacket. Peirol cast it out into the keep as he'd spin a flat stone across a pond, into the midst of the changelings. Then he cried out, the distress cry of the moor wolf, the cry that should bring the pack to savage anyone one trying to harm their fellow. The changelings hesitated, waving from side to side, then fell back. One bent, and Peirol thought it picked up the pin.

Peirol saw torchlight at one of the gaps in the ringwall. "What . . . gods above . . . where in the hells did *they* come from?" The voice was Aulard's. Someone shouted, and a spear arced across the keep, went through one of the changelings, clattered against stone. A musket slammed, and Peirol saw smoke rise in the moonlight.

The changelings turned and moved toward the torches. Peirol saw six or more armed men beside Aulard. Arrows spat at—through—the creatures of the night.

Peirol and Zaimis scuttled to their horses. The changelings were closing on Aulard and his men, and then a scream came, this one deep, from a man's panicked throat. Peirol's hands fumbled the reins free, and he pulled the horses toward the nearby gap in the wall. Then they were through, as clouds moved on and the moon shone down brightly.

Peirol heard the clash of steel, another scream, more musketry, angry shouts, and Aulard's mad raging.

Leaping into their saddles, they struggled down the steep rock face, horses trying not to slip, as near to panic as their riders, while behind them howls of triumph and bellows of agony grew in the night.

FOURTEEN

*

Of Love
and Messiahs

Peirol and Zaimis reined in by the small stone
building guarding the bridge into the walled
city of Isfahan. Two guards came out, neat if
not very warlike.

"Salutations, travelers," one said.

"And we greet you. It's nice to see a real city
again," Peirol said, again grateful for Abbas's language spell.

They'd ridden hard for two days after escaping
Aulard, not sure the changelings, whatever they were,
had completely destroyed him and his banditry. Seeing
no dust clouds behind them, they finally slowed their
pace. They passed through two villages large enough
to have merchants interested in gems. Peirol sold a few
small stones, traded for others, coming out a few gold
coins to the good. Zaimis had wondered why he'd

bothered, and Peirol explained it'd been so long since he'd done business, he wasn't sure if he was still able, or if a runny-nosed urchin could outbargain him.

They hadn't lingered in either village, since they had no inns as such. Peirol thought he'd as soon sleep in the open as pay a ridiculous amount for some peasant's flea-bitten feather bed, lumpy enough to suggest the feathers were still on the chickens, or sleep on the floor with the pigs. Zaimis kept looking at Peirol oddly. He had an idea why, but said nothing, waiting for the right moment.

It came a day's travel beyond the last village they'd traded in. It'd been a hot day. Near dusk, Peirol had seen a secluded place not far from a spring, with a small pool. He made camp, fed and tended the horses, and the two of them collected dry wood. He built a fire next to the spring and lit it. Peirol filled the horse's bucket from the pool, propped that over the fire on stones to heat.

"Now, my lady, your bath awaits," he said, bowing.

"So that's why you've made no approaches to me! You think I smell!"

"You do, my lady. And so do I."

"You surely are romantic, Peirol of the Moorlands. Now I know why I didn't wait until you knocked on my cabin on the *Petrel*. You probably would've checked me for fleas before you kissed me!"

Peirol waggled his eyebrows. "If you'll be so kind as to undress, while I modestly avert my eyes."

"Why are you suddenly so modest? We've been sleeping next to each other for days."

"There is a right way and a wrong way for everything."

Peirol looked away, heard clothing rustle. His body suggested this was, indeed, the proper time.

"Now what?"

"Take this dipper, and wet yourself."

Splashing.

"Now what?"

"Now you take the soap, and lather yourself."

"I don't understand your instructions, master," Zaimis said in a pouty voice. "Perhaps you'd better show me the way. But without peeking."

"As a master of the bath, that is easy." Peirol, ostentatiously looking off, took the soap from her, lathered her back and legs.

"You slighted an area, you know."

"You mean, here."

"Mmmh," she breathed. "Yes, that particularly needs attention. Now, I think I have learned sufficiently well, so it's time for me to become mistress of the bath, and you obey my instructions."

"As you wish, my lady."

Now the journey became an idyll, Peirol not wanting this happiness, after so much travail, to come to an end. But a day before he guessed they'd reach Isfahan, he woke, remembering a bare bit of a dream. He'd been once more in Abbas's study, and the magician was in his great carved chair, arms folded, silent, just staring at Peirol, and his gaze was hardly friendly.

After that they rode on more quickly, taking to the wide, level beach when it presented itself. And so they came to Isfahan. The city filled a canyon that sloped down from the hills to open on a small ocean bay. The waterfront, businesses, and warehouses were deserted. Fishing boats were beached, and rotting merchantmen tied up at the docks.

The canyon's mouth was closed with a stone battlement, and along the canyon wall were guard towers. They rode to the guardshack, were greeted.

"Welcome to Isfahan," the other guard said. "In the text of Makonnen, it's written that it's good to gift a stranger, for he might be the Redeemer." Peirol blinked. The guard unbuckled his sword belt, handed it up to Peirol. "And for the lady, I have but these few copper coins," he went on. "But the text of Makonnen says it is better to give from the heart than the purse."

A bewildered Zaimis took the coins.

"Uh . . ." Peirol managed. "Thank you. But . . ."

"It is the custom," the first guard said, "to respond to a gift with another gift, for as the text of Makonnen says, only he who has nothing will recognize the Redeemer."

"Oh. Well, here." Peirol passed the sword belt and coins back. "Uh . . . as my priest once said, the tools of a man's trade should never be far from him."

"I thank you," the guard said. "And your priest showed wisdom, but it is a pity that he has not been given the opportunity to learn from Makonnen, and thus will be doomed to be torn by demons, as all unbelievers shall be, when the Redeemer comes."

"Including us?" Zaimis asked.

"So the text of Makonnen says."

"Who is this Makonnen?"

"He is the one who came to pave the way for the Redeemer," a guard said. "We have been fortunate that he has chosen to remain with us, awaiting that day."

"Which is?"

"Coming fast," the other guard said. "But Makonnen says the exact day must not be asked, though it is soon. So you will have a chance to convert, to sing hosannas and be present when the Redeemer arrives."

"I note the docks and shipping areas seem deserted," Peirol said. "Is this a particularly special holiday for Makonnen or something?"

"As for the bigger ships," a guard explained, "trade by sea has been scanty since those damned Sarissans began their piracy. Makonnen has written this is yet another sign we are in the Latter Days. But why should we worry, if the Day of the Redeemer looms close, when all shall be as we wish, and no one's desires will be denied?"

"We are truly fortunate in arriving before such an exciting time," Peirol said, "We feel doubly welcome in your city, and know we shall be greatly enlightened."

The guards saluted, and they entered Isfahan.

"What happens if this Redeemer doesn't show up at all?" Zaimis asked.

"I think that might be a very frightening day indeed," Peirol said. "We should do our trading and be on our way before that happens. Let's hope the whole city isn't given over to this sort of silliness, which I fear it is, for what sort of business can I do if everyone simply gives things away?"

Isfahan was old, very clean, well designed and

solidly built, streets winding through the main canyon and up side draws. There were trees and parks, green oases with ponds that broke the heat reflecting from the tan stones of the buildings, the high canyon walls above.

Zaimis shook her head. "I wouldn't want to live in this gloomy place. They can't get more than a few hours of sunlight each day. And I'd keep thinking the walls were closing in on me."

They stopped a prosperous-looking merchant and asked him where a good inn might be found. "In the text of Makonnen, it's written that a humble abode with those you love is better than the finest lodging," he said. "But I would suggest the Place of the Contented Duck."

He gave instructions, and they rode on. Peirol listened to bits of conversation as they passed:

A child, to her friend: "Even though this is my favorite toy, I'll give it to you, for Makonnen told my mother giving is always better than owning."

A woman, barefoot, wearing nothing but a pair of loose-fitting breeches, to a laborer: "I'll freely give you my body until nightfall, for the words of Makonnen are that a woman's task is above all to give man happiness."

Zaimis snorted, but Peirol was a bit heartened at the response from the working man: "And I, in m'turn, will buy wine and p'r'aps gift you with some of the coppers m' foreman just give me, after I give him the gift of half a day's hard work."

A well-dressed woman to her friend: "I see you admiring my hat, which you must accept as a present, for the text of Makonnen says a happy person is a delight to the eyes of all."

That one set Peirol back, but the last exchange gave him greater hope, listening to a fat woman and an equally fat female vegetable merchant: "Of course I'll give you those cabbages, for doesn't Makonnen say there's no greater joy than that of others?"

"And I, in turn, will give you six coppers, for the same reason."

"Eight would give me greater happiness."

"But I'm sure you really want seven, for didn't Makonnen say the good man always is satisfied with less than his dreams?"

"Seven it is."

Zaimis started finding this nonsense funny. But Peirol wasn't sure whether he did or not.

The Place of the Contented Duck was quite a large inn, with a central courtyard and its own stables. The buildings were stone, like the rest of the city, but faced with wood stripping, carved and painted in fantastic colors.

They found a nearby money changer, and Peirol tried exchanging one of his smaller gems, an emerald, for the local coin, using the cabbage merchant's trick. It seemed to work—he got a dozen gold coins, twice that in silver, and three coppers—but the changer gave him dismaying advice:

"It's well I have remembered as much of the text of Makonnen as I've had read to me, and know a stranger is to be treated well and taken into your household as if he is one of your family, but I must warn you that if you're a man who traffics in expensive baubles, you might be saddened by Isfahan, for the text of Makonnen says when the Day of the Redeemer is close, expensive delights that give nothing should be put away, and among these are jewels, gold, dancing women, racing horses, and mansions."

That truly worried Peirol. But the innkeeper at the Contented Duck made only a mumbled reference to Makonnen and his greatness before naming what, in the old days, he would have charged for the best room in the house, and was quite happy to take exactly that amount as a gift without further moralizing.

The rooms were quite satisfactory—a huge bedchamber, a greeting room Peirol could use as his showroom, and an even larger bathroom, with water both hot and cold coming in through brass pipes, the flow controlled by levers, into both a cascade and a tub.

Zaimis waited until the keeper left, having put their saddlebags next to a great closet and accepted a coin. Then she walked over and tested the mattress.

"I'm not sure I remember how to do it in a bed. Perhaps you might come here, and we can attempt to remember together?"

"Perhaps I might, my lady."

He got up on the bed beside her. Zaimis smiled, lay back, and Peirol took her in his arms.

"I think," he said, "the memory is returning. Now, if you'll give me a hand with these buttons?"

"Oh, you are a *clever* man!" Zaimis squealed after a while.

Peirol noted he'd been promoted from dwarf—if,

in view of men named Aulard and Niazbeck, that was in fact a promotion at all.

The next day seamstresses were summoned while Peirol went out to do business. Peirol inquired about the finest jewelers in Isfahan and was given directions. The first jeweler mouthed more of Makonnen's platitudes and seemed uninterested. Finally he drawled offers on three of the better stones Peirol had presented, offers that would show no more than a few coppers' profit. Peirol, trying to be polite, managed to thank the man and left.

The jeweler's clerk, a sharp-faced sort, followed him outside and asked where he was staying. Peirol eyed him.

"The Place of the Contented Duck," he said. "On an upper floor, with barred windows. I might add I sleep very lightly, if at all, and one of the peculiarities of my past is, I sleep with a bare blade in my hand."

"Nay, nay," the clerk protested. "I'm not a scout for footpads. But I know a man—actually, some men and women both—who don't share my master's fascination with Makonnen. Though," he added hastily, "all are most religious, and wait the Redeemer eagerly. But they think, shall we say, it's well to have an interest in other matters."

"You, sir," Peirol said, "are entirely too sharp to remain a clerk for long."

The clerk bowed. "I thank you."

"I'm not sure I meant it as a compliment. But I'll give you ten percent of the profits from anyone who seeks me out with your recommendation."

Peirol found another lapidarist, somewhat more interested in trading, and turned a small profit. "And may Makonnen bless the both of us," the trader said as he bowed Peirol out.

"May Makonnen get foot rot up to his damned knees," Peirol said. But it was under his breath, and after looking to make sure no one was in hearing. He went back to the inn and found a corner booth. He considered whether they should ride on or keep trying.

The innkeeper, bowing as if he were a marionette, brought a richly dressed man to Peirol's table, whom he introduced as Nushki. Peirol stood, made an elaborate obeisance, asked him to be seated, and ordered a bottle of good wine. The man waited until the wine was tasted and approved, then sipped at his glass.

"I am delighted to be alive in these exciting days of the Redeemer," Nushki said.

"As are we all."

"I must say, however, there are certain . . . unusual circumstances no one could have predicted."

"Such as?" Peirol asked.

"Such as the difficulty, shall we say, of conducting commerce."

"I'm encountering that selfsame problem."

"So I understand," Nushki said smoothly. "Which is why a certain clerk of my acquaintance brought your arrival to my attention. Since you're evidently a stranger to Isfahan, perhaps you're unaware our populace can be extraordinarily excitable."

"In what way?"

"In seizing on enthusiasms," Nushki said. "And, worse, becoming enraged when, or rather if, those enthusiasms don't develop in the manner expected. I remember, when I was a boy, a rage for exotic nut bushes swept the city, and people spent outrageous sums to buy the latest and strangest. Of course, when everyone had at least one or more bush, was tired of selling on credit, and the market was flooded, prices collapsed. The man who began the craze was dismembered, his heart and genitals burned before his eyes while he screamed. Then the throng rioted, and no one knows how many hundreds died.

"My father, who was a wise man, which is why I was able to finance my businesses with a minimum of risk, had seen this coming. We fled the city before the riots, after he'd converted as much of his holdings into cash or transportable goods as possible. We stayed at an inn leagues beyond Isfahan, and we could barely see the smoke from the fires. When we returned, all was calm, although the city was a quarter ruined.

"They'd burned our house and several of my father's businesses. But because of his farsightedness, my father was able to reestablish himself quickly. And since his funds were liquid, he was able to take advantage of many opportunities in the depressed marketplace."

"I'd guess," Peirol suggested, "nut bushes weren't among them."

"As a matter of fact, I still can't stand to eat those meats. At any rate, I've been considering what is happening today, and, of course I'm wrong to even think this, to wonder about the greatness of Makonnen and the Redeemer, but a wise man takes precautions."

"One of the most transportable and easiest to convert of all assets is high-grade gems," Peirol said.

"Which is why I thought we might have a common interest."

"An excellent thought," Peirol said. "Perhaps we should adjourn to my chambers and discuss the matter further, and you might peruse some interesting examples of my craft?"

"Such would be my pleasure."

As they reached the stairs, Nushki, very casually, pointed out six armed men as his bodyguards and said that unfortunately the taproom couldn't accommodate all of them, so others were forced to wait outside in the back, near the stables, and in front, on the street.

Peirol gave him a wintry smile. "You'll find I'm no less honest than those you normally conduct business with."

"The thought never came," Nushki said, and bowed him up the stairs.

An hour later, Peirol was fatter by two bags of gold, and Nushki, quite delighted, had a palmful of gems, one Aulard's ill-omened opal.

In the days that followed other men and women, equally richly dressed, equally worried about Makonnen's prophecies and what would happen if anything went awry, came to Peirol and left with jewels. They swore him to secrecy, because those who displeased Makonnen were taken to a park and stoned to death. Several hundred people had already been made aware of Makonnen's displeasure. Peirol was more than happy to promise.

He had gotten rid of half his gems when the summons came. Four plainly dressed, well-armed men came to the inn, and announced Peirol of the Moorlands and his companion had been selected for a rare privilege. Makonnen himself was prepared to grant them an immediate audience and a blessing. Horses were waiting outside.

"Trouble," Zaimis whispered.

Peirol couldn't think of any way to put the men off and make an escape. Besides, he thought hopefully, perhaps this will really turn out to be a blessing.

It wasn't.

The house Makonnen lived in sat high on the canyon, near the city-circling walls. It had been given—honestly given—by a merchant prince, one of the first to accept the creed of the Redeemer. Makonnen now considered him one of his most trusted advisers. His former friends such as Nushki, of course, reviled him as a traitor to his class. But they did it very quietly. Isfahan was divided among the ardent believers, who included most of the peasants and a great deal of the upper class, the very quiet opposition, and those who simply got on with things and waited for the worst.

Peirol had expected the mansion to be laden with loot, all "gifts" to Makonnen. Instead it was bare as a penitent's cell, although the sparse furnishings were all of the finest woods and metals. Makonnen's household was all female, all good-looking, mostly young. Not all looked happy to be where they were.

"Godsdamned men," Zaimis whispered, and Peirol couldn't argue.

A bearded dignitary introduced himself as Kuphi.

"You should consider it a great honor to be personally summoned by Makonnen, the One Who Comes Before the Redeemer, to be asked to gift him."

"What sort of gift would be appropriate?" Peirol asked, hoping the payoff would be no more than a large diamond or two.

"I cannot say," Kuphi said. "But I know Makonnen wishes the city to prepare a great gift for the Redeemer, when he arrives, and I've heard mention a model of the world, done in gold and gems, might be the least offering."

Gems. Peirol tried not to let the wince show.

"I see," he said. "I am truly looking forward to this audience, for there's a question of a spiritual nature has been pulling at me, and only a man with the wisdom of Makonnen can answer it."

"Perhaps," Kuphi said, "you would wish to ask me, for I'm not unfamiliar with spiritual matters, and might be able to solve it for you, so Makonnen will not have to occupy himself with matters not on his plane. I don't mean that to be insulting, for all of us, as Makonnen has taught, think our own souls as depthy as the ocean, and perhaps we are right."

"No, no," Peirol said. "I know this question can only be dealt with by Makonnen. If not him, then I'll be forced to hold it for the Redeemer's arrival."

"I, uh, see," Kuphi said. "I bid you wait for a few moments, and then you will be called to dine, with Makonnen himself making the before-meal prayer."

He bowed, left.

"So they're going to feed us," Zaimis said. "Hogs before the slaughter?"

"I prefer lambs before the shearing."

"*You* can think in that manner," Zaimis said. "All *you'll* lose will be our gems. I might become one of this man's chattels and spend the rest of my life, at least until he tires of me, on my back with my legs in the air. I am very tired of being a possession."

Peirol nodded glumly.

"And what is this great question you've been waiting to ask Makonnen?" she asked. "And why haven't you puzzled at it with me?"

"Because I don't know what it is, yet," Peirol whispered fiercely. "Maybe it's why the hells the gods didn't make me a magician so we could fly right on out of here. Shut up and let me ponder."

A few minutes later, a rather dissonant gong sounded from somewhere in the mansion, and a woman came into the room and beckoned them to follow. They entered another almost bare room, empty except for a long table with chairs. Two dozen dignified men stood behind chairs, and they nodded to Peirol and Zaimis. At one end of the room sat a young woman with pen and paper.

There were bowls at each place, a spoon, a mug of water, and a half loaf of bread. In the center of the table was a great steaming dish. Peirol sniffed, smelled nothing but vegetables, which made sense. It was always good for those who prate of spiritual matters to disdain earthly things. Thus far, with the exception of the women, Makonnen was doing well.

Another gong came, and Makonnen entered. Peirol had expected a bearded, hairy charlatan of some sort, a village mountebank who'd fallen into a good thing. Such a one could be bribed with a single gem. But Makonnen was young, in his mid-thirties, sleek-haired, clean-shaven, with a handsome face, if the nose was a little large and pointed for some tastes. In keeping with the ascetic setting, he wore a white tunic, close-buttoned at the neck, white breeches, and simple white sandals.

Zaimis was looking at the man a bit interestedly.

Makonnen came to the only empty place at the table, held out his hands, palm up, and lifted them. "This day is blessed," he said, in a voice that was pleasing, mild, "for it is one day closer to the Redeemer's coming. I lift my voice in prayer to him, and to the gods and heavens he comes from, to give us ease, peace, and plenty, a life of great plenty, for all to savor and enjoy. For have I not written, 'Only in the Redeemer's graces can anything be enjoyed, and only when we are joined with him shall we know true happiness'? I now further add to that, by saying—"

The prayer went on and on. Peirol saw the young woman writing hastily as Makonnen spoke. By the time the prayer finished, the dish in the center of the table had stopped steaming.

"Be seated, my advisers, my guests," Makonnen said. "And allow me to serve us." He went around the table, dishing up bowls. No one began eating until Makonnen sat down and lifted his spoon, and then everyone followed, eating at a great rate. Peirol tried the dish, found it a lentil stew of no great distinction, with too many tomatoes and not enough garlic. He'd eaten better, he'd eaten far worse.

He ate slowly, paying more attention to Makonnen than the meal. Peirol thought the man very clever for avoiding the usual traps of impostors. He wondered why no one ever thought the young could be frauds. Certainly an old charlatan must get started sometime. He was at a loss as to what he might do, and then he noticed something. There was a peculiar glitter to Makonnen's eyes, and he never quite looked directly at anyone or anything, but beyond them, over their shoulder. He'd seen the look before, on the face of the gods-besotted. An idea formed.

Makonnen had finished about half his bowl when he put his spoon down. Instantly everyone else stopped as well. Zaimis had her spoon lifted, and Peirol had just taken a bite. She kicked him and put her spoon back down, obviously more experienced with formal state banquets than the dwarf. If this was Makonnen's way, no wonder his advisers gobbled so hastily. Makonnen made no gesture, but women swarmed, cleared the table.

"I greet my visitors," Makonnen said, without rising. He looked a bit past Peirol and Zaimis as he spoke. They ducked their heads, hoping that would be showing adequate respect. "I asked you to come here," he said, "because first, I'm always curious about outsiders who come to my . . . to the Redeemer's city."

Ah. A slip, there, Peirol thought.

"My agents report that even though you two come from the beyond, you have been more than respectful about the Redeemer's coming, and have listened with great interest to what humble teachings of mine have been presented to you. This is very good. Another reason I invited you was to ask you if you wished to become part of our family, as each gives to each, and thereby increases their worth in the eyes of the Redeemer. Each of you could choose to give a great gift, but one which will ensure your being in the greatest favor with the Redeemer, as these friends of mine here are and as I hope I am considered."

The advisers hastily cut in with "Of course you are," "You're the best of us all," and such phrases sycophants have always used. Makonnen waited until the chorus died away.

"However," Makonnen said, "before we discuss that matter, and perhaps pray for proper guidance, I understand from my friend Kuphi that you have a question on spiritual matters you wish to put to me. I am delighted to listen to it, but you must remember, I am but the messenger of the Redeemer, and what little power of thought I've been given comes from him, for his great mind can more than spare the mite he's given me, and"—Makonnen hesitated, regained his train of thought—"so it's not at all inconceivable the answer to your question might have to wait until the Redeemer himself walks among us. But that will be no great burden, for I have been told, through my dreams and visions, we have but little time to wait, although we all know what the gods and great beings call little time might be a lifetime to a man."

Again the chorus chimed agreement.

"Ask your question, if you will," Makonnen said.

"As I'm sure you know," Peirol said smoothly, feeling his palms bead sweat, "we come from a far distant land, and had intended to pass through Isfahan on our way to other lands, as our gods have dictated we must wander."

"I'd sensed," Makonnen said, "you were not traveling of your own will."

Got you, you lying bastard!

Zaimis was doing an admirable job of keeping an even face.

"We knew nothing of the Redeemer, nor of yourself. But even before we knew of you, Makonnen, just after entering this country where Isfahan is a dreamed-of paradise, we noticed the peasants and villagers we met treated us strangely."

"Not surprising," Makonnen said. "By now the two of you—one so fair, the other so unusual—must be used to curious looks."

"Of course we are," Peirol said. "But this was very different. Finally, in one village, we encountered a wonderfully knowledgeable village witch."

"I hold but little with magic," Makonnen said. "As I have written, 'Once the Redeemer arrives, such mummery and illusion will fade, and we shall all rejoice in the clear light of day.' "

Peirol waited until the claque finished.

"I know little of that, for I have nothing of the Gift. But this witch, who later told us of your coming, and the gifts of comfort and knowledge you've brought, explained why we were held in such, well, I don't like to sound cocky, but the only word I have is awe. She said it was the legend, or rather folk-poem, called 'The Dwarf and the Lady.' She said it was very old, hundreds of years."

"Since I, like yourselves, am not a native of this land," Makonnen said, "I know the legend not. Do you, Kuphi? Before I came, Kuphi headed the Colleges of Learning, and it was said that he knew everything."

"So it was put about," Kuphi said humbly. "But then I met you and realized the depth of my ignorance, Makonnen."

Makonnen smiled, pleased. "Well, what of this legend?"

Kuphi furrowed his brow, pretended to think. "I heard it years and years ago, either in my childhood or as a young student. I'm afraid the details have slipped my mind. But it is a very definite ancient country legend."

Peirol kept from grinning. "The witch taught us the rhyme that would begin any of the adventures of this dwarf and lady, which she said was always the same. I memorized it as a curiosity. But then, when I learned of you and the Redeemer, I determined I must, when we reached Isfahan, seek you out and ask what it means, for surely a legend that old must have some merit. My friend here and I vowed we would mention the rhyme to no one until you offered your wisdom," he said. "The verse goes, and I think I'm quoting it precisely:

> "First the oracle
> To set the way
> Then all await

The lady and dwarf, both fey
Come from afar
With baubles so gay.
To the heart of the land
Knowing not that they
Bring word of the One
Who'll bring peace to stay
Behind them a Time
A Time and one day."

The commotion was quite respectable. Men came to their feet, overturning chairs. Kuphi managed, "But that sets the day for the Redeemer!" and there was other, confused babble. Some men had expressions of bewilderment, some fear, others dawning hope.

Peirol had heard tavern tale-tellers describe someone as going green in shock, had always thought it wild exaggeration, until Makonnen. His already white face went corpse-pale, took a very peculiar tinge to it. He slammed to his feet, held up a hand for silence, didn't get it.

One man was on his knees, praying at the top of his lungs, eyes streaming tears.

Makonnen shouted. Then there was stillness. "Repeat that foolish rhyme."

Peirol did.

"It seems obvious, Makonnen," Kuphi said. "The Redeemer's arrival, hallelujah, has been foretold, and I'm embarrassed I remembered this legend not, for surely it would have made your task simpler, not that we know—"

"I said, silence!"

Makonnen walked to a window, looked up at the guardian wall above him. The only sound in the room was the scuff of his sandals. "Very well," he said. "As I've written, the arrival of the Redeemer will be a surprise, even for me. This legend does seem to have promised things, even though I'm not sure yet what those things are, and will need to pray and think for a time as to its significance, as shall you all. I bid you, my advisers, to say nothing of this to anyone, not to your kith, nor your kin, on pain of my most severe displeasure.

"As for you two, I must thank you for bringing me this legend." He sounded like he was gargling bits of glass in his happiness. "I will not be able to give you a proper interpretation tonight. But perhaps at another time, when we shall also discuss your gifts to the Redeemer, I shall be ready. In the meantime, return to your inn and say nothing of tonight, nor of that legend, to anyone at any time, until I personally give you leave to do otherwise."

"Of course, great Makonnen," Peirol said. "You'll note I've not spoken of this matter before tonight."

"I am aware of that. My guards will accompany you to your inn, and in the days to come ensure your safety."

They left, bowing, and the four escorts followed them back to the Contented Duck.

Zaimis leaned close as they rode. "You are a very fast thinker."

"Thank you, my lady."

"And a terrible poet."

"Hush. Your voice carries."

At the inn, the guards stationed themselves at the front.

"Now what?"

"Now I go to the innkeeper with gold, settle our accounts, and pay him well enough to ready our horses without telling those thugs of the True Thinker. You pack."

"We're fleeing?"

"As soon as circumstances warrant."

"Which will be?"

"I'd guess by tomorrow afternoon."

But it didn't take that long. By midnight, the streets were alive with people, some shouting, some singing, some with torches, some drunk, some fighting. Peirol watched from their room's window, saw the guards being called away by a superior. Clearly, some of Makonnen's advisers had talked.

"Now we ride," he said, and they went downstairs, saddlebags over their shoulders. The horses were waiting, and Peirol pulled himself up into the saddle.

He tossed more gold to the innkeeper, who bowed deeply, even though he kept glancing at the street as pandemonium built. "The gods be with you," he managed.

"I'm afraid, my friend, they're with you," Peirol said, and they made their way through madness toward the city gates. Twice Peirol heard shouts directed at them, once saw someone grabbing for a sword. But his own blade was ready, and the man came no closer. The gates were open, and the guards were staring into the heart of the city, paying no mind to anyone leaving.

Peirol of the Moorlands and Zaimis left Isfahan, leaving a powerful message of the spirit behind.

FIFTEEN

✳

Of the Road
and Bandits

I don't think," Peirol said, "I'm very fond of gods
or the people who associate with them. They've
brought me not much but grief."

"And I'm not very sure I like men," Zaimis said.
"For the same reasons."

"But what about me?"

"You're different."

"I'm a dwarf?"

"That, too. I meant you seem to actually care
about women."

"Of course," Peirol said. "Who doesn't?"

"Oh, I suppose that man on the ship would have
been one of those who don't, except in bed. What was
his name, Edirne?" Zaimis said. "The sort I'm always
attracted to, it seems. Aulard. Makonnen. My father.
Some other boys, men, whose names wouldn't matter

to you. It's a long list," she said sadly, then brightened. "You know, if that horrible Makonnen had done what I thought he was planning, he wouldn't have been around long enough to meet his Redeemer, not that I ever think there was any such anywhere but in his imagination."

Peirol lifted an eyebrow.

"I would have poisoned the bastard before he could've gotten his hand above my knee," she said fiercely.

Peirol felt the hair along his spine ruffle. He certainly would have approved if she'd said she would have stabbed him, or pushed him out a window, even if such would've been probable suicide. But poison? That seemed insidious, in the same way he dreaded snakes, possibly for the same reason.

"Let's not talk about that," Peirol said. "For Makonnen and the others are behind us."

She leaned across, gave him a hug. "You're a lovely fool, always expecting the best. Maybe that's your problem."

"Why do anything else?" Peirol asked reasonably. "The worst seems to always take care of itself. And isn't it easier to be cheerful than gloomy?"

Zaimis shivered. "Like you said, let's put what's behind us behind us."

They traded in two small cities, Peirol content with the small profits he made. Again, Zaimis asked why he bothered, and he quoted one of the maxims of the master jeweler Rozan: "Better quick coppers than slow gold."

They encountered no one from Isfahan. The few travelers who caught up with them said they'd bypassed the city, hearing turmoil within and seeing refugees fleeing in all directions.

A small boy whose parents were staying at their inn came by Peirol's table after he'd finished a successful trade with a local collector: one who knew the value of semiprecious stones, but not that of the scattering of precious gems he'd merely polished and left uncut.

The boy marveled over Peirol's stones, and the dwarf showed him how to use the glass, how the gems were cut. Zaimis got more and more impatient. At last the boy's mother called him away.

"Now what made you do that? We haven't eaten or drunk for hours, and I'm starving. Did you think the boy's parents were rich or something?"

"No," Peirol said. "I just remembered a journeyman jeweler named Ty Lanherne, who was nice to another boy a long time ago."

"What?"

"Never mind. Let's go find something cold."

Beyond the two cities, Zaimis's mood changed abruptly. She was short, testy, quick to anger. Peirol asked repeatedly what he'd done wrong, and whatever it was, that he was sorry for it. Zaimis said it was nothing, just a mood. And it passed in time. But still every now and then he caught her looking at him, as if evaluating his worth.

✼   ✼   ✼

"Do you realize something?" Peirol said gleefully. "We're off the Manoleon Peninsula."

"So?" Zaimis said, a little irritated. "I've got a blister on my behind that's just as important. Actually more, because it's not going away."

"I thought we'd never see the end of that land," Peirol said. "The things that happened to us . . . I hope the next time I visit it is never."

"Well," Zaimis allowed. "I'll admit it hasn't been wonderful to me, either. Although I never would have met you if I hadn't been sent here."

"True, true."

They watered their horses at a village well, and an old woman warned them there were bandits about. A caravan had passed through not more than a glass or two ago, and they'd best join it for safety. Peirol thought that an excellent idea, and they caught up with the traders by mid-afternoon. There were twenty of them, hard-faced men with ready pistols and swords, cargo concealed by canvas.

Zaimis and Peirol gave them a start, riding up from the rear, and there was a rearing of horses and worried shouts as the traders spun, hands on their weaponry, then recognized there were but two oncomers. Peirol asked to ride with them, for safety, and would be prepared to pay when they reached the next city and he was able to make some trades. He didn't want to mention the sacks of gold they already had, nor the sack of precious stones behind his knee.

"What are you trading for?" one man asked, pistol still aimed steady.

"What makes me a profit, the same as yourself."

"I don't think so," another man said. "First, the bandits of this country frequently send out spies who pretend to be travelers, join a group like ourselves, and then betray it to their real masters. Second, you've a woman with you, and we swore an oath to take no women on the road, to prevent trouble amongst ourselves.

"And you, dwarf, may have the weapons of a man, but I doubt if any bandit would see you as a threat, nor take longer than a heartbeat to spit you. We'd be lessening our capabilities by having to protect you."

"Right," a third said. "Ride on, you two."

"Thank you for your hospitality," Peirol said, and he and Zaimis trotted past the caravan. The traders stared suspiciously as they passed.

Zaimis turned in her saddle, cupped her hands, and shouted back: "For that, you shitbutts, I'll not tell you which village you passed through today had a poisoned well, and hope you spend the night puking out your guts!"

She spurred her horse, and they galloped off as a single arrow lofted through the air at them.

That night they dined off a fowl Peirol purchased at a roadside farm and drank wine from their saddlebags, then made love slowly at first, then fiercely. Their camp was above the road, hidden in brush, yet they could still see the valley from where they lay, Zaimis's head on Peirol's chest. The sun was just setting, a bit of its bright coin showing across the hills.

"I love this," Peirol said sleepily. "To lie here with

you, an unknown road winding ahead to cities and people and places unfamiliar."

"It's nice when it's like this," she said. "But what about when it rains? What about when it's hot and dusty and we're out of water, and the horses keep trying to bite us? What happens when a village turns us away because you're a dwarf and most likely a mad wizard?"

"That's not good," Peirol said. "But if there were no bad, how could you appreciate the good?"

"I'd manage," Zaimis said. "So that's your dream, a road that goes on and on, and there's always a new gem to trade for and people to chance your wits against? Hardly mine."

"What would be yours?"

"I don't know," Zaimis said after a time. "Maybe a world where I'm not at the beck of any man who lusts after me and has enough power to enforce his will. Maybe I'd like to be a queen. No, not a queen, for I couldn't stand having to listen to the problems of everyone who came to me, having to pretend I care if a peasant's crops are failing or if a merchant's been seized by pirates for ransom or if the neighboring king wants my land and what's between my legs to boot.

"I like travel, moving about, when it's nice like this. Or maybe I just like things to be changing, so I don't get bored. That was one reason my father wanted to marry me off without paying much attention to who my husband might be. Maybe I'd like to be a pirate queen, with my own secret island, that no avenging navy would ever find. I'd have my men, who were devoted to me, and when I chose I could take one as a lover, and when I tired of him there'd be no tears, no resentment, no anger. And everyone would know my name and fear me, but no one would know who I really was."

"A strange dream," Peirol said.

"Some say I'm a strange woman."

That night, Peirol dreamed a real dream. Again he stood in Abbas's study, and the sorcerer was staring at him. But this time, his expression was friendly.

"You have done well, Peirol of the Moorlands," Abbas said. "It has taken me two nights to find you with my magic, for you've traveled far since I last thought of you. You are now well on your way, and if my charts are right, you are two-thirds of the way to Restormel. My thoughts and best wishes go with you."

Abbas vanished. Peirol came slowly awake. He was happy at first, then realized there'd been no scent of jasmine or roses, no hint of Kima's presence. He felt guilt, wondered if the wizard's daughter had somehow sensed Zaimis curled against him and was angry. That was absurd. He'd made no commitments to her beyond the mildest of romanticisms. And that was two years ago. Most likely she was being happily wooed by a hundred of Sennen's richest youths. At eighteen, she might even be wedded to one, with her first child on the way.

But he had trouble going back to sleep, and woke at dawn feeling guilty and sad. He managed to avoid being grumpy to Zaimis, and they rode off, through a day that was overcast and humid, with flies buzzing around their horses. Zaimis was in no better mood, and

Peirol wondered if she thought she'd said too much the night before.

At midday Peirol's horse trod on his foot, and he spilled a jack of wine. He glumly wondered what else could happen to them on this ill-feeling day. An hour later they were taken by bandits.

There were eighteen of them, evil-eyed, scruffy as a nightmare. But their horses and weaponry were well groomed and polished. They ranged from teenage to their fifties, all men. Their leader was a large man whose beard and long hair were braided and tied incongruously with bright ribbons. He wore stained finery, evidently of the school of thought that expensive clothing doesn't need to be washed but can be worn until it falls away. At some time in his career he'd taken a club blow to the face, for it was dished in slightly, his nose flattened and leaning to one side. He carried four pistols in a sling across his chest, a sword, and two daggers.

His lieutenant wore an immaculate white linen shirt and unstained leather trousers and vest. His beard was dark and well trimmed. He was armed with a single richly engraved pistol and a dagger. For some reason, he reminded Peirol of the long-dead mate of the *Petrel*.

"Interesting haul," the large man said. "A beauty and a dwarf, eh? What riches do you carry?"

"Not much," Peirol said. "A handful of gold, for traveling money."

"Toss it over."

Peirol pulled out the small bag he kept ready for such emergencies, handed it across. The heavy man hefted it. "You're not nobility, or the bag would be a deal larger. What's your business?"

"We're fugitives," Peirol tried. "Leaving a place called Isfahan for a better place to live."

"I know it only on a map," the large man said. "The question is, what'll be done with you now? You needn't worry about better lives, but rather whether you'll have one at all."

A bandit licked his lips. "She could make all of us happy for a while."

Zaimis's hand was on her dagger. "You'll be the first I'll caponize if you try it."

The dark-bearded man chuckled. "She looks like she's capable of it, Bamian. In any event, she'll not entertain all, not as long as I've silver for the auction."

"Or if I choose to exercise my right as leader," the heavy man said. "She'd make a fine mattress for a fat man like me."

The bandits found this funny, laughed hard.

"Brave men," Peirol sneered, wishing he had better control of his mouth. "Eighteen against two."

"Actually," the dark-bearded man said, "eighteen to one and a half."

Again, the bandits laughed.

"So what's to be done with us?" Peirol asked.

"Generally, three paths exist," the bearded one said. "By the way, I'm Manco, and I serve as Urga's right-hand man. You needn't bother with your names until we decide if you'll be companying us for a while. As I said, there are three paths. The first, reserved for the poorer travelers, is to be stripped bare, used as we see fit, and left to welter in your blood.

"The second is for you to amuse us for a time, then we sell you at the first slave market. I rather imagine, lady, you know what form that amusement would take. You could be bought for a time by one of us at tonight's campfire, or if the lads are of a common mind, your services can be procured generally, if they choose to make the highest bid."

"An ugly fate," Urga said. "Better to choose one of us, and hope he has enough silver to buy you out."

"The third and best," Manco said, "is if you have people to ransom you. The greater amount they're willing to put up, the less damaged you'll be when we hand you over. You see, fair and equitable choices. Now, if you'll hand over your weapons, we'll take you to camp for the vote."

Peirol was deciding if he could send his dart into Manco's face, plant his dagger in Urga's gut, and then gallop on in the confusion when Zaimis shook her head. "None of those paths appeal to me."

"They ain't intended to," a bandit called.

"What about people who want to join you?"

The laughter was very loud.

"Lots of mice wish they were cats, when they hear the meow," Urga said.

"Those we accept into our band," Manco said, "are generally known as reputable rogues to our members. We're very selective, partly to avoid spies who might betray us to the Brown Men, but more practically because the more comrades, the more shares must be made."

"Suppose," Zaimis said, "suppose someone gives

you something, something of far greater value than even a ransom? Would that be a sufficient price?"

Urga coughed laughter, but Manco stroked his beard. "You interest me, lady. First, because you're not vaporing about your fate, unlike most of your sex. But also because of what you say. Go on."

"No," Zaimis said boldly. "You've not said you'd make such a bargain."

"We would," Urga said. "And I'd give my word you'd be undamaged, if—and I'll say if again—what you give us is truly valuable."

"I don't know about your word," Zaimis said. "But his"—and she looked at Manco—"I'd accept."

"I give my word as well, in front of my comrades," Manco said, sounding amused. "As for being able to join our band, we have a few women, but none as riders."

"We had two," Bamian said. "Before you came, Manco. Twins. Hellions, they were. Let no man touch them, and in a raid they showed no mercy. But they were taken and garroted by the brown bastards, what, four years ago?"

Another bandit said, "I remember them. Good fighters. So we'll let women in as full members of our band. If they can fight."

"I know how to use a sword," Zaimis said. "As does my companion. And I can shoot after a fashion."

"All this is all very well," Urga said, irritated. "But all we're doing is sitting beside the road, jacking our jaws. Just what do you have for us?"

Peirol was as puzzled as the others.

"Twenty traders," Zaimis said. "Heavily armed,

with a hidden cargo. Suspicious men, so I guess that'll mean what they carry is valuable."

"Twenty of them," Urga said. "We're eighteen. Plus, what, another score back at our camp. Close odds."

"Not if I can tell you just how to attack them where they're weakest."

Urga hesitated.

"What do we have to lose?" Manco said. "We can send for the others, listen to this woman's plan, lay in wait if it makes sense, and reach a final decision when—and if—the traders materialize."

"They will," Zaimis said. "I give my word on that. They're about half a day behind us, and there's been no cities for them to stop in or crossroads to turn aside on since we encountered them."

Urga looked at the bandits. "Well?"

"Let's see what the woman offers," a bandit said. "Something different, something new."

"And if it doesn't happen the way it should," Bamian said, "there's still Manco's three paths, now ain't there?"

The bandits were hidden in a draw, with scouts posted in both directions on the road, ambush teams dismounted between them and the main force. Zaimis and Peirol waited back with the horses, guarded by two men.

"You haven't said anything to me."

"I don't know what to say," Peirol said.

"Are you angry with me for being willing to betray those bastard traders?"

Peirol wouldn't have done it, but what of that? "No," he said honestly. "No, I'm not angry at you."

"Then what's the matter?"

"I guess I'm just surprised."

Zaimis looked at him, and her eyes were hard. "Surprised that I don't fancy being raped by these bastards, or becoming a springboard for that gross son of a bitch who probably hasn't bathed in a year?"

"I wouldn't have let that happen," Peirol said.

"But would we still have been alive after you set your plan, whatever it was, in motion?"

"Be quiet, there," one of the bandits snarled. "Don't upset your own cart, woman."

Peirol was happy to be silent, since he didn't like what he would have had to honestly answer. He wondered what Zaimis had noticed about the traders, and what secret plan she'd whispered to Manco while they were waiting for the other bandits.

Time dragged, the buzzing of flies in the clearing was loud, and the sun was very hot. A man came up from the road and waved to the two guards, and they trotted into the bushes. Peirol heard the clatter of horses' hooves, and a moment later a trumpet sounded. There were two great crashes, as of trees falling. Then came shouts, and musketry, and men and horses screaming. Again, the trumpet came, and more shots. Peirol thought he heard someone crying for mercy, the plea cut short. Horses' hooves thundered, and three single musket blasts came. Then all was silence once more, and the flies buzzed around.

Peirol saw Manco.

"You two! Come down here!"

They obeyed. The road was a scatter of twenty bodies, some downed horses. Ahead and behind the massacre, trees had been felled to block the road. The bandits were busy looting the horses' packs. Bamian was dancing around a corpse, waving a pair of tooled boots. "Just my size, and what beauties, what beauties, what beauties."

Urga was reloading his four empty pistols. One bandit lay facedown in the brush; another rocked back and forth, holding his arm, blood leaking between his fingers.

Manco bowed. "Very good, milady. You should have been a man, a warrior. You said they didn't watch their rear, and so it proved. And you've gotten us a treasure greater than your ransom, as you promised."

"What were they carrying?" Peirol asked curiously, trying to keep from looking at the corpses.

"Spices from the far south," Manco said. "More valuable for their weight than gold. We can sell these, no questions, in any city we choose. I doubt if there'll be much talk after this about the three paths. At least, not from me."

Peirol saw Zaimis had a pleased smile on her face, lips parted and wet.

"What do we do now?" Peirol asked. Zaimis seemed to be firmly in control. "We wait for them to vote, and then what, flee at the first chance?"

"First," she said, and the same smile was on her face he'd seen at the raid, "let's see what happens when the spoils are divided."

The bandits' camp was cleverly set up behind a

small village, in a rocky wilderness of lava tubes entered through a long draw, barely wide enough for two men to walk through abreast. The bandits could come and go as they pleased, the small store in the village could buy their supplies without arousing suspicion, and anyone prosperous taking the side road to the village would be prey.

Some of the bandits used the tubes to sleep in, others had built crude huts. When the raiders rode in, fires had already been built and two calves had been butchered and spitted. Other pots, tended by the bandits' women, steamed with spicy beans and a thick soup, while ears of corn roasted in the ashes. Peirol noticed three or four children scampering around, wondered what they'd grow up to be, wondered if they'd live to grow up, remembering from somewhere that bandits lasted about five years before meeting either the gibbet or a sword. Flasks and bottles appeared, holding everything from brandy to wine to unknown, brain-numbing concoctions.

Zaimis asked Urga when the vote would be held on their joining the gang. Urga frowned and said, "Certainly not this night. Tonight we celebrate victory, our new riches. But you've nothing to worry about." He leered. "I'll always be there to protect you."

Zaimis gave him a look that should have ignited his beard but said nothing until she and Peirol were alone. "That man is going to present a problem," she said. "I know what he wants."

"It seems obvious," Peirol agreed.

"That's why there's been nothing said about this vote. I'll wager he thinks the help we gave will be forgotten in a day, and then we'll be no different from any other poor soul they've captured. But he's in for a surprise if he thinks that will happen," she said grimly.

"Shall I go talk to Manco?"

"No," Zaimis said. "But maybe, a bit later, I might. We'll certainly not let either of them renege on the bargain."

Peirol made a face, but he had to agree Zaimis would be far more convincing than he would. The two set their bedrolls a bit away from the camp. Peirol took their horses to the edge of the bandits' lines, watered, fed, and curried them, and made sure they could be untied without raising an alarm. He filled plates with food, got a bottle of wine, and took this repast to where Zaimis sat. They ate and watched the bandits gorge and guzzle.

Three men produced a mandolin, a drum, and a flute and began playing while the bandits danced. Some danced with the camp women, some with each other, some by themselves, shouting abandon to the dark skies. Peirol barely noticed Zaimis slip away, then saw Manco lead her into the firelight, where they began dancing. Neither knew the other's style, but they quickly learned, both being agile. Peirol didn't like the way they danced, how the steps were, at least to him, like a wooing.

Bamian sat down beside him, handed him a bottle of raw spirits. Peirol thought about drinking deeply; he realized that was foolish, but let a swallow go down his throat, pretended to drink more.

"If she were mine, dwarf," Bamian said, "I'd not be happy, the way she's rubbin' up to Manco."

"We're friends," Peirol said, trying to sound casual. "No more. What we do is our own business."

Bamian shrugged, drank.

"I've got a question," Peirol said. "Twice now, somebody's talked about men in brown, bastards in brown. What are they?"

"They pretend they're poor mendi—mendi—beggars, travelin' from place to place, seeking charity an' practicin' good works. At least, those are the young ones, the new ones, who maybe believe in the shit they spout in the beginning. They're supposed to be like priests, I guess, but all belongin' to one sect, and damned if I know what their gods are, if they have any.

"There are others who wear brown, too, but they ride with soldiers who do their beck, an' they pretend to be enforcin' the law. But the only law they believe in is what benefits them. Nasty ones, they are. If you fall into their clutches, you're doomed. First a tribunal, in the nearest village, then the worst death they can imagine. Best, if you're one of us, to die with your sword in your hand, than finish with the death they'll grant. Needless to say, whatever loot you're taken with stays in their hands."

"Where are they from?"

"Far away. A big city, across some straits, called Rest'rmel, which I've never seen, and don't think anyone save maybe Manco has. The story is they're the real rulers of that city, or country. I don't know."

Peirol forgot about Zaimis. *"Restormel?* You know of it? How far away is it?"

"Who knows? Who cares, if the Brown Men hold

it? More than a week, more than two weeks. A month? Maybe a month to the ocean, maybe three weeks. Damn, but I'm getting drunk."

"Do the Brown Men have a name?"

"Yeah. They call themselves . . . uh . . . the Men of Lysyth."

"Just men?"

"Nobody's seen any women wearing brown," Bamian said. "When their nobles ride with the army, nothing happens, I mean they pretend to be high-'n'mighty. But there's stories from village wenches they're no different than the rest of us, after dark, when no one's about. Just godsdamned secrety about getting their wicks dipped."

"Have you ever heard about something called the Empire Stone?"

"Hells no. If I had, assumin' it's some kinda jewel, I would've been figuring a way to steal it."

Peirol asked for details about Restormel, but Bamian said he knew nothing more. "And you'd better not waste your time thinking about Rest'rml, or your friend'll be in Manco's bed before you notice." He got to his feet. "Speaking of which, I'm gonna go call on somebody myself. Take care of my own self. Here, dwarf. I'll leave you the bottle. Maybe you'll need it."

Peirol put it between his legs and watched as Manco and Zaimis danced on, ever more erotically, Zaimis coming close, darting away as Manco tried to pull her into an embrace.

Urga stumbled out of the shadows. "My turn t' dance."

Manco flushed; his hand touched his dagger and came away. "Your turn," he gritted.

Urga tried to dance like Manco had, and now the dance became a comedy as Zaimis flitted around him like a butterfly annoying a bear. The bandits howled laughter. Urga was red-faced, angry. But he caught himself, pretended laughter with the others. He glowered at the three musicians, and the music came to a ragged end.

"Late," he said. "Best we go to bed. Tomorrow we'll figure out where we'll market those spices. Tomorrow, boys, we'll all be rich!"

He grabbed a bottle from someone, upended it, hurled it far into darkness. Peirol heard it shatter on rocks. Zaimis bowed deeply to Urga, then to Manco, and ran around the fire to sit beside Peirol. Her face was sweaty, and she was laughing. "That was fun!"

She saw Peirol's expression. "What's the matter?"

Peirol almost said something, caught himself. "Nothing, nothing. I was just admiring the way you dance . . . and then I started thinking about other things. About our quest."

"Your quest," she corrected. "*Our* journey. And that's for tomorrow, or the day after. Come, Peirol. Tonight I want to love you."

They went away from the fire, to their bedrolls. Zaimis savaged Peirol insatiably, and the dwarf was hard pressed to hold with her. At last he fell asleep, waking once to find Zaimis was gone. A few moments later, she slid back in beside him.

"You're awake?"

"Umm-hmm. Where'd you go?"

"When you've been drinking wine like I have, where do you think I went? Come here, little dwarf. If we're awake, let's not let the moment slip away."

Finally she seemed to tire, and they fell asleep.

He was jolted awake by screams. It was after dawn. Peirol sat up, saw two women howling, leaping around the dying campfire. Men stumbled toward them, listened, began wailing.

"What is it?" Zaimis asked, frightened.

"I don't know. But get dressed quickly. Something's wrong."

Something was. Urga had died during the night. The bandits assembled, some still half-drunk, others wooziling through their hangovers, not improved by the camp women's keening. Manco got silence, found that one of Urga's women—he had three, none of whom had slept with him the night before—had tried to wake him gently with a potion guaranteed to cure a head filled with wine fumes.

"But he just lay there, lay there on his face, and I rolled him over, and saw his face, and oh gods, gods, I've never seen anything that awful, nothing, nothing, nothing ever like it," and she dissolved in tears. Peirol noticed the other two women were envious at her performance, then tried to equal it.

The band trooped to Urga's hut, one of the lava tubes he'd hung with silks and expensive rugs. It didn't smell nearly as good as it looked. Evidently the late Urga had some objection, possibly religious, to bathing. Peirol managed to slip through the crowd, looked at the dead bandit. The woman hadn't been exaggerating—Urga's face was twisted in a terrible rictus, and his clawed hands still pulled at his guts.

There was a cacophony of questions, theories. Urga's heart had given out, he was just too fat. No, it'd been the wine. Not the wine—had anyone seen how he ate? No one could gag down that much flesh without foundering. Aw, I'd seen him eat, drink more. Must've been something wrong with the meat, or something.

Peirol said nothing. He was the only one who'd seen a man die as Urga had, knew the cause.

Manco looked worried, shouted everyone out, said there'd be a burial ceremony in a turning of the glass, before the stink started. They'd give his body to the fire, since no one knew whether or not Urga had a religion.

"An' then," a bandit shouted, "we'll have an election, an' find a new chief."

"Manco!" someone shouted, and there were cries of agreement.

The bandits now had a new excitement, and like children they swarmed to get ready, some going for great balks of firewood from the outside village, others to make a proper bier for their dead chieftain. Manco's worried expression vanished. He let them scurry about, saying nothing. There was a bit of a smile on his face.

Zaimis went to him, bowed. "A question, Manco."

"Ask, Zaimis."

"When you are chief, will you remember your oath about us?"

"I don't know that I'll be elected."

"You will," Zaimis said positively. "Who else could lead these people?"

Manco looked at her, then at Peirol. "If that happens, I'd have an immediate vote on you two joining us, and I say again, there will be no problems. If you become members, would it happen that you perhaps have other ideas for the band? Other things you and your friend might have seen in your travels that might bring us gold? That would count mightily in the vote."

"I do," Zaimis said, and again she had a smile on her face, her lips wet, eyes shining. "You may rest that I—we do. Don't we, Peirol?"

"I, uh . . . yes, of course, Zaimis," Peirol said. "There's those jewelers we dealt with, I'm sure they could be robbed or, better yet, taken for ransom. I'm sorry. I'm just not used to thinking like a bandit yet."

"Like a bandit," Zaimis said. "Or a pirate. But you'll learn. You'll learn."

"I'm sure I will," Peirol said, voice oozing sincerity. He wondered how he could have been so brainless to have thought Zaimis stupid, back on the *Petrel* when he first met her. He was the stupid one. He vowed he'd never be so quick to make judgment again.

It took two turnings of the glass for everything to be properly arranged. All the bandits, even the sentries who watched over the draw leading to the camp, assembled for this, the funeral of their greatest chieftain. Someone who claimed he'd once been a priest's acolyte, before they caught him filching the bowl for the poor, said he could come up with a prayer. The musicians were ready, and the mourners were keening, thoroughly enjoying the moment as, again, the brandy and wine came out. First the ceremony, then the fire, then the meeting for the election, then a great feast. The musicians began playing, and the wailing reached up—or perhaps down—to the gods.

No one noticed as Peirol stealthily unhitched two horses, one he'd saddled as soon as he was able to get away from Manco, and led them away, out of sight of the bandits, to where his pack waited.

Clear of the draw, he mounted and set off in a league-consuming trot. He doubted if the single bag of gold he'd tucked into Zaimis's bedding would keep her from shouting the alarm.

Peirol had indeed seen that face of terrible pain before, back in Sennen, when a thief had set aside his woman for a younger whore. The jilted one went to a witch and bought poison.

He wondered how long Manco would live as bandit king and how long it would be before Zaimis became their queen.

A more disquieting thought came—if they'd not encountered the bandits, and considering Zaimis's growing dissatisfaction with Peirol and his way of life, how long would it have been before she started looking at *him*, thinking about the uses she could put that bag of diamonds behind his knee to and fingering her little bag of herbs?

He swallowed hard, then concentrated on putting the leagues behind him.

SIXTEEN

*

Of Diamond Mines
and Brown Ones

Peirol made the main road, turned east, hurtled past a dozen wagon loads of peasants headed for market, and galloped on.

A league farther, the road ran beside a brackish wetland. Peirol dismounted, led his reluctant horses into the mire, found a hidden copse, and went to ground. Prying branches aside, he could just see the road.

The peasant wagons creaked past. He waited on.

By the time he'd killed his eighteenth mosquito, horses galloped past. He recognized some of the horses, thought he saw Manco at their head with Zaimis beside him. He waited on, killing more bugs. Eventually the bandits came back, horses lathered and exhausted. He could hear shrill recriminations, couldn't quite make out who was accusing whom of what. He could imagine the mutterings about whether Peirol was a better horseman than any of them, or if they'd missed a turning, or if the villagers or peasants had been bribed to lie. Perhaps they'd check the road to the west.

Peirol made his way back to the road and rode off, pushing hard, walking beside his horses, then riding at a walk, then trotting, then on foot again. Dusk fell, but he didn't think of stopping. He reached a village, with welcoming gleams of yellow light and an inn. Inside would be food, fodder for his horses.

Peirol kept moving, stopping only when his and the horses' legs started to buckle. He moved off the road beside a rivulet, let his horses drink, pulled them away to keep them from foundering, unsaddled his mount, and let the animals graze. Peirol pulled handfuls of grass, curried his mount as best he could, then resaddled him. The horse nickered anger and nipped at him, and Peirol felt bad. But discomfort was better than death. Sword ready, wishing he had pistols like the bandits, he leaned against a tree, forcing himself to doze. He jumped awake a dozen times, realized the noises were normal forest sounds, and returned to his drifting stupor.

Before dawn, he rode on. He stopped in another village, fed and watered his horses, forced himself to eat something in the inn, unhurried, as if no one in the world were on his trail. He rode all that day, stopping in a village to buy a bag of grain, bread, cheese, and a small bottle of wine. Again he slept rough, did the same for two more nights, and then reached a small city. Now he might relax. He didn't think men with prices on their heads would chance a city, no matter how rich their prey.

The next morning, as he was settling his bill, there was a commotion outside. A dozen armored lancers were followed by as many musketeers, then two men in brown robes. They were middle-aged, their faces haughty, arrogant. Behind them rode a dozen more lancers. These must be the Brown Men, the Men of Lysyth.

The innkeeper was beside him, watching, face carefully blank. When the Brown Men had passed, he spat after them. "Bastards," he muttered.

"Why so?" Peirol asked. "I'm a stranger."

"They behave as if all cities, all villages, all lands, are secretly theirs, and they're but waiting the day to take them over. They send their damned beggars, calling them journey priests, across the straits from Restormel—that's the city they secretly rule—to do good works, helping farmers in the field, working on the roads, rebuilding bridges, and the like.

"Those are really damned spies, for behind them come the older ones, like those who just passed. They always know when to trade, when to buy, when to sell, when there's famine or feast. They have force of arms to back them, as you saw. If a village or town wants little to do with them, they'll find pretext for insult or injury, and the next visit will be with the gun and the sword.

"Our damned king, far distant, won't do anything. He's as weak as that child-king of Restormel and that whore who rules in his name. One day the Brown Men will usurp his authority, and then we'll all be under their lash.

"Not that they think there's anything wrong with their way, of course. For don't they know, absolutely damned know, what's right and what's wrong? And isn't their damned city the richest maybe in the world, which proves all men should obey their humble advice? Shit!"

The innkeeper, red as the handkerchief around his neck, stamped back inside.

It was summer, and the weather was pleasant. Peirol tried to keep from rushing on, eager to be at the end of his long quest, if Restormel indeed held the Empire Stone. He had no idea how to look for it once he reached Restormel, hoped for an advising dream from Abbas. But none came.

In the only dream he remembered, he was a very tiny being in a huge, empty room. Overhead was a great diamond that reflected rays of many colors, and when the rays struck around him, they seared the ground like fire. Peirol woke, sweating, legs moving as his body still tried to evade those killing beams of light.

But now the phrase "Brave heroes, who journey out" came without irony.

Peirol traded in two more cities, feeling his keenness return, driving harder bargains. He was infinitely grateful for Abbas's language spell; it gave him not only familiarity with the languages he encountered but the ability to sense irony and deceit.

All of Aulard's gems were now gone, replaced

with gold or jewels with equally dark traditions. He spent some of that gold for a brace of handsome pistols, each with a bore he could fit two fingers down. He also bought holsters, powder, powder flask, balls, molds, and lead ingots to cast new bullets from. He remembered what he'd told Abbas so long ago in Sennen about guns, wondered if things would have been better if he'd taken the ones he offered, decided not.

The roads were better now, and there were maps, good maps, so he could follow his progress to Restormel exactly. He encountered several Brown Men on his journey.

Once a company of soldiers, with three Men of Lysyth in the center, rode past, commandeering the road from shoulder to shoulder. A cart was slow to move aside, and a soldier's whip sang, snapping across the carthorse's withers. He neighed in panic and reared, overturning the cart into the ditch. The soldiers laughed, but the Brown Men kept sober expressions, as if only slightly attuned to this earth, vast spiritual matters filling their mind.

Another day, Peirol rode up on two Brown Men afoot. They were younger than Peirol. One turned, wordlessly held out his beggar's bowl as Peirol rode past. He was about to ignore it when he saw the expression on the man's face. It was not pleading, but demanding his due. Peirol found coppers in his purse, dropped them in the bowl, received a curt nod of acknowledgment.

If the Empire Stone was in Restormel, and if it gave riches, power, who would have possession of the gem? The child-king and his retinue, whoever they were? Or, as likely, the Brown Men, if they had as much power as the innkeeper said.

When he stopped for a meal or for the night, he tried to lead the conversation around to these Men of Lysyth. Who or what was Lysyth? What did these men believe? What god or gods did they serve? No one knew.

Peirol sat happily in the corner of the huge tavern. It was large, suited for a greater city than the one he traded in. He let the laughter, the drunken cheers, the off-key singing wash over him, take away the silence and chill of the forests. Perhaps, he thought, when he returned to Sennen with, of course, the Empire Stone, and Abbas made him rich, he might open a tavern like this. It would never close, and there would always be laughter and musicians, and cheerful wenches like the one who served him. He'd have low prices, brew the best beer, and there'd always be a roast on a spit. If the women wanted to make their own arrangements with the customers, it'd be none of his affair.

It was a pity, Peirol thought, swirling brandy around his mouth, thinking of the huge feather bed upstairs he'd shortly be wallowing in, sleeping alone with no desire for company, the window cracked a shade so he could listen to the hammering rain outside, a pity indeed that Kima was of the upper classes. She'd probably think such an investment stupid, and certainly never go into such a raucous dive herself. Ah well, Peirol thought, just a bit drunkenly, she might learn to like such a place. Or . . . or not.

Across from him, in a snug like his own, one of

the Brown Men was gravely surveying the room as if it was in his charge. A tiny glass of wine sat in front of him.

Peirol waved to his server, who bustled over, and he gave instructions. She looked at him oddly, but took a balloon glass of the inn's finest brandy to the Man of Lysyth. He looked surprised, then frowned. Peirol lifted his glass in a toast. The Brown One spoke to the woman. She bowed, brought the glass on its tray to Peirol, scowling.

"The August One," and there was a hiss in her voice, "said . . . well, do you want me to tell you what he said?"

"I do."

"He said, and I'm giving his words exactly, 'Tell that child-man over there his gold could be better spent on alms for the destitute, rather than numb-wit for this poor vessel.'"

"Well, take that brandy back and tell the son of a bitch to shove it up—never mind. I'll drink it," Peirol said.

"Guess that's your first turn with them," the woman said. "They're all snotty bastards. And they do need something up their—up theirs. Like a thorn-bush."

Peirol gritted teeth, took out silver coins, went to the poorbox, ostentatiously dropped them in. He went back to his seat, smiled at the Man of Lysyth, lifted his glass, refusing to let the smug pisshead ruin his evening. The man looked through him as if Peirol were invisible.

*　　*　　*

Peirol heard an odd tale from a jeweler: farther to the south, away from the road to Restormel, were vast diamond fields, recently discovered, well worth a visit. The jeweler said the miners were "unusual," and that the dwarf might be "interested in their customs." A bit wary, Peirol asked if they happened to be cannibals.

"No, nothing dangerous," the jeweler said. "Just . . . well, interesting."

Peirol could use some uncut gems when he reached Restormel, especially ones bought cheaply at a minehead. As for those interesting customs, he'd already met many people with odd usages, and thus far his hide was intact, his bones ungnawed. He inquired of other gem merchants, to make sure the jeweler hadn't been playing a joke, before turning south into growing wilderness. There were small clusters of huts here and there, barely enough to be called villages. All knew of the miners; some even had some gems they wanted to sell. But these were generally just polished, and the few crude attempts at cutting had ruined the stones' value, and so he politely passed, continued on.

Two days later, he came to the first mine. He heard it before he saw it, a large pit dug in a cleared field against the side of a hill. The pit was filled with men and women, all digging, all chanting aloud. After a while, he figured out they were praying. He saw a man resting to one side, rode to him, was informed about what was going on.

"Why the praying, admirable though it is?"

"If we pray loudly enough," the man said, "the gods will place the diamonds in our workings. But if we're not holy enough, not dedicated enough . . ." He pointed, and Peirol noted half a dozen abandoned sites around him.

"You choose the area by prayer?"

"By prayer of our priests, but mostly by the supplications of our workers."

"Prayer is everything? You don't consider where you found diamonds before and look for a similar site?"

"That would be sacrilegious," the man said. "Besides, the land is rich with these stones the men of the cities go mad for. Why should we question how the gods choose to guide us to riches?"

Peirol thanked the man, tapped his horse's neck with the reins, rode on.

Two days later, he rode out of thick bamboo jungle into cleared land, and into chaos. There was a village, larger than the ones he'd passed through. Its inhabitants were on the road, shouting "disbeliever," "heathen," "blasphemer" at a Man of Lysyth. He was young—not much more than twenty—good-looking in an aristocratic way, in spite of his shaven head, and fairly well battered.

The man shouted back that he was but a messenger of the Invisible Ones, the Real Gods, trying to save them from damnation and destruction. A beefy woman knocked him to his knees. Someone noticed Peirol and cried out. Peasants saw the dwarf, and there were cries of wonderment.

An old woman tottered out of the throng. "Who are you? Are you mortal?"

"Surely," Peirol said. "Do you think the gods

would choose someone of my deformity as their messenger?"

"They would," someone shouted. "For didn't Rivak come among us as a giant? Or Tuln work her greatest miracles as one without arms or legs? And the great Cohl came as a leper."

There was a rumble of agreement. A few people made obeisance to Peirol.

"Thank you," Peirol said politely. "But I assure you I'm no more than me. Might I ask what this Man of Lysyth did to offend?"

"He is a blasphemer," the old woman said. "For which crime, he must be punished."

"And that punishment shall be of the worst," a woman said gleefully. "He shall be tied to that stake you see over there, and his skin slowly stripped from his body. Our witch has placed a spell so he cannot lose consciousness, nor die until she wills it. While he hangs, bleeding, his toes and fingers shall be cut off. We'll slice away his genitals, boil them in front of him, make him eat them. Then we shall continue his dismemberment, a joint at a time, as we butcher our lambs when our gods tell us it is time for the sacrifice.

"His eyes will be burned out, his tongue cut away, sticks driven into his ears until he's no more than a red-bleeding egg. Then we shall make a cut into his spine, drain out and drink the fluid that drips, and then, perhaps, he'll be allowed to die."

Peirol tried to keep from making a face. "That seems fairly thorough," he said mildly. "I suppose you don't have many blasphemers in these parts. I assume this death means that he's being sacrificed to your gods."

"Of course," the old woman said indignantly. "Do you think we're barbarians?"

"Certainly not," Peirol said. "And I assume the sacrifice has consented to what you are going to do?"

There was confusion.

"Consent?" the old woman said. "The man'd be a fool to agree to a death like that."

"Not where I come from," Peirol said. "Our priests inflict deaths worse than that, but because of the great glory, we never lack for volunteers."

The villagers looked at each other in amazement.

"You must come from a very holy place, dwarf."

"So it is said," Peirol said, trying to look pious. "But I would not take on such airs of gods-granted holiness, for I know each day must be spent working hard for greater enlightenment, rather than arrogantly wallowing in what one thinks salvation."

"You yourself are a priest?"

"No," Peirol said. "A mere merchant. But I've always had an interest in religious matters. Tell me this. Might I ask the sacrifice a few questions, to enlighten myself before the ceremony begins?"

"Not really a ceremony," someone grumbled. "We're just killing the brown bastard. Giving him to the gods is the salt on the roast."

"Go ahead," someone else said. "But make it quick. It's midday, and we want him dead before midnight."

"Tell me, Man of Lysyth," Peirol asked. "What sin, in your eyes, did you commit?"

"None," the man said, struggling to his feet. "I

serve the Invisible Gods, without Shape or Form, who must be worshiped, or the world will be destroyed and all in it cast into eternal fires. That is why I, and men like me, go forth into desolation, to carry the Word, and do what we can to help the benighted."

"I'll benighted you," a heavyset man snarled, about to strike the Brown One. Peirol held up his hand.

"Do you have a name?"

"I do," the man said. "Perhaps, if you go to Restormel, you might go to the Great Temple, and tell them Ossetia, son of the High Priest Warleggen and the Lady Broda, grandson of the Supreme Priest Kaitbai, died in the faith, doing his duty."

"You sound noble."

"My family has been exalted in service to the gods, it is true."

Peirol considered Ossetia thoughtfully. "Forgive me, you people. For my question is in ignorance, not meant to insult nor injure. Would you consider accepting a ransom for this Ossetia, good red gold, perhaps, or something equally valuable, in exchange for his life?"

There were shouts of no, yes, possibly, overridden by Ossetia's lusty bellow: "No! That would be cowardice, and no Man of Lysyth dies a coward!"

"Ossetia, be silent," Peirol said. He looked at the old woman. "In the confusion, I couldn't make out what the answer to my question would be."

"In the past," the woman said reluctantly, "we *have* ransomed those who've only slightly offended against our customs, since we're a truly tolerant people. But I don't see how we could ransom this one, since all others that we have allowed to live and go their way have repented, and this man is firm in his sin."

"In my righteousness," Ossetia shouted.

"Hmm," Peirol said, stroking his chin, pretending great gravity. "Considering the holiness of you villagers, I should not dissemble further. I am, as are you all, a great enemy of the Men in Brown. They have despoiled all that I've come on in my travels, and as a man who studies the gods, I look at their arrogance without affection. When I saw you tormenting this one, my heart leapt within me, although I must say, if he were in my hands, he would think the death you propose to be quite gentle."

"You can do worse?" someone asked, incredulously.

"I can do worse," Peirol said firmly. "For as that man there correctly saw, I have some magical talents, although little compared to the wizards in my homeland, which is why I wander as a merchant. I can, for instance, start a fire burning inside a man's bones, slowly consuming him, day after day, as he writhes in agony. Like your witch, I also know spells forbidding death.

"That is but one death that occurs. Another might be to summon demons, who'll use him as men use women, save with barbed genitals that rip and tear, instead of giving pleasure. Such a man, given to those demons, will die beyond all gods, so whatever the Men of Lysyth think comes after death will not be allowed. Instead, the demons will have his soul to use, day after day, year after year, until the end of time."

The peasants were silent, shaken. Ossetia glared defiantly.

"But these ideas," Peirol said slowly, "pleased me not, for my faith insists on justice. It is you men and women who've trapped this creature of the depths, and if you are not given the pleasure of killing him, you still should reap benefits, which is why I asked about ransom. Let me suggest something. I am a merchant, a trader, as I said. I came to buy the stones you bring from the ground. But I could provide you with a greater gift, if you would give me this Ossetia as a slave for a moment of time, then I shall kill him as no man has ever died before."

"What are you offering?" a young man asked.

"I have learned, when you seek these gemstones, the manner of your search. I could teach you a prayer that would prevent you from wasting time on barren fields that offer only blisters and pain, a prayer that would almost always take you directly to the great underground tubes where diamonds proliferate, if made with sufficient devotion and in the correct place and time."

"Wouldn't that offend the gods? Don't they send the diamonds to us when we've shown sufficient sincerity?" someone asked. "What say you, Abdi?"

A woman stepped out, not old, not young, but with the light of authority in her eyes. Peirol supposed her to be the village witch. She held her hands to the north and south, then turned, extended them once more, eyes closed. She opened her eyes, lowered her hands.

"I see no reason," she said in a calm contralto, "for the gods to object. They have never found it ill that we use shovels to dig, instead of our bare hands, for instance. And who knows at what time the gods choose to seed the fields for us? Certainly not I."

"Dwarf, would you be willing," the old woman who'd spoken to him first said cannily, "to linger in our village while we learn this prayer, and make sure it works? For if it does not, we would have to consider you a blasphemer like this wretch, and give you a similar doom."

"I'll teach you the prayer," Peirol said, stomach sinking a little. "And I'll remain with you, giving you a chance to try it not once, but three times, for the gods don't always grant success on the first try."

"If it works, no shoveling our hearts out, starving, while other villages get rich," a man said softly.

"Our children won't ever be hungry," a woman breathed.

The old woman looked around. "For that great boon," she said, "we'll grant you the life of this Brown Man. *If* it works. If not . . ."

The witch Abdi was chosen to learn the secret prayer. By the time the choice was made, Peirol had written a page of gibberish to teach her. While she memorized it, Peirol rode around the countryside, making careful notes. He was heavily guarded by spear-carrying men, to make sure he didn't escape.

Ossetia did not have an easy time of it during those days. He was kept in a bamboo cage, where everyone who passed by was advised to spit on him or pelt him with offal. He was fed garbage and drenched with a bucket of water twice a day, for bathing and drinking both.

When Abdi had the prayer committed, Peirol told her to be ready an hour before dawn. The two walked a league away from the village, flanked by guards, until Peirol reached the area he'd chosen.

"The gods who grant us diamonds in my land love yellow over all other colors," he told her. "I should think that would hold true here, as well. You see this rocky waste has yellowish clay? That's pleasing to them. Now, you'll take a small trowel, which represents the digging your village will do, and dig a small trough for each foot, ankle-deep. This is to connect you with the great mother of us all, earth, where the diamonds will occur. If you have secured a blessing, you should find some blue or gray rocks in your diggings. If not, find another field of yellow, and try once more.

"Now, these men and I will go out of sight, and you repeat the prayer three times, loudly, to the heavens. Then you may summon diggers and begin work."

Peirol and his guards moved off. After a time, she came to him. "I achieved no enlightenment."

"Because you have not yet dug," he said.

Abdi told a man to call the villagers with their tools, water, and food for a day's work. "What sort of pit should we dig?" she asked.

"The same sort as you always have."

The men and women set to work. It wasn't that warm, but Peirol was sweating gently. But the sun hadn't climbed more than a finger-width before the first digger shouted in joy, ran to Abdi and Peirol. In her dirty hand she held a few unprepossessing dull, greasy pebbles.

"And there you have it," Peirol said. "You should never have doubted my prayer."

The villagers cheered. The old woman came to Peirol. "There is such a thing as luck," she said. "Would you chance lingering on to see if that prayer works a second time?"

"I promised three trials," Peirol said, and it was now his turn to pray, although he didn't know who he was praying to.

The second attempt yielded only some sorry stones, but diamonds they were. Peirol told them to try again, and this time the field was rich with diamonds. He said he was now interested in trading for those gems. The ecstatic villagers didn't bargain, but took whatever he offered in silver and gold. His saddlebags laden with uncut gems, Peirol made ready to leave.

"I thank the gods for your coming," Abdi said. "And for this secret prayer, and for the conditions for its use." She eyed him thoughtfully. "I, of course, would be stoned by my own people if I wondered what would happen if I went to a field of yellow clay, dug until I made sure bluish stone was under my feet, and then said "habble, habble, habble, habble" or other nonsense before I dug."

"A deserving fate for being an unbeliever," Peirol said, hiding a smile.

"For what you brought us, regardless of what surrounds it, Peirol of the Moorlands, take your slave and go."

Peirol had Ossetia bound, seated on his packhorse, and they rode away, the villagers cheering. An hour later the priest spoke.

"Know, demon, you'll have no joy from the screams of your slave, for I know I can withstand the most terrible torture without giving up my faith or my strength."

"I'm glad you're so sure of that," Peirol said. "And, by the way, you can leave off this slave nonsense. I free you, I free you, I free you, or whatever nonsense it takes in this land to manumit a fool." Ossetia goggled. "We'll stop at the next river," Peirol continued, "and you can wash your filth off and clean your robes. I prefer not to travel to Restormel with someone as smelly as you.

"And by the way, the next city we come to, I'll loan you the money for new robes, or whatever you want to wear, which you'll repay me for when we reach Restormel, just as you'll give me gold for what I spend on your meals and lodgings. Perhaps magicians can provide such for free. But we poor traders have to keep our books balanced."

As they rode north, then turned east, Peirol welcomed Ossetia's questions, at least those that encouraged him to think a certain way about Peirol: Of course he wasn't a magician, nor even a man particularly gifted by the gods. He felt that was a matter for those properly called, and it was but his lot to serve. Well, he was a bit of a nobleman, actually the second son, which was why he was traveling, rather than tending to the family estates. No, being a merchant, at least a merchant dealing with certain items, such as gold or gems, wasn't regarded as disgraceful in his land.

Why was he journeying to Restormel? First, of course, to see its marvels, marvels long fabled in Peirol's homeland. He hoped while he was there to show the nobility of the city some of the interesting things he'd constructed with gems and precious metals.

How long did he plan to stay? Who could tell? If he was welcome, if the city fathers felt he was adding to the greatness of the city, who knew? A year, forever. Certainly no longer than Restormel wanted him around.

In turn, he found out much about Restormel and the Order of Lysyth. Lysyth was the name of a great battle, fought centuries ago, but Ossetia knew, or admitted knowing, little about it. Once Peirol asked, as casually as he could, about something he'd heard called the Emperor Stone, or something like that.

Ossetia's lips went thin. "Talk of something such as that is forbidden, for the Men of Lysyth have no time to truck in childish legends."

Peirol wanted to caper wildly. He was getting very close.

They reached the straits, and took passage on a plush ferry to the great island across. There were two galleys escorting it. Ossetia said the Sarissans had not only raided this far east but, rumor had it, attacked and conquered lands beyond Restormel. Peirol noted the galleys and their sweating slaves, shuddered, and suggested they find something to eat.

Two days later, the ferry sailed into Restormel.

SEVENTEEN

✳

Of Religious Caterpillars
and Poor Rich

Restormel sat a league upriver from the wide mouth of the Sugat River, on the north bank's steep and easily defended hills. Here the river widened into a tidal pool, which over the centuries, as Restormel grew, had been dredged into an admirable harbor, nestled away from pirates and winter storms. As time passed, wizardry had compacted and solidified the marshy southern shores, and skyscraping tenements, some as high as eight stories, were built. Most of Restormel's poor lived there.

Restormel ruled the huge island it sat on, and was huge, more than twice as big as Sennen, its population estimated at two, three, no, four million. Peirol doubted if even the Sarissans, with all their strength, could invade the city. The mostly wooden houses, three or more stories, leaned together for support. The streets below, some narrow enough for a man to touch either side with his outstretched hands, twisted like writhing snakes. This was deliberate, Ossetia told Peirol: "Back when men were superstitious, they built like this to keep demons from being able to run amok through the streets, for all know that demons cannot easily turn."

"I wonder how *that* was determined," Peirol said. "Did a succession of wizards evoke evil spirits and test them until one magician escaped by dashing into a maze?"

Ossetia, who Peirol had already decided had little humor, looked at him strangely.

There was only a scattering of open squares in Restormel, since land was at a premium, but the waterfront was open, paved, and had bandstands, speakers' podiums, stone planters, and statues of fabulous beings and heroes for the citizens to stroll past.

The first thing to strike Peirol as the ferry closed on Restormel were the number of spires: each a temple, Ossetia told him. The gods of Restormel may have been invisible, but that didn't mean they were in short supply. Ossetia said there was no greater reward for a citizen than to build a temple or to donate a house, the larger the better, to the gods.

"And there," Ossetia said proudly, "is the very heart of my order."

He pointed to a large, light brown octagonal tower high above the other pinnacles of Restormel.

"Does it commemorate anything special?" Peirol asked politely.

"Our great victory at Lysyth, where we earned our name," Ossetia said.

"Doesn't appear to be very big," Peirol said. "Do you meet there in rotation, or are there great cata-combs underground, where you go to work your magic?"

"I assume you jest," Ossetia said without a smile. "The tower is just a . . . a symbol, no more. We have palaces, retreats scattered throughout Restormel."

Peirol wondered why the momentary hesitation before Ossetia chose the word "symbol," but shrugged it away, looking to the other side of the hillcrest, at the royal palace, its huge stone walls looming over the city. Here, Ossetia told Peirol, was the home of the Dowager Custodian and her royal charge.

The ferry tied up, and its gangplanks dropped. Traders hurried off, travelers looked for kin or friends, stevedores began unloading cargo. One of the escort galleys had sped to Restormel during the last night, carrying messages of arrival, and so Ossetia was look-ing for someone. An old, bearded man beside a small, somewhat battered carriage waved frantically. The monk burst into tears and fell into the man's arms, re-covering enough to introduce him as Turmaf, his fam-ily's head servant and oldest-serving retainer. Ossetia's family was waiting impatiently, Turmaf said, and there was a great feast laid, so they must come at once.

Their baggage was loaded into the carriage, horses tied behind, and they made their way up steep cobbled streets through the city. The second thing to strike Peirol about Restormel was the number of religious sorts. He saw robes of white, red, green, black, the more familiar brown of the Men of Lysyth, others. Some were parading, some chanting, some praying, others singing.

"We're proud," Ossetia said, "to serve all of the Invisible Ones who choose to reveal themselves, with new ones appearing regularly to lucky prophets. There's an example," and he pointed to a dozen men wearing red striped robes, swinging incense burners and singing a rather pleasant song. "I know not who they serve, for instance, since I didn't see any robes like theirs when I set forth on my mission half a year ago."

"What prevents," Peirol said, thinking of Makonnen, "a false prophet, seeking only personal gain, from claiming he's been enlightened by the great god Hoola-Hoola who wants all to serve him?"

"That," Ossetia said, his lips pursed, "is one of my order's responsibilities. For if all of the Invisible Gods are equal, as we preach, some are given powers greater than others. The god I serve, who must be nameless except to initiates, has granted us the powers and right to examine these claimants, using magic, our intellects, and if necessary, physical means."

Nice deities, Peirol thought. Like most. And their disciples seem even nicer. But he didn't voice his thoughts. Nor, as they crossed a square, and he counted four different processions going in as many directions, did he say the winding columns reminded him of nothing so much as industrious caterpillars.

* * *

They were forced aside into a tiny square as half a dozen armed horsemen cleared the way for an elaborate carriage almost too big for the street. There was a postilion with a trumpet on the lead horse, four footmen on the carriage's boards, and two drivers. The carriage, all gold leaf and red enamel, slowed, and the postilion blatted with the trumpet to clear the way of whatever blocked their passage.

Peirol wondered who was the high dignitary. Peering into the window of the carriage, he saw a very young, dark-haired woman, wearing a black lace gown that would've done a lover's bedroom proud. She eyed him interestedly, allowed a smile to come, and leaned slightly forward so her deep cut dress gave away as much as possible. She saw Ossetia, and her haughty manner broke with a giggle. "Ossetia, my love! You're back!"

Ossetia bowed, didn't answer.

"I *must* visit you," she said, as the carriage moved slowly past, "for I'm bored and without adventure these days. Perhaps hearing yours will content me. And I *must* meet your friend, who looks very . . . interesting." And the carriage was gone.

"Who was that?" Peirol asked.

"A vampire," Ossetia said fiercely.

"Out abroad in daylight? Your vampires are a hardier breed than the bloodsuckers of our legend. Prettier, too."

"I didn't mean that literally," Ossetia snarled. "Yes, maybe I did. That's Sereng, who should be Baroness Sereng by now, since she was betrothed to Baron Agar of Sancreed when I left Restormel. She's a year older than I am, but we were playmates. When she got older she played another game with some of my friends, sucked away what she wanted, and left them brokenhearted. I suppose I was lucky, having the Invisible Gods to guide me, so I was no more than tempted. I didn't think the baron would keep her from her old tricks. Bored and without adventure indeed!"

Peirol somehow doubted Ossetia had been only momentarily tempted, considering the vehemence of his words. "I assume her husband is rich, gouty, and old," Peirol said. "No doubt jealous and easily cuckolded."

"What makes you think that?" Ossetia said in an irritated voice. "In fact, he would be about thirty, and was considered one of the best officers in our army. Rides out every morning and is obsessed with sports, the harder the better. Although he did impress me as the possessive sort."

"Ah well," Peirol said. "There goes the ballad I was thinking of. Obviously they're wealthy."

"Certainly," Ossetia said. "The baron is from one of the richest families, very close to the Dowager Custodian."

"I would definitely like to meet Sereng," Peirol said.

"Why? Aren't you listening, dwarf? She must not have seen all of you, for I know what she likes, and how partial she is to athletes and warriors."

Rather than shaven monks, Peirol thought.

"Careful," he said mildly. "I have both a name and a title, and I'm not fond of being considered a nameless freak. Don't get arrogant now that we're in your world. Remember where you were, in a bamboo cage with garbage, and where I was, not many days gone."

Ossetia glared, then looked down. "You're right," he said, forcing humility. "That's one of my greatest sins, pride, speaking from my station, whether it's warranted or not, and I pray hourly that I shall learn not to give in to conceit but remember my place before the gods." But the grandson of the Supreme Priest Kaitbai didn't sound as though he really meant it.

"I still would like to meet this Baroness Sereng," Peirol said, remembering the glitter of rings on her fingers, a diamond necklace, bracelets, and earrings. "We might find we have much in common."

Ossetia snorted, looked pointedly out of the carriage.

The carriage entered the gates of High Priest Warleggen and Lady Broda's grounds about four leagues beyond Restormel, following a dirt road curving through a league of freshly harvested orange trees, through the house gardens, and past sprawling outbuildings toward a single-story mansion, painted white, surrounded with open porches.

"How much farther do your parents' possessions extend?"

"This estate," Ossetia said, carefully not emphasizing the word, "goes on for another two leagues to the north, another two leagues inland. We have other lands farther from the city, all devoted to agriculture."

They pulled into the great house's drive, and a swarm of cheering, crying servants ran to meet them. All seemed honestly glad to see Ossetia, which lifted him a bit in Peirol's estimation. They were led into the house, a huge, open, high-ceilinged mansion built of various hand-fitted woods. Peirol noticed the tile floor was cracked in some places, and that paint was peeling a bit here and there. Peirol began to develop what he hoped Ossetia's parents might find an interesting proposition.

The meal was sumptuous, seven courses, with two servants hovering behind each diner. Besides Ossetia's father and mother, there were two teenage brothers and one sister, about nine. Ossetia's parents were a study in contrast. Lady Broda was huge, little short of a giantess, and the High Priest Warleggen was a thin, emaciated mite, no more than a foot taller than Peirol. He ate as if he had an all-consuming fire inside, but Lady Broda only picked at each course before nodding to a servant to remove the plate.

After dinner, all adjourned to a wide porch, and sweet wines and fruits were served. Ossetia's siblings were fairly dancing with impatience, and at last Warleggen asked about Ossetia's doings across the straits, as casually as if he were inquiring about a visit to a nearby town.

Ossetia must have been trained by his order to report clearly and concisely, as unemotionally as if his preachings, rejections, conversions, and dangers had happened to someone else. Of course, the perspective was how terrible the unbelievers were, rather than the alternate explanation that they had disliked someone meddling in their private spiritual matters. At last Ossetia reached the point of his capture and maltreatment in the diamond miners' village.

"I knew I was doomed," he said. "And then the gods sent this man, Peirol of the Moorlands, to rescue me." He went on to accurately give most of the details of what Peirol had done, and didn't attempt to laud his own role. He told them how Peirol had paid all his expenses after they escaped the village, and Ossetia considered himself in vast debt to Peirol.

"Of course," Warleggen said, "we'll repay you."

Lady Broda flickered, as if worried about what that would do to the family accounts.

"I thank you," Peirol said. "Certainly I jested with your son about the great interest I would charge him once I returned him to the bosom of his family. However, while I might have wanted repayment—of the actual debt only, of course—I've reconsidered the matter."

"Oh?" Warleggen's voice was a bit suspicious.

"Let me word it as precisely as I can. I'm a newcomer to Restormel, and wish to have as much goodwill as any outsider can expect, not only among people but with the gods who rule this land."

"The Invisible Gods rule *all* lands," Ossetia said firmly. "This is the truth."

"My apologies for misspeaking," Peirol said. "You must be right, or we would all be punished for heresy. So, honoring these Invisible Gods, I would like whatever sums I spent freeing your son to be considered a sacrifice from a newcomer, who hopes to live in their graces. If that's permissible?"

Ossetia looked at his parents. Warleggen sat in silence, thinking. "Yes," he said. "Yes, I think that might be acceptable. And I thank you both personally and as a priest in the Order of Lysyth."

"But it certainly leaves us still in your debt," Lady Broda said.

"That has been repaid by meeting you, and by the friendship, I hope, of your son," Peirol said. "Although there is a small matter you might help me with. I am a merchant, as you know. Perhaps less a merchant than an artist, since trading permits me to indulge my interest in rare stones. I'm aware Restormel thinks trading is never a proper pastime for nobility, even for such a lesser lord as myself, but I would think this great city wouldn't be upset if an outsider practices his own customs, without infringing on those of his hosts."

"Your reasoning is correct," Warleggen said. "Although I will have to say the fact that you do indulge in trade would most likely keep you from being presented directly to King Proclus, the Dowager Custodian Jeritza, or to the Inner Council of my own Order of Lysyth. Some might call those people overly traditional, others might even consider their behavior a bit arrogant.

"I am merely stating facts, Peirol of the Moorlands, and hope you do not take offense. Those, however, are the only limitations I can think of, and see no reason, in time, assuming you continue to behave as nobly as you have thus far, you might not even be presented in open court."

Peirol stood, bowed. "I would, of course, be deeply honored by that." He resumed his seat. "To continue with my request. I assume noblemen and women of Restormel are like others I've met, and own jewelry."

"Of course," Lady Broda said. "As do most of the Men of Lysyth, we are human."

"Such a display, properly made, gives glory to the Invisible Gods," Warleggen said, and Ossetia nodded agreement.

"I would propose," Peirol said, "to establish a shop, in the proper location, where I could repair jewelry, or recut and reset gems that are no longer in style or favor. I also brought a fair number of unset gems with me, which I will use to create my own unique designs. I might also consider making outright purchases of gems that are no longer wanted. However, I would hardly be so vulgar as to advertise my services, so I must depend on my merits being heralded by satisfied customers.

"If the Invisible Gods are good, I would like to make repayment to them. But I certainly wouldn't want to make vulgar sacrifices of bullocks and grain, such as I've seen peasants make to their gods, but rather more discreet offerings. The problem, as I see it, is how I might make such offerings, say a tenth of my profits, and be sure they don't end up in the wrong hands or misspent."

"The solution's easy," Ossetia said eagerly. "Just pass it to the Men of Lysyth."

"That *is* one way," Peirol said. "But that seems so . . . impersonal."

Lady Broda leaned forward. "Son, would you mind fetching me a glass of the charged water from our kitchen? This wine doesn't suit my palate at the moment."

"Of course, Mother," Ossetia said. Broda waited until he was out of the room.

"Go on," she said, voice as sharp as any tradesman.

"Perhaps," Peirol said, "a way that would solve my problems is to hand these donations to you, Warleggen, since you are a high priest, to handle their dissemination."

Warleggen frowned and started to say something, but Lady Broda spoke first. "That is, indeed, a good idea. Fifteen percent was the sum you mentioned, I believe?"

"Such could easily be the amount," Peirol said. He lifted his glass in a toast. "Thank you, my lady. And thank you, Warleggen, as well. You have not only treated a stranger in a wonderful manner but have solved what few problems I have."

And so Peirol's scheme, hatched when he saw the shaven-headed man struggling with a mob, came to fruition, and the Warleggen family became his agents in Restormel.

Peirol rented a tiny shop with an upstairs apartment on one of the streets leading up from Restormel's waterfront, a street lined with expensive dressmakers, armorers, furniture makers, and other artisans catering to the rich. Most importantly, a rear window opened on an alley not connected to the street. Peirol bought rope and small round balks of lumber and built a rope ladder, which he hid under his bed. He replaced the tools he'd lost, adding a lathe sorcerously driven that required its spell to be recast every seventh day, brought in showcases and carpets, and was ready for business.

It was not long in coming. Customers came, considered his works, bought, and sold. Peirol was soon busy enough to hire a clerk, who he trained to be as loftily arrogant as he was, as the master jeweler Rozan had trained him to behave around the rich. There were other jewelers in Restormel, of course. But none seemed to have the proper obsequity, stock, skills, or knowledge. He cordially ignored these competitors, and they reciprocated.

Peirol chafed a bit, wanting to ask about the Empire Stone, but repressed his impatience. Two Times passed. He kept to himself, finding a quiet tavern to drink in, three or four discreet restaurants. He made no friends, sought none, ensured he made the "sacrifice" promptly to Ossetia's parents. Ossetia came by every now and again, and they had dinner. Some women and a few men suggested they would be interested in visiting Peirol's bedchamber, but he made light of the offers.

Restormel felt like a trap waiting to spring on an unwary dwarf, who could well stand to discipline his vices for a time anyway.

He recognized the woman when she entered, went to greet her, bowing low. "Baroness Sereng," he said. "You honor me deeply."

"The monk Ossetia told me where your shop was. . . . Oh! You're a—"

"A dwarf, Baroness."

"I didn't notice when you were in the carriage, you were sitting down, and I'm—well . . ." Her words stopped in confusion.

"And you're very beautiful," Peirol said smoothly. Evidently Ossetia had been right: Sereng was attracted to the athletic type, and Peirol's stumpy legs had just ruined his attractiveness. She *was* beautiful, hair curled, falling below her shoulders. She wore a red velvet dress, possibly cut lower than the gown she'd worn before, with white lace ruffles around the front.

"I, well, I thank you," she said, trying to recover. "I, uh, came here because I have this brooch whose clasp has broken, and no one seems able to fix it without possibly damaging the center stone."

"May I see it? Thank you." He picked up a glass, examined the bauble. The clasp had been snapped quite recently—broken metal gleamed. An excellent excuse for going to a jeweler that a woman might show her husband. "There won't be any problem. I'll do the work myself, right now, if you care to wait."

"No, no, I'll come back."

"I'm afraid I can't let you leave without showing you the gems I have brought from afar, Baroness. It's the least toll you could pay."

"Well . . . all right. I have a few minutes."

Peirol showed her jewels, brightly chatting as he did, hinting of hilarious scandals he'd been told but of course could never repeat, telling a few stories of his travels, letting her talk about her friends. She said, mournfully, that her husband thought she spent too much on fripperies, which was the reason she couldn't buy any of Peirol's wares. Peirol told her men are like that, not understanding what is important but always ready to buy a new sword or gun or horse.

She grew friendlier, and Peirol fixed the brooch.

"One favor you might allow," he said, taking out a bracelet she'd particularly admired. "In my own land, I frequently make use of a model—I don't think that's the correct word, but I know no other. By model I mean a woman who must be not only beautiful but vivacious, witty, belonging to the highest levels of society, who goes to balls and other events. I give, or rather loan, this model a piece of jewelry. A different one every Time, or more often, if she goes out frequently. She wears my wares to parties, to feasts, and her friends admire them, hopefully ask where they can be obtained.

"If my model wishes to purchase a piece she's been loaned, I allow her to buy them at my cost, no more. And since I like to think I'm a generous man, when something wonderful happens to me, I make sure the woman who made it happen is rewarded as well."

"One's husband would never know," she breathed.

"Why would a husband talk to a dwarf?"

"I don't think of you, Peirol," Sereng said, "as being a dwarf at all anymore."

Peirol bowed, clasped the bracelet on her wrist, was rewarded with a kiss on the cheek. Sereng bounded out into the autumn sunlight, letting the rays reflect through the gems, laughing like a small girl. A charming woman, Peirol thought. And, if Ossetia was right, as dangerous as a serpent.

But still . . .

* * *

Two men in brown asked the clerk for Peirol the dwarf. Peirol asked how he could be of service.

"I am named Damyan, and understand you have been seeking a magician," one said. "We are of the Order of Lysyth, protectors of Restormel, and are naturally curious why a stranger needs wizardry, and must ensure it is for the good of all."

"Might I ask," Peirol said, "how you heard of my quest? Although I freely admit to the truth of it."

"The Men of Lysyth never reveal their sources."

"I see. You said magic used must be for the good of Restormel. My plans can be justly described in that way," Peirol said, and explained he needed a thaumaturge to help with his jewel designs, told them how he'd put magical fire into the heart of gems, used magic to enhance the beauty of his stones in other ways.

"Hence your noble men and women appear even greater, more glorious, and the name of Restormel is even more loudly praised, which must be considered all to the good," he finished.

"My first thought," Damyan said, "is that this idea of yours is perilously close to unseemliness." The other man nodded thoughtfully.

"Perhaps I misstate myself," Peirol said. "As I'm sure you're aware, I've been favored by High Priest Warleggen, and when I consulted him about the idea, he didn't see any problems. However, let me offer a specific example of what my craftsmanship and a Restormel wizard might do for the Men of Lysyth."

"Are you suggesting a bribe?"

"Certainly not," Peirol said indignantly. "Merely to clarify what my intent is. Of course it's blasphemous to suggest anyone make an image of the Invisible Gods here—unlike some of the heathenous nations I've passed through—which is admirably sophisticated. But wouldn't it be possible to suggest the glory of these beings by, say, taking crystal, or even a large stone, if one were presented to me? Cut it properly, so it gathers the light. Then put a bit of magic within and let the fires burst forth, as if from nowhere.

"Hang this in a temple, and it would be glorious, even more so than glass stained in brilliant colors, such as I've seen in your tabernacles. If *I* meditated on such an object, I think I would become closer to the gods I worship, hence more religious, and Restormel would be glorified. That's but an example of what I propose."

Damyan considered. "If High Priest Warleggen approves—and your idea brings other thoughts to me—"

"Which," Peirol interrupted, "I'd be pleased to hear if you choose to share them, and hopefully we could arrange for such a project to become financially possible."

"No," the monk said, "no, I was wrong in thinking you capable of evil, as was the erring soul who mentioned you to us. There's no stink of heresy or of dangerous matters here. Go your way, Peirol, and I hope you succeed, for the idea of having such a fiery symbol in one of our order's churches, or in a cloister, sounds most wonderful."

Peirol escorted them out, came back, wiping his forehead. "Take the store," he told the clerk.

"Yes, sir. Might I ask where you're going?"

"To that tavern that serves triple-distilled brandy, to meditate on which bastard jeweler might've tried to doom me."

He spent time with Ossetia, found out more about the Men of Lysyth. He asked what temporal authority they had, beyond determining real from false god-discoverers. Ossetia told him that their power was almost total, with their ability to know what was right for Restormel and their authority to detect and punish those who would do it harm.

"I assume there are provisions for denouncing an evil man or woman to the order?"

"Certainly."

"Then the miscreant is taken in hand by your order," Peirol said, "and brought to trial?"

"After he's questioned, and confesses."

"What means are used to gain such a confession?"

"I know little of that, being hardly more than a novice in the ways of Lysyth. There are special members who dedicate their lives to uncovering the truth, and I know they use prayer, contemplation, and, in the most extreme cases, physical force."

"Torture?"

Ossetia nodded reluctantly.

"I assume the informer is rewarded?"

"Yes, with a share of the guilty one's goods, after he's punished by the fire, or in minor cases with a term of imprisonment. His property, by the way, is always seized, and added to the glory of Lysyth and Restormel."

"Ah," Peirol said. "What's to prevent false accusation from, say, jealousy?"

"If the accused survives our ... investigation without making a confession and without further evidence," Ossetia said, "then he is in turn rewarded with the goods of his accuser. But that happens but seldom."

"I would expect so."

A few days later Peirol passed a small apothecary's shop and noted the door was sealed, with two ornately carved beams nailed into the door frame. Between them was a brown parchment:

✼

This Establishment

Has Been Seized

As the Law Orders

By the Men of Lysyth

Its Owner Has Been Tried

Condemned and Executed

And All His Works Are Forfeit

All Praise the Gods of Restormal

✼

He was the only one who stopped. All others hurried past, looking studiously elsewhere.

* * *

Peirol bought a small, very fast sailboat that could be crewed by one man. He also paid for sailing lessons, and spent an hour a day tacking back and forth in the tidal pool until it wouldn't be completely suicidal for him to use it. He carved a secret compartment in the back of a hatch, hid gold and gems there, and hired a man to sail it from Restormel east to a small fishing village known for its honesty. More gold went for dry provisions, casked water, and to have the boat dragged out of the water on rollers.

Peirol would rather have hidden a fast horse somewhere, but that would have left him across the straits from the way home. At least the boat, like the rope ladder, made him feel less trapped.

He also refilled his tiny knee-pouch with gems and strapped it on.

Baroness Sereng's friends and acquaintances flocked to his shop, and Peirol was hard-pressed to have a new creation to amaze them. He was forced to take another building in a poorer district, hire half a dozen artisans to do the cruder work, and even, most quietly, buy acceptable finished works from smaller craftsmen.

He'd listen to the gossip from these rich customers, laugh heartily or pretend pleasant shock, sympathize with their troubles rather than suggesting that being found wearing the same gown as another wasn't the end of the world, and offer solutions to their travails without ever sounding authoritarian. Baroness Sereng came in frequently, always alone, flirted, selected her latest piece of jewelry, and left in a short time. If she was a vampire, Peirol was unblooded, and slightly regretted it.

Peirol now knew a great deal about Restormel, about the real workings of its rulers: how the king had died in a fall from his palace's battlements, leaving no heir. A child, the king's distant cousin, had been chosen by the nobility of Restormel to take the throne. While he grew, the throne would be held by a Dowager Custodian. That child had died of a sudden sickness. Another, even more distant relative, only five years old—Proclus—had been recently selected. Until he reached his majority, all agreed it would be wise for the Dowager Jeritza to continue. Jeritza ruled Restormel and the island of the same name through the army and an array of officials, all owing their appointment to her court. The Men of Lysyth were thought to be the most honest of her advisers, stealing not as individuals but as an entire order. All this was very interesting, and Peirol wondered where the next heir-apparent would come from when Proclus had his own accident.

He noticed that when he brought up the Brown Men, very little was forthcoming. Even more interesting, when he mentioned the Empire Stone, he got one of three reactions: blankness; a very rapid change of subject; or, two or three times, a polite, low-voiced request to ask no more on that matter. The people who gave him the latter response were highly regarded at court, and one was the Baroness Sereng. He wasn't sure how he could pressure her into telling what she knew, or what she thought she knew.

* * *

The man could have posed for a sculpture as a great hero or a warrior god. He was almost twice Peirol's size, wearing soldier's garb in silk and the softest leathers, gold-trimmed. But his sword and dagger, even though they were lavishly engraved, looked well used.

"Dwarf," he growled, "I think you've been trying to seduce my wife."

EIGHTEEN

*

Of Marriages
and Secrets

Peirol could guess who the bruiser might be but was hardly stupid enough to fan the flame by greeting him by name. "I beg your pardon?"

"You damned well should! Trying to make love to my wife behind my back!"

Peirol heard a choking from his clerk, imagined the sexual position, tried to keep from laughing himself. "Might I ask your name, sir?"

"Don't be cute, you—you less than a man!"

"I rather resent that remark," Peirol said. "Such behavior can, in certain places, provoke a challenge. Please identify yourself, if you would. Only a blackguard or a scoundrel refuses such a request."

"I am, as you damned well know, Baron Agar."

"Under different circumstances, I would be pleased to meet you. Your wife, the noble baroness, has done great good helping me be part of Restormel's society."

"So you admit it?"

"I admit nothing, Baron Agar," Peirol said. "And I have a suggestion. Let us go, you and I, and find a wizard. Let us put up, say, five thousand gold coins each, and hire him to sniff my sins out. Surely a great city like Restormel has a magician capable of such snoopery. Let whichever one of us is wrong forfeit what he put up to a charity to be named by the other, less the wizard's fee.

"Further let whichever one of us is wrong placard Restormel, with an admission of that calumny, and if there's a further penalty due, according to the customs and laws of Restormel, let him surrender himself to the proper authorities for judgment. Is that not a better plan than you storming about, maligning a great and noble lady? I think it is you, rather than me, who is going behind someone's back."

Agar stepped back, anger visibly leaking away like water from a shattered vase. Peirol waited, while the idea ran through the baron. "You," Agar said weakly, "would be willing to—ah, but you're a magician yourself, capable of blocking another wizard."

"Don't be an ass," Peirol said. "If I were, wouldn't I have cast a spell when I first laid eyes on the lady, turning you, say, into a kitchen spider to be cast into the fire? Or perhaps a spell of withering, so your fine talents on the athletic field—and perhaps in the bedroom—disappear?"

Agar whitened. "No, I guess, I mean, yes, if you were a magician, you'd do something like that, I guess."

"But I'm not and I haven't," Peirol agreed. "Now, shall we go in search of a sorcerer?"

Agar hesitated. "Perhaps, well, no, I wouldn't. . . . I must think on this!" He stormed back out. Peirol watched him gallop away, four retainers at his heels, then went upstairs and made sure his rope ladder was ready.

The next day Sereng came in, her usual bright, flirtatious self. Evidently Agar had said nothing to her, or she was excellent at dissembling. As usual, she turned back a piece of jewelry, selected another, giggled, and said she'd see Peirol in a week, for there was a big masked ball approaching, and he might want her to show off something very special.

Peirol said, as a matter of fact, he would like for her to return the very next day; he had something in mind, but it was quite unusual and must have her approval before he went to the expense of fabricating it. Her eyes widened, and she quickly agreed.

After Sereng left, Peirol hurried out of a side entrance, jumped onto the saddle of the horse he'd tied there, and followed her, wearing a drab cloak with a cowl. Her carriage went through winding streets, away from the waterfront into a working district. It stopped in front of a large two-story stone building, which was a little shabby. Sereng got out and went inside, and the carriage left. Peirol tied his horse, started into the building, then listened to the sound of thumps, clangs, and shouts from inside.

He remembered what Ossetia had told him of her tastes, went to the rear of the building, and waited. In about ten minutes his patience was rewarded, and he followed Sereng to her eventual destination. He was just a little bit shocked.

Peirol returned to the stone building and went inside with a small bag of coins. When he came out, the bag was empty and his questions were answered. Thoughtfully, he returned to his shop and prepared for the morrow.

When the baroness came in, bubbly and curious, he suggested she might accompany him to the tavern around the corner. Sereng lifted an eyebrow coquettishly. "La, sir."

"La indeed," Peirol said. "For what I propose for you might be best said over a glass of wine."

"I am," Sereng said, "a married woman, as I'm sure you remember."

"Oh, I do, I do," Peirol said, and his voice was a little more grim than he liked.

The tavern help had been well bribed before to pay no attention to Peirol or his guests, and a small, closed booth in the back waited. Peirol had made sure Agar wasn't doing something imbecilic like following Sereng. He ordered wine for her, a brandy for himself.

"Now," Sereng said, "what is this bauble that's so unique as to be presented in this romantic secrecy, as if we were a boy and girl about to become lovers?"

"The bauble for next week, milady," Peirol said, "is yet unmade. The bauble I propose to discuss is your reputation."

"I beg your pardon?"

"And well you should," Peirol said, holding back

anger. "Although you are lovely and charming, and have done well for me in some regards, I'm not happy with you at the moment, not happy at all. I despise the way you've used me as a cloak for your—shall we say, recreational?—habits."

"What does *that* mean?" Sereng hissed nicely.

"I am not much interested in who you futter," Peirol said tiredly, "nor whether they're male or female, nor if you like to do it in threesomes. But I do not like it when your husband, who's far too big, angry, and well armed for me to feel comfortable around, boils in and accuses me of being your lover."

"How dare you?" Sereng was half on her feet. Peirol thought she was enjoying this drama.

"Sit down, baroness," he said, still calmly. "And if you waste that wine by throwing it in my face, I'll spank you. Now, sit down. Good. Drink this brandy. Suddenly you look a bit shaken. So we may avoid various hysterics you might have in mind, let me tell you that I followed you yesterday afternoon to a certain gymnasium in a laborers' district. I went to the rear and had the pleasure of seeing you leave with a man and a woman about your age, both of extremely athletic build, to a nearby inn, which has large bedrooms for rent. You were not below stairs in the tap room when I chanced looking in. I made inquiries.

"You may be pleased that the inn would not tell me how many times you'd visited their establishment, nor who your guests might have been. However, the gymnasium, once a bit of money had changed hands, was more than willing to tell me about your habits. Forgive me for embarrassing you, but did you know you're known there as 'The Workout Queen?'

"Yes, I thought you'd like the brandy. A moment, and I'll get another for you."

When Peirol returned, he found Sereng experimenting with tears. "What . . . what do you wish me to do? I'll do anything to keep my husband . . . or anyone else . . . from knowing . . . even though there's been some dreadful mistake, and there must be someone in Restormel who looks just like me."

"No doubt," Peirol said.

"What do you want from me?" Sereng took a deep breath, put on another mood, licked her lips. "I can show you things that will make you very happy."

"You, my love," Peirol said gently, "are indeed going to make me happy. But not how you think."

"You want money instead of—you want money?"

"Not at all."

"Then what?"

"I just want you to find out what you can, as quickly and quietly as possible, about the Empire Stone."

Ossetia, very upset, came the next day and took Peirol out, away from the inn. "Because I owe you my life," he said, "I'll give you this warning. You've been denounced to the Order of Lysyth. I went to certain officials, as did my father, and we told them of your virtues, and how you'd been a good friend not only to us but to the Order. I think, at least for the moment, without further evidence, you won't be arrested."

"Who denounced me?"

Ossetia shook his head. "That is forbidden."

"At least you can say whether it was a man or a woman."

"A . . . a man." Ossetia said reluctantly. Peirol gave a name. Ossetia nodded.

"Thank you for the warning," Peirol said. "And thank your father for the character witness."

"What are you going to do? I know—I'm sure—you're innocent. I'll . . . we'll do anything we can to help you escape, if you decide to flee."

"Being innocent, I see no reason to run," Peirol said. "However, I think I should deal with this immediately, and see the matter is permanently closed."

"How?"

"First, I'll visit my local sorcerer."

Peirol made a small object of wax, took it to the magician who ensorcelled his gems, and had a small spell cast. The magician thought the idea was very funny. Peirol decided, if it worked, he would as well.

Baron Agar slunk into his shop minutes after Peirol opened it the next day. Peirol sent his clerk out for a tray of sweetmeats, told him to take his time in coming back. "Yes, Baron?"

"How could you?" Agar sounded broken. "You said . . . you were no magician."

"Perhaps I lied," Peirol said. "I certainly could deny knowing what the hells you're going on about. But a better question is, How could you go to the Men of Lysyth with a lie? Have you no honor, sir? Have you no morals? Have you no decency?"

Agar reddened, started to snarl something, stopped himself.

"I told you," Peirol said, "I am not sleeping with your wife. I offered to have a magician prove it. Instead of believing me, or challenging me like a *man* does, you slunk behind my back like a scoundrel." Agar said nothing. "That is why, perhaps, a certain small wax image arrived at your door, in a box that had a spell on it so only you could open it with no witnesses present. When you opened that box, I assume you might have been shocked at the . . . indecency of what was inside.

"I would guess you might have been further shocked when it smoked, flamed like a tiny candle, and vanished. Did you feel a part of your body shrink at the same time? Become limp, sagging, like it belonged to an ancient? Did you attempt to make it behave otherwise, to make it stand like a proud soldier, only to fail? Did you test yourself with your charming wife?

"Don't bother replying. I might just know the answer and imagine that you would visit me, thinking I'd sent such a small doom against you, and that you would be willing to do anything to prevent such an awfulness from happening to someone as manly as yourself? Sir, you've gotten no more than you deserve.

"I have a new suggestion," Peirol went on, pleased at his eloquence. "I now suggest you and I present ourselves to the Men of Lysyth and have them put us to the question. I, sir, have been trained and am experienced in undergoing pain. You are a soldier, and should have the same talent. Let them take us to their dungeons and determine who is lying about that accusation leveled against me. I understand someone who confesses to wrong in front of them forfeits all that he has.

"Look around. What you see is all I own. I am willing to chance its loss, to prove you a liar. What do you own? How many leagues of farm, how many rich castles, how many horses does your family hold? Do you want those to be forfeit? Who will chance the most in those dungeons?

"Have you ever been tortured? No? I have," Peirol lied. "It was . . . not uninteresting. Would you like me to tell you what they did to me with fire, with iron, with leather and ropes? I withstood them once. I think I can do it again. Do you have the same confidence?"

Agar was growing steadily paler. "That's a different kind of pain than a soldier faces," Peirol said. "I recommend it to no one, would have no *man* undergo such torment. But when I am being dealt with in an underhanded manner, I play by the same rules as my enemy. Perhaps you want to return home now and, however you choose, discover I cast no spell, at least no spell that would linger.

"Then I think you would want to return to the Men in Brown and tell them of your error, and how you wish to recant your accusation. I'm sure, if you accompany your apology with gold, they'll forget about the matter."

Agar's hand was on his sword. Peirol laughed in his face, a hard laugh. His hand, unnoticed, was on the dart behind his belt. Agar turned and almost ran out.

Peirol rubbed his face, catching his reflection in a nearby mirror. "I did not realize," he said to no one in particular, "what a complete bastard I can be." He didn't sound terribly ashamed.

* * *

"The Empire Stone," Sereng whispered, "is the way the Men of Lysyth secretly rule Restormel. But they only consult it in time of great crisis, for the story is they're afraid of its powers."

"Some of that I already knew," Peirol said. "What is it?"

"I've never seen it, nor has anyone I know. I know it's a gem of great quality and size."

"Is it a clear stone that catches and reflects colors, many colors, not just the ones we know? Is it round, and cut with many more facets than any diamond?" Peirol's voice was excited.

"I don't know. You seem to know more about it than I do."

"Where is it?"

"I don't know that, either," Sereng said. "But there's a man, a singer, once an acolyte to the Men. He drinks too much, and I heard he doesn't hold his tongue, like sensible people do. His name's Yasin."

"Most interesting."

"That's all I was able to find out," Sereng said. "Please, Peirol, don't make me keep asking. A Brown Man came to me, said he'd heard of my curiosity, warned it was not a good thing for a noblewoman like myself to be talking about or being interested in. *Please*, Peirol, I don't want to see the inside of one of their dungeons."

"I hope I have enough information, and I thank you," Peirol said. "If I do, I free you from your debt."

"Why are you asking about the stone, anyway?"

"When I return to my home," Peirol said, "I want to

be able to tell of my travels. Being a jeweler, having heard rumors about the great stone, I wanted to be able to tell my fellows about it. No more."

Sereng looked at him askance, and Peirol realized he'd better come up with a lie better than that one. He decided to change the subject.

"Now," he said, "may I ask another question, having nothing to do with jewels?" Sereng nodded. "This is a very personal question," he said. "Has your husband, the Baron Agar, been, shall we say, especially, umm, romantic of late?" Sereng blushed, looked away.

"Ah," Peirol said. "Just curious. Now, about this gem I'm designing for you . . ."

As he described the jewel, Peirol wondered about that small phallus he'd made. There had been two spells cast, but only on the box: one to prevent anyone but Agar from opening it, and one to create the flames after the box was opened. Everything else had been in the Baron Agar's mind, or what passed for one. Peirol found that interesting.

It took a bit of searching to find Yasin, and the trail led steadily downward—and physically upward, for the poor of Restormel occupied not only the tenements on the former marshland across the tidal basin but the heights of the city as well. The tavern was much like the thieves' dens of Sennen: dark, smoky, with nooks and snugs to whisper illegal business in, and no doubt half a dozen exits in case the watch showed up looking for someone.

Yasin was a big, thick man with an angry, torn face. He was scrupulously clean, in worn, well-mended clothes that might've been a priest's habit. He wore a neatly trimmed beard and hair as short as a prisoner's. His voice was wonderfully ranged, from a rasping base to a near-falsetto, and he accompanied himself on a multistringed instrument held flat on his lap. His songs were of the past and the present, most of the contemporary ones sly digs at the nobility, at the Dowager Custodian, at the annoying habit kings had lately of dying, even at the Men in Brown.

His audience was mostly laborers or those who made their living in the shadows, with a scattering of slumming nobility.

Yasin kept a bottle beside him, and when he finished his set, the bottle was empty. He upended it once more, had no better luck, muttered "Shit," and made his way to the bar, where Peirol waited.

"On the ticket," he growled at the bartender.

"On my ticket," Peirol corrected, and spun a gold coin across. "Whatever your taste is."

"Not this swill," Yasin said, glowering at the empty bottle then tossing it over his shoulder, paying no attention to the yelp as it smashed on an unaware customer's table. "The ten-year-old. I used to drink that when I was . . . better off. Two glasses, man. If I can't buy you the next, at least I can share your generosity."

"No need," Peirol said. "I have my brandy here."

Yasin ignored the glass put in front of him, drank off about a quarter of the bottle. "Whuf," he said. "That died easy. I forgot what real liquor tastes like."

"You sing well," Peirol said.

"I know," Yasin said. "I guess if I believed in gods, I'd be grateful that the voice hasn't gone, given how I punish it. So what do you want, little man? I warn you, I know no songs about dwarves. Small kings expend my repertoire in that direction."

"I'm not interested in songs about me or mine," Peirol said. He leaned a bit closer. "I heard you've no fear of anyone."

"That's a lie," Yasin said. "I fear my landlord, if I can't find the coins for the rent of my room. I fear all three of my ex-wives. Sometimes, when I've my wits about me, I fear . . . others."

"Men who wear brown?"

"Those might be in that category."

"You were of them once."

"Which is why I fear them."

"I'm interested in songs—or stories—about something called the Empire Stone."

A look of fear flickered across Yasin's face. He drank the bottle halfway down in a draught. "I'm not drunk enough to remember if I know any songs about that."

"I'm from a far country," Peirol said, "and a man who's interested in rare gems. Why don't the rulers of Restormel allow it to be exhibited?"

Yasin lowered his voice. "The rulers of Restormel—the real rulers—know where it is and where it can be seen, and have no interest in what others think or want. Plus, they're a little afraid of it themselves."

"The Men of Lysyth?"

Yasin didn't answer, but drank. Then he stared into Peirol's eyes, and his gaze was sober, cold. "No. I'm not that drunk, by far. Nice try, little man."

Peirol took another gold coin from his purse, tossed it to the bartender. "Make sure my friend here doesn't have to rot his guts with the cheap stuff." He slid off the stool. "I doubt if I'll get tired of listening to your songs, Yasin. I'll see you another night."

Peirol was halfway home when the two men rushed from an alley. One had a sandbag, the other a dagger in each hand. Peirol took the sandbag on his left arm, numbing it, spun away from the man with the knives. His sword whispered out of his shoulder sheath, and he pulled his pistol, grateful he'd kept the slow match burning and shrouded. The man with the knives came in, while the other man jumped away. The knifer gasped once as Peirol's blade flicked in, out of his lungs, stumbled back.

The sandbag came down on empty air, and Peirol pulled the serpentine. He'd intended to take the man in the shoulder, but he missed, and blew a significant hole below his ribs. Guts spilled steaming on the cobbles, and the man screeched and fell.

The man with the sandbag gurgled long, then died. Peirol checked the other, found him already dead. He went through their pouches, found a few coppers, no more. Thieves. But his mind jeered at the easy explanation.

That night he dreamed of Kima, sitting on the mossy bank of a pool. She was naked, and the sun gleamed on her oiled and shaven body. She had a yellow flower in her hair. She saw Peirol, smiled.

"I am here," she said, "in that vale you told me

about, though I've seen it not in real life. This is a spell cast for me by my grandfather. Hurry home, Peirol, for Abbas has forbidden me to marry or go with men while you still live. This is not a punishment for me, Peirol. I've dreamed of you. I hope my dreams will be nothing compared to the real you, when you return."

She came easily to her feet, opened her arms, and Peirol moved toward her.

Then he was in Abbas's study. The wizard looked worried. "Good morrow, Peirol of the Moorlands," he said, and his voice echoed. "I have been trying to touch you for a week now, without success. There is something . . . someone . . . blocking us. I thought I could go deeper, use . . . another symbol . . . and that might work. Evidently it has. I can feel magics swirling around this spell of mine, and am exerting great power to keep it from being broken. This is a great spell someone has cast, or possibly more than one wizard. Be careful. I think you might be in range of the Empire Stone, and that whoever possesses it is worried. Or perhaps you've disturbed the twig that holds a trap cocked. I cannot tell. I also sense that—"

Abbas vanished, and Peirol was beside the pool as Kima came into his arms. He felt her body's warmth, breasts just touching his cheeks, nipples firming.

Then he awoke in his apartment, in Restormel. He went to the windows, looked out, saw no one in the predawn blackness. Peirol went back to bed, but still felt as if someone, something, was watching him.

Another thought came, and he considered, a bit disgustedly, the depth of Abbas's lust for the Empire Stone, and how he would use anything, even his own granddaughter, to further that ambition. Or maybe he was being too cynical. Maybe Kima was telling the truth about her feelings. He snorted in total disbelief. After all this time, after all these betrayals, didn't he know better?

"A small secret," Peirol began, sheepishly realized what he'd said as Yasin snorted ale across the table and shouted laughter, fortunately missing him.

"Let me put it another way," he said. He'd gotten into the habit of dropping into Yasin's tavern, trying to find information about the Empire Stone. Yasin seemed to enjoy not only the free drink but the duel of wits.

"There was a king once, long ago and far away, who had the Empire Stone," Peirol began. "He carried it, the legend goes, in a two-handed scepter, proud for all the world to see."

"And someone came and took it from him because of that." Yasin added.

"Well, yes," Peirol said. "The men of the black ships."

Yasin looked at him in surprise. "So, unless there's two sets of black ship sailors, that would mean they had the Stone for a time, and then we here in Restormel took it from them at the battle of Lysyth."

"Interesting, is it not?"

"If I were of a suspicious mind, which I'm not," Yasin said, "being only a humble singer of bad songs and drinker of worse potions, I might think you've come to take the Stone back to its rightful owner. A proper quest, worthy of great ballads."

"Dwarves don't qualify for ballads," Peirol said.

"And the city that king ruled, long ago, is ruined, and no one but wolves and serpents live in its desolation. I swear that is the truth."

"And of course," Yasin said, "being a humble man, I believe anything anyone tells me." His smile twisted, became bitter. "Which is why I was stupid enough to swear to the Men of Lysyth that I wanted to become one of them. I still believed in truth back then, and thought they knew the path to it."

"Anyway," Peirol went on, "my question is this: Why would one ruler keep it in the open, others hide it? Restormel surely has nothing to fear from raiders, not even those Sarissans the rest of the world seems in terror of."

"Rule one is as I suggested," Yasin said. "Out of sight, out of lust, to create a phrase. If that's really the case. But I have a better puzzler. As we've agreed, I know nothing at all about the Empire Stone, correct? However, consider this. If the Empire Stone gives power and riches to he who holds it, what does it get in return?"

"What?"

"Think about it, little man. Nothing goes for nothing in this world. The diamonds you sell, for instance. They take in light, correct? Then they reflect it back, in various colors, to please the owner's eye, correct? But they get something out of it, right?"

"Like what?" Peirol said. "I've been dealing with stones for most of my life, and I've never had a diamond thank me for a sunbeam yet."

"Aaargh," Yasin snarled. "Conversations like this are what I thought I'd get when I entered the Order. I left it, partially, because I got answers like the one you just gave me. A diamond, or other cut stone, absorbs heat when it's in the sun, correct?"

"Of course."

"Well, who's to say that doesn't make its stony little soul happy?"

"You're drunk."

"I am not, especially as sluggardly as you are in buying the rounds. I'll explain simply. The Empire Stone, if it exists, was created by god or demon, or was a normal stone of earth, given a spell by god, demon, or wizard."

"That seems probable," Peirol admitted.

"So things—feelings, thoughts, whatever—are attracted to it, and the owner of the Stone can use the knowledge he gains for his own purposes. I don't know how he learns those things. Maybe by contemplating that rock."

"That's what the legends say."

"What does the Stone keep?"

"I still don't understand."

"All right," Yasin said. "Try another comparison. When you were a babe, I assume you blew soap bubbles. First you dipped the circlet in soapy water, then blew, gently, regularly, and the bubble grew and grew. At the correct moment, you twisted the circlet, and the bubble drifted away on the wind. What happened when you blew too much?"

"The bubble burst, of course."

"Now think about this Empire Stone. Think about all those centuries it's been, well, listening, to all the evils and plans of mankind, maybe even before that, to the schemes of the gods, for if there are gods, their lusts and plots must be greater than man's. Slowly, slowly, the Empire Stone has been filling up, as one of your stones gets hotter and hotter in the sun. What happens when it gets full?"

Peirol considered Yasin for a long time. "That isn't drunkenness talking," he said finally. "It almost sounds like a theory someone might have come up with who'd been around the Empire Stone. Maybe not you, but maybe somebody in the Order."

"Maybe someone, very old, very senile, who babbled long to a very young acolyte," Yasin said, looking away from Peirol. "Someone who, when they died, left a big hole in a boy's life." His voice lowered. "Something that still hasn't been filled by man nor woman."

A day or so later Peirol, taking his midday meal at one of the stone benches, saw Ossetia pushing through the throng. He stood, waved. Ossetia looked straight at him, then away, as if he'd seen nothing, and kept moving, even faster than before. Curious, Peirol thought; and he heard in his mind the whisper of sands running through a glass.

Yasin was drunker than usual that night, or rather that morning. He'd growled at the barkeep, at the tavern manager, even at Peirol before stumbling up to the low stage. "Before I do my usual songs, I want to sing something I just remembered. A song from when I was a boy—yes, I was a boy, damned good-looking too. If anyone laughs, I'm liable to remember another part of my boyhood, and give lessons on how to fight with a razor."

The tavern, even though it was late, was full. Thieves keep hours citizens do not. But it was suddenly very silent.

"This isn't a very good song," Yasin went on. "And I'm not sure I learned all of it, for the verses aren't the same length. And the rhyme ain't the same. This is what they call a people's song, which is why it's so shitty. Also, I won't sing the chorus every time, like it's supposed to be done, to keep you from getting bored. I'm singing this for a good friend of mine. Two good friends, really. Only one of them's here. The other's dead. Been dead a long time."

He swept a hand across the strings:

>"We saw them as they closed
>On our stricken land
>
>Their ships were black
>Their hands were red
>Their demons darker still
>And they knew no mercy, O
>
>And they were guided by a stone, lads
>They were guided by a stone
>
>Our ships went out to fight them
>They were smashed against the shore
>Ten thousand men died that day
>Ten thousand men or more

With bloody swords they landed
And marched along the strand
Old men stood against them
A tattered forlorn band

And they were guided by a stone, lads
Guided by a stone

The jewel flamed as they closed
Death was on every hand
The old men stood, not afraid
To die upon the sand

Then held forth a wizard bold
Who cast a mighty spell
Against that stone and its wights
No mortal sword could quell

And they were guided by a stone, lads
Guided by a stone

The magic took the stone
And turned it in their hand
Flames roared out against them
Breaking what they'd planned

They stumbled back
They turned away
Abandoning the stone
And to their ships they ran

The beach was black with corpses
Their ships they fled away

> *Their demons burned and capered*
> *Around the stone that day*
>
> *The old men took the stone*
> *To the proper place*
> *To guard against the ships of black*
> *And keep us in our grace*
>
> *And now we're guided by a stone, lads*
> *Guided by a stone.*"

Yasin broke off, raked the back of his hand across the strings, laughed harshly. There'd been a stir when Yasin began the song: Peirol'd seen two men at a table near the door get up and leave.

Yasin sang a dozen other songs somewhat listlessly, ending to scattered applause. He came back to the table. "There," he said. "I suppose that's done it. Tonight I am drunk enough not to give a shit about the Men of Lysyth. Now, do you want me to show you where the Empire Stone is hidden?"

"At least," Yasin said as they came into the clean night air, "it's a nice walk to where the Stone's hidden, and no strain on the heart. I found out where it is from that certain old man. I wasn't supposed to learn that secret, or any of the others of the Order, until I'd grown gray in its service, and knew nothing else and wanted nothing else."

Strangely, his drunkenness had vanished as he left the tavern.

"We'll just stroll along, and I'll point things out,"

Yasin said, "and you'll curse yourself for being a thick-headed foreigner, not realizing where it was all the time, and then you can buy me another—"

They swarmed in from the night. Peirol had time to pull his pistol and fire it into the mass; a man yelped, went down. Someone knocked him rolling, and when he came up the pistol was gone, but he had his dagger in one hand. A man swung with a broadsword, and Peirol went under the blade, put his knife up into his heart, danced free as he fell.

He heard Yasin whoop, and a man went down.

A mist that he later remembered as red, but it couldn't have been, came across his eyes. He head-butted another attacker, had a free moment, and drew his sword. He feinted with the blade, drove his dagger into his opponent's groin, found the scream like music. Someone shouted in anguish and there was a man there, sword pulled back for a killing stroke, back to Peirol. Peirol spitted him through the back of the neck. The man spun, pulling the sword from Peirol's hand, and the dwarf saw the reddened blade sticking out of the man's mouth as he went down.

Someone cut at Peirol, took him in the arm, but it was a superficial wound, and he ducked around another attacker, pushed him into the first. The two stumbled back, and Peirol cut the first's throat, grabbed a pistol from the man's belt, and shot the second man in the face.

He saw another pistol on the ground, had it, and there was another man coming at him, a man bleeding, breathing hard. Peirol pulled the serpentine and the weapon fizzed, misfiring on damp powder. A blade burned through his thigh. He yelled in pain, reflexively struck with the haft of his knife, thumbed the man's eye, and he roiled back. Peirol killed him with his dagger, scooped his sword from the ground, not knowing how he knew it to be his, and there was no one left to kill. He heard the footsteps of men, more than one, running away.

Peirol saw Yasin lying on the ground, a broken sword blade in his chest. The dwarf picked up an unfired pistol, held it ready as he knelt over the singer.

"Fughpigs," Yasin moaned. "Should've known they would've been watching."

Peirol wondered whose set of fughpigs it'd been.

"I'll wager," Yasin said, breathing hard, "you being a bright dwarf, educated and all, you'll figure out—"

He was quietly dead. Peirol got to his feet. He was swallowing hard. He found his pistol, reloaded it, found another, still charged, looked around at the corpses.

One—he supposed the man he'd shot when the fray began, since he was a distance from the corpse-scatter—wore a brown habit. Your fughpigs, not mine, he thought. But there were two others he saw, well dressed for back-alley thugs, and he wondered once more. Maybe the fughpigs teamed up.

Yes, he thought. Yes, Yasin. I *have* figured out where the Empire Stone is. Now all I have to do is steal it before they kill me.

NINETEEN

✴

Of Empire Stones
and Temblors

The oldest godsdamned trick in the book, Peirol thought, staring up at the octagonal brown stone tower commemorating the Battle and Order of Lysyth. Hide something in plain sight. Then he wondered how many people would want the damned Empire Stone, anyway.

The tower was about a hundred feet in diameter, three hundred feet tall. There was a small, barred entrance, and he assumed winding steps upward on the inside, guarded by some evil monster or other. At the moment, his bloodlust still unslaked by the battle, he wouldn't mind encountering a monster or two—or better, a Man in Brown. He rubbed his hastily bandaged thigh, hoped the superficial wound wouldn't make muscles stiffen any more than they already had.

Pick the lock, and—and he saw the two sentries

standing next to the entrance, completely motionless in the shadows. He hoped they were drowsing, rather than professional and extremely watchful. Perhaps he should cast a pebble, wake them, and have them do their duty and make a sweep around the tower, which was about a hundred feet in diameter. Then he saw the roving patrol—another pair of men—come into sight, and muttered unhappily.

Peirol stayed in the alley mouth, thinking for a time. His best chance, he knew, would've been to make an immediate assault on the tower, before a hue and cry could be set for a murderous dwarf. But it didn't seem possible, without certain pieces of equipment and considering the guards were most alert.

The sky was graying, and Peirol moved farther into hiding, staring hard at the tower, wishing he had a telescope to examine every inch as if he were next to it. Then he spotted a way in. Or hoped he did, at any rate. It was just a bit chancy.

Better to escape Restormel, find his boat, and sail west. To face what? Abbas's wrath if he made it back to Sennen or, more likely, a sea monster he'd send the moment he found out Peirol'd abandoned his quest?

Besides . . .

Besides, this would be the theft of the century. Peirol thought about all the deaths, all the weary miles, all the pain, and bristled. The *hells* he'd even think about giving up. He'd be back. At nightfall. Peirol slid away, toward his store and quarters, to secure gold for the purchases he'd need.

* * *

But the Men in Brown weren't entirely dilatory. Two patrols, ten men each, of armored horsemen, a cowled monk or priest at their head, were patrolling at a walk through his district. Cautiously he went to a building close to his store, climbed upstairs to its roof, and peered across. The ornate crossbeams had already been nailed over his door, and the brown parchment sign flapped in the early morning wind. Peirol hoped his clerk hadn't been grabbed by the Men of Lysyth to scream his life out in their torture chambers, knowing nothing of Peirol.

He thought perhaps he could go through the alley and chance climbing the drain spout into his apartment, but he decided to watch for a while. It was well he did, for a man appeared at the window for a minute, then ducked away. But that minute had been long enough for Peirol to identify him as Damyan, the Man of Lysyth who'd first accused him of heresy.

One sanctuary gone. Peirol thought of his lost tools, his gold and silver, the gems cut and uncut, shrugged, forgot them. Jewels, gold, and such can be replaced.

A life cannot.

The blacksmith looked at him oddly but took his silver without question. Peirol tucked what he'd had made into the burlap sack containing his other acquisitions. He'd found a store, bought drab gray clothing, gone across Restormel using alleys whenever he could.

Peirol wondered why there was no hue and cry, then realized the Men of Lysyth would hardly want someone other than the "proper authorities" to take him, possibly thought an alarum would send the dwarf fleeing into the wilderness. No doubt all city exits and the ferry boarding points were well watched. Peirol didn't know how he'd escape Restormel after ... if ... he got the Empire Stone. He would worry about that when the time came.

There were other problems. It was several hours until darkness, and a blond-haired dwarf wandering the streets was sure to be seized. Peirol wiped away sweat. The day was still, muggy. He considered where he could go to ground, remembered a tavern he'd wandered into by accident, gone back out of much more quickly.

He was halfway to his destination when the ground shook a little. He thought it was a heavy freight wagon passing, saw no such vehicle. A pair of rats scuttled out of a building, stood in the middle of the street, looking at him, unafraid.

The shaking came again, and across the street a flowerpot in an upper window fell, shattering on the cobblestones.

The sign was in very discreet script:

✠

The Place of
Man's Reward

✠

Under it was a tiny rendering of a cat-o'-nine-tails. Peirol saw he was unobserved, entered.

A young man, quite muscular, stood inside. He

wore leather breeches and was bare-chested and shaven-headed.

"You desire?"

"A quiet, curtained booth. Iced water. Do you have food?"

"Later there'll be a roast."

"I'll be here for a time, so I'll eat then."

"You know we have facilities in the rear if you prefer greater privacy. And other arrangements can also be made."

Peirol tossed the man two gold coins, followed him down a long line of snugs. The young man's breeches lacked a seat.

Peirol glanced into the occupied booths as he passed. Only one held a woman, and she too wore leather. A thumbscrew sat on the table in front of her. The other patrons were all men, some dressed as soldiers, some as seamen, one bold one as a Man of Lysyth. Their tools of romance were on the tables, advertising: a whip, twisted ropes, long pins, tiny vises, leather straps, rubber devices.

The young man showed Peirol to his booth. Peirol drew his dagger, put it on the table. The young man glanced at the knife, shuddered, but said nothing.

The hours dragged past. Three or four times men walked by, eyed the dwarf with interest, saw the dagger, passed on quickly. Occasionally he heard a scream or a laugh from other booths or from the rear of the building.

The roast, when it came, was quite rare, which fit well with the surroundings. He had little appetite but forced himself to eat. He wanted wine, knew better, and three hours after sunset dropped two more gold coins on the table, left unhurriedly.

Peirol watched the guards around the tower, counted the time of their tour three times. Then, when they moved out of sight again, he darted across. He had a count of a little over three hundred to become invisible. He'd tied the burlap sack so it fit like a knapsack over his shoulders, and it held his sword, his pistols, and his purchases. A small hammer was stuck into his sword belt.

The tower was built of well-fitted large stones. Peirol, when he'd studied the building, thought the spaces between the stones deep enough for finger holds. They were. It wouldn't be the easiest climb he'd made, but it wouldn't be the hardest. The ground shook for an instant, and he thought he heard a distant rumbling. Perhaps a summer storm in this strangely humid fall night. Alley cats wailed in mournful anticipation of the storm.

He pulled off his shoes, stuffed them in the pack, took a breath, and started up the vertical wall.

He climbed slowly, rhythmically, body well away from the stone, fingers and toes finding niches, moving upward. The stone wore on his skin, and he knew he'd be bloody by the time he reached the top. By the count of three hundred, he was invisible, twenty feet above the ground. He heard the slight shuffle as the guards passed beneath, froze, climbed on, still counting, pausing when it came time for the patrol to pass underneath.

Twice he stopped, clinging by his toes and the fingers of one hand while he reached in the burlap pack, took out one of the steel spikes he'd had the black-smith make, tapped it softly into place, put another above it, climbed up, and used that for a foothold. He'd need them for another purpose on the way down.

Peirol started once, as dogs howled below. But no shouts of alarm came, and he climbed on, not looking up, not wanting to know how much farther he had to go, not looking down, not wanting to know how far he would fall. Then his upreaching hand touched smooth stone and metal. The top of the tower was also octag-onal, set equidistant from the main tower angles. Eight windows, with eight sides, appeared to give entrance. There was a guardrail across them. Peirol eeled over the rail, forcing himself not to rest until he peered through the dusty smoked windows and saw nothing of an interior guard.

Of course not, he thought. Magical beasts never materialize until their prey's at hand.

He sagged against the stone, dug into his pack for his sword and a small flask of brandy-flavored water, drank deeply. He allowed himself a count of a hun-dred to rest, then considered a window. He saw no way it could be opened, clambered around the tower, saw no catches on the other panes.

Why should there be? Jewels don't need a view.

He hadn't thought there'd be glass, had seen no reflection, so hadn't brought putty or a cutter. He tapped gingerly with the butt of his dagger, felt the pane yield.

Glad of that. It'd be like these bastards to put in panes thick as their arms.

He tapped once, twice, struck hard, and the glass shattered, tinkling down to stone a foot below on the inside. Peirol waited for an alarm, broke out the rest of the glass.

This is easy. Far, far too easy.

Sword in one hand, dagger in the other, he slid inside. He could see in the dimness a domed pedestal, which would reach to the chest of a man but was head-high for him, in the center of the room.

Peirol started toward it, and as he moved, the world changed. There was light, but he knew no one could see it but him—a dimness. It was as if he were walking underwater, or better yet, under oil, for his vision was clouded. He stepped slowly, each motion deliberate, unable to move faster. He felt pressure in his ears, not unpleasant. Then he'd reached the pedestal.

He leaned his sword against it, sheathed his dagger, and somehow knowing what he should do, carefully lifted the top of the dome away.

The Empire Stone was there, just at eye level. As he stared into it, it began to glow, to refract, and he felt a humming within his bones.

He picked up the Empire Stone, turned it about.

"Double the size of both m' fists."

Bigger, really.

"A clear stone that catches and reflects colors, many colors, not just the six we know, but colors that aren't like any others on this earth."

The Stone was alive, and colors that Peirol had never known, had no names for, knew no artist could label, shot out against the stone walls around him.

"Round, cut perfect. They say it's got a thousand facets. . . ."

Nothing came from the shadows to attack him.

I guess the Magical Guardian that any self-respecting evil gem's got must have gone out for a glass of wine or a human sacrifice, he thought to himself. He tried to keep from laughing, tucked the Stone under his arm, picked up his sword, and, moving as slowly as before, walked deliberately to the broken window and stepped through it.

A cat yowled below him, then more across Restormel. He paid no mind to the noise, any more than he did to the exultation of his mind.

We're only half there, he thought. *Now for the escape.*

He took the Stone out, was about to put it in his pack, then reconsidered. Again, he looked deep into the Stone, and again the colors, many colors, flared. He was looking down, at the square and buildings below. There were guards there . . . there . . . over there . . . half a dozen hiding inside that building. He knew their orders, could, if he wanted, have told their names.

Peirol lifted his gaze, looked across the city heights, at the royal palace almost a league distant. He saw the young king turn in his sleep, dreamed with him, dreams of fear and death. In another chamber, a fat woman sat awake, though her thoughts might have been dreams, too: of a processional, and the Supreme Priest, and a diadem lowered onto her head.

Peirol brought his mind back across the distance, knowing the thoughts, the dreams, of the people sleeping below him in shack or manor. He turned away. What he'd heard of the Stone was no more than the truth. A tiny part of him lusted after the knowledge it would give, but the rest screamed in horror, welcoming ignorance or innocence. That was for Abbas. Let him have the Empire Stone if he wanted it. Peirol wanted only peace and his life.

He hastily stuffed the Stone in the burlap sack, wrapping it in the toweling he'd brought. Peirol took rope out of the sack, ran it through the railing. He sheathed his sword, shouldered the sack, then looped the doubled rope over his shoulder, down his back, up between his legs and over one thigh. Then he began walking, backward, down the face of the tower, moving slowly. He'd seen men try to go down fast, seen them slip and fall to their deaths.

Simple, simple, my gods, how simple this was....

A shout: "Hey! Look! Up there!"

Another shout: "Son of a bitch! That's him!"

He saw his shadow, as lanterns and torches came to life. There was a bang, and a musket ball whined off the stone three feet away. Another musket fired, and the ball went who knows where.

"For the love of the gods, shoot him down!"

Peirol knew that voice for Baron Agar. A volley rattled, and balls sang around him. He felt pain flash in his side, almost let go of the rope, knowing he'd been shot, then realized it was a bit of stone, flung off by a ricochet.

There was nothing else but to keep moving downward. His foot found one of the spikes he'd driven in, then the next one. Quite methodically he pulled the rope down from the rail above, redoubled it over the upper peg, went on. At the last peg, he decided, he'd turn, chance a jump down into them, and hopefully be able to break through the melee and escape. Or at least take some with him, starting with Baron Agar.

Then the great noise came, a groaning, a rumbling, and the tower swayed. He swung free for an instant, back, forth, almost fell. He recovered, though the tower still shook, and the rumbling ground at his soul. Someone screamed, and Peirol looked down. It was only thirty feet to the cobbles, but they were moving, as if they weren't stone but seawater. The tower itself was whipping back and forth as the earthquake tore at Restormel.

A roaring came, and the ground parted, a gouge running across the square, almost swallowing two running men. Peirol slid down to the bitter end of the rope, jumped, landed in the cleft—soft muck—as the world shook around him. The night air shimmered, moving, as the buildings around him swayed. The man who'd screamed stared blankly at Peirol, then began whimpering, while the ground tossed, swayed.

Peirol saw the tower shatter and the stones cascade down, and all his mind could wonder was, Did I cause this, did my taking the Stone bring this about, or was there other magic? Are the gods laughing at their new game?

TWENTY

*

Of Sea Waves
and Ruin

Peirol rolled close to the tower's base, and the stones fell around him. He heard a scream, cut off in the middle, then nothing. Deafened by the shock, ears ringing, he stumbled to his feet, ground still shaking. He wanted to cry out to the gods for it to stop, for the solid earth to be still, not roll like ocean waves, for this was madness. The stars above seemed to be moving. Then everything stopped. And the screams began.

Peirol peered through the haze at the tower stones littering the square, buildings lying askew, beams, furniture everywhere. The city below was dark, and then flames began flickering here, there. The night was very bright, without a cloud, and he looked around dumbly.

Over there, along the hillcrest, was the royal

palace he'd looked into with the Empire Stone. Or, rather, where the palace had been. Its stones had poured down the steep hill, crushing buildings as they went. It was as if a child had built the huge palace of pasteboard, then crumpled it in boredom.

He came back to himself a bit, realizing that the Stone was still safe in the burlap sack on his back. He hastily pulled his sword, sheathed it across his back, struck flint and lit the slow matches for his two pistols, slid the covers back on, and stuffed the weapons into his belt.

Another shock came, this one shorter but more violent. Peirol fought for his footing, stumbled, went down. As he got up, the ground across the river rippled, and he saw the high tenements totter and crumble in silence. A moment later, the smash of their collapse washed over him.

A uniformed man, an officer by the gilt on his armor, stumbled toward him, sword in hand. Peirol went on guard, but the man was no threat. He was sobbing as if he'd lost his closest, and brokenly muttering, "What do we do, what do we do, what do we do?"

Peirol shook him with his free hand, and the man fell silent, stood swaying.

"There are fires," Peirol shouted. The officer nodded. "Are there fire companies?" Again, a nod. "Take me there. Get your men and take me there." The man went back into the swirling dust, shouting orders.

"Here," the officer said. "Here's where the company was." The building the firemen lived in had collapsed around them, but wagons stood untouched in front of the ruin.

"Where are their horses?" Peirol demanded.

The officer looked about dumbly at the thirty men he'd gathered.

"Back there, I guess," someone said, pointing to what might have been a stable once. "Under everything."

"Do you know how to work this apparatus?" Peirol asked the officer.

"Yes . . . yes, I saw an exhibition once. There are mains the wagon has hoses to hook into, but they'd be torn by the earthquake, so that's no good, no good at all," the man said. "But each of those wagons has a tank."

"Come on," someone shouted. "We'll pull the hogfutters to the waterfront, fill 'em up there."

Peirol pointed to the shouter. "Yes! Do it! Now! You're in charge!"

The man looked at the dwarf, then shouted to his companions to find harness, and they by the gods *could* drag the wagons down, three of you on the brake, there.

Peirol went down into the city. He wasn't sure where he was going, what he was doing, but his mind kept thinking perhaps he'd been responsible for this nightmare, and he must do something as recompense.

Peirol found other soldiers and men of the watch, gave them orders to find other fire companies and fill their wagons. He told half a dozen of the men, who still held muskets and appeared to have their wits with them, to come with him.

They came into a street that was burning along one side as looters, already half-drunk, smashed into stores on the other. The men with him didn't seem to care. Peirol saw a man tearing at a screaming girl's clothes, drew his pistol, and shot him without a qualm.

"'At's good," one of the men beside him muttered as Peirol reloaded.

"You and three others," Peirol said. "Go grab three, of those bastards. Bring them back here." The men obeyed. "Line them against that wall," Peirol said.

One of the looters struggled, and Peirol leveled his pistol at him. The man started whimpering.

"No, no," another said.

"Shoot them," Peirol said, and the muskets came up, and three of them fired. Two looters lay motionless, the other writhed with a ball in the lungs. Peirol blew his brains out, loaded once more. "Go find other men of the watch or soldiers, or even men with their wits about them" he ordered. "Do what I just did to any bastard who tries to harm or steal anything but bread. Smash any wine casks you see. There'll be time for drunkenness when this is over."

Peirol went on downhill. Fires were breaking out everywhere he looked, and the screams of the buried, the wounded, the crazed rang from everywhere.

He looked down a street, saw men and women carrying the injured on improvised stretchers, laying them out in the center of the street, as buildings crumbled on either side. Other men and women were tending to them, heedless of the fires. A pillar of fire burst into life at the far end of the street, and Peirol felt the blast against his face.

A tall bearded man, wearing robes of an order Peirol'd never seen, walked toward the fire, arms spread wide, shouting an incantation—a wizard. The fire licked out a finger, swallowed him, roared pleasure. Then it sprang down the length of the street, taking women and men, both the hurt and the caregivers, capering for an instant in the flames, then falling, black, charred, forgotten.

Peirol went on, wondering at his calmness. By rights he should start screaming, running to and fro as everyone else seemed to be doing, but he felt no panic pulling at him. He realized he was heading, vaguely, toward his shop, turned away, went on toward the water. He passed a corpse, a soldier, stopped and took his belt pouch, put the Empire Stone in it, strapped the pouch on firmly.

Peirol reached the huge open esplanade and found more madness. People thronged the grounds they'd walked, had picnics, fallen in love in, now milling about, half shocked, half panicked. Here and there statues had fallen, sometimes with corpses lying under them.

Peirol recognized a man on a horse, the High Priest Warleggen, and started toward him. Yet another tremor pulled him down, this one very sharp, continuing for almost a minute. Peirol thought it came from a new direction, from the sea. He came to his hands and knees, picked himself up.

The advantage of being a dwarf, his mind said mockingly, *is you don't have as far to fall.*

Somehow Warleggen had kept his seat. He saw Peirol. "Help me!"

"To do what?"

"Get the people down here, out into the open, away from the buildings! We'll have to let the fire burn out, then we can start worrying about rebuilding!"

"Good," Peirol said, turned to obey, gaped at the tidal basin. Water was receding from it, leaving bare mudlands, rushing out to sea even faster than the river could replace the flow. Peirol thought it was some sort of strange tide, then remembered a tale from a seaman, back aboard the *Petrel*.

"Get them out of here!" he shouted to Warleggen. "Get them to high ground!"

"What?"

"The sea! The quake's struck it!"

"You've gone mad, dwarf! Now do as I order!"

Peirol started to argue, remembered what else the sailor had said, knowing there was no time left, and ran, cursing not for the thousandth time his short legs. He ran up a street away from the square, fire on either side, not turning to look as a great roaring built behind him. His lungs seared fire, his legs were rubber, but he pushed on until he could run no more, stopped, panting, and others ran past him, abandoning children, whatever goods they held, seeing the newest doom rush on them.

A great wave swept toward Restormel, a wave taller than any of the waterfront buildings, a wall of water moving faster than a horse could gallop. Peirol ran on, not knowing how he managed, and then the wave crashed, and he could hear nothing but its coming. A wind pushed against him, almost knocked him down, and he glanced back, saw the sea foam over the waterfront, spray flying high. A statue of some soldier or other fell, and Peirol thought, more likely imagined, he saw Warleggen and his horse sent tumbling by the wave, then buried.

The wave rushed on, swallowing people, wagons, horses, buildings, came up the street toward him. Peirol saw a lamp standard and clung to it, both legs wrapped around it, and the sea washed around him, came to his shoulders, foaming, and then receded, pulling at him, trying to tear his grip away. A woman with a baby in one arm floundered toward him, was pulled under, was gone.

Peirol looked down at the esplanade, washed clean, saw the rubble of a city clogging the bay. He stood numbly; then the rest of the sailor's story came, and he ran on, always uphill. Twice more the wave came, and each time part of Restormel died with it.

Dawn finally came, a harsh twilight, and it was more terrible to be able to see—see the ruins of a city.

Another aftershock came, this another lingering series of tremors. Peirol was looking across the bay, at the ruins of the tenements, wondering how many had died there. He gaped, seeing yet another way for the earth to strike man, as the ground around those tenements, once marsh, became liquid, and the remaining buildings and their ruins leaned, fell, and were sucked down to disappear in the jellylike mire, swallowing all, until there was nothing but a roiled flat.

Peirol found men, gave them orders to start

putting out the still-spreading fires. He found women and men, told them to set up nursing stations, ordered other people to stop the looters by any means necessary. Some of those who gladly, grimly, took muskets or halberds were women, a few children.

Then it was almost dark, he dimly realized, and he was pulling at stone, trying to free a child, a girl, who was beyond tears, beyond fright, staring. Someone shouted, knocked him aside, and as he rolled, reaching for his pistol, a cornice fell, crushing the child.

Peirol next remembered filling a flask he'd taken from somewhere with brandy, remembering his orders about drink, not giving a damn, swallowing half the flask and refilling it from the stove-in barrel.

Then it was night, then it was day, and he could never put together the order of things.

He was pumping hard at a fire wagon, water spraying on a fire, then the wagon catching fire and he and some others running;

He was standing over the body of Ossetia, a dagger in its chest, a dead man lying nearby, Peirol's pistol barrel still smoking;

A harridan was offering him her body, because he was the lucky dwarf, and it'd be good for her, let her live another day;

Someone was telling him the young king had died in the earthquake, but the Dowager Custodian was, gods be thanked, still alive and healthy, and Peirol couldn't stop laughing;

Half a dozen men were pulling in unison at a beam, a man winkling his way out of burial, getting up, smiling, saying, "Thanks, friends," walking a dozen paces, and falling dead;

Trying to sleep, but alcohol was the only thing to offer relief, vomiting the food he reluctantly swallowed;

Realizing it was never night, never day, the fire and the flames the world's sun and darkness;

A high-piled stack that might have been logs but was bodies flaming up, and the sweet smell, oddly like roasting mutton, spreading over Restormel;

Standing on the waterfront, flames still spreading in the city, thinking for an instant that at least certain districts here and there were safe, realizing they were dark because there was nothing left to burn;

Making love to a woman in a burned-out house, both of them crying, and he didn't know why or who she was;

Half a hundred men cheering him as they ran past, some with axes, some with soaked burlaps, against another flare-up.

All he could remember was that he worked when someone told him to, or told others what to do when he saw something that needed doing. The rest was a haze of pain, blood, and brandy.

Then someone called out, and it was if nothing had happened, no time had passed, since he'd come down from the tower of the Men of Lysyth.

"You! Dwarf!"

He was in a small square, having no idea why, where he was going. Across the square, on horseback, was a grimy man in armor, Baron Agar of Sancreed.

"You bastard, my wife's dead, and it's because of you!"

Peirol stared in bewilderment as Agar slid from his horse and stumbled toward Peirol, drawing a sword. "Die now, die you will," Agar shouted. "Pull sword and fight me, you demon son of a bitch!" He was running.

Peirol reached to his belt, took out a pistol, cocked, aimed, and pulled the trigger as he realized the match had gone out. He frowned at his carelessness, took out the other weapon, realizing Agar was almost on him, but there was more than enough time for proper aim, and the pistol went off. Agar's head slammed back, red and gray sprayed the air, and he skidded sideways on his face, sword spinning high through the air.

Peirol stared at the body, felt nothing in particular, slowly turned, hearing another shout. He saw the rest of Agar's party, wondered how they'd managed to stay together since setting the ambush at the tower, and if they'd been looking for him, him and the Empire Stone. He recognized the monk Damyan.

"Take him," the monk screeched, rushed at him with a leveled halberd. "He's a demon-spawn, and the one who's stolen the—"

Peirol knelt unhurriedly, picked up a broken cobble, and threw it full into Damyan's face before he could finish. The man screamed, spun, and fell, kicking.

A musket went off, and the ball went by his ear. Peirol ran, zigging, toward a smoldering building. A ball bounced off the cobbles, and he was in the ruins, running through them, feeling burning under his feet, going toward a street still in flames, hearing the clatter of pursuit. He darted past a collapsed house, jumped a flaming beam, and was gone—the smoke, the fire, his friend, Peirol a small furry animal whose hide was the destroyed city.

Then he was back at the waterfront, and it was dusk, and he was wondering how many times in the past days—however many days there'd been—he'd come around and around in a grand circle. There was a small boat tied not far distant, painted green, one of the boats that ferried people across the bay to the tenements, now swallowed by the returned marshland. He jumped down into it, surprised no challenge came, found one oar, no other.

Peirol untied the painter, pushed himself into the current, felt the chop rock the boat, tried to steer it away, downstream, toward the open sea. He looked at Restormel, still flaming, smoke blanketing the sky, a city still writhing in its death agonies, and sat down carefully, worried about tipping the boat.

The village had not been touched by the sea wave at all. Peirol's boat still sat on its rollers, and there were men around the village who'd help him launch it. He couldn't remember if he'd slept or eaten. He must have, for he felt healthy, even if everything seemed somewhat distant, as if he were looking through a smoked glass.

There were people staring at him, at his tattered clothes, his ready weapons, concerned, friendly, asking things, wondering. But he would have little to say, other than to buy whatever foodstuffs and drink they would sell, to have them launch his boat, and give him a course west through the straits, toward Sennen. Once through the straits, once beyond the island of Restormel, then he'd drop sail, wash the stink of fire, smoke, and death off his body. Then he'd sleep.

When he was safe.

TWENTY·ONE

Of Sennen and
a Certain Vale

The tiny, battered sailboat tacked into Sennen's inner harbor, making for a finger dock to one side of the bustling commercial wharves. Peirol dropped the sail, let the boat drift silently to touch the dock, stepped ashore, and tied the craft to a bollard.

"Handily done, sir," a lounger said.

Peirol nodded thanks, dropped down into the boat's small cabin. He put on his sword belt, wriggled at the now-unfamiliar weight, belted on the pouch that held the Empire Stone, and went up the dock. He felt as if the ground was still moving, like the deck that had been his world for four Times.

He should have been handy with the boat after this time. Peirol had sailed south and west from the fishing village, hugging the coast. He'd put into small ports four times for supplies, quickly returned to the sea.

The ocean wasn't his friend, just the least hostile place he could think of. He'd almost been dismasted in a sudden blow, nearly pitchpoled, and twice he'd seen sails of the galleys of Beshkirs, once a small formation of the Sarissans' ships. But either they hadn't seen him or, more likely, thought him scanty prey, and they had sailed on.

Peirol hadn't touched or even looked at the Empire Stone since leaving the ruins of Restormel, afraid of what it might bring.

He'd sailed down the Manoleon Peninsula, remembering his travails as an escaped slave, passing Isfahan, Tybee, through the straits between Parasso and the peninsula. Rather than follow the route of the *Petrel*, he'd chanced sailing due west, across the Sea of Cotehl. Here he'd almost lost his boat, but the storm was short-lived. He passed through the Straits of Susa by night, lying up in the shelter of uninhabited islands by day, and the pirate villagers hadn't seen him.

Then, in calm early spring weather, he'd managed the Ismai'n Sea, seen the ruins of Thyone, and sailed upriver to Sennen.

Peirol thought briefly of stopping for a glass of the bitter beer of Sennen he'd never much savored, but now sang happily of home, of buying new finery, of a meal.

He considered finding a shop that might carry a green silk scarf like the one Kima had given him, the one that'd been taken by that Beshkirian pirate years ago, but it wouldn't look as battered as the original should. Besides, she was no doubt happily with another by now.

He set all that aside. He'd been gone for what, three years? First was the ending of the quest.

The gate to Abbas's tower was shut, and the two small cannons were wheeled into position, facing through holes in the grating, powder kegs and balls ready beside them.

"Ahoy the house," Peirol called. There was no response. He shouted again.

A tiny casement opened. "Peirol of the Moorlands? Is that you?"

"It is, wizard, and I've returned with what you sent me for."

"Wait."

Peirol stood obediently for a very long time. He was growing angry when the door swung open and Abbas rushed out. The sorcerer had changed somewhat. His black beard and hair were streaked with gray, and his belly had grown much larger. But his eyes still burned, and he moved with the swiftness of a young man.

But then, Peirol had changed, too. He noticed a pistol stuck in the waistband of Abbas's gown. The sorcerer stopped about ten feet away. "I call you once, I call you twice, I call you three times, as Peirol of the Moorlands," he intoned. "If you are a false image, a demon, a spirit, I summon you to battle against me or to dissolution."

"I'm just Peirol. No demon. What's the matter, Abbas?"

The wizard examined him carefully, lips moving in another incantation. "Yes," he finally said. "Yes, you are Peirol. Welcome home, lad. Welcome home!" He pressed certain studs on the gate, it clicked open, and Abbas clasped Peirol in his arms.

"Now," Abbas said. "Now, I've fulfilled my duties as a host, yes?"

Peirol drained his second beer, pushed aside the empty plate. He wondered where Kima was, wondered if he wanted to know. "You have."

"Then may I see it?"

Peirol, a bit reluctantly, unbuckled the belt, passed the pouch to the magician. Fingers trembling, Abbas unbuckled the ties, opened it, took out the Empire Stone. It sprang to life, feeling his touch, and Peirol flinched inadvertently as all colors flashed around the wizard's study. Abbas turned it in his hands, holding it as if it weighed nothing. Once he laughed, almost a miser's cackle, staring into it, lips moving. He caught himself, looked up.

"Yes," he whispered. "Yes, you have brought me my dream. For this, Peirol of the Moorlands, I shall make you as rich and powerful as any man on this earth, second only to me!"

"I think," Peirol said, starting to feel at ease, "I damn well deserve it." He poured another glass of beer, sipped at it.

"I owe you an apology," Abbas said, trying to be polite, though his eyes kept straying to the Stone.

"For what?"

"Times ago, I came to you in a dream, the last

time I was able to communicate with you, telling you about a great spell, great magic, that was building."

"I remember."

"I lost you, and couldn't manage to find you, using all the devices I had, including the one that had worked before." Peirol remembered Kima naked in a green vale. "But nothing came. I didn't know what had happened to you. But that great spell lived on, and then I sensed it moving west, and I thought perhaps you'd failed, and whoever cast that spell had managed to sense me, and the doom was coming for me, since I'd sent you out to steal it. It came closer, and closer, and so I prepared defenses, such as those loaded cannon, and certain . . . servitors of mine being armed for any eventuality, corporeal or spiritual. I also had that pistol, loaded with a ball given magical powers, at hand.

"That was why I challenged you at the gate. But you proved yourself real, Peirol, and I no longer feel the presence of any spell."

Quite suddenly it came to Peirol. The great spell Abbas had sensed hadn't been cast at all but was the Empire Stone itself. He remembered Yasin's warning about the Stone, filling with evil, perhaps overfilling, as a soap bubble before it bursts.

"I know not what happened to the spell, but it does not matter," Abbas went on. "Such is the nature of the spirit world, not operating on our standards or by our rules. I've learned to not question the unquestionable."

Peirol almost told Abbas what he'd realized, of Yasin's, or rather an unknown dead priest's, theory. But he said nothing.

"Forgive me, Peirol," Abbas said. "I have difficulty talking about other things than the Empire Stone. I wish you would leave me for a time, let me examine my treasure. Besides, there is someone below stairs who wishes you to take her to a certain place."

Peirol turned the horses off the narrow path at the tree he remembered that twisted like a man's hand, and went downhill slowly, through green brush, grass growing knee-high on either side of them.

"I see why no one ever found your vale," Kima said. "I'm quite lost, myself."

Peirol allowed himself another look back. She was very beautiful indeed; in the years since he'd seen her last, she'd blossomed. She wore a riding outfit of green, almost the shade of her eyes, and there was a green scarf around her neck like the one she'd given him years ago.

They rode through a screen of brush, and the tiny vale spread before them. The pool bubbled from the spring, and wildflowers had already sprouted here and there on the moss. Peirol heard a splash, and a fish jumped into the air, away from the hunting otter. It was silent, except for the singing of birds.

"Oh, my," Kima breathed. "Oh, my. It's as I dreamed—no, better. It's magic. Real magic, not like the sort my grandfather casts."

She slid from the saddle, walked to the pond, looked down into it. "Even the fish are magical," she said. "There's one that's striped red and white. I've never seen one like that."

Peirol dismounted, walked up behind her, chanced

putting his arms around her waist, kissing her back. She put her hands over his, slid them up, over her breasts, larger than he remembered.

"This is something else I've dreamed of," she whispered, guiding his fingers to the buttons. They unfastened easily, and she slid out of the blouse, letting it fall on the bank of the pool. "Now," she said. "You sit over there, on that moss."

Peirol obeyed. Kima sat on a rock, pulled off her thigh-length boots, unfastened her breeches, slid out of them. As in the dream, she was shaven, oiled, wearing only the scarf. "Am I as pretty as you hoped?"

"More so," Peirol said hoarsely.

"Do you want me?"

"More than anything."

"More than the Empire Stone?"

"I never wanted that."

"Good," she said, and came to him. "Now, your sandals . . . yes, and those horrible sailor's breeks . . . your shirt. We'll have them burned. Oh, Peirol. You're . . . more than I'd dreamed. How long have you been without?"

"Since . . . since forever."

"Stand up. Yes, and take my hand. Over here, by this tree. We want this to last, my love."

Peirol leaned back, closed his eyes, and her lips, hands, caressed his chest, moved lower.

"Now," she said. "Let us lie together."

She curled like a cat, back on the moss. Peirol went to her, knelt, and kissed her, tongue going deep into her mouth. Kima sighed, put her arms around him, lay back, with Peirol half across her chest. He smelled jasmine, roses. "Now, love me."

They lay naked, side by side, on the moss.

"There is a picnic in our saddlebags," Peirol said.

"I can have food anytime," Kima said.

"Well, as far as I'm concerned, you can have me anytime, too."

She laughed, stroked him. "How many women were you with since I met you? I sensed one, maybe another."

"I don't remember. No more than I had to."

"I don't mind," Kima said. "One of us has to be experienced." She sat up. "You laughed."

"I snorted."

"Don't you believe me?"

"I *always* believe you," Peirol said.

"I could get very angry!"

"Why? I said I believed you."

Kima lay back down. "Well," she said, poutily, "there were only . . . four, maybe five. None after I met you. Well, none but one, two, and I'd had too much wine then. Does it matter?"

"No," Peirol said honestly. "No, it doesn't."

"There won't be any more," Kima said. "I'll be the most faithful wife you've ever known."

Peirol covered his reaction.

"How many children do you want?" she asked. "Three? Four?"

"I hadn't really thought about it," Peirol said, blanching a little.

"Can you imagine the power our children will

have? I found out they won't necessarily be like you, although if that happens I'm sure I'll try to love them as much as the others. I know you'll probably scoff, but the sons and daughters of a wizard's offspring and a dwarf—I know, and I don't know how I know, they'll have great powers, maybe as wizards, maybe as kings!"

"Roll on your stomach now," Peirol said, desperately wanting to change the subject. "I have a certain power I want to show you."

Kima obeyed. "Oh, you do, don't you," and she squealed.

"Uh," Peirol asked, "is your grandfather going to object to what we did?"

"Why should he? He's as interested in an heir as I am."

"Oh."

"Besides, you're living with us now, and in my bedroom, so how do you think we could keep it a secret?"

"Oh."

She rode closer. They were entering Sennen's outskirts. "Something, oh husband-to-be, I wonder. What do you want to do after we're married?"

Peirol picked a safe answer. "Screw all day and all night."

"Ha ha. I mean, are you still wanting to open that silly store, like some kind of merchant?"

"I *am* a merchant."

"Not anymore, you aren't. You're the husband of Kima, granddaughter of Abbas, the ruler of Sennen."

"Pardon me?"

"Now that Grandfather has that Stone, don't you think he'll use it? Oh, Peirol, it'll be so exciting, seeing how he'll remake the city into perfection, into something the gods will think is a dream."

"Yes," Peirol said slowly. "Exciting." He remembered the dream the Men of Lysyth had made of Restormel, and what had happened.

"So of course you don't want to be a stupid shopkeeper," Kima said. "Perhaps you can do your designs, with any kind of stone you want, and those I get tired of wearing you can turn over to merchants and let them sell them. Not under your own name, of course."

"Of course not," Peirol said, a bit numbly. Then he asked, "What about travel?"

"Oh, I think that'd be wonderful," Kima said. "We could build a villa somewhere, perhaps not far from Thyone, and maybe have an upcountry house as well, for when the city gets too hot in the summer. A place where we can raise horses, and our children can ride for leagues and leagues. I have it. We'll put up the smallest little cabin, back at our pond, where just the two of us, and maybe a single servant, can go when we want to get away."

Peirol thought of the vale, of the trees being cut for lumber, the mosses leveled for the cabin's foundation, a workman shooting the otter for his skin.

"That isn't what I meant," he said, remembering a conversation with Zaimis. "I meant *real* travel. Going somewhere we've never been, just the two of us, wondering what's over the next rise. Maybe looking for new, different jewels that I can work, for you to wear."

He realized there'd been a hard note in his last sentence, hoped Kima hadn't noticed.

"Now why," Kima said in shock, "would anyone want to do that? That sounds dangerous!"

"Yes," Peirol said. "Yes, it does, doesn't it."

TWENTY·TWO

✳

Of a Jeweler's Scribe
and the Road

Peirol leaned across a boulder, on a high hill
overlooking Sennen. Behind him were three
horses, one saddled, two with packs. Dawn
was coming fast. The river was a bright silver way,
leading to the sea, past the ruins of Thyone. He looked
across Sennen to the dark finger that was Abbas's
tower.

He'd been in Sennen for just two weeks, living,
somewhat uncomfortably, at the tower, although the
old man, when he noticed Peirol, called him, abstract-
edly, "Son-in-law." Thinking of a wizard as a father-
in-law made him even more unsettled.

Kima had spent the time either enthusiastically
telling Peirol what their future would be, or with equal
enthusiasm in bed, eagerly learning the tricks of Reni,
Ellena, Zaimis, showing him some others of her own.

That at least was wonderful, better than anything he'd ever known. But still . . .

Three nights ago, Abbas gleefully announced the time was close when he would use the Empire Stone for the first time, three days distant, just at dawn. They'd all had a little too much wine at dinner, and Kima had pressed Abbas to tell Peirol what he planned. The wizard had been reluctant, then grew enthusiastic.

"First, of course," he said, "is to deal with my enemies, those few I haven't had the powers to already take care of. I've approached the rulers of the city at various times, and sounded them to see how they feel about some of my ideas on government. Some favor my ideas. Some, the more malleable or stupid, I think I can live with. But others must be removed, either for being set in their ways or too ambitious. Sennen as a whole, as a living entity, must change, will be growing beyond its present borders, and no one can stand in its way.

"There are those who think Sennen should move in other directions than the ones I know to be right, or worse, they want the city to be mired as it is for all time. They too must be removed. That shall be the first change I shall make. By the time you two waken, Sennen shall be as a new city."

"Then what?" Peirol asked.

"Then I shall proclaim my majesty," Abbas said. "For with the Stone, none can stand before me."

"No," Peirol agreed. "You'll reign supreme."

"Tell him, Grandsire, what other changes you'll make, once you hold the throne."

"I'll need no throne, none of earth's trappings of velvet and nonsense," Abbas said. "What I have here is more than sufficient."

"Not for me."

"Then we'll build the two of you a palace like the world's never known," Abbas said agreeably. He chortled, poured more wine. "Then I'll rebuild Sennen. We'll have no more crime, no more criminals. The Stone can scent them out, punish them as they deserve, without need for judges, trials, or prisons. The diseased, the cripples, the misshapen—not, Peirol, of course, the poor folk who're like yourself—but the others, will no longer trouble our eyes. The poor—those that are willing to work, and work hard, to improve their lot—they'll become one with the rest of Sennen. The slums, the tenements, the thieves' district, they'll all be razed, and new buildings, buildings that I've designed, will be erected.

"Sennen shall be a place where all work together, to my and their great glory. It shall be a city where all men, everywhere, shall envy us. I'll go further. The gods themselves will be jealous!"

Kima was looking hard at Peirol. He avoided her eyes, came to his feet, glass raised. "To the new Sennen! And to you, Abbas!"

Peirol had, the next night, talked to Kima about one of his problems. He walked in his sleep, and was afraid he'd stumble into one of the traps or magical guards he knew Abbas had set within the tower. Kima told him he had nothing to fear—the wards were only set for intruders. The three of them were safe, no matter where they went, at what time. They could even go out of the tower and the grounds. Her grandfather was hardly foolish enough to build a trap he himself might step in.

"Besides," she said, "I plan on keeping you so tired you'll never have the energy to somnambulate."

Laughing, they'd rolled onto the bed, clothes falling away.

The next day Peirol had visited Sennen, outfitting horses and packs, finding a stable on the outskirts of the city to keep them hidden. All that remained was buying one tiny tool, from a fellow jeweler who was most envious of Peirol's new lot.

The final day had passed quietly, peacefully, and Kima and Peirol had eaten lightly. Abbas was fasting. He told them the next day, the day that would mark the beginning of real power, there would be a feast. In fact, that would be a good time to announce the wedding.

Kima squealed happily, Peirol pretended equal joy. "I think," she announced, when they were alone, "we should stop our constant lovemaking until we're married."

"Why?"

"Because I want you—and myself as well—to be as fevered as we were that first time by the pool, when we go on our honeymoon."

"I think that's an excellent idea," Peirol said, and Kima had looked a bit surprised, then smiled happily. He doubted if he would have been able to perform at all that night.

"I'm going to *love* being your wife, Peirol. I can't see why we'll *ever* have an argument."

When Kima's breathing became regular, Peirol had dressed, except for his sword belt and shoes, which he carried and left beside the door.

He moved carefully, using all the skills he'd seen thieves use, past Abbas's bedroom, up into his study at the top of the tower. Peirol looked for the Empire Stone, saw it not, panicked for a moment until he saw a crystal case on a table, a case he'd never seen before.

He opened the case and took out the Empire Stone, keeping his eyes turned away. Peirol took his tiny tool, a jeweler's scribe, from his pouch, and gouged the Stone deeply along one facet. He felt the groove with his fingernail, chanced deepening it once again.

He saw, through the window, a lamp go on below him, quickly replaced the Empire Stone, put it back on the table. Peirol found a corner, crouched until the gleam from Abbas's bedroom below went out.

Very silently, thinking as a mouse, he crept downstairs, taking his sword and shoes, to the main door. He unbarred it without a noise and went out, closing the door behind him. The gate clicked when he pressed the studs in sequence learned from Kima, and he closed it. He pulled on his shoes and sword belt and trotted off toward the distant stables.

Now he sat, waiting, beyond the city.

The sky grayed, lightened.

Peirol felt his guts tighten. Abbas would be awake. He hoped he was leaving Kima to her sleep, fearing to let any outsider near when he was working great magic. He hoped the magician couldn't sense the unbarred door and gate, Peirol's absence.

It grew lighter still.

Peirol, having nothing of the Gift, felt his skin crawl, thought it probably his imagination, but knew Abbas was casting his spell.

On the far horizon a beam of light lit the world, the sun's first herald.

In that instant, a greater ball of flame exploded atop Abbas's tower, grew like a sun aborning, blinding Peirol for an instant. No sound at all came.

When his sight came back, the morning was growing, and birds were singing. Far across the city—he could see it as clearly as if he were within a third of a league—Abbas's tower still stood. But its upper works were blackened, ruined, torn away.

Peirol was almost positive the room he and Kima had shared was below the damage.

Yasin and his nameless mentor had been right. The Empire Stone had been full, full of man's and maybe gods' evil. Maybe that was what had brought on the earthquake, the sea waves at Restormel. Or maybe the disaster had further filled the Stone with death and grief.

Perhaps it would have exploded anyway when Abbas's spell struck it.

Or perhaps not.

Perhaps the cut Peirol made had weakened the Stone's crystal, as a cut against a diamond's grain can make it shatter under the first, gentle strike of the cutting hammer.

Or perhaps not.

Peirol thought about things. He could go back into Sennen. There would certainly be a reward for what he'd done, if he chose to claim credit. He could find a wizard who'd testify to the truth of his tale. That would make him rich, honored.

Desirable, even as a dwarf.

As for Kima . . . Peirol realized he was the fool, for having created a person from a conversation lasting but a brief moment. She was hardly to blame for not fitting the mold of his dream. As for her ambitions, were they any worse than those of any nobleman's daughter? In time, assuming she yet lived, she'd no doubt forgive him.

Or perhaps not.

He shuddered at *that* thought.

He didn't think he was much of a brave hero, but as for journeying forth . . .

Thoughtfully, Peirol of the Moorlands mounted his horse. Somewhere out there, in the welcoming wilderness, full of brigands and rogues, would be the diamonds of Osh.

Or even greater marvels.

Peirol laughed, tapping reins on his horse's neck, and it broke into an eager trot east.

CHRIS BUNCH is the author of the best-sellers THE SEER KING, THE DEMON KING and THE WARRIOR KING, from Warner Aspect. He's written other science fiction and fantasy books, including the LAST LEGION series and co-authoring the STEN series, which has sold more than a million copies, worldwide. He's a former journalist, magazine editor, and screenwriter. Bunch lives with his best friend, Karen, overlooking a commercial fishing port in the world's smallest Washington town. He is currently working on a fantasy titled CORSAIR, to be published by Warner Aspect.

VISIT WARNER ASPECT ONLINE!

THE WARNER ASPECT HOMEPAGE
You'll find us at: www.twbookmark.com then by clicking on Science Fiction and Fantasy.

NEW AND UPCOMING TITLES
Each month we feature our new titles and reader favorites.

AUTHOR INFO
Author bios, bibliographies and links to personal websites.

CONTESTS AND OTHER FUN STUFF
Advance galley giveaways, autographed copies, and more.

THE ASPECT BUZZ
What's new, hot and upcoming from Warner Aspect: awards news, best-sellers, movie tie-in information . . .